STEEL DRAGONS MC BOOK ONE

DRAGON SLAYER

C.A. RENE

Copyright Dragon Slayer © 2022 C.A. Rene

www.careneauthor.com

Edited by: ProofsbyPolly

Cover design by: Black Widow Designs Co

Paperback ISBN: 978-1-990675-52-2

DEDICATION

For Jocey,

Thank you for helping me brainstorm this world, it wouldn't exist without you.

Diego is yours.

Love you dearly.

CONTENT WARNINGS

There are instances of violence, drug use, and alcohol consumption. There is a detailed torture scene and mention of off the page SA.

This is a *Why Choose* story which means the female main character can have more than two partners without having to choose.

If you are triggered by any of these things, I would suggest reading no further.

Reader's Discretion is advised.

GENEVIEVE
BMW Motorrad Milano

PROLOGUE

This room I'm in is dark, the air fetid, and the temperature bone-chilling. I can hear the *drip, drip* of water leaking somewhere close by, the sound slowly driving me to the brink of madness. My skin feels tender against the cement floor and walls while my bound wrists and ankles are rubbed raw by the abrasive twine wrapped tightly around them.

My throat is dry, and my mouth is like sandpaper as I suffer with something beyond thirst. I don't know how long I've been stuck in this basement, but I haven't had anything to eat or drink since I was thrown down here. Screaming for help ceased when my voice disappeared a long time ago. Even *he* stopped his daily visits, probably because he prefers it when I scream.

Now I lie here waiting for someone to find me or for death to take me.

Death sounds like the easier choice because I don't think I'll ever be the same if I leave this basement alive. No amount of therapy could erase the horror and humiliation of the situation I'm currently in. There's no life to go back to. This room is where my life ends. Everyone I love no longer exists, and if I do walk out of here, there's only going to be bloodshed for the ones who believe they've gotten away with what they've done.

My father depended on me to lead, to pull ahead, and

endure the torture he knew I would face. He prepared me, or so he thought anyway.

I'm failing.

My chest seizes with the pressure of a sob, only it can't seem to work its way up my throat. My eyes burn as they try to force tears, but I'm all dried out. There's nothing left.

There's nothing left of *me*.

PART ONE

Six Months Earlier

GENEVIEVE
BMW Motorrad Milano

ONE

"Genevieve!"

My brother, Jaeger, strides toward me, his black, wavy hair swaying in the breeze, and his near-black eyes aflame with anger. His leather vest looks freshly oiled as it reflects the sun's rays, and his ripped jeans are dusty, telling me he just got in from a ride. My breath gets trapped in my chest as his tattooed hands curl into fists.

Shit, he's pissed.

"Where were you today?"

He stops right in front of me, his chest heaving with labored breaths, and his leather cut sporting a new patch. *Vice President.*

"Mall," I answer quickly, my eyes never wavering from that patch.

"Try again."

No way. There's no way he knows. We were careful.

"Jaeger…"

"Genevieve…" He steps in closer, his chest now touching mine. "I called you ten times. Do you know who else I tried to call?" Our eyes finally meet in a clash of indigo and ebony. *This is it.* "Quinton." My brows crash together in confusion as my head tips to the side. He must've been on the road for a long-ass time because he's making no fucking sense. What the fuck is he talking about? "Were you out with Quinton?"

"Quinton?" Surprise courses through me, making me rear back my head. "Why would I be with Quinton? He hates me."

Quinton is Jaeger's best friend, his lap dog who would do anything he asked, and a jerk to top it all off. The fact that Jaeger even thinks Quinton and I speak is outrageous. He has his head so far up Jaeger's ass, he wouldn't dare spare me the time of day.

"You've been caught." His long finger points at my face. "I can see the fucking fear."

"Fear?" I push him back with my hands on his chest. "Are you insane? That's disgust you're seeing. Quinton is an asshole."

"I see the way you look at each other, and I warned you, Genni. No fucking my boys."

Now it's my turn to step up to him, our chests bumping once again. Jaeger is tall, at six and a half feet, but I'm tall too, standing at nearly six feet.

"Watch your fucking mouth, Jaeger. No one tells me who I can and can't fuck. If I wanted to hump every cock in town, I'd do it." I stand my ground, uncaring if the neighbors see me and my brother fighting in our driveway.

His face turns an abnormal shade of purple as anger burns through his eyes. His lips pull back taut against his teeth as he prepares to douse my flames with accelerant. Playing with fire has always been a hobby of his.

"Kids," Dad's deep drawl sounds from the side of the house. "Knock it off and get inside. Your mother needs help with dinner."

Jaeger's hand grips my chin as he yanks my face closer to his. "You're fixing for a fight, Genni." His spit flies on my cheeks as he speaks the words. "Don't start something you can't finish."

He lets me go with a sharp shove, making me stumble

backward, my ass hitting Ma's car. My body vibrates with anger, each muscle stiffening as I contemplate knocking him the fuck out, but I need to bury it down because Ma's anxiety will kick in the moment she realizes we're fighting.

"Genevieve," Dad calls out, coaxing the flames of my anger. Jealousy burns inside of me because he made Jaeger Vice President. "Come here."

My feet obey before my mind registers, because no one says no to Victor Varga, President of the Steel Dragons Motorcycle Club. I may have a filthy mouth on me, and more times than not, it lands me in hot water, but I have a will to live, and mouthing off to Vic is a sure way to end up six feet under. Daughter or not.

I find my father leaning against the side of the house, a cigarette hanging from his lips, and a black bandanna wrapped around his long, graying hair, though the ends are still a dark brunette, much like my own. His long legs are crossed at the ankles, and his muscular arms are crossed over his chest.

The leather cut hanging from his shoulders is worn with spots of faded black decorating the edges. He's had this cut since he was a prospect, and the day it leaves his shoulders will be when it's folded inside his coffin or hung up in retirement. His skin is dark and weathered from long days on his bike in the Arizona sun, and lately, his face has been gaunt. He's looking *old*.

"Let him believe you were out with the Chino kid. It's better that way." He takes a long drag of his cigarette, exhaling the smoke in circular plumes, and his eyes stay focused on the grass at his feet.

"You made him Vice." My hands land on my hips and I can't control the whiney tone of my voice.

"He's my only son." His shoulder tips, his answer pissing me off.

"Jaeger is not your blood." My chest is still tight with anger, and the words fly out of my mouth before I can stop them. We don't speak of blood in this house. We've been raised to be full siblings. Jaeger is my brother, nothing less.

He drops his cigarette and crushes the butt with the tip of

his boot, only to reach into the pocket of his cut to light another one.

"I adopted him when he was ten years old, Genevieve. He's my son." I watch as he takes another long drag of the cigarette, his words sounding slightly exasperated. "What would you have me do?"

"Those are going to kill you," I snap.

"Your mother said it would be a bullet to my head." He chuckles as if he just told me a fucking joke. "I believe her predictions."

He means my birth mother. She died when I was three from ovarian cancer. *Fuck cancer.*

"What was the point of our talk today if you went and made him Vice?" I fall against the wall beside him with a sigh. I'm confused, irritated, and still cresting the high of fighting with my asshole brother, but everything we did today is making less sense. I was told I would be the most prominent figure in the MC when the time came. I watch him as he continues to smoke his cigarette.

I thought Dad meant Vice. I was sure he wanted me to be the one to stand next to him. Minutes pass by before he speaks again and what he says shocks me to my core.

"Because you will be Prez."

THIS BODY IS
TEMPORARY
BUT THIS SOUL IS
ETERNAL
JAEGER

JAEGER

Genevieve has always been a pain in my ass. I enjoyed being an only child, but Ma had to go and fucking ruin it by marrying a man with a cunt for a daughter. My teeth snap together as I slam the front door. I don't mean that. She just knows all the fucking buttons to press to piss me off. She's the only person I let get under my skin.

She's my baby sister. I'm just trying to protect her from the world she's living in.

I step up beside Ma in the kitchen, watching as she cuts into the roast, then I give her a kiss on the cheek. No matter how angry I'm feeling, Ma doesn't deserve any of it.

"This smells amazing, Ma."

My mother is a petite woman, but what she lacks in size, she has in personality tenfold. She's tough and fiery, and always ready to knock a motherfucker out. Claire Varga makes a perfect Old Lady, and one day, I want to find one just like her. We share the same raven hair, but that's where our similarities end. The rest belongs to a man I'd rather forget. Her bright green eyes are like jade in the sunlight, and I've always wished I inherited those too, instead of the demon-like orbs of my father's.

"Yeah, well, you go wash up before you sit at my table. I don't need blood or pussy on my new kitchen set."

I chuckle as I head upstairs to my childhood bedroom, finding the bed made, and my window open. Ma likes to clean and air it out on the nights I stay at the clubhouse. She says it gives the place time to breathe. I'm rarely home nowadays anyway, and soon, I won't be here at all.

As Vice President, I need to live at the clubhouse with the rest of the guys, keeping an eye on them, and keeping a presence of authority. With how the Steel Dragons are going lately, I'll need to keep up morality too. That means hitting the road and bringing in new prospects. It gives the older men pride in knowing the club will carry on after them.

My fingers brush over the new patch, the roughly sewn edges rubbing against my skin. This is what I've been waiting for. Vice President is just a small leap to President.

President has been my dream since the day Dad led me into the clubhouse at fourteen years old. I can still remember the way it smelled, like tobacco and whiskey. The men were all intimidating, but I looked up to every one of them. I still do.

My shoulder hits the wall beside the window as I reach into my pocket to pull out my pack of smokes. I flick open my Zippo and watch as the flame ignites the tip of my cigarette just as voices float up from down below.

It's Genevieve and Dad, they're voices are both distinct in the silence around us. I take a drag on my cigarette as I hear Dad light another one of his. At least the smell of mine burning won't be obvious. The man smokes like a fucking chimney.

"Those are going to kill you," Genni snaps. Her voice has become a bit huskier this last year, coupled with how much her tits and ass have filled out means I'm going to have trouble keeping her in line. Not to mention how often my knuckles will be busted from bouncing off my brothers' faces with each look they give her.

My teeth clash as I think about Quinton and the way he's been eyeing her lately. The way he calls her annoying and bratty doesn't fool me, not with the way his eyes stay trained on her ass. He's my brother, but she's my baby sister. He will be buried in the desert if he keeps it up.

"Your mother said it would be a bullet to my head," Dad says with a chuckle. "I believe her predictions."

He's talking about his first Old Lady, Genni's mom, Wendy. My mother isn't delusional. She knows what that woman meant to him. She was his first love, and if I dare say it… his last. I know he cares about my mother. She's been good to him, but they aren't crazy in love, not like he was with Wendy.

Ma's better off here with Vic, and she knows it. My abusive, asshole father did nothing but drink himself into a hole and send my mother to the ER. The night of my ninth birthday was the last straw for her. He got belligerently drunk and then put his cigarette out on my arm, his abuse moving on to me.

My eyes flick down to the small, circular scar, nothing but a drop in the sea of scars on my body, but it was my first. Most are now acquired from club jobs or war. That night, when he finally passed out, Ma packed us up in our piece of shit car and left him for good.

She drove straight out of New Mexico, not stopping until we arrived here in Arizona. Vic found her cleaning rooms for the rundown motel we were staying in, gathered us up, and gave us a proper home with my very own little sister. Genni was eight at the time. The rest, as they say, is history.

"What was the point of today if you went and made him Vice?" Genni asks her father, her voice filtering up toward my window as they stand directly below it.

I take a drag of my cigarette and tilt my head toward their voices. What does she mean? Where the fuck was she today? And why does she care if I'm Vice? I'm his only son, after all.

"Because you will be Prez."

Those words are clear as day, but I'm struggling to understand them over the white noise blaring through my ears. He couldn't have said that. I'm fucking imagining things. No woman has ever been President of the Steel Dragons MC. I have never heard of a woman Prez period.

"Have you lost your mind?" Genni asks in a hushed voice. "Dad, you've completely gone off the rails."

"It's your legacy as my blood," Dad states.

He's fucking serious. His words rip at the long-buried trauma I have inside. Daddy issues are a bitch to deal with. I stub my cigarette out on the windowsill as anger courses through me. This was supposed to be *my* legacy. He's been saying that for the last ten years. He walked me into that clubhouse at fourteen and announced to everyone that I would one day be his successor.

What changed?

Because we aren't blood?

I never cared much for blood, considering the man I share blood with treated me like shit beneath his shoe. Blood doesn't automatically equate to respect. I can see it now. I was used as a place card to protect the bitch who would steal it all from under me.

That won't happen, I won't let it.

He may think we'll all succumb to his decision, bow down to the Prez who's clearly losing his mind, but he'll be in for a surprise.

No woman will take what belongs to a man, and what rightfully belongs to me.

"How was the mall, Genni?" Ma asks as she passes me the mashed potatoes.

"Yes." My lip curls into a sneer. "Tell us how the mall was."

Genni's eyes narrow in on my face, but I give nothing away. The man currently sitting to my right at the head of the table taught me how to do that.

"I bought new boots," she snaps.

"That's nice," Ma hums as she scoops up a spoonful of potatoes.

After getting an earful of Dad and Genni's conversation earlier, a few things are becoming crystal clear. Genni has always sat on the right side of Dad at the table. It seems stupid to some, but in our club, that means that person is your right-hand man, the second to your first. That's where I sit—unless Genni is present. In this house, she's always on his right-hand side. I missed it and never paid much attention until today.

Genevieve Varga is the heir to the Varga throne and always has been.

I may have the man's last name, and have the cock and balls between my legs to be the leader, but Victor Varga had no intention of giving me everything. Just enough to one day say he cared, that he saved Ma and me. The legacy is Genevieve's alone.

"You okay, Son?" Dad asks with concern, pointing his fork at my hand that's wrapped around my knife. "You look like you're ready to kill someone."

I am.

"Yeah," I snarl and release the knife, letting it clatter to the plate. "Just a rough day."

"Did you and the brothers get the information you needed?" His eyes look at my busted knuckles as I raise a brow.

We don't ever talk club business outside of the clubhouse, so his line of questioning is leaving me a little fucking stumped.

I can feel Genni's intense stare on the side of my head, making me turn to look into those midnight blue eyes. "Yeah."

"Your sister and I will be going for a ride tomorrow. Make sure you clean up the mess and get the guys ready for a trip." He begins to cut into the roast on his plate.

He's taking Genni for a ride.

She doesn't even ride a cruiser. Her bike is a sports bike, nothing like the bikes we ride in the club. His Harley Softail couldn't keep up with her Honda CBR1100XX Super Blackbird. It's another reason the guys at the clubhouse find her *interesting.*

She zips around our small town on her flashy, yellow bike, catching the eye of men, young and old. I hate that they all look at her like she's more than just my baby sister. To me, she's still the annoying little shit she was when she was eight.

When I became old enough to learn to ride my first bike, Dad bought me my own Harley, and Genni cried for one too. We thought she would grow out of it, but when she became of age, she begged for a bike.

Dad was adamant, no girl should have her legs draped over a bike unless she had a man in front of her, but Genni was persistent. She had saved up from her part-time job at the local theater and bought a fucking dirt bike.

A week later, she wiped out and suffered a broken arm. Dad was pissed, but he realized it wouldn't stop her from jumping back on when she could, and he feared the next time, the extent of her injuries could be worse.

So he taught her how to ride, just like he had taught me. I should've seen it for what it was back then. He was grooming his next President.

My cell rings from the pocket of my cut, and I stand from the table when I see Quinton's name flash on the screen. "I gotta take this," I murmur.

"You haven't even finished your dinner…" Ma's voice trails off as I leave the kitchen.

"Where the fuck were you today?" I growl into the phone as soon as I pick it up.

"Fucking your mother."

"Bro…" I try to keep the smile out of my voice, but don't think I managed it. The cheeky fucker. "Do you not give a shit about your life?"

"Sometimes mommy pussy is worth a torturous death."

"Jesus," I hiss. "Seriously, I need you to be honest with me. Where were you today?"

"I was sent on reconnaissance by Vic. Why?"

I want to be able to tell my best friend everything, especially what I found out today, but I can't. Quinton Chino has been a part of my life since I was ten years old, and yet, this would devastate him. He's been promised the Vice position when I become President.

"I need help with cleanup back at the club. I had a hard day of breaking bones and cutting flesh while you were banging my mother… Vic's fucking wife."

"It's dangerous being this fucking irresistible."

"Just meet me at the club." I hang up the phone and chuckle to myself. The asshole is always going on about fucking my mother.

"Son." Dad's voice comes up behind me. "Are you heading over to the club?"

"Yeah." The humor bleeds out of my tone. I turn slowly and stare into his blue eyes, nearly identical to his daughter's. I search them, trying to see the deceit he's been creating. "I'm going to clean up my mess."

"Let Quinton know he has the day off tomorrow."

"Sure." I nod. My throat begins to swell with emotions when his hand lands on my shoulder.

"Thank you for doing that today." His hand drops, then slips into the pocket of his cut, withdrawing his smokes. "What did you find out?"

"Hell's March is taking over distribution for the cartel." I take a smoke when he offers me his pack and both of our Zippos hiss as we light the tips. "They have plans to take it through here, then into Phoenix."

It's a smart plan. We have the police in our pockets here, and they wouldn't bat an eye to see a nondescript tractor trailer roll through.

"Looks like Hell's March needs a reminder of who owns this town."

I give him a nod as I exhale the smoke from my lungs. They do, but the more I let his and Genni's earlier conversation sink in, the more irate I become. I'm no rebelling adolescent, but I can feel the mutiny rising inside of me.

Vic's first mate is about to take control of the ship.

GENEVIEVE
BMW Motorrad Milano

TWO

Dad is cruising on his bike like we have all the time in the world. I'm trying to stay with him, but my bike is purring between my legs, begging me to open her up and burn rubber. We've been on the road for half an hour now, and I'm beginning to feel the burning ache on the inside of my thighs. I want to fly, I hate cruising.

I want to fly along the asphalt.

Dad's sharp whistle grabs my attention, and I turn to see him point ahead to an abandoned-looking warehouse in the desert. My heart rate kicks up in my chest, and I swallow down the lump forming in my throat. After he told me his plans yesterday, I've been a ball of nerves wound so tight that it's been hard to think straight.

I know what they do to rival bikers who cross territory lines or to cops who decide they can force them to obey the law. Is that why we're here today? Am I going to torture and kill someone?

With a little nudge, my bike shoots forward ahead of Dad, and I pull up to the warehouse before him. The place is a fucking dump of beer cans and broken windows. I haul my helmet off and shake out my long hair; the strands skating along my cheeks.

Dad pulls up behind me just as a large, garage-like door

begins to roll up. We're not alone. My hands tighten on the handle of my bike, and I feel the rapid patter of my heartbeat in my chest. I'm not a confrontational person. I don't like to fight, but it doesn't mean I don't know how. I know how to break a nose if need be. Weapons are another story. I don't know how to use a gun to save my life.

Quinton stands in the opening, his arms crossed over his wide chest, and a cocky grin on his sinful mouth. I've always hated the man, but it's never stopped my pussy from wanting him. He's a gorgeous asshole, and my brother's best friend.

His long, black hair is tied back into a braid that hangs down to the middle of his back, the dark strands shining in the sun's rays. The sepia tone of his skin makes the hazel of his eyes pop from behind thick, black lashes. All-in-all, Quinton Chino is a lady killer… he certainly slays me.

"What is he doing here?" I hiss to my dad as he pulls up beside me.

"What?" He tips his head to the side, unable to hear me over the roar of his engine. I give him a look, and his chest vibrates with a rumble. "What?" he asks again once his bike is quiet.

"What is Quinton doing here?"

"He's here to help with your training." Dad gets off his bike and stretches, his back cracking in the process.

"He will tell Jaeger. They're best friends."

"Not if he wants to live," he answers nonchalantly. "I'm his President, that trumps even his mama."

It's true. Every member is sworn in to lay their lives down for the President, no matter who *he* is. The thought alone has my insides quaking. Would they lay their lives down for me?

According to Dad, they won't have a fucking choice.

"Kid!" Dad calls out as he removes his bucket helmet. "Did you bring everything?"

Quinton's honeyed gaze roves over me as I unzip my jacket and shake out my legs.

"Yeah, Prez." His voice hardens as I stride forward behind my dad. "Is this for her?"

"Are we going to have a problem?" Dad's voice lowers to a deathly growl, making Quinton's arrogant face fall.

"No, boss."

"Good." Dad's hand lands on my shoulder. "Now, teach my girl how to shoot."

"Dad!" I snap my head to glare at him. "We did that yesterday."

"Baby," he says, his hand patting my cheek roughly before continuing, "those were tin cans. You need to learn with moving targets. Now, stop fucking questioning me." His voice softens a bit for me.

I swallow down the rest of my protests, refocusing my attention on my brother's best friend, his annoyance hitting me in potent waves.

"Let's go." He gestures behind him.

"You'll be fine with him," Dad assures me. "I'll be back in a few hours."

I want to beg him not to leave me with the sadistic fool who loves shooting anything in his path, but I force it all down, attempting to act brave. My dad is entrusting me with his most important asset: His club.

Quinton stands beside me as Dad gets back on his bike with a lit cigarette in his mouth. His lips tip up around the stick as he tosses me a wink. I want to feel as confident as he looks by this whole situation, which I still don't fully understand. Why he's making me President of an all-male motorcycle club makes no sense, and every time I question him, he tells me to trust him.

I'm not even sworn in.

"You have a stalker after you or something?" Quinton's gruff voice hits me as we both watch my dad pull away.

"Or something."

I can feel his penetrating stare hit the side of my face, and neither of us moves until the rumble of Dad's bike slowly fades away. He has questions, I can feel them, but unfortunately, I don't have a single answer.

"Let's go," he grunts out, turning on his heel and heading into the darkened warehouse. I watch him walk away, his tall stature strong and his steps confident. The braid resting down his back swings with every step and the eagle feather hanging from the tip blows slightly with the breeze, an ode to his Apache heritage. "We don't have all day, Varga," he calls out. "These things won't shoot themselves."

Wait… Dad said *moving* targets.

The moving targets ended up being mannequins on tracks, thankfully. I haven't hit a single one, and my shoulder is aching from holding my arm up for too long. I keep my mouth shut though because Quinton would take any opportunity to scream at me. He's been doing enough of it for the past two hours.

"Your grandfather was the founder of this MC," he huffs out as I miss another mannequin. "He could hit a rat from a mile away."

"First of all,"—I point the gun at his face—"that's a fucking lie. And second, shut the fuck up."

"Get that out of my face," he snarls. "Knowing your aim, you'll shoot my fucking shoulder."

"Nah." I let out a chuckle, and drop the gun to my side. "That would be a target I wouldn't miss."

A trickle of sweat rolls from his temple down along his cheek. It's fucking hot in here, and I've stripped down to my crop top long ago. Quinton hasn't done the same. No member can remove their leather cut while out in public, and even though this is an exception because we're inside, he's still wearing his. He's been running to reset the targets and yelling at me while slowly melting.

I hope the fucker passes out.

"You'd think with your lineage, you'd at least be able to hit something." He rolls his eyes, ignoring my jab.

"Nope, *princesses* aren't supposed to be able to shoot," I snap back, then grab a handful of my pussy. "I have a vagina."

He chokes on a surprised laugh, then immediately clears his throat, giving me an annoyed look. God forbid he finds me funny.

"It's your stance." He moves behind me, his heat hitting my back in thick waves. "You stand like you're waiting for a latte in a Starbucks line."

"Fuck you." I move to turn when his hand slips into my hair, fisting the strands in a deathly grip. My body vibrates with anger at the way he's manhandling his President's daughter.

"You stand like the privileged daughter of a MC's President. Like nothing can hurt you." His words are like vitriol, stabbing through my chest to ignite my anger further. "What size do you take, princess? Venti?"

He presses in close to my back, his hot breath on my neck, and his hardening cock at my ass. With a slight curl of my hips, my ass pushes in closer, eliciting a groan from the unfeeling man. His arm wraps around my waist as I chuckle once more.

"It feels more like a tall to me."

Quinton releases my hair and steps back with a curse while his hand hits me between the shoulder blades with force. "Keep your shoulders up, widen your legs, and line your eye up with the barrel."

An hour later, Dad returns, finding me sprawled out on the filthy warehouse floor. Quinton is putting away the mannequins as Dad's chortle echoes around the cavernous space.

"Smells like the pits of Hell in here."

"Dad!" I sit up excitedly, a proud smile on my face as I look at him. "I got one!"

"She hit the pregnant one," Quinton calls out with a snort.

"Look,"—I roll over and slowly stand to my feet—"she was undercover, and that was a pillow up her shirt."

"She hit her square in the belly. Two birds, one stone," Quinton continues to rub it in, his eyes shining with mischief as he winks at me.

"You're sick!" I hiss at him.

"You killed an infant, not me."

"I'm going to kill your Sergeant at Arms," I proclaim to Dad.

He laughs at our banter, pride shining through his blue eyes. "We'll line him up for you. Make sure you don't move, Chino."

It doesn't matter how much they poke fun at me; I shot my first moving target. Yes, it was after the asshole corrected my stance, but I still did it.

VUITTON

QUINTON

Something strange is going on, and if I want to keep my life intact, I can't question any of it. This situation with Genevieve is unsettling. Her need to learn to shoot isn't on a whim. Prez wants me to teach her a few times a week for the foreseeable future. This isn't a quick lesson in self-defense, this is a honing of skills.

Still, I need to keep all my suspicions to myself… It's kept me alive thus far. Last year, Vic announced me as his Sergeant at Arms when my father died in a shoot-out, making me the youngest in club history. I'm proud of my position, and I intend to keep it by ensuring Vic is happy. Even if that means playing cops and robbers with his daughter.

I've known Genevieve since she was two years old, and when Jaeger and his mother came into the picture, I got to know her as she grew. Jaeger became my best friend. It helped that our fathers were in the same club, but he and I clicked, giving me a front-row seat to the life of Genevieve.

Was I being too much earlier by calling her privileged? Not by a long shot. Genni's lived a life of comfort, constantly cushioned, and kept safe away from any nasty shit this town's faced. She zips around on her foreign motorcycle, playing at being a badass when in actuality, she's a fucking baby. She whines, demands attention, and her attitude grates on my last nerve. Until today, I always saw her as a lazy princess, waiting for someone to serve her every whim.

I watch as she speaks to her father, her arms animated, and her face bright with excitement. Today I saw another side of her, one that's working hard toward impressing her dad, and she didn't mind getting dirty to learn.

I just wish I knew what the point of all this was, and I can't ask Jaeger unless I want a bullet to the head.

It feels off that Vic is keeping this from his Vice, and I don't think it's because he feels it's no big deal. There's something I'm missing.

"Thanks for this." Vic comes to stand beside me, lighting

a cigarette.

We both watch as Genevieve heads toward her bike, hauling on her leather jacket.

"No problem."

"You probably have a few questions." He takes a drag of his cigarette, his eyes still on his daughter.

I shrug my shoulders, not wanting to look too eager to hear his explanations. "I'd want my daughter to know how to defend herself too."

"With Hell's March pushing their way through our town, and the war I'm about to rain down on them, she's my weakest link." Smoke exhales through his lips in a thick plume. "I need you to promise me something, Chino."

"Anything, boss."

"If something happens to me, I need you to protect her."

My eyes snap from his daughter to the side of his face. "What?" Confusion courses through me at his strange request.

"Protect her as if she were me, your President."

His words send a wave of shock through me and I feel my mouth fall open in surprise. He's asking me to swear my life to her, like I did to him when I was sworn into the club.

"Dad!" Genevieve whines from her motorcycle. "Let's go. It's a long ride back, and I'm tired."

Vic's eyes meet mine, his reflecting something I have never seen before. Fear.

"I promise," I whisper.

His large hand clasps my shoulder and gives it a hard squeeze. "Your father is proud of you, Son." With that, he saunters over to his daughter, giving her a quick kiss on the temple before straddling his bike.

I just swore my life to Genevieve Varga, and all I can think about is how Jaeger would kill me if he found out.

The gates swing open, and I nod to the prospect standing in the booth. The music is blaring out of the compound, and I grin as AC/DC sings about the "Highway to Hell." I park my bike in its place beside Jaeger's and haul off my bucket helmet.

"Heard you were given the day off," a gruff voice says.

I look over my shoulder to find Laith leaning against a picnic table, a smoke hanging from his lips. He's our Road Captain, and the toughest motherfucker around. He's not much of a talker, letting his fists relay most of his thoughts, but he's loyal to a fucking fault.

"Yeah." I get off my bike to walk over to where he stands. "What's the rager for?" I jut my chin toward the compound.

"We're riding out tomorrow," he grunts out, the slightly visible scars on his cheeks moving with his words.

Laith was shot in the face during a shootout with Hell's March a few years ago. Luckily for him, it entered through one cheek and right out the other. Now he has a matching set of dimples and some gold teeth to replace his missing ones.

"Right." I forgot about the ride we're taking to Phoenix tomorrow. We need to scope out the cartel's warehouse where Hell's March will be dropping off their runs. "Looks like we'll be hungover too."

"Maybe you little girls will be," Laith retorts. His hand comes up to pull the smoke from his lips, his massive, completely tattooed-covered bicep bunching with the motion. He flicks it out onto the gravel, just missing a few of the strippers as they walk by, having come from Glitz, the club we own. A giggle sounds from one of them as she watches Laith closely.

"It's going to be one of those nights." I whistle as Carrie, one of my regulars, gives me a wink. I'll be balls deep in her asshole later.

"Great." He pushes himself off the picnic table, standing to his full height. Fucking six-foot bastard. "Not only will you little bitches be puking, but you'll stink like rotting fish too."

I let out a laugh as he makes his way back inside, his wide body having to turn sideways to fit in the door. Laith has been with the Steel Dragons since he was fifteen years old, having come down from Phoenix alone, and with no family who cared. He was sworn in and prospected for two years. Now, ten years later, he's an important part of our organization. Not to mention completely feral when he's let loose.

He took a fucking bullet to the face and still killed four men afterward.

"Look who finally came home," Jaeger says, snickering as he comes outside, a beer in one hand and a spliff in the other.

"Give me some of that." I motion to the joint.

He offers me the J, and I grab it eagerly, taking in a deep inhale. The smoke burns its way down my throat, making my lungs stall with the intrusion. I don't smoke cigarettes, but weed? I could smoke it all day.

"What did you get up to today?" Jaeger tries to sound nonchalant, but I can hear the suspicion in his tone.

"Rode up to Fort Apache to visit my family," I lie. I do it with ease, but I fucking hate lying to him.

"How's the reservation? Did you bring me back anything?" He's fishing.

"Nah, I spoke to my mom, then came straight back." Jaeger nods, but I can see his eyes are narrowed from my periphery. He doesn't quite believe me, but there's nothing I can do about that. Vic is where most of my loyalty stands. "What made you want to throw this tonight?"

"We may die in front of the cartel's machine guns tomorrow." His dark eyes light with excitement. "Thought we'd fuck warm pussies one last time."

"Fuck, yes." I hold out my fist, waiting for his bump. "Are we tag teaming?"

"Only if you do that thing with your tongue I like." He waggles his eyebrows. "You know, like the time we were fucking Sandy."

"That was a fucking accident," I snap, looking around us and finding us alone. Thank god. "Watch your fucking mouth."

"Her pussy was tight and warm, and your tongue had the perfect pressure as it flicked against my balls—"

With his joint still firmly between my lips, I shove away from him with a glare, leaving behind his stupid fucking chuckling. I don't need any of the other guys hearing about me accidentally licking his balls while he was pounding Sandy from the back, I would never hear the end of it. Not to mention, a few of them probably wouldn't mind the same treatment.

The club is smokey and loud when I walk inside as the song changes to Def Leppard's "Pour Some Sugar on Me," and a few of the girls begin stripping on the bar. We cater to the older brothers a lot, letting them have the music choices and first pick of the girls. Vic has been working on turning over all the important roles to us younger brothers, hoping it makes the club more appealing to prospective members.

We need more men. We've lost a lot to the territory wars with Hell's March and to old age, both battles we'll be forever fighting.

I find Laith sitting on a stool at the bar, his back to the wood as the women dance behind him. He's an odd one, he doesn't partake in any club pussy, and he doesn't give women the time of day. He's not necessarily rude to them, just doesn't entertain them. I take a seat beside him as Carrie drops her panties over my head, making a few of the brothers closer to us laugh.

"Take some Penicillin later," Laith advises. "You don't know how many men were in those tonight."

I drop the spliff to the bar top, the cherry long gone out, and haul the fabric of the panties to my nose, taking a deep inhale. "Smells like pussy to me."

Laith gets up off his stool with a shake of his head and a grumble, leaving me laughing behind him. A hand taps my shoulder, and I look back to find Chip, our bartender, offering me a glass of Jack. I down it in one swallow then motion behind him.

"I want the bottle tonight."

JAEGER

JAEGER

Quinton is hiding something from me.

I've known him too long not to know what he looks like when he's lying, not to mention how his eyes droop with guilt. There's something he's not telling me, but I won't be pulling it out of him tonight. Nope, this is my night to forget everything I learned this week. Everything that took the world I've known and spun it on its axis.

I will never be President of the Steel Dragons.

Is it stupid that this was my one and only dream? Maybe. But I grew up knowing nothing else except for Vic and how he sat at the head of the table. The way his enormous fist would grasp the gavel to pound into the wooden tabletop, announcing the end of Church.

I wanted to be him, and he let me believe I would be one day.

The tip of my boot digs into the gravel around the picnic table as I give myself exactly one minute to wallow. How the fuck am I supposed to follow a female? No one in this club will bow down to her willingly, especially not the older brothers. A pussy is there to fuck, not to lead.

I don't disrespect women, not by a long shot. I worship them for hours with my talented tongue and big dick. But when it comes to this MC, to any MC I know, women are not members. Their highest position is to be an Old Lady to a brother, that's it. I didn't make the fucking rules, but that's what they are. Vic is putting his daughter in danger, and I can't figure out why.

No one here would ever view her as their leader, their President, no one, and eventually, they'll all leave. We're already down on members because the older generation is getting too old to ride, and prospects are few and far between.

I'll have to take care of this, take the future of this MC into my own hands, and save it from the disaster my father is about to make.

The gates swing open at the sound of an approaching bike. By the sounds of the rumble, I can tell it's Vic's Harley. One of the guys must've called him about the party because he usually stays home with Ma the night before a ride, otherwise, he'd have already been here and partying with us.

He parks his bike beside mine, at the top of the row, and slowly gets off. I can see his age showing with how slowly he's moving nowadays, but it's worrying because he's not that old. He looks tired all the time, and he grimaces often as if he's in pain. I know a few of the brothers have noticed too, but like me, they don't want to risk a bullet to the head for being too nosy.

Vic drops his helmet onto the seat of his bike, then reaches into his pocket to pull out his cigarettes. His eyes meet mine as he lights it, smoke funneling out of his nostrils like the dragons we're named after. A quick shot of apprehension skates down my spine, but I steel it. He's my father, not the enemy.

At least I don't want him to become my enemy.

He makes his way over to me, each step exaggerated by his slow swagger, his long, gray beard swaying in the wind.

"A party, huh?"

"We usually do it the night before a ride," I reply, watching as he drags on his smoke.

"A party, yeah. This is looking like a rager."

I shrug my shoulders, making him chuckle.

"Let me do most of the talking tomorrow. I want you to sit back and observe," he says as he squints through the smoke. "I want eyes everywhere."

"You got it." I nod while my insides quake with anger. What would be the point of me observing him and his actions?

Unless… he wants me to teach my fucking sister how to lead when the time comes. I go rigid as the thought settles inside me. There's no way he would spit in my face like that. He's my fucking father.

"We haven't had a full-out war with Hell's March in years," he continues. "There's been a little peace, but if they insist on traveling through our town with cartel drugs, it will be war."

"What if we run into the March tomorrow? Are we prepared?"

"I don't see why we would need to be prepared." His eyes narrow. "They don't know we're going to scope this place out."

"Right."

"We're speaking to a few of the guys in charge of running that warehouse. They're employed by the cartel and have nothing to do with the March. Why would the March even show up?"

"Yeah, you're right," I placate him.

There really would be no point in Hell's March showing up at the cartel warehouse. They're only working a job for the cartel, not manning the place themselves.

Not unless someone told them what was happening anyway.

QUINTON

THREE

I'm being suffocated, and it's dark as fuck. My hand shoots out in front of me, my palm meeting warm, clammy flesh. I crack an eye and slowly peel my face away from whatever I'm suffocating on, only to find a large pair of tits. Dusty rose nipples stand erect in front of me, and I grin as I suck one into my mouth.

Fucking best way to wake up.

Carrie moans as she arches her back, pressing her chest closer to my face. My hand glides down over her stomach, then between her legs, and I find her soaked. It's a quick maneuver, getting her on her back and her leg hooked over my arm. Her eyes finally open, the lids heavy as her blue irises meet mine. The column of her throat stretches as her head tips backward on a moan.

"Yes, Quinton. Fuck me."

My cock is nestled between her wet pussy lips, the warmth of her flesh enveloping my length. I glide through the silky folds, my head settling at her entrance just as a hand whacks down on my bare ass cheek, the sound reverberating around the room.

"No time for that now," Jaeger's voice breaks the silence. "We need to get up."

Carrie curses as I roll off of her to look at my best friend and whine, "Are you fucking kidding me?" He just lays there on the bed with a shit-eating grin on his face.

"No." He gets up and starts retrieving his clothes off the floor before putting them on. "I'm sure she'll find another brother to fill her cunt while we're gone."

A whimper sounds from beside me, and I turn to find another female, completely naked with cum crusted along her tits. Could be mine, or it could be Jaeger's. When we drink this heavily, we end up fucking girls together, passing pussy back and forth.

With a groan, I haul myself up and out of bed, my hard cock jutting out straight in front of me. I grumble under my breath as I search the floor for my fucking clothes, stopping when I hear Jaeger suck in air like he's struggling to fill his lungs.

My eyes find him first, then I follow his line of sight toward the bed. The girls have found each other, their plump tits pressed together, their tongues tangling, and their fingers exploring each other's cunts.

I pull on my boxers and then slap Jaeger on the back of his head, forcing him to tear his eyes away from the heavenly vision on the bed.

"What the fuck?" he growls out, sending me a glare.

"We could've been in between them, and it's your fault we're not," I snap.

I find my cut folded and placed on a chair next to Jaeger's. No matter how drunk we get, we never disrespect our cut. That rule has been embedded into our souls. It's never to touch the floor.

With a hard shove, I push Jaeger out of the room and give one last look over my shoulder. Their moans of pleasure are increasing as the sounds of wet, sucking pussy fills the room.

"I fucking hate you," I mumble at my best friend as he chuckles, pulling a pack of smokes out of his pocket.

"Pussy is easy to get, but a meeting with the guys running the cartel warehouse? Not so much."

Jaeger heads toward the bar while I dip inside a bathroom.

I smell like a whorehouse, and it'll only get worse the longer we are on the road in the Arizona sun. I wash my face and brush my teeth, then braid my long, black hair back. I'm in desperate need of a shower, but I need to be ready for when Vic shows up. I'll shower when we get back.

Most of the guys are standing around the bar when I emerge from the bathroom, but the clubhouse is still a mess. There are naked females sleeping on the pool table, the couches, and even one on the bar top. One brother currently has her tit in his mouth and a coffee in his hand. There are articles of clothing, beer bottles, and cigarette butts everywhere.

The place smells like a fucking petting zoo.

I stand beside Laith at the bar because he's chosen a stool farthest away from the naked female whose pussy is leaking copious amounts of cum. He's drinking a small cup of espresso, and his scowl is firmly in place when I sit beside him.

"How was your night?" I ask him as I raise my hand for Chip to bring me a coffee.

"Quiet and STD free. I will live well beyond the rest of you," he says as he brings his dainty cup up to his mouth for a sip.

"You have the willpower of a saint." I chuckle as Chip drops a cup of steaming black coffee in front of me.

"One day, one woman will have my sole attention, and she'll be deserving of it."

"You're a romantic." I snap my fingers, as if a lightbulb went off, with a laugh.

He shrugs, unbothered by my teasing while he drinks the rest of his espresso. The doors fly open, bringing in the blaring, midday, Arizona sun. A few of the brothers groan with the sight, but I soak it up. The sun has always revitalized me.

"This place is fucking disgusting!" Vic hollers as he walks in. "Women! It's time to get up and get the fuck out of here."

Claire comes in behind him, her nose screwed up and wearing her *property of* cut. She never has to worry about Vic straying, he never partakes in the females, and he always goes home to her. But he enlists her on days like today to gather up some women to clean up after our debauchery.

She's hot. I would be making sure to get my ass home to her as well. I wasn't playing when I told Jaeger I'd marry his mom if she ever left Vic.

Even risking the wrath of my President.

What shocks me even more is Genevieve stepping out from behind her and into the club, her eyes wide as she looks around at the evidence of our most primal behavior. She's never cared too much about the club and its parties before. I don't know why, but I have the strongest urge to grab her and drag her back outside. This isn't something she should see as the Prez's daughter.

Instead of shrinking back at the filth displayed in front of her, Genevieve strides right up to a naked woman sprawled out on the pool table and smacks her ass.

"Get the fuck up and out," she barks, making Laith whistle beside me.

Then she looks down at her hand with disgust, turning on her heel and heading toward us at the bar. Laith and I both watch her as she steps behind and begins to furiously wash her hands in the small sink.

"Who knows what the fuck was on her damn ass," she mutters to herself. "Fucking men and their nasty-ass dicks."

Laith snorts while he watches her, and I grin, knowing how uncomfortable this all must be for her. Jaeger steps up next to her, his dark eyes looking as hard as obsidian.

"Is the princess about to get her hands dirty?" he sneers.

"Maybe." She shrugs while drying her hands, looking at him from the corner of her eye. "Is daddy's little boy gonna become a man today?"

She shoves by him as he glowers at her, his face as hard as his eyes, and I try my best to hold in my laughter as I choke with the force. He reaches his hand over to hit the back of my head, making Laith snort again.

"Shut your fucking mouth," he retorts.

"I didn't say anything," I grumble indignantly.

"Let's ride out!" Vic calls, and the brothers all start to move.

Genevieve comes back into the room with a disinfectant bottle and begins to spray the females still sleeping.

"Get the fuck out, skanks!" She's growling the words as she works her way around the room.

The strippers slowly begin to wake up, a few of them tossing nasty looks at Genni. The guys are standing around and chuckling at her display while Claire looks on like a proud mother.

I leave the scene, laughing at her antics. Maybe she could handle the shit this club gets up to. She'd make an alright Old Lady one day.

"Hey…" I shoulder bump Laith, making him roll his eyes. "You could make Genevieve your Old Lady."

"Nah," he responds, sticking a piece of nicotine gum in his mouth. "Too young."

We all roll out in our formation and set off for Phoenix. It's a long ride, but I love the wind in my face and the vibration of my bike between my legs. This is how life is meant to be.

GENEVIEVE
BMW Motorrad Milano

GENEVIEVE

When the last of the strippers leave, I begin to help Ma with cleaning the floors and throwing out the random thongs I find scattered around the place.

"This is so fucking gross. These men are fucking barbarians," I whine as I find a used condom on the floor.

"Put on gloves before you touch that," she says quickly. "At least some are using condoms. My son better be, at least."

The thought of Jaeger fucking anyone makes me want to gag, let alone the thought of him contracting some sort of cock rot.

"At least you don't have to worry about Dad being in the middle of this shit," I mumble as I wipe an unknown fluid off the bar top with a rag soaked in disinfectant. Thankfully, Ma made me put on gloves.

"There was a time when he did join in," she confesses, and I stop to look at her. She's standing there with a forlorn look on her face. "You and Jaeger were young, and Vic was still getting over Wendy." My mother.

"And you stayed with him?" I ask incredulously.

"It's hard to explain." She stops and rests her gloved hands on her hips. "I appreciated him, but I hadn't fallen in love with him yet. I was coming out of a dangerous situation, and trusting men was a work in progress. He gave me the space to do that, so I gave him the space to grieve your mom."

"I'm glad he found you, Ma," I tell her, my voice wavering. She was exactly what he needed.

"I'm glad too," she replies, giving me a smile. "He gave me the sweetest daughter a mother could ask for."

We get back to cleaning, and I can't seem to stop the worry that's been plaguing me lately. There's something my father is hiding from me. This situation he has cooked up by making me President of the Steel Dragons feels like a last-ditch move, especially because he has a son who's been trained and more capable for the job.

Then there's the urgency behind training me and piling it all in such a short period of time. It feels like we're running out of time, and I don't know what from. I can't figure out what's looming on the horizon, but whatever it is, it feels like it's going to be life-changing.

This ride they're taking today to Phoenix also has me worried. My father didn't say much about it, but I could see the look of uncertainty in his eyes. I wanted to beg him to stay home because this ride felt more dangerous than any of the others he's taken.

"Hey, Ma," I call out. "Did Dad tell you what they were doing in Phoenix?"

She pops up from behind the bar, her skin flushed from scrubbing the floor. "No, of course not." She shakes her head. "They never tell me anything."

That's the usual for women in an MC. They aren't privy to any club information. The highest position for a woman is being an Old Lady to the members. Then sometimes, they have more responsibilities in the club, but never do they know the inner workings of it. My father is expecting to change that dynamic, and I can only imagine the blowback.

"Dad seems tired lately," I say out loud. "Has he been staying here late again?"

"Yes." Ma clicks her tongue. "I've been telling him he needs more rest, and to quit the damn smoking. But he always gives me the same line—"

"He'll do it when he's dead," I finish for her, and we both look at each other with a laugh.

"Yeah." She nods.

"Oh!"

I look away from Mom and turn to the voice that just popped in out of nowhere. My eyes automatically zero in on the stripper, Carrie. She's walking into the room without a stitch of clothing on, while her other stripper friend is scratching at the hair on her head, also as naked as the day she was born. Both of them look around expectantly. Maybe they're used to the party continuing into the next day.

"Will you put on some damn clothes?" I snap. "Then get the fuck on out of here?"

"Who are you?" The other stripper's eyes narrow as her hands hit her waist.

"That's Jaeger's little sister, Angel." Carrie snickers as she steps into her tube dress and pulls it up her body.

"Don't worry, honey." *Angel* gives me a smarmy look. "I took care of your brother all night last night."

"You better watch that mouth and listen to my daughter." Ma pipes up from behind the bar, her voice filled with disgust. "I don't need to be hearing anything my son did with any of you whores. Now git!"

A nice, deep red color coats both of their cheeks as they hastily pull on the rest of their clothes and rush out of the compound without bothering with their shoes.

"If my son catches any-damn-thing," Ma growls out as she watches them leave, "I will kill him as a treatment."

My head tips back on a loud, obnoxious laugh, and soon enough, Ma is joining in. "I could smell the yeast from here," I add on.

"Oh, shit." Ma retches then covers her mouth. "Do they lose their sense of smell when they drink?"

"All of them lose every damn sense," Mariam retorts from the hallway as she comes into the room with bright yellow rubber gloves to her elbows and a mask over her mouth. "Especially the common kind."

Mariam is Cash's Old Lady, he's the club's medic, and he's nearing an age where he'll have to retire from his bike. Mariam is at least twenty years his junior, and clearly, by the look of her hazmat get-up, she's learned a lot about sanitation from him.

"Those bedrooms are disgusting," she snaps, dropping a garbage bag to the floor. "How the hell are they sleeping in there and not dying of mold inhalation?"

"I can't." I hold up my hands. "This place is a fucking sty."

"Men are pigs, baby," Ma says with a snicker.

I vow it here and now, when I become President, I will change everything about the condition of this place, and how they abuse it. No longer will there be all-night ragers and fucking strippers on every surface or letting their sleeping quarters get so disgusting that we need hazmat suits to traverse through them.

I know it'll only add to how much they'll hate me, but I might as well do it all at once.

"You look like you're full of plans," Ma remarks as she sprays disinfectant in the air.

I wish I could tell her everything, the plans Dad has made, and what it'll mean for my future, but I can't. Not yet, anyway.

"Only to kill the men that inhabit this shithole."

romântic
THIS BODY IS
TEMPORARY
BUT THIS SOUL IS
ETERNAL
永遠
JAEGER

JAEGER

We pull up to the dilapidated warehouse, our hair coated in sweat from beneath the bucket helmets and our faces lined with dust from hours on the road. We put our bikes in neutral and sit here idling for a few minutes, looking at the nondescript building.

Something has been nagging at me this whole ride, and the feeling only increased when my eyes landed on this place. Vic taught me to listen to my gut and to follow my instincts, and they're screaming at me to pay attention. My eyes skip along the area, taking note of the large boulders and red sand. Things look too calm.

We shut off our bikes in tandem as the silence stretches around us.

Finally, Vic looks at me and says, "Watch the door. I'm going to head inside."

I give him a salute and continue to watch his back as he saunters into the warehouse. His gait is slow, his shoulders slightly hunched forward, and his hair is hanging limply around his shoulders. I want to tell him about how I'm feeling, but it wouldn't stop the mission we need to complete. The only thing I can do is make sure he's as safe as he can be, regardless of how I feel about him right now. He's not just my President, but my father as well.

"Something about this feels off," Quinton says as he reaches into the pocket of his cut to pull out his pack of smokes. His long fingers are covered in tats, each one a Totem Pole design representing his tribe and ancestors.

"I'm going to go check around the back," Laith grunts as he gets off his bike. My eyes follow his wide back as his long legs eat up the space toward the warehouse.

Quinton's instincts are telling him the same thing mine are. He may be our Sargeant at Arms, but he's also our fucking hunter when we need one. He can sniff anyone out of anywhere, and I never take his observations for granted. I nod, letting him know I sense it too.

I lean back on my bike, fishing into my cut's pocket to pull out my pack of smokes when Quinton clears his throat. "Brother, I've been watching Vic lately. Do you think something is up with him?"

"What makes you say that?" I hold the tip of the flame to my cigarette, watching as the cherry burns bright.

"I don't know." Quinton kicks at the red gravel under his feet. "He's just been weird."

"I'm gonna need to know what he's doing in order to tell you if I think it's weird or not," I push, because I know there's something he's not fucking saying. Quinton has been quiet lately, like he fears if he speaks too much, something might slip.

"Never mind." He waves me off. "I'm just acting like a female."

"True," I agree and take a drag on my smoke.

"I don't hear any gunshots in there," Quinton muses as he looks over his shoulder toward the warehouse. "Shall we check it out?"

Laith reappears from behind the warehouse, a smoke burning bright between his teeth, putting emphasis on the scars that his beard can't disguise. "Place looks clear." He drops the smoke to the ground, crushing it beneath his boot. "Too clear."

I get off my bike with a grunt, flicking my half-finished smoke across the gravel. "You think something's up? Should I go inside?" I ask.

"Nah, you're VP. We need to make sure you stay safe." Laith shakes his head, a few light brown strands escaping his hair tie. "I'll head inside."

We watch the tank of a man make his way inside the warehouse, then he disappears into the shadows, the black void eating up his form.

"Maybe we should have brought more guys," Quinton murmurs.

"Vic doesn't want to worry the club. Plus, there are two different rides today."

Most of the club is out driving our freshly cooked meth to our distributors in the neighboring town. We couldn't break too many off from them to come here with us. It would be too suspicious. Not to mention unsafe for the other group.

"Do you hear that?" Quinton's gruff voice breaks through my thoughts.

The both of us become deathly silent as we watch the distant horizon while listening, and sure enough, there in the distance is the soft rumble of motorcycles.

"Motherfucker," I curse.

"Do you think that's March?"

"I don't know." My hand snaps to the gun clipped to my waist. "But if it is, and they're trying to run up on us, I'm going to shoot as many as I can."

"Should we get Vic?"

"Nah." I shake my head and listen as the bikes grow closer. "He's safer inside."

I stand at the edge of the road, watching as dust kicks up over the rocks in the distance. The best and worst thing about being out in the desert? Stealth is nearly impossible; the sand will always give you away. The rumbling gets louder, and I sense Quinton coming to stand beside me.

"We should have brought the machine gun," he quips.

"Going to avoid a bloodbath if I can." I give him a look from the corner of my eye.

Bikes appear up the road, three of them. As they get closer, I can see that it is indeed Hell's March. Their helmets are bright orange with red flames, the sun's rays making them look like they're actually on fire. Another thing that gives them away. They refuse not to be ostentatious.

"Only three," Quinton scoffs. "Who the fuck do they think they're coming for? The seniors' home?"

"I mean, most of our guys are geriatric."

"But those fuckers are tough at heart," Quinton replies while chuckling as the bikes pull up in front of us.

The first to remove his helmet is Bernard. This must be important if The March is sending him. He's one tough son of a bitch, and they call him Bear for a reason. He's so fucking big that I don't know how the tires are fucking holding up on his bike. His cut is tight around his arms, his biceps like boulders. His hair hangs to his shoulders in black, greasy strands, and his face is hard, etched with a permanent scowl. He has a scar running across his throat from side to side. They say the President of The March tried to slit his throat. When he survived, their President made him Sergeant at Arms.

"What the fuck are you guys doing here?" he asks, his eyes brimming with anger as he's looking between me and Quinton.

The other two don't take off their helmets, the visor on the front blocking parts of their faces, but I know who they are. One, especially.

Malik Charles has the exact same face as Laith. Malik's just missing the scars… The very same scars he put on his own brother's cheeks. Two brothers, once so tight that you couldn't rip them apart. Now, they're on opposing sides in rival motorcycle clubs.

"This place belongs to you?" Quinton asks, thumbing the warehouse over his shoulder. "We're thinking of setting up an ice cream parlor."

"You know fucking well this is ours," Bear growls.

"Is my brother here?" Malik asks, his voice a deep baritone.

"Yeah." I give him a grin. "He's inside. Wanna take a peek?"

He knows as well as I do that if Laith ever comes face-to-face with him again, he'll shoot him between the fucking eyes.

"We came here to talk to you," the third guy says. His name is Diego Montez, and he's a medic for Hell's March.

Diego is educated. He was supposed to become some

fancy surgeon up in NYC, but his daddy was Hell's March. It doesn't matter what you want your career to be, when you have MC in your blood, that's your legacy. Lucky for Hell's March, they now have a medic who can perform surgeries. They'll need it if they keep up their bullshit, because I'm about to pump them full of fucking bullets.

"Talk to me?" I ask. "Or Vic?"

"We were told to find you specifically," Bear says, leaning on the front of his bike. "Let's talk."

"Vic will be out any minute," Quinton says. "So will your brother," he tells Malik.

"Nah. The boys in there know to keep them busy a little while longer." Malik gives him an eerie grin, his black lacquered nails stroking through his short beard.

I meet Quinton's stare through my periphery and give him a subtle nod. "I'm going to go with them."

Quinton's jaw tightens with frustration, but he won't go against me. I am his Vice after all. In his mind, one day, I'll be his President. Maybe that's the only reason I'm giving these assholes a chance to talk. I'm irritated, fucking pissed, and maybe something inside of me is ready to prove I can be President. I *should* be President. I can handle these fucking pussies.

"Who am I talking to?" I look at all three.

"Me." Bear gets off his bike and motions for me to follow him. "Let's take a walk."

The sun's bright rays reflect off the metal siding as I follow Bear to the side of the warehouse. He pulls a joint out of his pocket, sparking the tip, and the heady scent of weed surrounds us as he squints at me through the smoke. "What are you guys really doing here?"

"I can't tell you that." I shrug my shoulders, pulling my smokes out of my cut. "Why don't you start by telling me what you guys are doing here?" I bring the flame of my lighter to my cigarette.

"Aren't you at all worried about how we knew you were

going to be here today?" he asks.

"Crossed my mind."

"Let's cut to the chase." He takes a long drag off the spliff. "How's your pretty little sister? Genevieve, right?"

GENEVIEVE
BMW Motorrad Milano

FOUR

Jaeger won't look me in the eye.

We've been sitting across from each other at the table eating dinner nearly every night this week. He's been coming home because Ma's been begging him to spend more time with us, but he's not really here. His single-word responses and animalistic grunts to her questions are starting to irritate Ma. I can see it in the way she constantly rolls her shoulders or tips her head. The way her cheeks grow pink with anger and her eyes narrow. She doesn't like to be disrespected, and he's real close to being called out with a slap to the cheek.

Dad has also been similarly quiet. Something happened on that ride, as I knew it would. I had a gut feeling that not everything was as it should be, but because I own a pair of tits, I'll never know what it was. Or at least, I don't know *yet*. With Dad's bigger plans for me, maybe he'll let me in on what's going on.

Tomorrow morning I have to be up early. I have another shooting session with Quinton, something I'm not looking forward to. I wish Dad could teach me himself, but he says there's no one as good as Quinton with a shot, just like I know there's no one as good as my brother when it comes to a bomb or fire. The way he's been looking at me lately, I wouldn't be surprised if he put those skills of his to use. It's as if he wants to see me incinerated.

Right now, from across the table, he's glaring at me.

Those black eyes pierce straight through to my heart, proving if looks could kill, I'd be a corpse. I can see by the set of his plush lips that he's angry, but I don't know what I did wrong. We used to be so close growing up, inseparable. He was the big brother I always wanted, and he protected me with little thought. Then, two years ago, it all changed. He no longer wanted to hang out. He stopped laughing at my jokes, and I became a nuisance. I'm not going to lie and say I didn't care. It broke my heart, but I chalked it all up to his rising through the ranks of the Steel Dragons. No longer could he be friends with his little sister.

His hand brushes through his tousled black hair. Even so, his eyes don't waver from my face.

"Genevieve," Ma says, breaking our stare down. "You've been gone a lot lately. What have you been up to?"

Dad's fork hits his plate with a resounding clang, and Jaeger's eyes just burn hotter on me, like he already knows what I've been up to.

"Hanging out." I shrug my shoulders as I pick at the food on my plate.

"Have you considered college yet?" Ma asks. She's been at me for the last year about extending my high school education, and even though I agree with her, I don't know what the fuck to study. Now it's even more confusing with my being my father's successor. Do I look and see if the local college has a course on how to dismember someone properly?

"No," I reply, shaking my head. "I don't know what I want to do." My eyes skip to meet Dad's, his fist curling tightly as it rests on the table.

I don't have to look at *him* to know he's still staring at me. Those black eyes are probably searching for any lie I hold, and I fear if I look up at him, he's going to see them all.

"I feel like all our children are gone now, Vic." Ma reaches over, clasping his fist in her hand. He finally relaxes and opens his palm, linking their fingers together.

"I know, Claire," he says with a touch of sadness in his voice. "All children are meant to fly the coop. I just pray they remember to check in on their parents now and then.”

“I haven’t left to go anywhere,” I remind them, my voice ladened with sarcasm. “I still live here.”

“I gotta go.” Jaeger pushes back his chair to stand, leaving behind his still full plate of food.

“What are you up to tonight?” Dad asks him.

“Me and Quinton are going to go take care of that thing you wanted us to do.” He gives Dad a pointed look, then he heads out of the kitchen, and I hear his boots thudding up the stairs. I begin to rise slowly, my dinner long done.

“What about dessert?” Claire asks as she rises to stand.

“I’ll grab some later.” I pat my stomach. “I’m full.”

She sits back down with a disappointed look. “All right.”

I head upstairs, taking the stairs slowly one at a time, my mind racing with thoughts. I’m so lost in everything in my mind that I don’t do the one thing that’s been ingrained in my mind since I started training with Quinton… I don’t observe my surroundings.

As soon as my foot hits the top stair, a hand wraps around my throat, and my back meets the wall.

“Little sister,” Jaeger growls out. “What are you hiding?”

“Get off of me.” I hit his wrist as surprise coats my words, but he doesn’t budge. “What the fuck do you want?”

“You’re not a very good liar, and you’ve been lying a lot lately.” His face is slowly turning red with anger.

“So you think you can just choke me at the top of the stairs, and I’ll tell you everything you need to know?”

He steps in closer, his body heat radiating against mine, and my head falls back against the wall. We stand nearly eye to eye, which I’m thankful for because to most, his height is intimidating, but to me? He’s just fucking annoying.

His hot breath hits my cheek, and his lips pull back taut against his teeth. “I’ll find out what you’re hiding,” he says, “and then I'm going to make you regret whatever it is you're doing."

"Regret?" My brows crash together with trepidation. "Are you threatening me?"

"I'm warning you." I shove his chest, and this time he lets me move him as he takes a few steps back.

"That's not a warning, it's a threat, and I'd be careful if I were you." My eyes narrow on him.

We stare at each other, our chests heaving, our eyes narrowed. His fists are opening and shutting, the veins on his forearms protruding with his irritation. But his eyes... They can't hide the threat. No longer do they shine with love for me. Right now, they're deep, inky pools of hatred.

He steps forward again, crowding back into my space, and I step back instinctively, my back meeting the wall once more. He bends down slightly, so we are truly eye to eye, and suddenly, his hand hits the wall beside my head, the loud *thud* startling me.

"You may be the princess of this house, the apple of this family's eye, but beyond these walls? You're nothing." Each of his words is spit out with vitriol. The boy I once knew as my brother doesn't reside inside Jaeger. He's drawn the line, and he's made one thing very clear.

We're enemies now.

He steps back to adjust his cut, flicking the Vice President badge, and turning on his heel. He walks away from me, and I watch as he leaves, the Steel Dragons' emblem on his back moving with his steps. My heart is crashing around inside my chest, my stomach like a liquid pool of lava, and then, when he's completely out of sight, I slide down the wall, a sob escaping my throat. I don't know what changed between us. Sure, we went from kids to moody teenagers. But now? As young adults, it feels like we're head-to-head, and there's not a single doubt in my mind. He would never support me as President of the Steel Dragons.

The sun shines in through my bedroom window, searing through my thin eyelids, and forcing me awake. A scowl comes over my face as I look at it with a groan. I hate when I forget to close the curtains, and then another groan sounds when I remember what it is I have to do this morning. I have to face Quinton; I have to hold a gun, and I have to shoot at things moving around me. My concentration is going to be shit today because all I can see is my stepbrother's dark eyes filled with hatred. All I can hear is his palm hitting the wall beside my head, and all I can feel is my broken heart.

I drag myself out of bed, forcing myself to shower, and once I'm dressed, I head downstairs to the kitchen. Ma's at the counter, putting together my favorite waffles and strawberries and lays it on the table.

"Your father said he had to run an errand this morning and that you could take yourself to your appointment." Her eyebrow raises. She wants to ask me what this appointment is, and I don't blame her. It feels top secret. If I was in her position, I'd be curious too.

"Just an oil change for the bike." I shrug, my eyes downcast and staring at the waffles on my plate. The thought of her hurting because of my lies makes me feel queasy.

"All right," she drawls, setting a glass of milk beside my plate. "I'm thinking of going to the spa today. Lord knows I need some sort of relaxation. Will you be home for dinner?"

"I should be."

"Okay, sweetie. Have a good day." Her heels hit the tile floor, the sound breaking up my thoughts as she walks away. I'm suddenly feeling like scum. Nothing good comes from secrets. They isolate you, pulling you away from the people you love. The guilt eats at you, tears up your insides, and burns you with acid. I hate secrets, but there's absolutely nothing I wouldn't do for my father. *Nothing.*

Once my breakfast is sitting heavy in my stomach, I get on my bike and pull the helmet down over my head. I pause, looking down at the yellow color, running my hands along the paint. This bike has been my baby for years. I don't want to have to give it up. Would I have to ride a Harley like the old men in the MC? I can't imagine myself on a cruiser. The thought sends a shudder through me.

I start up the bike and pull out of the driveway, heading toward the vacant warehouse. This time my ride is solo, giving me a lot of time to think. I try to piece together why my father would want to put this on me. Nothing about it feels like a privilege. It scares me because it feels like a declaration of war. My shoulders are buckling from the weight of the burden, and I'm too afraid to tell him I'm scared. I'm scared for me, I'm scared for Ma, but mostly, I'm scared for him.

The respect he's gained, that he's worked tooth and nail for, will all be washed out in a second. The very moment he announces me as the future President of the Steel Dragons MC, everything he's worked for will be washed down the drain. There's no situation, there's no reasoning that I can think of for him to do something so drastic. Then there's the time frame, the rush of it all. It feels like I need to learn so many things in such a short period of time. The fact that I have to work with guns and shoot at inanimate objects is telling me one thing. He's making me into a killer. One that will shoot first and ask questions later. He wants me to be able to take a life without remorse, to wear a cut, and blend in with the men who ride behind him through thick and thin. No matter the weather, they endure it for him. I can't see that happening for me.

The thought of having to kill anyone makes me feel sick to my stomach. To point a gun at someone's head, intending to blow it off, makes my hands shake with trepidation. I can't see any amount of training changing that. I was raised to have humanity, to regard life as precious, and to live every day like it's my last because life is a gift. A hard lesson taught through my mother's passing.

Jaeger wasn't raised the same. He was raised to kill or be killed, to have a switch on his humanity and turn it on and off at will. His ruthlessness and his utter disregard for life are what's going to make him an amazing Vice President for the MC though. He shoots first, and I doubt if he ever asks questions. I can't see him standing beside me while I'm President. There's no way he would support that, not with how tumultuous we are, and I may be the one on the wrong side of his gun when he finds out.

I pull into the warehouse, the sound of my engine pulling Quinton from the inside. He stands at the doorway, his hands on his waist with his cut hanging over a black T-shirt. His jeans are scuffed and dirty, a little loose around the waist and hanging low while his belt buckle shines with a steel dragon, the surface reflecting the bright sun. He has his hair braided back away from his face, shining with blue highlights. I haul off my helmet, setting it on the bars, but I don't make a move to get off my bike. I watch him as he watches me, both of us, silent and scrutinizing. His skin is like bronze in the Arizona sun, his cheekbones high and protruding, and his nose is prominent and straight. Then that sinful mouth. The top lip has a harsh dip in the center as the full bottom lip cushions it, creating a perfect balance. His jawline is covered in scruff, almost like he hasn't shaved in a few days, giving him an intimidating look.

I get off the bike and dust off my jeans. No matter where you go in Arizona, there's no avoiding the dust. The sand just floats in the air, attaching itself to anything in its way. Slowly, I walk toward him and watch as he drops his hands from his waist, his posture relaxing.

"Are we ready to shoot down some innocent bystanders today?" A small smirk lines his mouth and his eyes hold a teasing glint in them. "Maybe a few pregnant women? We can see if there's some squirrels in the back?"

"Sure." I shrug my shoulders and walk by him into the warehouse, boredom etched in my tone.

"Hey, what's eating you?" he asks as he comes up behind me, handing me an extra hair tie. "You need to tie up your hair."

"Can you just get me the gun? I want to get this over with," I say as I snatch the hair tie and pile my hair up on top of my head.

He stands there watching me without moving, and I do all I can to avoid his eyes. But as the silence stretches, it begins to get uncomfortable, so I finally turn to look at him. For once, Quinton's not picking on me or laughing at me. Instead, he's looking at me with curiosity.

QUINTON

QUINTON

The ride to the warehouse today was wrought with irritation, and it all stemmed from the fact that my brothers got to sleep in. Me, though? I had to drag my ass up at the ass crack of dawn to come here and deal with a petulant child. As I stand here and look into her eyes, I stand corrected. She looks sad, and maybe a little scared. It hits at the protectiveness inside of me, and I feel it clawing its way out as I try to push it back down.

The longer I look into her eyes, the more I want to wrap her up in my arms and promise her nothing bad will ever happen. Instead, I break eye contact and stride forward to grab the gun she used last time. I load it with bullets as she stays in the same spot, looking down at her feet.

"Gen," I call out to her, her face rising to look at me with curiosity. "Did you wanna get started?"

"Do you know why I'm here?" she asks, not moving from her spot.

"Yeah, to shoot at targets. Well, in your case, any innocent bystander." I wave my hand around, pushing her to get to the point.

"My father didn't tell you why I'm here? Or why we're doing this?" Her head tips with the inquiry.

I place the gun back down on the table and turn to face her. My hands press into my waist as I exhale a frustrated huff. "I don't know exactly why, Gen." My brow lifts. "I don't ever question what my President asks of me."

"Any President?"

"What do you mean?" I tip my head. "The President of the MC. Whatever he tells me to do, I do it without question."

"What about if my father was no longer the President?"

"Then, whoever the new President is, which is most likely going to be your brother since he's Vice. I listen to everything he says too."

"Do you promise?" she whispers.

With an earnest look on her face and the scared sound of her words, I'm hauled into yet another predicament. There's a secret here somewhere, and I don't know if I have the energy to decipher another Varga puzzle. So I turn my back to pick up the gun and hold it out to her.

"I don't know about a promise, Gen," I answer truthfully as she grabs the gun from my hand. "We're all sworn to it. It's what we have to do."

"I see," she murmurs, walking toward the targets.

She doesn't see shit. She doesn't know what this life is about. She doesn't have a fucking clue about the oaths we take as prospects and carry through to the end of our lives. When our dead bodies meet the dirt of our graves, then our oaths are declared kept. She doesn't understand it's not a promise, it's a declaration. Hell, it's a fucking law.

The consequence of breaking the club's laws? Exile. To some, that may be no big deal. So what if you have to leave town? I know most men in clubs who face exile would rather choose death. There's no coming back from that, and your life is over, anyway.

I lean against the table, watching Genni as she shoots at the targets. They're just paper cutouts since I haven't started up the machines for the moving ones yet, but her stance is better. She has the perfect width between her feet, her back is straight, and her shoulders are relaxed, her arms are loose but steady. It's only been a few days of lessons, but already I can see that she's absorbed everything and puts it to use. When she starts firing at the targets, I can see her bullet holes are a little closer to the bullseye than it was the day before and the day before that.

Again, I'm stuck with another puzzling predicament with the Vargas. What's making her learn to shoot? To absorb all the information and enact it? What threat could there be that Vic would summon an emergency training for his daughter? If someone was after her, we'd be on a ride. If there was any kind of threat, we could take care of it. Shit, Jaeger would bomb the place. He would burn the town to the ground before he let anyone threaten his sister.

So that leaves another question. What is this Varga hiding?

A few days ago, when Jaeger took a walk with Bear from Hell's March, every hair on my body stood up on end. How did they know we were there? Why didn't they come for a fight? It was almost like a meeting was planned between Jaeger and Bear. Which doesn't make sense. Jaeger doesn't talk to them. I mean, I don't think he does, but my heart was in my throat the whole time. The whole *fucking* time. I was just waiting for Laith to step out of that warehouse and see his brother. Then I'd be in the middle of a shootout. Fuck, Vic would've started the shootout had he walked out first. But then it felt like as quickly as it had begun, the meeting was over as both men walked back toward us. Jagger sat back on his bike, stubbing out a cigarette while we watched Bear sit back on his, putting his helmet on and starting up his bike. I looked between them and I remember thinking… Is this where we start shooting? Instead, they popped their helmets on and rode out in formation, like we were at the fucking PTA meeting.

It made no sense. It still makes no sense. And when I asked Jaeger, *"What the fuck was that about?"*

He told me, *"It's all good, man. I'm taking care of it."*

I wanted to ask him, taking care of what? What the fuck did our rival want with you? Because they certainly came here looking for him. Before I could rant or run off my questions, Vic and Laith came out of the warehouse. Perfect timing, if you ask me.

For the past few days, all I have running through my head are questions, and every single one of them pertains to a Varga. Whether it's Vic, Jaeger, and now, as I watch this girl shoot a bullseye straight between the eyes of her target, without a reaction, I'm beginning to question her too.

"Hey, looks good. Looks like you could shoot someone if they're standing still," I call out, needing a reaction. But instead, she keeps looking forward, giving her shoulders a shrug. "Let's set up the moving targets," I declare as I push off the table. I walk toward the tracks that hold the mannequins. "I'll give you one hundred bucks if you can hit the pregnant lady again."

No reaction. Her face remains stoic and her gun is still aimed ahead as she waits for me.

I usually don't let this shit get to me. I don't care what

people think, what they're feeling, or how their day is going. I don't give a fuck. But today, I'm giving a fuck. Why? I don't fucking know. Maybe I'm bored, maybe these Vargas are getting under my goddamn skin.

She reloads the gun and holds up a hand. "Don't start those yet. I haven't been able to hit that target." She points her slender finger with her pink nail toward the last paper target in the warehouse. It's far. It's the hardest to shoot, and if you're a beginner, it's a slim chance you'll hit it.

"Leave that one," I tell her. "That's a difficult one."

She ignores me as her jaw hardens, and she aims the gun, uncaring if I'm within the target. Irritation is bleeding from her pores, another similarity she has with the Varga men. Competitive as fuck. She shoots two rounds, her jaw only growing tighter, her eyes narrowing, and her body stiffening. She's not going to hit shit like that. So I come up behind her and her arms drop to her sides, along with her gun. I run my fingers along the thick, mahogany curtain of her hair, gathering it up and pulling it to the side, revealing the thin column of her throat. My eyes land on her pulse, and I can see it fluttering against her skin. I know I was looking for a reaction, but this wasn't it. Fuck if I can ignore it though.

I bend down and run my nose along the space between her shoulder and her neck, breathing in her scent. Something close to vanilla and a bit spicy hits me. An enigma, just like Genni. Her body finally relaxes and her head tips back to touch my shoulder. She releases a long sigh; the stress radiating in the space around us.

My cock is hard, straining in my pants, and like most times, my mind loses control. The things I want and crave take over. No more logic, just primal need. So I step into her, my groin lightly brushing her ass, and she lets out a moan. She arches her back, pressing that delicious ass farther into me, and I close my eyes, opening my mouth, readying to lick my tongue along her skin when her voice breaks me out of my lust-filled need.

"Why don't you bend me over the table, Quinton?" she husks out, making my cock jump against my zipper. "Or wait, why don't you call Carrie? Or is it Angel? How would you like to be between them?

At the sound of the Club Bunnies' names, I pull back, my spine straightening and my surroundings coming back in crystal clear definition. Shit. What the fuck was I doing?

"Leave that target," I snap, then walk over to the machines. "We're working on the moving ones right now. I don't want to be here all day."

"Okay."

I was expecting her to snap, to react, to retaliate. At the very least, be punctured by her words because she's so good at tossing them out. But instead, she readies her stance, and that jaw tightens again. That's when I realize something bad is happening to Gen. It's a gut feeling, and I don't ever want to ignore it.

"Hey, Gen. You know, if you needed anything, I would help you, right?" I tell her. She turns to look at me, her eyebrow in the air. I get why she has doubts. It's not like I've ever had to help her before. I mean, she hasn't asked for any help, and I haven't been the nicest, but regardless, she's family. "Seriously, if something is wrong, you can tell me." She turns away from me again and begins to reload her gun, avoiding eye contact.

"I'm fine, Quinton," she calls out as I start the motors for the tracks. "Let me see if I can win that $100 from you."

And she does.

She wins $300 by the time we're done.

JAEGER

JAEGER

My hand wraps around his bloodied neck, his nose dripping like a fucking fountain, and the bright red crimson flows over my hand. He's tied to a wooden chair, the thick ropes cutting across his chest and stomach.

"I'm going to ask you one more time, motherfucker. Where the fuck is our money?"

"I just need a few more days." The guy shakes like a fucking leaf.

My fist connects with his cheek, the chunky rings I have on my fingers, splitting the skin open along the bone. "You've had two weeks," I snarl as I grab his cheeks again, pressing my fingers into the delicate skin and watching as the blood pours from the newest wound. "Two weeks. I need that ten grand."

"I was robbed," he begins to say while sobbing hysterically. "I had your money. I had the interest, but I was robbed."

"And how is that my fucking problem?" I bend down into his face, spit landing on his forehead from the force of my words. "How the fuck is that my problem?"

"It was a Hell's March prospect," he sobs out. "He knew I had your product. He knew I was pushing your product, so he broke into my house. He took a fucking bat to my face."

"Hell's March?" I question as dread settles in the pit of my stomach. "You sure about that?"

"Course I'm fucking sure." The blood runs down between his teeth and dribbles out over his bottom lip. "I saw the cut he had on."

I release him with a shove and turn with a curse. Hell's March is coming into our territory way too frequently lately. It's starting to really fucking piss me off with how often they're coming into our town, slipping beneath our noses, and leaving a trail of shit behind them.

I said as much to Bear when we had our little talk, when

he shocked me with the information he decided to share. I want to say I had a hard time believing what he was telling me, but after the shit I found out this week, anything is fucking possible.

If this was a few weeks ago, I would have immediately dismissed it. I probably would have shot him in the head, to be honest. Now I'm questioning everything. I'm questioning my brothers and my father, but most of all, I'm questioning my sister. I'm suspicious of her. I want to believe none of this is her doing, but I can't.

"Listen." I crack my bloodied knuckles and look Junior in the face. "There's a reason I gave you the shit I did. You told me you could distribute it quietly." I hold up one finger. "That you wouldn't let anything happen to it." I hold up a second finger. "And that I would get my money." I hold up the third and final finger. "That didn't happen, Junior."

"Look, I know." He holds out his hands, his face a mottle of blue, red, and purple colors, and blood drips off his jaws onto his white T-shirt. "I don't know how they found out I was running for you guys."

"Obviously,"—I raise my brow and grab my smokes out of the back pocket of my jeans—"you ran your mouth to someone." I open the case and pull out a cigarette, the blood on my fingers soaking through the thin paper. Wouldn't be the first time I smoked bloody tobacco.

"No, Jaeger." His eyes roll into the back of his head, proving he's gripping on to the last vestiges of his consciousness as his words slur. "Listen to me. I didn't tell anyone. Why would I? I have a rap sheet the length of this room. Why would I want my parole officer finding out I'm running shit for you?"

I won't deny it… he does have a point. I pop the cigarette in my mouth, flip open my Zippo, and take my time lighting the tip of my smoke. I snap the lid shut, the sound bouncing off the walls as we're both silent, dropping the case and the light back into my pocket. I take a long drag, inhaling the smoke into my lungs, praying it gives me some patience, and then I slowly exhale, blowing out rings as I keep staring into his eyes.

"Do you have a theory?" I ask, mainly because I'm curious, but there's a part of me that's a little lost here. Everything he's saying sounds legit. I've just pummeled his face and chest for the past hour. I'm pretty sure his jaw is busted, his nose is broken, and maybe even a few ribs. Despite that, he's kept his story straight.

His head drops, his chin hitting his chest. "I don't know, man." He shakes his head, his blood flinging out in a perfect arch around his seat. "I think you have a mole."

"You think…" I step up to him and grab a handful of his wet hair, forcing his head up to look at me. "One of my brothers betrayed us? That my family here is fucking us over?"

"I told no one, Jaeger." He begins to shake again, fear emanating out of him and filling the room with potent energy, feeding the primal beast inside of me.

I take the last drag on my cigarette, holding his head steady as I press the burning hot cherry into his cheek. His screams filter around the room, the echoes slamming into my body, only heightening the beast a little more. Unfortunately, with all the blood and sweat on his face, the cigarette goes out way too quickly.

"So, who do you think betrayed me?" I ask him, bending down and looking deep into his bloodshot eyes. The brown of his irises is nearly blending in with the pink. "Tell me, Junior. Who outed you? Who betrayed their family?"

It's at that moment the door opens and in walks Kennedy, our Enforcer. He's a lanky fucker. Skinny with protruding cheekbones. He looks like a fucking druggie waiting to suck off the next dealer for his last fix, but it's only a front. The greasy, black hair that hangs to his shoulders, the long, nearly gray beard that hits his stomach, and those beady, bloodshot, black eyes are only a disguise for what lurks just beneath the surface. There's a reason why he's our Enforcer, and he does his job real fucking well.

"You called, boss?" he says as he strides into the room, letting his vest slip off his shoulders and down his arms. He hangs it up next to the door on the hook beside mine and comes over to stand next to me, where I still have Junior's hair in my hand.

"Got ourselves a situation here, Ken," I say without breaking eye contact with Junior. Mind you, it's not much contact.

His eyes keep rolling back into his head, and I fear I won't have much longer getting the information I need. "Junior here has lost ten grand of our crystal."

"Is that right?" Kennedy begins to excitedly crack his knuckles, his body coiling for what he knows is a treat today. He's a hard one to decipher, but I can see the way his eyes shine with eagerness, and right now, he's a fucking kid in a candy shop.

"Get this." I bark out a laugh, releasing Junior's hair. "He says Hell's March stole it from him." It's only for a split second, but I catch it. Kennedy's eyes flick to me, widening slightly before they slip back to look at Junior's lolling head. "That's not all," I supply. "He also thinks one of our brothers let the secret out."

"So, what you're telling me," he says, his voice monotone, not the slightest lilt detected in its depth. "This man is looking to commit suicide?"

I chuckle as I run my hand down my face, feeling the blood coating my fingers transferring onto my cheeks.

"You gotta give it to him," I reply with a laugh. "It was a well thought up story."

"I think Junior here enjoyed a little too much of our crystal himself," Kennedy suggests.

"Possibly." I nod as I shake out my hands and head over to the wall to grab my cut. "Possibly," I repeat.

"Leave the rest up to me," he says as Junior groans.

"Let me know what you find out." I shrug on my cut and walk to the door. "And when you're done, make sure a prospect is in here to clean the place up."

"You got it, boss."

I leave and shut the door behind me. Not two seconds later, Junior's wails filter through the large, industrial steel door.

I'm in the clubhouse's basement, in a section we've named The Slaughter Room. Steel floors, steel walls, steel doors, all easily cleaned on the days we have a butchering. Like today.

I head back upstairs, and as I get closer to the main room,

I hear Mötley Crüe playing "Girls, girls, girls." It means the older brothers are up there and maybe a few of the younger ones too since we all seem to tolerate their era of music and such. Sure enough, I find a few girls dancing on the bar top, and a few of the older brothers lounging on the couch, watching them as they pass a spliff back and forth. They don't ride much anymore, and their day of running product is over, but their membership is forever, and they're always welcome here. I would still lay my life on the line for them, because we wouldn't be what we are today without them.

I find Laith at the bar, drinking from his fucking weird little cup filled with coffee again, and I snicker as I sit down.

"Man, you and your little fucking teacups."

"Shut the fuck up," he snarls as he downs the rest of his Turkish coffee, putting it back on the bar top. "Looks like you were having a good time." He gestures to my blood-soaked shirt and jeans.

"One of us has to deal with all the fun." I raise my hand for Chip to bring me a beer. "Have you seen Quinton?"

"Nope." Laith shakes his head. "He's been slipping out a lot lately."

He has been.

I'm not sure what he's doing, and when I question him, he gives me some fucking lame excuses, like he's visiting his family or at his father's grave. You know, excuses I can't call him out on, because if they're true, it'll make me even more of a cunt. He's not just my best friend, he's my fucking brother.

The bottle of beer lands in front of me, and I crack it open, the hiss releasing from the mouth, giving me pause. Suddenly, it feels like something ominous is about to happen. I take a drink of my beer and sit in silence with Laith, because that's what he's good for. He listens, he keeps quiet, and he keeps his fucking opinions to himself. I respect that.

I pull my cell phone out of my cut, bringing up Quinton's number. I call him for the fifth time today and get his voicemail yet again. When his recorded voice sounds through my ear, I hang up the phone with a curse.

I'm starting to feel like the glue that's always held us together is slowly fading. Vic isn't around as much, spending a lot of time with his daughter or my mother, and I can't complain about that. He made me Vice to fill in for his absences. I'm trying to do that and keep up the morale, but also maintain our reputation. It's hard when I feel like the family around me is crumbling.

It's hard to hold this position, knowing there's no further I can go. There's no chance I'll ever be President, not unless I contest Vic's decision. Not unless I look my sister dead in her eyes and challenge her. It would mean certain death for one of us. It would mean certain death for *her*.

"Quinton said something about seeing my brother," Laith breaks the silence as I take another swig of my beer.

"Yeah, we saw him."

I don't know why my heart begins to pump a little bit faster. Maybe it's those twin scars he sports on his cheeks, given to him by his twin brother, that cripples my insides with unease. I was never hiding the fact that I saw Malik from Laith. I just hadn't had the opportunity to tell him yet.

"What did he want?" he asks.

"They were monitoring the warehouse, and when we pulled up, they rode out, wanting to know why we were there."

"Quinton said something about your father not knowing."

I'm going to kill Quinton.

"I'm Vice now, Laith. Some things I got to handle for him. He's getting old, and I need to ease him into his retirement while convincing him I can handle the job."

"You're going to be a great President." Laith taps my shoulder, then he gets up off the barstool and heads toward the bedrooms.

Kennedy appears from the basement looking like he's washed up. His hair's wet, combed back over his head, but as he gets closer, I don't miss the dots of blood that appear on his face and arms.

"Well?" I ask him, as he leans against the bar, his heavily ringed fingers tapping along the surface of the wood.

"If I were to make a guess," he starts, those fingers, *tap, tap, tapping*. "I would say he was being truthful."

"Fuck," I hiss.

He shoves off the bar and gives me a nod, then heads to the bedrooms.

If it's true, then Hell's March is slowly taking down our distributors. It means they're infiltrating our market, hoping to distribute here in our place. Which means they're looking to start another war, and they're confident they'll win.

Is this newfound confidence because of what Bear told me?

My fist hits the bar, my growl of frustration making Chip snap his head my way, his brow rising. I get down off the stool and stride outside, anger radiating throughout my chest. My hands clench and my teeth grind together at the fucking situation I find myself in.

I get on my bike, shoving my helmet on my head. I wish I could go to my dad and question him, telling him I overheard everything, then make him tell me what's happening. Because right now, I'm feeling so fucking alone and the burden on my shoulders grows heavier every day.

The sound of another bike approaching has me settling in my seat and my eye trained on the gates. When Chino's bike pulls into view, his arm lifts and a prospect runs to the gate to open it.

I haven't seen this fucker all day, and with the anger already burning through my body, the temperature only rises at the sight of him. I could have used his help today, but instead, I found myself alone and that's been happening way too much lately. Fuck his family. I'm his family. This club is his family.

Chino cruises by me, giving me a nod as he parks his bike in his spot. He cuts the engine and pulls his bucket helmet off his head.

"What's up, brother?" he calls out. I keep my mouth shut

as I bite into the skin of my cheek, the taste of blood coating my tongue. My fingers itch to grab the piece strapped to my belt, to pull it out and cock it, then point it at his fucking head. "Jaeger." He gets off the bike and slowly moves toward me. "What happened?" I finally break eye contact and rev my engine, pulling out of the spot without giving him another look. "Wait," he calls out, but I'm already gone.

Quinton Chino is a loyal brother, but right now, that loyalty is no longer to me.

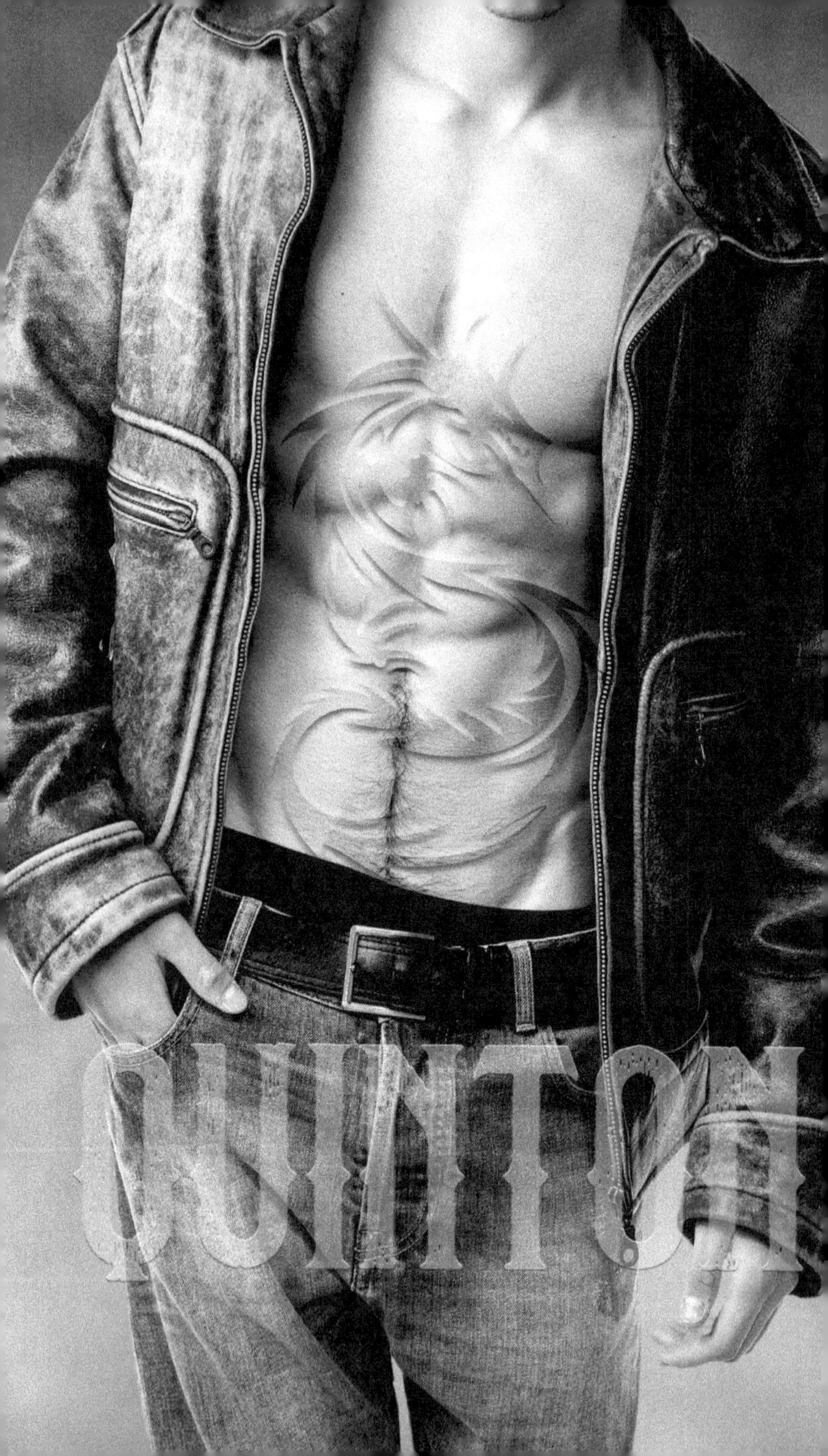
QUINTON

FIVE

Jaeger leaves the lot, his cut blowing in the breeze behind his back, and I stand here like an idiot watching him leave. He's pissed. I knew he would be, but what else can I do? Vic is asking me to train his daughter. I can't say no to him. Then there's my best friend, my brother from when we were ten years old, who is slowly drifting away from me because I've been absent. I can see the mistrust building in his eyes, and it kills me.

I kick at the gravel, then saunter inside the clubhouse. It's quiet tonight. A few brothers are around the pool table, their eyes on the girls dancing in front of them, and another couple are sitting at the bar, but besides that, the place is empty. With a few nods at the guys, I head to the back, toward my room. The place smells cleaner, and I know we have Claire and Genni to thank for that.

Genni.

There's something about her that's just been gripping me and slowly sinking past my toughened exterior. She's worming her way inside of me, and I know it's because she's yet another mystery my mind wants to unwrap. She's been practicing with a gun the days she's not with me, because the target she was hitting today should be well beyond her expertise.

I open my bedroom door and see my fresh bed linens perfectly made up. The condoms that were lining the floor are now gone and the room's been given a vacuum. I shrug off my cut and fold it, placing it on top of my dresser, then I head into my small bathroom. Turning on the light and blinking through the bright fluorescents, my mind once again drifts to the Varga family as my fists land on the counter around the sink.

Vic and my dad were close, best friends even. My father worshiped Vic, and he proved it by jumping in front of a bullet meant for his President. He died selflessly, and the thought makes me proud.

I would do the same for Vic or Jaeger.

Maybe even Genni.

My mother wasn't so accepting, so when my father died, she tried to pull me out of the club and move me back to the reservation. Vic wouldn't let her. I wasn't just a prospect anymore, I was a full-blown member, and I even refused to go. My family is here in this clubhouse.

I don't think she's ever forgiven me fully for it.

I'm an only child, so when Jaeger came to live with Vic, I was overjoyed. We clicked instantly and we've rarely been apart. A few days here and there. If Jaeger has to go on a ride and I'm not accompanying him, or vice versa, but otherwise, we're here together at the clubhouse. We eat together; we ride together; we kill together, and we fuck together.

But he's drifting.

Maybe I'm drifting? My assignments have changed. Now I'm teaching the Varga Princess how to shoot a fucking gun while my brothers are out riding, causing mayhem, and cleaning the streets.

My fist drives into the counter as I growl through my teeth. What is the point of all this?

I pull off my clothes and start the shower, waiting for the steam to rise above the shower curtain. I slowly unbraid my hair, letting the long strands hit the bottom of my back, the raven color shining stark under the fluorescents. With my hair down like this, I look like the man my father once was, and it makes my heart ache. I miss him. I'd love to have him here now, to give me some words of guidance, because I don't know what the fuck is going on. Intuitively, I have my suspicions.

Vic is worried about his daughter. Something's going on with Genni, something important, possibly dangerous. He's teaching her to take care of herself, to fight for herself, and ultimately, to protect herself. His eyes have been heavy with fear as he tries to act nonchalant. He knows something the rest of us don't and being president, that could be the case. I just don't understand how it involves his daughter.

Lately, Vic's focus hasn't been on Jaeger and coupled with my absences, Jaeger's probably feeling pretty neglected right now. I bet he's feeling alone.

Guilt eats through me as I step into the shower, letting the hot water pelt down over my face and chest. Now my thoughts wander toward the youngest Varga. The way her mahogany hair fell out of her hair tie today, the thick strands refusing to be held up, and her skin reminding me of the creamiest coffee. Saliva gathers in my mouth. I won't deny it. I've always wanted a taste of Genni Varga.

It doesn't matter that she's my brother's little sister. As soon as she grew tits, and that ass of hers ballooned, my fingers itched to touch. I know Jaeger sees it, but he's kept out of my way, only because I haven't acted on any impulses. But now I'm spending time alone with her, long periods of time, and I can feel myself weakening. When I stood behind her today, smelling her skin, I almost gave in. Consequences be damned.

My cock hardens, and I drop my head to look down as my hand wraps around my length. It's been a long time since I've fucked my hand. There are enough Club Bunnies to go around, and even if there weren't, I can call whoever I want over here.

But none of them would be Genni.

I think about the way her midnight blue eyes blaze with heat when she's angry, how her cheeks blush when she's about to lose her temper, and then those plush lips pursing when she's ready to give a verbal lashing.

My hand pumps steadily along my cock, my balls tightening as I imagine her here, kneeling in front of me, begging for just a single drop of my cum. I would deny her, fisting my hand into the scalp of her head, and yank her up until we were face-to-face. Then I would spin her around to push her face and chest into the tiled wall.

Both of my hands would grip into the thick globes of her ass, spreading her open. Her cunt would glisten with arousal, the juices dripping down her thighs and mixing with the water from the shower. I would slam inside of her without a barrier between us. No condom… nothing. She would feel every inch of my cock, taking each thrust I'd pound into her, and my fingers would jam into her mouth, sealing off any noise she'd be trying to make.

I'd fuck her roughly, her face bouncing off the tile, her ass reddening from the slaps of my palms, and her fucking pussy weeping around my thick cock. She'd be begging me to stop, trying to speak around my fingers, but I'd hold her tongue in place, my fingers sinking into the tissue and forcing her to shut the fuck up.

I continue to fuck her without abandonment, uncaring of her pleasure and only chasing my own. My balls tighten as my cock thickens, my cum working its way up my shaft. My pelvis is slapping off her ass, the loud, smacking noises reverberating around the shower, and then I'm coming with a shout as tears escape her eyes.

I release my cock and open my eyes to find myself completely alone with thick ropes of my cum dotting the tiled wall in front of me.

"Fuck," I hiss out as I turn off the water. This is bad.

The more time I spend in Genni's company, the more I fear the weakening of my resolve. I consider myself strong. There's not much that can sway me.

Except for a nice pussy.

Anger simmers in my veins as I open the shower curtain. I can't get caught up in Genni now. My ambitions in this club trump my President's hot daughter. I need to somehow tell Vic his daughter can shoot the fucking gun and that she doesn't need any more lessons from me. Snatching the towel off the wall, I wrap it around my waist and head back into my bedroom.

I grab a clean pair of jeans, another black T-shirt, and then put my cut back on before I leave the room. It doesn't leave my body, except for the times I'm sleeping or when I'm dead.

Some guys have put on some better music in the main room as I head inside. The sun is setting as Chip slips behind the bar, serving beer to a few of the guys, and then he's pouring coffee into a tiny little cup. That's when my eyes fall on Laith. He rarely drinks now, not since he took that bullet to the face. Sitting beside him is Kennedy, our club's Enforcer, and a sadistic son of a bitch.

I sit on the stool on the other side of Kennedy and both he and Laith turn to look at me, each sporting a small smile on their faces.

"You missed the fun today." Kennedy snickers as he takes a drink of his beer.

"Oh, yeah?" I quirk a brow at his words.

"Jaeger had Junior by for a visit." Kennedy's smug voice hits my ears. "I got to have a little fun."

"What?" My eyes skip to Laith, his shoulder tipping up to his ear. "Why did Jaeger have Junior here?" Unease courses through my chest as my voice drops.

"Seemed like the kid was stealing the merchandise. Not paying his dues," Kennedy supplies.

Fuck. I'm the one who suggested Junior to be a drug runner for the club. He's a loner, quiet kid, doesn't get himself into too much shit. No wonder Jaeger is pissed.

"That's not like Junior," I say as I motion for Chip to bring me a beer. All of this is so disconcerting.

"He was adamant he was robbed by a Hell's March. He said it was a prospect," Kennedy speaks like he's dishing out some hot gossip, when in fact, all of this will probably be what signs my death certificate.

Junior was my responsibility. I dropped the shit off, and I was supposed to pick up the money. That was supposed to be last week, the day I was teaching Princess Varga how to fucking shoot. So I guess Jaeger picked up my slack today.

"Where's Junior?" I ask. My skin breaks out in goose bumps as Kennedy chuckles, the sound like an ominous church organ fraying my last fucking nerve.

"I chopped him up into little, tiny, itty, bitty bits."

"Fuck!" I slam my beer bottle on the counter and stand from the stool. "I need to call Jaeger." My outburst has Kennedy snickering while Laith groans.

"Wait!" Laith calls out, standing from his stool. "It's not a good idea, man. He wasn't in a good mood. I think you should just let him stew." He's always giving sound advice, but his calm suggestions aren't going to work this time.

"Something interesting came up," Kennedy continues, giving me a sly look. "Jaeger said something about a mole in our compound. Would you know anything about that, Chino?"

The way he says my name sends shocks of static electricity over my skin, and the need for violence overwhelms me.

"Why the fuck would I know anything about that?" My chest puffs in anger as my jaw tightens to the point of cracking.

"Guys." Laith puts his hand on my chest as I take a step toward Kennedy. I don't care if he's a sadistic motherfucker. I'll fight him right here and now. "Cool off." Laith taps my hard chest.

"What's going on over here?" My spine stiffens at the sound of Vic's voice. He's not usually at the clubhouse in the evenings anymore. He likes to spend his time with Claire and let us younger brothers chill out.

"Nothing's going on, boss." Kennedy rises off the stool, slinging his arm over my shoulder. Just the scent of him has murderous intent rolling through me. "I was just telling Chino about my day."

I shrug his arm off of me in frustration and turn to find Vic, his face looking haggard and his eyes drooping with exhaustion. Concern soon wipes out the irritation I'm feeling.

"Pres." My eyes rove over his face. "Are you okay?"

"I actually need to talk to you," he tells me, nodding his head toward the corner of the room. He turns and leads me over to the single door. It has a large, golden plaque in the center, and the word *Mass* in large capital letters embossed on the plate. "We need some privacy," he says as he unlocks the door, swinging it open and motioning for me to go ahead.

We don't use this room besides meetings. We talk about our agendas, what we're selling, profits, losses, battles, war. This room has heard and seen it all, but I haven't been in here without it being a designated time for Church. So the fact that he's hauling me in here, and soon after the shit with Junior has gone down, makes me feel like I'm in deep shit.

"It's about Gen," Vic says after he closes the door.

"What about her?" I'm relieved this isn't about Junior, but it being about Genni is just as bad.

"I think she's shutting down, getting overwhelmed." Vic falls into his chair at the head of the table with a worried sigh, his fingers wrapping around a large gavel that sits on a thick, wooden disk. I've only ever had to see him pound that thing into the table twice. Both times, the brothers were getting rowdy and on the verge of fighting each other.

"There's not much I can tell you because I don't know what's going on," I admit to him as I sit in the chair to his right. The chair that's belonged to Jaeger for as long as I can remember, and just sitting here gives me a sense of pride. "I noticed she was quiet today," I admit to him while I scratch my chin in thought.

"She doesn't have any friends," Vic confesses. "I mean, none that I see stick around. She's a free spirit, and I feel like I'm breaking her."

I open my mouth, then close it, then open it again, but I don't have an explanation for him, because I don't know what's going on, or what exactly he's doing to break his daughter.

"Maybe ease up on this heavy shit. Does she need to learn how to shoot right now? Three lessons in a week feels like overkill. Is she in danger?" I ask him as I lean back in the seat. I wouldn't mind not having to teach the brat any more shit.

"My family will always be in danger. They are my weakest point, but no, she's not in immediate danger." I can see how troubled he is by the set of his mouth, the corners dipping downward harshly.

"I think maybe easing up on the shooting. You know, and the defense shit. It's not usually a girl's thing," I try to advise him. "Maybe she needs friends to hang out with, go to the mall or something. Girls love that."

He chuckles and I watch as he runs his fingers through his beard. "Yeah, someone should take her out to the mall."

"Yeah, what else do girls like? Ice cream and shit?" I suggest as I wave my hand between us.

"Yeah. Ice cream. That's a good idea." I watch as a slow smile works its way over his mouth.

My chest heats with pride. It's me sitting in here with the President, advising him on what he should do to help his family. I bet my father is smiling down on me right now.

"Come by the house tomorrow evening. I'll let her know someone is coming to take her out."

"Wait, what?"

GENEVIEVE
BMW Motorrad Milano

GENEVIEVE

Dad left for the clubhouse about fifteen minutes ago, and Ma decided to have a wine night at her friend's house. So that leaves me here alone in this house, wallowing in self-pity. I could continue practicing my shooting like I've been doing every day, even when I'm not with Quinton, but I've also grown bored with that.

Nothing feels the same anymore. The things that I used to find pleasure in all feel dull and inconsequential now. I know it's the mounting responsibilities gathering on my shoulders, along with the stress of the position that's been thrusted onto me.

President of the Steel Dragons Motorcycle Club.

I fall back onto my bed, exhaling a long breath and staring up at my ceiling. The more time I spend with Quinton, and the more time I'm at the clubhouse cleaning up after the filthy men, the more afraid I become. How would I ever be accepted into that position? How would I be able to walk through that clubhouse as the brothers are fucking the Club Bunnies, and then discarding their used condoms on the floor? It's true when they say there's no place of power for women in a motorcycle club.

It makes me feel angry. Why would Dad put me in this position? My hands clench and my teeth grind in frustration.

My thoughts are interrupted by the sound of a bike coming up the street. There are only three bikes on our street. Mine, Dad's, and Jaeger's. It's too soon for Dad to be home, so that leaves only one other person.

I jump up from my bed and run to my bedroom door, quickly shutting it and turning the lock. Ever since that night Jaeger cornered me in the hallway, I've been fearful of him. He wasn't himself, and even though I've stood up to my brother many times over the years, I saw something different in his eyes that night.

I haven't seen him since. He's been busy with club business, I'm sure, but I knew the peace couldn't last forever.

The engine cuts in the driveway as my heart pushes its way up into my throat, pounding out a quick rhythm and making it hard for me to breathe. Now I regret telling Ma I'd be fine here alone. I'm twenty-two years old. It's about time I start acting that way, but right now, it feels like the boogeyman is coming through my front door.

The loud bang resonates throughout the house as Jaeger slams the front door, and then his boots hit the wooden stairs. *Thump. Thump. Thump.* I scramble back onto my bed and bite my fist to hold in the whimper that's threatening to escape from inside my chest. My eyes stay trained on my bedroom door as his footsteps come down the hallway, approaching my bedroom. I pray he passes by and goes straight to his room at the end of the hall. He knows I'm here. My bike is parked out front, but maybe he doesn't want to look at me tonight.

His footsteps stop and the shadows of his boots line the bottom of my door. I hold my breath as he continues to stand there. The longest ten seconds of my life goes by, and then he continues on down to his bedroom as I exhale with relief.

Of course, it's short-lived. Just as soon as I relax and take in a breath, my door is kicked in. The wooden slab bounces off my wall and the metal door handle sinks into the plaster.

"Jaeger!" My body startles and I sit up with a frightened yell, yanking my blanket up to my chin. "What the fuck?" He doesn't say anything as he walks into my room, the tips of his fingers running along my dresser. But his eyes, those dark pools of tar, are staring straight through to my soul. His silence finally pushes me to my breaking point, the oldest intimidation trick in the book is successful at making me feel small. "Get out of my room and fix my fucking door," I snap, my voice shaking slightly with fear.

He stops in front of my window, the last remnants of sunlight dancing through the black strands of his hair. His jaw is tight, the joint pulsing with agitation, and his shoulders are straight and stiff. I can see his leather cut through the reflection of the window, with that Vice President patch glaring bright white against the backdrop of black.

"I thought we were a family," he finally mutters. Even

though his body is radiating with tension, his words sound sad.

"We are family," I try to reassure him. "Now you need to fix my door." I infuse my tone with authority. He's going to need to start seeing me as an equal.

He turns those dark orbs back on to me, and that's when I notice how much his beard has grown in, like he's neglected to shave it recently. His hair is also a little too shiny, like he's exerted a lot of energy recently and hasn't bothered to wash it properly.

He takes two steps toward my bed, and I flinch before I can stop myself, folding my legs up in front of me and wrapping my arms around my knees. One side of his mouth tips up quickly, then falls back into place. Of course he noticed my reaction.

"I've loved you like my little sister, as if you were my blood," he puts emphasis on blood, and the sound makes my own pump rapidly through my veins. "I took care of you. I protected you. I only ever wanted the best for you." His eyes continue to burn holes into my skull, never wavering as he spits pure gasoline on the fire burning between us.

I can't figure out if he's inebriated or if this erratic behavior is stemming from something he's having to deal with. So I try to empathize, hoping that maybe it'll talk him down off the ledge he's flirting with.

"Jaeger, what is going on? Talk to me."

"Talk to you." He lets out a snort before taking a few steps closer to me. "Is that an order?" His words are lined with sarcasm and dripping with disdain.

My mouth turns down as my eyebrows crash together in confusion. An order? What does he mean by that? He sees the look on my face and laughs, a loud, boisterous sound that leaves my heart palpitating in my chest as he closes in on the last bit of distance separating us. His hand reaches out slowly and his fingers curl into the thick strands of my hair, the nails scraping along my scalp.

I gasp at the sudden pain and try to rear my head back, but he doesn't relent. I whimper as a few strands break off from his brutal hold.

"Jaeger, let go of me." I gasp with surprise as my hands grip onto his forearm, my nails sinking into his skin.

He bends down and yanks my head back so we're eye to eye. There's nothing left of my brother inside those obsidian pools. His jaw is like granite, the muscle ticking as his anger grows, and his nostrils flare with each breath. He really does hate me. His other hand grips my chin, the tight squeeze pursing my lips, and forcing my cheeks between my molars.

Fighting the hold only forces the skin on the inside of my mouth to break open and blood to rush over my tongue. Tears begin to pull at my eyes as his dark chuckle washes over me, making every hair on my body stand on end.

His knee hits the bed beside my thigh as he leans over, forcing my back to the mattress. The hand in my hair moves as his fingers grip my cheeks tighter. His other hand brushes over my shoulder and down my arm, and when those fingers meet my ribs, I stiffen. One touch is hard while the other feels soft, almost reverent. Both only fuel my fear further.

"Genni, Genni, Genni," he taunts, his voice like liquid steel. "Always getting what she wants." I want to rebuke that statement. I want to tell him I'm not getting what I want right now, but speaking is impossible as his fingers clench even tighter on my cheeks. "You've always wanted all the attention, didn't you?" he asks. Again, it must be a rhetorical question, because there's no way I can speak around the grip he has on my mouth. I try to shake my head and use my eyes to plead with him, hoping he sees the sister he was raised with. Fear of provoking him further leaves me frozen to the spot, all the fight escaping me.

My efforts are futile, because once he releases my face, that same hand wraps around my neck, crushing my windpipe and sealing off any air. I feel like I'm going to die here at the hands of my family and the only thought that runs through my mind is how it will devastate my father and Ma.

"Stay out of my way, Genni." Spit flies from his mouth, landing on my cheeks as they flare with the effort of trying to breathe. "If you don't, I will fucking kill you." My eyes roll around as I struggle with my burning lungs, but he must take that as me being bratty because he taunts me one more time "Don't believe me?" I watch through blurry eyes as he raises a brow, waiting for an answer that I'm unable to form. "Do you know how easy it would be to wait for you to be home alone? To come in here, tie you up, and slit your throat? No one would ever believe I would do such a thing to my sister. Dad would believe Hell's March came here and fucked with his family. And do you know what, Genni?" His mouth lands at the shell of my ear, his tongue skating along the edge of it as my nails sink into his wrist, trying to pry his hand off my throat so I can breathe. "I would pretend to grieve you, set out on a revenge mission, slaughter men in your name. All the while, your blood would be staining my hands."

With one final squeeze, he releases me, but not before he shoves my head down into the mattress farther, and then stands to look over me as I gasp and choke for air. Pure hatred lines his eyes, and tears course down my cheeks as I grip my throat, both hands clawing at the surface.

"I dare you to tell Dad." He gives me a mocking grin before tilting his head. "Go tell the old man, and I will make that scenario happen. Be careful how you act, Genni, and watch your fucking back."

My mouth gapes open as I suck in mouthful after mouthful of air, wishing I could ask him why he's doing this, but my throat throbs, and speaking is next to impossible right now. I let my eyes do the talking as I glare at him, hoping he sees that I still have some fight inside of me.

His boots thud along my carpet as he leaves my room, the smell of sandalwood and nicotine lingering in the air. A scent I once felt comforted by, but now? It will haunt my dreams at night.

Why does my brother hate me?

QUINTON

SIX

Jaeger didn't come back to the clubhouse last night. I waited for him as long as I could, but as soon as the sun started to rise, I knew he wasn't coming back.

I've barely slept, tossing and turning in this bed. I feel like something bad is about to happen, and Jaeger is at the center of it. I've neglected our friendship, I admit that, but we're brothers, and our bond goes beyond friendship. We're there for each other no matter what, but right now, he's sealing himself off from me, and I'm going to find out why.

A loud banging on my bedroom door has me startling in bed.

"Chino!" Vic's voice booms through the thin, wooden slab. "Get out here, man. You've got a date."

I grab my phone off the side table and squint at the screen. Damn, it's noon.

The banging starts up again as I flip the blankets back. "Yeah. Yeah!" I call out. "I'm coming."

I guess it's another day of teaching Genni how to shoot, and another day that forces Jaeger and me to split further. I'm hoping I'll be able to tell him exactly what's going on. Shit, I'm hoping Vic tells him exactly what's going on, because all this secretive shit, this isn't what our club is about.

I hop in the shower quickly, rinsing my body and washing my hair. Then I stand in front of the mirror and begin to braid it slowly.

The length of a man's hair is a representation of his strength. The longer our hair, the longer we've survived. My hair touches my ass crack, and I'm so proud of it. I slip the Eagle feather into the bottom, the same one my father found when I was four years old. Even though it's ragged and old, I wear it every day. It represents the strength my father witnessed in me, and I refuse to let him down.

I meet Vic out in the main area. He's leaning against the bar with his arms crossed over his chest, and that's when I notice how much weight he's lost. His cut is hanging loose, his jeans look a little too cinched at the waist by his belt, and the most worrying part is the stress that's so apparent in his eyes.

"What do you need me for today?" I sidle over to him and hold out my hand.

He clasps it in one of his and hauls me in, patting my back. "You're taking out my daughter today."

I look around the club and breathe out a sigh of relief when no one is near enough to hear his words. "I thought this shit was a secret," I whisper to him as he releases his hold on me.

"We talked about this yesterday." His brow flicks up. "Remember? She needs someone to take her out."

"Oh, fuck no." I step away, shaking my head and raising my hands up. "There ain't no fucking way I'm dating your daughter, Vic."

"You're not good enough for my daughter." He narrows his eyes and points at me, his nicotine-stained finger nearing my face. "You're not dating her. I just need you to get her out of the house for a day."

"So, what you're telling me is, your Sergeant at Arms, the best shot you have in this Motorcycle Club, the man who can take down a body over fifty-feet away, is now a babysitter?" I ask incredulously as my hands lower to the table.

"Hey, if that's what I want you to be for the day, that's

what you'll be." He shrugs, his finger still wagging between us.

"Come on, Vic," I groan out and brush by him to lean against the bar top. "What is happening, man?"

He turns and picks up my braid from my back, holding the Eagle feather between us.

"I was there the day your father found this," he says quietly. "I miss my brother."

"I miss him too," I say, my heart sinking into my stomach. My father would want me to respect the man sitting in front of me. "Fine. I'll go get her."

"She's at home." He drops the braid and it swings back down to rest against my back. "I don't even think she's out of bed yet. I'll leave that to you."

His tired laugh dissipates as he walks away.

"What are you up to today, Chino?" Laith says as he strides into the room.

"Fucking babysitting," I snap and shove off the bar and begin to pace.

"Should I know what that means?" he asks as he slips onto a stool.

I turn to look at him and his strategically placed beard that hides the large scars on his cheeks. "No. Top secret Sergeant at Arms shit."

"All right." He nods.

Laith is only a few years older than Jaeger and I, but his maturity and the experiences he's been through makes him seem a lot older. He's had a tough life, and it doesn't help that his twin brother, who is now running with Hell's March, our rival MC, tried to kill him the last time they came face-to-face.

It just goes to show you that sometimes blood isn't always thicker than water.

"Man, I'll see you later." I groan as I slap the bar and stride toward the door.

"Hey, Chino!" Vic calls out from the couch he's sitting on. "No funny business, huh?"

"Fucking gross," I grumble lowly as I stalk out the door, hearing him chuckle behind me. "Asshole," I growl out as I get on my bike, slamming my helmet onto my head.

When I pull up into the Varga driveway, I cut my engine and look at the house. It's dark and quiet, too quiet, almost like no one's home. Her bike sits in the driveway, but that doesn't mean she's here… right? I can only pray that's true, and when I walk up in there, Genni won't be home. Maybe she found herself some new friends, and I won't have to fucking babysit her. I drop my helmet onto the seat of my bike and walk up onto the porch. It brings back so many memories of being a kid. Of me coming here to call on Jaeger to go ride our bikes. Back then, we had a two-speed each, but we pretended like our legs were wrapped around steel dragons as we soared into battle. The nostalgia hits me in the chest, and it becomes a little hard to breathe when I think of how much I'm deceiving my brother. So when I bang on the door, it's a little harder than I expected, the frustration leaking out through my fisted hand.

There's no answer, so I bang again. I wait for another minute, and when there's still no answer, I try the knob. The door opens inward, and I curse because someone better be fucking home if the door is open. You don't run with the Steel Dragons and leave yourself open to external threats.

I step inside, closing the door softly, and peek around into the kitchen.

"Genni!" I call out.

There's no answer. So I kick off my dirty boots by the door and walk into the living room. Everything is pristine here, screaming of Claire and her cleanliness, but the cleanliness isn't the only thing I'm noticing. The place is also empty. My eyes gradually move up toward the ceiling, and I let out another exaggerated sigh. I could leave now and say I attempted, that I couldn't find anyone and no one was home. I could say that, but as I'm telling myself this, my feet move of their own accord toward the stairs, and I take them two at a time, making sure to keep my steps hushed. I pause on the landing to listen, and when there's no noise, I continue onward, fear spiking at the thought of her missing or the house having been broken into. I know which one is Genni's room. I've been here enough to know where everyone's room is. I head that way, but what I find when I get there has my stomach knotting and my breath leaving me in one fell swoop.

The door looks like it's been kicked in, a large boot print is cracked into the wood paneling, and the door latch is completely broken off. I rush inside, her name on the tip of my tongue when I find her laying there in the center of her bed, the blankets up to her ears and her eyes shut as she faces the ceiling.

"Genni." I rush over to her, yanking the blanket down.

"Don't," she says tiredly and turns around quickly, grabbing a pillow to put over her head. "Just leave." The T-shirt she's wearing is riding up over her bare thighs.

"Can't do that, Princess," I tell her as I gently pull the pillow off her head. "I'm on orders to be here. Rise and shine, we have a date." When she doesn't move, I grab her shoulder, pulling her over, and when her face finally turns toward mine, I let out a loud growl. "What the fuck happened to you?" I snap as I pull her up to get a closer look, her pain-filled blue eyes meeting mine.

She has finger-shaped bruises indented on her cheeks, which look swollen and red. That's not the worst part. Her throat is lined with fingerprints as well, as if they were wrapped around her neck, gripping as hard as they could. Her face slowly hardens the longer she sits there under my scrutiny.

"Never had rough sex before?" She attempts to be snooty, to look like she's unaffected. The longer I stare at her, the further her face falls, and then she loses her composure altogether. A sob erupts from her chest and her bloodshot eyes fill with tears. Her arms wrap around my waist as her face burrows against my stomach, her tears soaking through my shirt. I try to breathe, to tamper down the rage that's threatening to consume me. My hands curl into fists at my sides and I let my nails bite into my palms.

"Who was it?" I try to keep my voice low and even, but it shakes with barely contained anger. She shakes her head, her tangled hair brushing along the leather cut. "Genni, I'm gonna need a name."

"I need your help." Her words come out rushed and slurred from crying as her face is pressed into my stomach. "I need you to teach me how to defend myself, how to fight. And if I have to, I need you to teach me to put a bullet between someone's eyes."

I tip my head back and close my eyes, praying I don't lose it here. I don't want to traumatize the girl more than she already is. I wonder if Jaeger knows what's happened. When she grabs my wrist, her nails biting into the skin, I reach into my cut to grab my phone.

"Please don't call him." She pulls back and releases me from her hold.

"He's your brother—"

"No. Quinton, I'm begging you. Please, don't tell anyone," she cuts me off, her words rushed with concern.

I don't know what it is about those dark blue eyes of hers, how they brighten just a fraction when she's crying, or her swollen, red lips and the way her teeth are biting into the plush flesh. I don't know what it is, but I drop my phone back into my pocket and turn around, yanking open her closet door. I pull out a hoodie and a pair of those stretchy pants that girls love to wear, throwing them at her face.

"Get dressed, we've got work to do," I tell her as I turn on my heel and stride out of her room, past the broken door. The wooden splinters dot along the floor, and I continue to breathe as I head for the stairs, slowly making my way down. I count backwards from ten, three times before I reach the kitchen. When I open the patio door, I step out into the backyard, close the door behind me, and take one step down off the deck, my socked feet hitting the grass. I tip my head up, facing the bright, blue sky, and a loud scream wrenches from my throat, ripping through my vocal cords. Searing pain floods my throat as I scream to the sky, letting loose the frustration building inside of me. I need her to feel safe with me, because she is. I need her to trust me, because she can, and then, after all of that, I'm going to need her to tell me who the fuck did this.

I fall to my knees on the grass before moving to sit back on my ass, crossing my legs as I continue to stare up at the sky. I was raised to believe women are sacred, their bodies a symbol of rebirth. Some days, yes, that belief fades, especially when I take women to bed and leave them the next morning, but never have I struck a woman. It's against my very nature.

And that's how Genni finds me ten minutes later when she steps out into the backyard. I hear the door slide open behind me as I continue to look up at the sky.

GENEVIEVE
BMW Motorrad Milano

GENEVIEVE

"Quinton?" I call out as I step down onto the grass, my arms wrapped around my waist.

His back is rigid, his legs crossed with his hands clenched into fists on his knees. I'm so fucking scared he'll say something to Jaeger, and then my brother will feel more incensed to finish what he started.

Quinton is looking up to the sky, his head tipped, and his strong, straight nose aimed toward the clouds. The end of his braid kisses the ground as the slight breeze moves it back and forth, rustling the Eagle feather nestled inside the tie.

"I'm not going to ask you any more questions," he says quietly, the words barely distinguishable. "I won't tell Jaeger, because honestly, what's one more secret when you're sitting on a mountain of them? But Genni? I will promise you this, if I see another mark on you,"—he turns to face me finally, his eyes boring into mine—"you will tell me everything." I swallow down the fear that's clogging my throat and give him a nod because even though speech is difficult, the emotion he's bringing out of me is snatching up any intelligible thought I have. "So, are we going back to the warehouse?" he asks as he stands, straightening to his full height. He steps in close to me, his height a little taller than Jaeger, but not by much. My forehead meets his mouth as he towers over me, the few inches making me feel protected. His chest brushes mine as he takes a deep inhale.

"Yes, please." I nod, my voice sounding rough.

He nods back and motions for me to follow him. "You're riding with me." He saves me the embarrassment of having to ask, because the thought of getting myself anywhere right now only serves to amplify my exhaustion.

We pull up to the warehouse about half an hour later, and I unwind my arms from around his waist, setting my feet back on the ground. He reaches behind without looking and clasps his hand on my thigh, giving it a squeeze. I feel safe with Quinton, but at the same time, I know he's Jaeger's best friend, and if he was forced to choose, it would be the man he's regarded as his brother for most of his life. Whether I'm President or not. The thought has my chest tightening in sadness.

He takes off his helmet and hangs the strap on the handlebar of his bike. I remove mine and swing my leg over to stand beside him. His jaw clenches as he looks at my face and throat, his eyes burning like fiery lava. He can barely stand the sight of me because of the bruising, making me feel both ashamed and curious. I've known Quinton Chino my whole life, but never has he given me the time of day. I was the annoying kid who chased him and my brother around the yard. I was the girl who wanted to play on bikes and pretend we were riding steel dragons. When they got their motorcycle licenses, I wanted mine too. There wasn't much they did, which I didn't envy, but I never once thought he actually cared about me.

"We're gonna start with some basic defense," he grunts out as he strides toward the warehouse.

"Okay," I whisper, my voice still hoarse as I follow after him.

We get inside, and he turns on the lights, the fluorescent overhead blinking slowly throughout the vast room. Images of the last time we were here float through my mind. How I felt shooting at targets, becoming slightly bored, and truly contemplating the plans my father has for me. I was questioning whether it was all worth it, but as I stand here now and look around, seeing the targets I used the last time, I'm starting to believe it is. The holes are so close and on the bullseye, proving I can do this. That sense of pride flushes through me, and I grip it tighter, clinging to it with everything left inside of me. Nothing will be easy, but from here on out, I'll be damned if I find myself on the receiving end of Jaeger's ire again.

"You're going to want to be comfortable." He points to my leather jacket. "Take that off."

I do as he says and fold my leather jacket, placing it beside his cut on the table. My fingers glide over his worn leather, touching the Sergeant at Arms badge with admiration. He's come a long way, and I bet his father would be proud of him as well.

"First things first, you need to make your throat inaccessible." His words are clipped, heated, and low. I stand beside him, and he slowly wraps his hand lightly around my neck. Despite that, the slight pressure has me cringing. "Are we going to do this? Or are you in too much pain?" His thumb begins to glide up and down over my pulse point, which I'm sure he can feel fluttering rapidly.

"I'll be fine." My voice rings with a false bravado. I give a brief nod and swallow past the tightness of my throat. The thought of having another hand there, leaving me at the mercy of someone again, scares me, but I refuse to let it cripple me. Instead, I'll use it to strengthen myself, and then later, I'll spit it in Jaeger's face, showing him he didn't break me.

"Keep your chin to your chest." He demonstrates the move before continuing. "The neck is one of the most vulnerable places besides your stomach. If you're stabbed or sliced open, there's not much you can do to save yourself."

"Okay." I drop my chin to my chest, exactly how he showed me.

"Hold it tight. Keep your eyes up and always keep your eye on your opponent's hands."

He takes me through a couple of basic self-defense moves, and by the end, I'm able to crack my fist against his wrist and elbow to break his hold on my neck. I'm able to maneuver myself out of certain capture holds, and he's taught me a few punches and the most effective places to use them.

We're hopping around each other as I dodge hands, fists, and chokeholds. Then suddenly, a laugh erupts from my throat as I imagine how the both of us would look to someone watching.

He stops and puts his hands on his waist, tipping his head to the side, his braid brushing along his arm. "What's funny?"

"We look like we're dancing." I laugh again, and this time, his eyes brighten with humor as they skim over my face.

"It's nice to hear you laugh," he says, giving me a smile. The way his lips curl upward, his cheekbones accentuated, and those dimples winking at me... All of it just takes my breath away.

"Remember my first high school dance?" I ask him as a smile coats my mouth. "The one you and Jaeger crashed?" My hands curl together under my chin.

His head tips back with a laugh, the sound echoing around the warehouse. "Yeah, you were dancing with that pimply-faced asshole."

"Darren was sweet." I roll my eyes at his description of my date that night.

"He was shorter than you and he was scrawny," he replies, chuckling again.

"Most guys are shorter than me." I shrug. "I was lucky if any guy paid me any attention. I was the beanstalk."

"Nah, they were just intimidated." He waves me off.

"That was the first time I saw you dance," I remind him, the grin on my face increasing into a wide smile as I let the memory slip over me.

"Yeah." He snickers and steps closer, his eyes running over the length of my body. "It was our first dance together."

"It was our *only* dance together." My brow lifts as he starts humming the tune to 'Baby, I love Your Way' the Bob Marley version. "Oh God, Quinton." I laugh as he begins to gyrate his hips.

"But don't hesitate 'cause your love won't wait," he sings, and it's my turn to take up the humming of the tune.

My hips move in time with his, and soon we're both singing and dancing, "Ooh, baby, I love your way." "Wait," I say with a laugh as I run to my jacket and pull out my phone. I pull up my playlist and find the song, playing it and turning up the volume. As soon as the singer's voice starts crooning through the speaker, my hips move, and I pull my hair tie out of my hair, letting it cascade down around my shoulders. My arms end up above my head as I dance, and when I leisurely turn around, I find Quinton's heated eyes on me. They slip from the top of my head, slowly, all the way down to the tips of my toes. Then he drags them back up. When our eyes clash, he lifts his hand and hooks his finger, gesturing for me to come to him.

My heart pounds, but my feet move before a single thought

penetrates my mind. There's no denying Quinton Chino, not when he looks like his fingers could incinerate me with a single touch, or when his tongue slips out and glides along his full bottom lip, the movement turning my insides into liquid lava.

As soon as I'm within reach, his fingers curl into my tank top, and he pulls me in against him. His head tips downward, and mine tips back so we can maintain our eye contact, but our hips move in sync, brushing along each other, the fabric of our pants kissing, and our chests brushing.

He's mouthing the lyrics of the song, and suddenly the temperature in the room escalates, creating a wave of inferno around us. Everything around me disappears, except for him. His breath washes over me as he sings along with the lyrics, and the hand that was fisted in my shirt slowly glides down over my stomach, creeping around my waist before finding purchase on my lower back. A moan escapes me, and as soon as he hears it, his eyes darken. He hauls me in closer, intensifying his scent, spice and musk, as it just envelops me in its warmth. It's been so long since I've felt wanted.

My hands slip up under the front of his shirt, my fingers skimming over the ridges of his abs, causing him to flex them as he takes a deep breath. I don't stop there though. Instead, I keep going and fan my fingers out as I move along his stomach, slipping over his obliques.

"Genni," he whispers, his mouth drawing nearer to mine. "What are we doing?"

"Dancing?" It comes out like a question because I'm not so sure anymore either. All I know is, the closer his mouth moves to mine, the more I long to find out how he tastes. This is all types of wrong. He's my brother's best friend and completely off-limits. I'm toeing a line that's been drawn a long time ago, and right now, I want to obliterate all the rules.

With that thought in mind, I pull him in the last few inches and our mouths brush together just as Bob Marley croons about *wanting to be with you every night and day.*

His hand moves up to the back of my head, his fingers slipping in through the thick tresses, and then he's holding my head while our bodies are completely flush. I open my eyes to find his boring into mine.

"Genni," he says, his lips moving against mine, "once I do this, that's it. There's no turning back."

I feel two things at once simultaneously, pure and intoxicating lust intertwined with concern. They course through me, threatening to wipe all logical thought from my mind, but the concern flares brighter as I take a deep swallow. The ache in my throat throws a vivid picture of Jaeger's face in my mind. If he knew what I was doing right now with his best friend, I have no doubt he would lose his cool.

My first instinct is to back away, but it's the flick of Quinton's tongue and the subtle shake of his head that has me pausing.

"Too late, Varga."

Then his velvety, supple lips are on mine, the brutalizing pressure of his kiss a direct contrast. My body bows backward as he forces himself on me, devouring my mouth and forcing his tongue between my lips to tangle with my own.

One hand still holds my head, but the other slides from my waist to grip my ass, the rough press of his fingertips bruising the soft flesh. The sounds escaping from my throat sound animalistic, but they only prove to spur him on as his erection presses against my lower stomach.

Quinton backs me up, and soon enough, the backs of my thighs hit the table. He lifts me, setting my ass on the top of it and spreading my legs before stepping between them, and then pulls his mouth off mine, resting his forehead on the top of my head.

"Shit," he hisses. I nod, feeling his forehead move with the motion. I can't speak. I can't think beyond the press of his hard cock between my legs and the scent of him all over me. My lips throb with the bruise of his kiss, and my hands have somehow wound themselves into his T-shirt, the fabric tight around my fingers. "He's going to kill us." I know who he's talking about, and after what happened last night, I know Jaeger would kill us both for what we're doing. A whimper escapes my throat, causing Quinton to step back. He looks down at me, his finger dipping under my chin to force my face up to look at him. "With how I'm feeling right now, I'm ready to say fuck it," he confesses.

He doesn't know how that could never happen, because one day, I'm going to be his President, and he'll hate me. I wish I could tell him right now, laying all of my father's plans out in the open so it's not such a betrayal when the time comes, but I'm sworn to secrecy. So instead, I haul him back into me, pressing my heated core to his hardness.

"Kiss me," I husk out. "Just kiss me."

He doesn't immediately fold. His honeyed eyes rove over my face, and his thumb rubs circles into the bruises on my cheek. I can see the wheels turning in his head, the way he's weighing out his options blatantly on his face. Is she worth it? Is this what I want? Who's more important? I can see them all, like a kaleidoscope inside those amber eyes. My heart stalls in my chest, feeling like it's about to slip down into my stomach.

This is my life now. Forever isolated and always wondering where I fall in the chain of importance. Before those questions stop circulating in his head, I push him back and slip off the table. I don't want him to have to decide, nor should he ever choose me above the club. Not yet, anyway. Still, it leaves me feeling alone and bereft.

"Please take me home," I croak out. My throat is still sore, but it's my emotions that are getting the best of me.

Quinton stands still as I grab my jacket and shrug it on. I can feel his penetrating stare, but I can't bring myself to meet his eyes. I don't want to crumble under his scrutiny. I don't want to give in and make our lives that much more difficult later. Right now, he's blissfully unaware. That leaves me to be the one to make this decision for us both since I know all the cards before they're revealed.

I turn my back on Quinton Chino and walk out of the warehouse while he watches me, never once trying to make promises he can't keep. I should be grateful he's making this easy for me, only my heart doesn't agree with my head. She's screaming for someone to love me beyond my responsibilities. To have at least one person look at me with some sincerity without seeing the things they could use me for.

Sometimes our desires need to be buried and shoved to the back burner because survival for a woman in a man's world is a full-time job.

THIS BODY IS
TEMPORARY
BUT THIS SOUL IS
ETERNAL
JAEGER

JAEGER

Whenever I see Laith and those man-made dimples I know are hiding just beneath the surface of his beard, I seethe for my brother. It used to be hard for me to imagine what it was like to have someone you considered your family, or your *actual* family, turn on you like that, but I think I'm beginning to understand.

These last few days have proven really difficult for me to keep up the ruse. Looking into Vic's eyes only makes me angrier, and even the slightest scent of Genevieve's perfume sends me into a red rage. I know I bruised her. I know my fingers left their mark on her sensitive throat and possibly her face, but I haven't been back to that house to confirm it. I'm coming to terms with this monster inside of me, the part of my blood that sings to the same tune my father sang. My real father, the one whose tainted blood is coursing through my veins.

"What are you thinking about?" Laith asks, his body turning a little in the stool. His large bicep rests on the bar top, and that tiny fucking teacup is perched between his forefinger and thumb.

"Loyalty," I admit to him. "I'm thinking about loyalty, and if I'm being completely honest with you, I'm struggling."

"Struggling how?" He flicks the corner of his cut off of his lap so he can fully turn in his stool to face me. I can see the worry etched upon his features, and my first instinct is to expel that. To convince him everything is okay, but I just don't have the energy anymore.

"Maybe I'm just aging." I grin at him. "Time is feeling like it's running forward at a breakneck speed. Now I know what you old guys go through every day."

He laughs, the sound like dark chimes tinkling in the air around us. "I'm not old," he huffs. "But I agree with you about time. Some days, I feel like I don't have enough of it to accomplish everything I desire."

I know what he means. I can feel the pressure mounting, feeling as though time is flowing as fast as water, and I don't even know what for. There's a part of me that wants to convince Vic I'm worthy. I just don't know how. I don't know what I did wrong to begin with and I don't understand what made him disregard me and turn to his frail daughter, expecting her to run a motorcycle crew.

"If you were given the choice," I say as I sit beside him at the bar. "Would you remove those scars from your face?"

His eyes don't move from the rim of his cup as he slowly lifts it to his mouth and takes a sip. I watch as the corded muscles in his throat work on his swallow, and then, again, he slowly lowers the cup back to the wooden surface of the bar top. His demeanor is at ease, his shoulders relaxed, and he seems unaffected by my question. Except, I see the tightening of his jaw beneath his beard.

"No." That one word is spoken gruffly, spat out like a mouthful of poison.

"Why not?"

I know I'm poking at him. I know this subject is difficult for him to speak about because he rarely does. I can imagine what it's like to be betrayed by your sibling, fuck, I'm going through it right now, and even though Genevieve hasn't held a gun to my face and pulled the trigger, it still feels like she's slammed her fist into my chest and decimated my heart.

"They serve as a reminder." His fingers tap along the bar. "They remind me never to trust a single soul, and that blood runs just as thin as water."

I clap him on the shoulder, squeezing the muscle, and let out a long exhale. "My blood is as thick as mud, brother."

A deep chuckle escapes his mouth, almost in surprise, and I can feel his tension breaking up.

"I made a promise," he grunts out, his mouth turning down into a frown. "If I ever saw him again, I would blow his brains out."

"I don't fucking blame you—"

"I choked," he cuts me off. "It was a few weeks after I got out of the hospital. My fucking jaw was wired shut, and I was eating from a straw."

"Where?"

"Outside of the compound." His chin juts toward our gates. "He was casually sitting there on his bike. I reached for my gun, and he just spread his arms out, like he was begging me to do it."

"Why didn't you?" I lean forward, my eyes meeting his.

"Because sometimes living with the shit you've done is a crueler fate than death."

"Nah." I chuckle with a shake of my head. "I would've shot him on the spot. Blood or not."

"The more lives you take, the heavier your soul will become. Especially if your life is intricately intertwined with theirs. Before you take your next life, consider the weight it'll add on your shoulders." Laith gets up from the stool, setting the tiny cup on the counter, and rapping his knuckles a few times on the wood. His words are slowly seeping past the anger I'm feeling and settling deep inside me. The whole time we've been speaking about betrayal, I've seen Vic and Genni's faces in my head. Mostly Genni's, and if I'm being honest, popping a bullet in her head has been an ongoing fantasy of mine these last few days. "I can see you're troubled, and maybe it's because you have a burden to carry with this club and the men in it, but I hope you hear my advice. There's only one life to live, brother."

He lumbers off outside, tying his bandana on his head, and smoothing back his long, brown hair. It's been hard to get Laith to open up. He's been through so much betrayal, so I don't push him too hard. I feel like he and I are finally forming a bond.

I won't lie and say his *advice* isn't affecting me. From the moment my fucking fingers wrapped around Genni's neck though, the desire to finish what I started has only grown. She's taking everything from me, and still, she acts like a spoiled brat. Her fake ignorance is getting to me, and I can't seem to muster up any feelings for the girl I loved as a sister.

The girl who used to look up to me, follow me around like an annoying pest, and worshiped me as her brother. As I robbed her of her breath, I saw nothing left of that little girl in her eyes. She's scared, and it wasn't just from being on the verge of death, it was because the cushioned life she once had was being ripped away from her.

All I could think of at the time was *good*.

I can hear Laith's bike start up outside, the deep, rumbling roar of the Harley as he pulls it through the gate and up the street. Lately, I feel like my brothers and I are all spread out on single missions or split up for drop-offs. There's a rift forming, and I'm right there in the center, sinking into the black abyss.

"You okay, boss?" Chip's hand lands on my shoulder. "Do you need a coffee?" I shake my head and get up from the stool.

"Nah, I'm good. I'm heading out."

He gives me a salute and goes back to cleaning down his bar. He's always had pride for this one corner of the room. It's the same corner of the room his father took pride in as well, pouring his brothers' drinks.

That's our goal here. It's how it's meant to be. The son takes over his father's legacy, and then one day, if he's lucky, he can pass that legacy onto his own son. Nowhere, when I look around this room, do I see a female in a Steel Dragon cut.

It just makes me rage more and solidifies exactly what I'm doing today. I know I'm playing with fire, but I always did love a good blaze.

I step out of the compound and stride toward my bike, the black paint shining and reflecting the sun's rays. Just as I sit on the seat, another rumble comes up the street, the sound gradually growing as it comes closer to the compound. The creak of the gates opening has me turning my head just as Quinton's bike rolls in. He's another one I feel like I'm losing, and I can't tell if it's because of the shit I'm going through, or if he has some shit of his own. What I do know is that neither of us is talking about it.

He pulls into the spot beside mine, his hands covered with leather gloves, the tips cut off to reveal his tattooed fingers. Right now, the knuckles are white as he grips the handlebars, and he has yet to look at me. Instantly, I know something is wrong. This has been my best friend, my brother, for more than half my life. There's nothing he can hide from me that I wouldn't find out… eventually.

He switches his bike off, drops his stand, and hauls the helmet off his head, his long braid swinging with the motion, that Eagle feather still firmly grasped in the hair tie.

"Where have you been?" I ask him, trying my best not to let my irritation bleed through my tone.

"Busy," he spits out, his face still averted from mine.

I could sit here and argue with him, find out what has him acting like a fucking bitch, but I don't have the time. I can't miss this secret appointment, not when I'm so close to getting what I want. So instead of pressing him, I watch as he gets off his bike, straps his helmet to the handlebar, and without a backward glance, strides inside. I shrug and let the attitude roll off my shoulders. It's just a matter of time before I find it all out.

I get my bike out of the parking spot, and the prospects have less than ten seconds while they're scrambling to open the gate before I fly through the small opening. As soon as my tires hit the asphalt, I open her up, and it's just me and the road.

Three hours later, the black-painted brick structure looms up ahead. The blacked-out windows and barbwire fencing cast an illusion of terror, but once you've been bred from a monster and raised by a soldier, there's very little on this Earth that'll invoke terror. I see it for what it is, a nondescript clubhouse belonging to Hell's March.

I shrug off my cut and fold it up, slipping it into the back compartment of my bike, and then lock it up. I'm never supposed to take it off in public, but I find myself breaking all the rules lately, and they're justified with reason. I sit on my bike, waiting in the exact spot I was told, and pull my phone out of my jeans pocket. Nothing. No messages from any of the guys, and definitely none from my supposed best friend. The last time he went weird like this, he had found pussy outside of the clubhouse. She was some rich, prissy bitch, and he was too afraid to bring her around. Chino's tastes always did run a bit on the decadent side, and that's why I know those looks he's been giving my fucking sister are more than just passing glances.

I'd fucking kill him.

The roar of engines in the distance has me sitting up straight. I was only supposed to meet one person here, and that sound is more than one bike. I reach for my gun at my belt and lean over the front handlebars, clasping it in my grip. I'm making it obvious I won't hesitate to use it.

My reputation precedes me. They won't need to see the gun to know that anything could trigger me. I don't play games and I never hesitate to pull the trigger.

Two bikes come around the bend, and I curse under my breath. Not that I'm disappointed. I didn't expect anything less from Hell's March. When we made these plans to meet up, I considered every possibility, and I knew without a doubt, not all of my demands would be met.

I let the tension in my shoulders bleed out through my body, giving the illusion that I am relaxed as they pull up in front of me. Even with the bandanas covering the lower parts of their faces, I know I'm looking at Bear and Malik Charles. My gun stays trained on both of them.

It's as if Laith is looking back at me. It's eerie how identical they are. Even though they haven't seen each other in a long time, their hair is the same length, same color, tied back with a black hair tie. It's fucking crazy.

"Brought yourself a friend!" I shout as Bear takes off his helmet.

"He saw me leaving and followed me like the dog he is," Bear says with a laugh, but Malik doesn't join in. My penetrating stare does nothing to Malik. Instead, I see the way his cheeks start to rise, as if he's grinning under that bandana. The man's veins run with ice. How else would he be able to shoot his own twin brother in the face? "Have you thought about what I told you?" Bear calls out. "About your sister?" I continue to stare at Malik, my fingers gripping the gun a little tighter. Right now, I could shoot a bullet between his eyes. I really fucking want to, but I think his brother should have that honor. "Don't worry about talking in front of him," Bear says. "Like I said, he's my dog. He won't say anything." He makes a panting sound to drive the point home.

"If I agree to this,"—I push myself to sitting on the bike, the gun still firmly in my hand—"you, Hell's March scum, will get the fuck out of our town?"

"Watch what you say, boy," Malik warns. He gives me a dark smile, one filled with murderous intent.

"You have my word," Bear says as he pulls the bandana down from his mouth, his face solemn. "When do you want this done?"

"Two weeks," I say as I start up my motorcycle and holster my gun. "I'll be in touch."

If any of my brothers found out how I was doing this, how do they put it, cooperating with the enemy, I'd be exiled. I kick my stand up and put my bike into gear, spinning out and shooting dust up into Bear and Malik's faces. There may be something we currently agree on, but it doesn't mean I fucking like them. This isn't some budding relationship or the start of a fucked-up friendship. I will hate Hell's March for the rest of my life. That will never change.

I speed back down the road, my conscience trying to start a war with the rage that's still simmering low inside of me.

I refuse to feel bad for this, and any outcome that arises, I blame it on my dad.

GENEVIEVE
BMW Motorrad Milano

SEVEN

My forehead hits the pane of glass, and it immediately cools my heated skin. It's been four days since I've seen Quinton, and every time I think of him, my body flushes with need. Each time, it takes longer to convince myself not to call him or seek him out at the clubhouse. Yesterday, I came home to find my bedroom door fixed, and when I questioned my father, he gave me a lopsided smile and a shrug of his shoulders. He was looking at me with pity, thinking the responsibilities he's putting on me are causing me to spiral, as if I took my aggression out on a wooden slab.

I let him think that.

It's a lot easier if he believes I'm some emotional twit who's still throwing tantrums at my age than to look him in the eye and tell him the son he adopted almost killed me. There's also the risk of him not believing a single word of the truth, and just maybe, he'll think I'm using any excuse I can find as a cop-out for the role he's pressing on me.

Jaeger hasn't been home since that night, but I never let my guard down. I barely sleep, and when I do finally drift off, it's because my hand is wrapped around a steak knife I pilfered from the kitchen drawer. Would I use it if he broke back in again? I don't know. When I think of Jaeger, I remember everything we've been through since we were children. He was my big brother who protected me, and I can't figure out when that changed. I know I annoyed him, I know I *still* annoy him, and even though we've been distant the last few years, I never once doubted that he loved me… until recently.

I'm not stupid. There's only one reason he would treat me this way, and it's because he knows. He knows what my father has in store for me and the MC, I just don't know how. Dad and I have been discreet. We don't talk about it in this house, and we go out of town for my training. There's no way he would have heard it from our mouths.

So the common denominator is Quinton.

But Dad assured me, from the very beginning, that he has told no one besides me what he has planned. Quinton thinks he's training me for self-defense and granted, he probably believes I need it after the state he found me in a few nights ago.

Covering my bruises has been difficult. Claire stares at me a little longer than usual, her lingering looks telling me my makeup and turtlenecks are only doing so much. She hasn't brought it up, but it makes me wonder how she would feel if she learned her son had become just as abusive as her ex-husband. That his blood gave in to its genetic makeup and fit the mold his father created. It would destroy her, and I couldn't do that to the woman who's been the only mother I've ever known. We may not share blood, but I love her just the same.

I have no doubt in my mind that if my mother is watching from heaven, she's happy that Claire is here, loving me and providing guidance in ways that only a mother can.

The rumble of a motorcycle has me jumping up and pulling my forehead off of my window, leaving a smudge of my skin imprint behind. The way my heart pounds and my breath quickens is a warning for me to get away from the window. Instead, I stare up my street, waiting for that single headlight to appear, and once again, I'm home alone.

As the noise grows louder, my chest grows tighter and my lungs begin to burn as they scream for air. I'm having a panic attack. Everything Quinton taught me flies from my mind as I frantically search around my room for a place to hide. He may see my bike outside in the driveway, but that doesn't mean I'm home.

I run forward and slam my fist into my light switch, dousing my room into blackness, then I do the one thing I haven't done in years. I slide under my bed and hold my hand over my mouth, praying I don't betray myself tonight.

Two minutes feels like two hours as the roar becomes louder, the vibrations of the engine somehow finding its way to me, slipping past the thin barrier of my skin and coursing through my muscles. My body trembles in time with the rumble as the bike shuts off, and I hear the ding of my cell phone from above my head. I left it on top of my bed when I went to look out the window.

With my heart up in my throat, I scramble back out from under my bed with a single thought in my mind: I need to have proof. I need to show my father exactly what Jaeger is doing. It's the only way he'll believe me.

I grab my phone quickly, swiping it to the camera without checking the messages that are lining my screen, and set up the video, placing my phone on my dresser right across from my bed. The front door slams shut as a whimper escapes me, making me dive back under my bed. I slap a hand over my mouth as I begin to suck in air through my nose at a rapid pace.

Boots hit the stairs in loud, unmistakable *clops*, one after the other, the ominous sound resounding around my room and hitting me in the chest. With each stair climbed, my anxiety peaks, and when those boots stop at the top landing, my soul nearly leaves my body. I should have known he would make his appearance tonight. Ma is spending the night in Phoenix at a work conference, a gathering of accountants, and Dad is at the clubhouse.

My heart is beating so hard, each pulse reverberating off the floor and pressing into my chest. He's probably here to finish me off, to seal those hands back around the yellowing bruises on my throat and finish what they started. Fear has me in its tight grip, and the only means of escaping is through the second-floor window. It looks like death is imminent on either end.

His heavy boots resonate with each footfall as he comes closer to my door. My breathing becomes harder and my eyes swim with tears as my nails grip the wood floor, trying to find purchase on the slippery surface. Even though I'll lose, I will have to fight him. There's no other choice.

The handle of my bedroom door shakes as a heavy hand lays its firm grip on the metal, as if they're checking for a lock. He knows there's no point. Lock or no lock, he can get through it. He's already proven himself capable of destroying a thin, bedroom door, no matter how new it is.

The hinges protest a little as my brand-new bedroom door opens, those boots finally landing inside the confines of my room. My lungs scream with pain from me holding my breath, but I don't dare suck in any air. Maybe I'll pass out and he'll leave thinking I'm not here. Four steps into my bedroom brings him next to my bed, and I squeeze my eyes shut, knowing I won't be able to take the sight of his boots and not give myself away.

The slight squeak of his soles on my hardwood floor alerts me that he's turned on his heel, and now he's heading toward my bathroom. I open my mouth, sucking in a lungful of dusty, bedroom floor air, but I keep my eyes shut. I begin to internally plead for the monster to leave. I should have known God would never answer my prayers. He watched as my brother nearly killed me, so maybe that's what's meant to be. This is God's way of telling me I will die at my brother's hand and join my mother sooner than I thought.

The footsteps come back toward my bed as a sob hits the palm of my hand; the sound leaking out between the fingers. *Fuck!* There's no way he didn't hear me.

Jaeger knows exactly where I am now, so I drop my hand from my mouth and let my palm slap the hardwood floor. I've done what I've shamed every female movie star for doing in situations like these my entire life. I just outed myself to a lunatic killer, when instead, I should have called the cops right away. Who cares if my dad and Jaeger own the cops? I could have put up enough of a stink that my dad would have come home, then I would've told him everything.

Instead, I'm the stupidest heroine that's ever lived.

I can hear him bending, his leather cut crinkling with the motion. He lets out a grunt as his hand wraps around my arm, and I scream at the top of my lungs while I'm being hauled out from under the bed. His fingers dig into the bones of my wrist, and I open my eyes at the same time my other palm slams into the soft skin of his throat. Shock tears through me as my assailant lands on his ass, his thick, tattooed fingers wrapping around his throat with surprise. The sounds of him struggling to breathe filters around my room.

"What the fuck, Genni?" Quinton rasps as he rubs his sensitive skin.

"I thought you were an intruder!" I scream at him. "You know what happened to me last time!" He has the sense to look ashamed, an apology shining through his hazel eyes. "What are you doing here?" I ask between pants as he gets to his feet, his fingers still working the tender flesh of his throat.

"Came to check on you," he admits, and then a stunning smile lights up his face as he lets go of his throat. "You did what I taught you."

"I didn't have any other choice since you broke into my house!" I snap at him.

"The front door was unlocked... again." His brow slightly raises as his mouth turns down. "Do you not lock your fucking door?" he says with disbelief.

What does a lock matter when the monster in your life has a fucking key?

There's no point explaining or giving him my reasons why I didn't lock the door, so I shrug my shoulders and sit on the bed.

"You've checked on me. I'm fine." I give him a tight smile as memories begin to flood of the last time we were left alone together. I have feelings for Quinton Chino. I think I always have, but I won't be some conquest. The President's untouchable daughter to become something he brags about later. My heart's barely withstanding the damage he inflicted on me at the warehouse. He takes a step closer and kicks off his boots, sending them skating across the floor toward my bathroom. "What are you doing?" He doesn't answer me, but his eyes are full of heat and an undeniable desire simmers in his amber orbs. "Chino." I lift my hand in warning.

He doesn't heed it. Then again, he's never been one for

obeying the rules. He steps in closer again, linking his long, tattooed fingers through mine, and then he's nudging my knees apart, wedging himself between them. Now my heart is beating fast again, but for a different reason. His musky, spice cologne tantalizes my senses as I fall back onto the bed, hauling him down with me. His fingers are still tightly interlocked with mine while his other hand presses into the mattress near my head.

"Tell me, princess..." His voice is deep and husky, the smooth tone like honey coating my body. He grinds his cock into the apex of my thighs, and a moan escapes my mouth as my eyes begin to close. "Don't you dare close your eyes. I need to ask you something." I look up at him, only to find his pupils dilating, the black slowly eating away at the amber like burning coals in a summer bonfire. He grinds into me again, and my jaw slackens as he bends down, his mouth ghosting over mine. "Do you want this tall inside of you?"

It takes me a minute to figure out what he's talking about, but as soon as the memory of my Starbucks reference clicks, a laugh bubbles out of my mouth. His lips tip up in response, and the deep dimple in his left cheek winks at me.

"I was hoping for more of a grande," I reply with a snicker. "A tall doesn't do much for me anymore." His lips hover over mine as his tongue slips out, running along my bottom lip and making my body tremble with need.

"It's all good. I'm a grower."

My chuckle ends in a long moan as his lips land on the column of my throat. His five o'clock shadow scrapes deliciously against my sensitive skin, and I find myself widening my legs, just so I can feel him closer to where I want him.

Quinton's lips continue over my collarbone, the tip of his tongue dancing along my heated skin, the feel of velvet making me arch my back, begging for his mouth to seal around my aching nipples.

He leans up, his eyes slipping up and down, staring at the bruises on my neck, and then traveling down over the satin camisole and small, matching shorts. His eyes widen like he's just now realizing how I'm dressed.

He pinches the creamy fabric between his thumb and forefinger, rubbing it together in achingly slow circles.

"This is how you're dressed while you're alone at home?" His voice is gruff and his cock jerks between my legs as he slowly drags the shirt up. Inch by inch, he reveals my trembling stomach, and his tongue comes out to glide along his bottom lip, moistening the plush flesh. My nipples are hardened peaks, the sensitive tips feeling almost assaulted by the silky fabric.

Quinton's eyes slip down, those long, thick, black lashes resting against his cheekbones as he takes in the rapid rise and fall on my chest, accentuating my heavy breasts. Again he licks his lips as his head descends, and I arch my back to close the distance. The heat of his breath warms the material covering my nipples, and I whimper as I crave for something more.

"You're so fucking hot, Genni," he husks as his hands press across the skin of my stomach. I don't know if he means how I'm dressed or the temperature of my skin, but I don't care. I am hot and so fucking bothered.

His fingers skim upward again, grabbing the hem of my shirt and lifting it just under the swell of my breasts. "Can I?" he asks, his eyes looking slightly vulnerable. I nod as nerves steal the very words from my throat. Quinton Chino is known as the playboy of the MC. I know he sleeps with the Club Bunnies, and considering most of them are strippers, their bodies are skinny, perfect, with perky fake tits, and bleach blonde hair. I don't compare with my natural body. I may be toned and have long legs, but otherwise, I'm nothing more than average.

You wouldn't guess it though by the way his eyes widen a fraction and his lips part with a breathy gasp as he exposes my breasts, hauling the shirt up beneath my chin. The satin feel of the fabric slips against the skin of my neck, his perusal making me feel skittish.

"Genni," he breathes out as he bends forward, his breath coasting over a nipple. "You're so gorgeous."

My nails drag down the back of his shirt, and when I reach the hem, I grip it tight in my fist, dragging it up over his head. He chucks it across the room while I feast my eyes on his toned stomach and chest, the area nearly covered in tattoos along with his large dragon branding. My finger skims over an intricate feather inked between his pecs, the colors gleaming with beautiful oranges and browns. He tugs on my shirt, and I lift up slightly, helping him to pull it over my head. I fall back down, my back meeting the mattress and my chest completely bared for his perusal.

He takes his time, his fingers ghosting along my collarbone and slipping down between my breasts. The touch causes my skin to pebble and my stomach to quake. I can feel the shorts gathered between my legs growing damp as my wet pussy presses against the satin.

Quinton's fingers meet my belly button, the tip of his forefinger dipping inside, pulling a groan from deep in my chest. "Please," I plead, not sure what I'm begging for.

My hands land on his belt buckle and I begin to pull it open as his hands land on mine, stopping me.

"Are you sure?"

I nod because words are impossible around the swelling in my throat. Emotion clogs any room for speech, and I hope he can see the sincerity in my eyes as he bores down into them.

I arch my back, letting the moist area of my shorts skim along the bottom of his stomach, and he groans, his eyes darkening as he gives me one brisk nod. He gently nudges my hands out of the way to undo his belt quickly, those long fingers deft and sure, and my hands grip the sheets of the bed. The buckle is undone, his button unclasped, and the zipper slipping down, all before I could take my next breath.

The dark trail of hair leading from his belly button and disappearing inside his underwear has my mouth pooling with saliva. I've seen Quinton without a shirt before, but he's never been this close, and I've never been able to touch what I have lusted over many times. I want to go slow, making sure to commit everything to memory, because this may be our only chance, but I also have next to no patience. The need to have him inside me is too overwhelming.

It's as if he can sense my desperation as he falls over me, his mouth brushing along mine and his hot breath heating my lips as he chuckles.

"We have all night, Genni," he whispers. "Your brother and your father are on a scouting mission, and they won't be back until the morning."

"Is that why you came here?" I ask. "Because you knew no one would be home, and you could have your way with me?"

My nails scrape along his cheek, my fingertips tingling from the rough surface of his five o'clock shadow.

"No." His mouth tips upward again and that dimple makes my stomach flip. "I came to check on you." He swipes a finger over the bruise on my cheek and then down over my jaw, along my neck where a few others are dotted. "I didn't want you to be alone."

I swoon, literally, like every romance movie and book when the heroine realizes she's in love, and all it took was for the man to say some simple words. It just happened to me, the same thing I've scoffed at multiple times in the past.

I lean up and sink my fingers into his braid before pulling his mouth down to meet mine because the thought of not kissing him for another second feels akin to torture. This time, the kiss isn't sweet, it's rough. Our lips collide, driving my teeth into his, and our tongues tangle in a heated war. I've never been so enraptured by someone else before. Everything about how I'm feeling is new, and I almost want to stop everything in a still frame, freezing time so I can pinch myself to ensure this isn't another one of my useless fantasies.

I feel him push off his jeans, the belt, and whatever he has in his pockets, hitting my floor with a loud *thunk*. The sound drives my anticipation to new heights, but it's also laden with fear. If we do this, which I'm saying we are, considering there's only two very thin articles of clothing separating us, it could change everything.

His and Jaeger's relationship would be destroyed if my brother found out. My father would go ballistic if he knew Quinton Chino was inside his daughter in his own home, and then I would have to face my villainous brother and look into his eyes, accepting the fact that I'm dancing on my own grave.

Even as all of that runs through my mind, my legs widen, curling up around Quinton's waist as the heels of my feet force him in closer. There are levels to being suicidal, and I can admit death doesn't scare me nearly as much as not having this moment with Quinton.

So when he pulls away from my mouth, I whimper at the loss, licking my tongue along my lips to gather whatever is left of his essence. I accept that death is a likely outcome.

His face glides down past my neck, his tongue dipping out to drag along my skin, the smooth velvet feeling making my core clench painfully. I release my legs from around his waist to let him move freely, unencumbered by any of my limbs, and he rewards me by sucking a nipple into his mouth. The sensation instantly skates across my body, forcing my back off the bed and my fingers to sweep along his scalp. Another chuckle comes from him as my cheeks coat with heat, but the embarrassment is short-lived when those fingers slip down beyond my belly button and to the waistband of my shorts.

"I'm not spending my night dry humping, princess." His words are garbled around my nipple as his teeth sink into the sensitive flesh. "I'm taking these shorts off, then mine are going to follow, and your pussy is going to eat every hard inch I feed it."

His words have my mouth running dry, my throat squeezing as I try to breathe and swallow at the same time. Every bit of fear is wiped away when that sinful tongue of his trails from the bottom of my belly button, following a line as he pulls down my shorts. The moment the tip of his tongue hits my clit, I scream to the ceiling of my bedroom. Suddenly my voice comes back, the sound bouncing off the walls and slamming me back in the face as his two large hands spread my thighs. Then he's devouring me like I'm his last meal.

Maybe he senses the same thing that I do, that we're both sitting on death row.

Quinton's fingers pull open my folds, his tongue lashing against my clit as the coil tightens in my lower belly. I feel the familiar tug of an orgasm, only this time, I know it's going to be like nothing I've ever experienced before. He doesn't use his fingers; he doesn't penetrate me, he just sucks, licks, and bites my clit in quick succession. He pulls away just as I've reached the edge, my toes dangling over into the pleasurable abyss. My muscles tighten as I'm ready to take off, and those honeyed eyes look at me with amusement as he blows air on my exposed pussy.

"You should see the way she drips," he tells me as he leans in, flattening his tongue and swiping a straight line up and over my mound. "This pretty pussy is fucking weeping for me." He smirks. "Did you want to come, princess?"

I refuse to give in to him. I won't feed his ego. Even though my pussy throbs, pulses, and begs for release, I still don't give in. My fists grip the sheets of my bed, and I bite into my bottom lip until blood coats my tongue.

"Chino," I snap as I finally collect my thoughts. "Either finish or move out of the way so I can do it myself."

His startled laugh has his head dipping downward, and he's once again secured onto my clit, pulling me slowly back to that edge, teasing me as every muscle tightens. That coil is just about to snap, and when I feel him withdrawing, I grab his hair by the handfuls and shove his face back where it belongs. If he dies of suffocation tonight, that's his own fucking problem.

His hands slide under the globes of my ass, forcing my hips upward, opening me up farther so he can latch onto and suck my clit, and taking a mouthful of my pussy in the process. Then it's game over. I'm thrusted into that abyss, pleasure coursing through every muscle and releasing in an orgasm so intense, I fear I'm about to black out.

My heart's pounding as I struggle to take in a full breath when I feel him climbing over me, shucking his boxers to the floor. My hands land on his shoulders as I gently run my fingertips over his skin. My right leg is wound up over his arm as he lines himself up to my entrance, which is a sopping mess, my release sticky on the sheet below my ass.

"I don't have a condom, princess," he grits out as he runs the tip of his cock along my folds, teasing my entrance with shallow pumps. "Tell me I can fuck you without a condom."

I've been taking birth control since I was thirteen, but I know pregnancy isn't the only risk right now, and none of those guys in the MC are as careful as they should be. He sees my indecision and groans, his chin hitting his chest. "I'll be right back."

He pushes off the bed, padding his way to the door and throwing it open. I lean up with confusion until it dawns on me... He's going to get a condom from Jaeger's room. So instead of waiting here, like a good little girl, I spread my legs and let my fingers feel the evidence of the pleasure he gave me.

He rushes back in, ripping the foil on the condom wrapper, to find me two fingers deep in my pussy and my other hand working a nipple. He stumbles to a stop, the hand holding the condom wrapper falling away from his mouth as it gapes open, his eyes widening on my movements.

"I told you I could get myself off," I say with a smirk.

The growl that erupts from his chest is purely animalistic, sounding on the edge of primal as he stalks forward, making me squeal as I try to scramble up the bed. But I'm not quick enough as his hand latches around my ankle, yanking me back to the edge. He gets the condom ripped open, slipping it down over his length in record time, and before I can say anything or do anything, he falls over my body, forcing my legs apart. He lines himself up to the opening I was just inside and gives me a cheeky wink.

I open my mouth to say something because everything feels like it's moving too fast, but he's already working himself inside of me, his head pushing in and moaning about how tight I am.

He grabs the fingers that were inside me and sucks them into his mouth as he slams the rest of his length into me.

I scream, the strain on my vocal cords burning, my neck elongating up toward the ceiling, and my legs stiffening with the immense pain. I feel like he's doused me in gasoline and then lit me on fire. He doesn't move as he looks down into my face, his mouth still sucking on my fingers. The crease between his eyebrows tells me he knows there's something wrong.

My mouth stays open long after the scream has ended, and he takes that as an invitation to invade it with his own. The act of kissing me spurs him on as he continuously slams into me.

Over and over, our skin slapping, the sound of wet suctioning echoing around the room, mingling with his moans and groans, but all I feel is agony.

With each thrust of his hips, scorching pain erupts and travels through me. All I can do is grit my teeth and bear through it. My eyes flick over his features, taking in how his lashes are kissing his cheeks, the shadows dancing on his skin with each movement he makes. His mouth is slightly open, his tongue pressed to his top lip, and his shoulders flexing each time he rams inside me.

"You're so fucking wet, Genni." His euphoric bliss right now is a product of the worst pain I've ever felt. "Your pussy is gripping me so fucking tight," he moans. "I'm catching feelings, Gen."

He grinds against me, rubbing into my clit, but I feel nothing over the throbbing in my pussy. So as his thrusts become sloppier, I pray he's nearing his end, and with one last thrust, his forehead lands on mine. He mutters my name, his cock jerking and sending flames of torment throughout my body.

He pushes up, straightening his arms to look down at me, and when I finally unclench my jaw to look up at him, I find him staring at me with confusion. His fingers brush along my cheek, and for the first time, I notice they're both soaked with my tears.

"Genni?" he asks. "Was I too rough?"

I shake my head, hoping he just withdraws so I can get up and take a cold shower. He pulls out, dragging a whimper from my mouth, and stands at the end of my bed. When he doesn't move, I lean up to find his face ghostly pale, and his eyes widened in shock. I already know what he's looking at. I feel destroyed down there, and I can only imagine it's a fucking crime scene.

I lean up and look between my legs. The sight of all the blood gives me pause, the bright red dark against my cream sheets. My thighs are coated. His cock, still wrapped in a condom, is bright red, and the tops of his thighs look like he took a bath in blood.

"You were… Fuck, Genni! You were a virgin?"

"What did you think?" I sneer as I push myself off the bed. "When did I ever get the chance to date without Jaeger threatening someone's life?"

QUINTON

It's a fucking bloodbath in here.

I stare at the bed in total shock. The filled condom is bloodied and hanging on my cock, and everything below the navel, just above the knee, is coated in blood. I ripped Genni in two, my big ass, motherfucking cock, ripped this girl in two, and the only thing I can think of is, both Vic and Jaeger are going to string me from a beam in the club's basement, and use my body as a punching bag.

Genni brushes by me, waddling to the bathroom as I stand staring at the blood-soaked sheets. I really didn't know she was a virgin. How would I know? I'm not that invested in her life. Sure, I noticed my best friend's gorgeous younger sister as she blossomed into a woman. I'm human. I'm a fucking man! I didn't keep tabs on who she dated, when she dated, or if she dated.

Fuck, I'm really dead.

"Quinton!" she calls out from the bathroom. "Get in here and wash the blood off of you." My fingers grip the latex of the condom, the surface slippery with her blood, as I pull it off my dick. I've never been one to be squeamish at the sight of blood, but this, I don't know what it is. Maybe it's the fear that my days are numbered, the amount of breaths I take, the minutes slipping like sands through an hourglass. I'm on borrowed time. "Stop thinking so much," she calls out again. "Get in here."

Oh fuck, what if she wants to have sex again? I turn my head to look into the bathroom. No, she can't. She couldn't want it again after that. Once again, I find myself staring down at the huge bloodstain on the bed. None of that looks pleasurable.

My feet take me toward the bathroom, but my mind stays transfixed on that stain on the bed. I've never taken a woman's virginity before. Clearly, the lack of finesse is evidence of that. I just didn't think there would be that much blood. Where did it come from? Did I rip her? *Fuck, I ripped her.*

I step into the bathroom to find her filling the tub, her ass looking plump as it's stuck up in the air. Her body bends over to feel the bathwater as it fills the tub, and my mouth waters at the sight. Can someone explain to me why I'm painfully hard again, while still covered in her virginal blood? I'm a fucking monster.

She straightens to standing and winces. That's when I take the focus off her bloody ass and stare at the blood on her thighs.

"I'm so sorry, Genni."

She turns to look at me, her eyes softening when she sees my expression. "You didn't know, Quinton. It's not your fault. I should have told you."

"Why didn't you tell me?"

"I guess I'm at an age where I just wanted to get it over with, and I was afraid if I told you, you wouldn't have gone through with it."

"So you just used me." I tip my head to the side as I widen my stance to unstick my thighs. I stare at this woman in front of me with shock. "For the first time in my life, I've been used, and I think I like it."

"I didn't use you—"

"No." I hold up my hand to cut her off. "You did, and I am putting up an offer from here until indefinitely. Genevieve Varga can use me all she wants, even when Jaeger makes me into the most beautiful corpse."

Her giggle rings around the bathroom as she turns off the running water and steps into the tub. I know with the amount of blood on her that water is going to turn pink real quick, and I'm craving to see the sight. It's almost like a masterpiece I've painted, using only her blood and juices, and my cock as a brush.

"Why are you standing there and looking like that?" Her brow raises as she eases herself into the tub. She lets out a hiss as soon as her pussy hits the water.

I walk up to the edge of the tub and bend over, my fingers gripping the edge. "Does it hurt?" My eyes soften on her as my stomach rolls with concern.

As soon as that sweet ass of hers hits the bottom of the tub, and her white-knuckled grip loosens from the edge, she looks up at me with a small smile. "That enormous cock of yours destroyed me, baby."

There's no question that there's something happening between us, something more than me dipping my cock into a forbidden honeypot. I've always been fiercely protective of Genevieve. She's my best friend's little sister, my President's only daughter, and I've watched her grow from a young girl into a young woman. I would have killed for her out of obligation, but now the circumstances have shifted, and I can see myself doing just about anything for this girl. This feeling is so fucking dangerous.

I will admit, I'm a love 'em then leave 'em type of guy. I don't like clingers. I like to have a girl who knows she can't form any strings with me, and that's why Carrie has been my go-to for a long time. She doesn't push for more and she eagerly accepts what I give her. Just like every other guy, I thought I could fuck Genni once and get her out of my system, but my bloody dick is hard at the thought of having her again. Maybe I just want to make it good for her, you know. I don't want to leave her thinking sex is a torturous activity after her first time.

"Chino." She snickers as she flicks some of the pink water at me. "You look like you're trying to solve world problems. You and I both know you're not smart enough for that."

"That's it." I give her a devilish grin as I stand up and rub my palms together. I don't miss the way her eyes skim down over my body, landing square on my cock and widening at the sight. "You're in trouble now."

I jump into the bath with her, making her scream as the water splashes up into her face and over the edge of the tub. "Quinton!" she squeals.

I set my ass in the tub, watching how the water darkens a little further. "This feels nice." I smile at her.

"We need to change the water." Her nose crinkles as she runs her fingers through it.

"Did it hurt?"

"Hell yeah, it did." She laughs. "But I expected that."

"You should have told me." I wag a finger at her.

"You were already on the edge, teetering on whether or not you should give in and risk it all or tuck your tail between your legs and whimper back to my brother, begging for forgiveness. If I told you I was a virgin, you definitely would have been his little bitch."

I can feel my jaw drop as my eyebrows hit near my hairline. Genevieve has always had a sassy mouth, but this time, her words hit something deep inside me. I don't like being referred to as Jaeger's bitch, but even I can admit, I can see how she sees that.

"It's the way the MC works," I tell her when I finally catch my bearings. My finger dances along the surface of the water, my eyes downcast as I mutter the words, "Your brother is my Vice President."

"You are Sergeant at Arms." She leans forward, her hand landing on my chest. "That's still someone of importance."

"Oh, I know." I grin at her. "But I'm no President."

She falls back against the edge of the tub and lets out a long exhale, her face suddenly sad as emotions flicker across her features.

"I'm tired, Quinton," she says as she stands, the blood now cleared from between her legs. "I'm already so tired, and my life hasn't even begun yet."

Her words have stuck with me the entire ride back to the clubhouse. I wanted to stay with her for the night, but she begged me to leave, not wanting to deal with the stress of her father and brother coming home early. She looked so weary, so I gave in, but now I'm feeling guilty about that decision. There's a part of me that didn't want to face Vic or Jaeger after just fucking Genni. I pull up to the clubhouse, seeing both Vic's and Jaeger's bikes missing, and park next to the empty spots. While I pop my helmet off, I reach into my vest for my pack of smokes just as Laith comes out. He gives me a once-over and then his lips lift with a smirk.

"Who'd you just fuck?"

I chuckle and shake my head as I light my smoke. "Carrie."

He leans against his bike that's parked beside mine, crossing his arms over his chest. "Is that right?"

"Yeah." I nod, taking a long drag. "You know how bitches get when you stay away for too long, beckoning you to come over and shit?"

"Mmm," he hums, that smirk still firmly on his face. "Tell me, Chino, does Carrie have a twin sister?"

I tip my head back in a laugh, dragging my fingers through my hair, reminding me I need to braid it back up. "Why man? You about to break open that chastity belt?"

"Nah." He thumbs over his shoulder. "Because Carrie's inside. She's been here all night."

Shit, I should have thought of that. My eyes don't waver from his, and the mischievous look doesn't erase off his face.

"Who is she?"

"No, I'm no… I wasn't seeing any chick." I shrug.

"I know that look. Your slack face, hooded eyes, relaxed posture…" His finger points from the top of my head down to my feet. "You just got laid."

I flick my smoke to the ground and give him a slap on the shoulder. "Why are you so obsessed with me, man?"

We both laugh as I head into the clubhouse, Laith coming up behind me. "She must be someone important if you gotta keep her a secret."

"She's not a secret." I open the club doors and look at him over my shoulder. "This one's a little different."

"Not Old Lady material?" His question gives me pause as my eyes peer around inside the club. Carrie is there, along with her friend, Angel, both of them fucking two of the older members.

I watch the globes of Carrie's ass bounce on the bare thighs of one of my brothers, while I continue to ponder Laith's question. "If you gotta think that hard, then the answer is probably no," he says.

He's wrong. That's not why I'm thinking so hard. It's because Genni would make the perfect Old Lady. She's sassy, can hold her own, and she already knows every man in the club. They respect her because of who her father is, and she's obedient. I know that sounds weird. No female should be described as obedient, and I don't mean it in any derogatory way. I just mean she knows when to let someone else lead when she's unsure of the situation.

"Nah." I shake my head. "She's not Club."

"Don't get too attached then."

He brushes by me and heads toward the bar, probably to fill up another one of his baby teacups. The man drinks coffee like the rest of us guzzle whiskey, only he's got a little more class, and none of it dribbles down into his beard.

I walk into the club, a couple of the brothers hauling me in for a quick hug, and then I sit on the stool in front of the bar as Chip hands me an ice-cold beer. Carrie's eyes finally meet mine, her full red lips tipping up as she grinds and gyrates, her hips circling over my brother's cock.

"I'll see you in a minute, baby," she calls out, then turns her attention back to the man whose dick she's riding.

Laith chuckles beside me as I cringe. There's no way I want my dick inside of her after it's been inside Genevieve. It would make no sense to throw away a pearl for a handful of pebbles.

I really should head out back and begin to dig my grave, because I really won't survive what's to come. I can already feel how strong my feelings are for her, and it's just the beginning. There are only two choices I can see in front of me. I could go to Vic and talk to him about me dating Genni, or I stop this thing before it's even started. The thought of letting her go makes acid pool in the bottom of my stomach though, burning its way upward, but I'm also not ready to settle down. I'm on the cusp of something great. The youngest Sergeant at Arms in the club's history, and with Vic muttering about retirement, Jaeger will become President, and then I'm Vice.

Maybe Genni wants a family someday, maybe she wants a quiet life. It's not like she spends much time here at the clubhouse. This isn't her scene. I will never be able to have a quiet life. My family will always be a target, and I am forever tied to this club.

The choices are blaring in front of me as Carrie pops off my brother's dick, the condom he has wrapped around it glistening with her juices. She saunters over to me, the apex of her thighs sticking together with her release. I know I have to let Genni go, so as Carrie steps between my thighs, I let her, wrapping my arm around her slight waist. The feel of her bones is nothing like the waist I gripped earlier, and I haul her in closer, my mouth landing on the corner of hers.

"I came here looking for you." Her hand slips inside the cut to press against my T-shirt. "Where were you?"

"Out," I answer as I pull back to look into her eyes. "You kept yourself occupied."

"I did," she remarks.

"Did you enjoy it?" I see Laith leaning against the bar beside us, amusement lining his features as he watches us.

"Yes." Her chin lifts a little in challenge.

My hand grabs her jaw, that small chin of hers fitting snugly between my thumb and forefinger as I push off the stool. While I walk her backward, I don't miss the look of fear in her eyes as they widen. It makes my cock swell so fucking fast. What better way to get over someone than to be inside another?

When Carrie's back hits the pool table, she lets out a whimper of discomfort, and I bite into my lip. My eyes warn her that this is only the beginning. Her blood red fingernails dig into my wrist as she tries to pull my hand away from her face.

"Come on, Carrie," I taunt, grinding my hard cock into her naked body, eliciting wolf whistles from the guys around us. "Remember what you said a few nights ago?" I ask her, running my tongue up the side of her face. "Harder the better, Chino." My voice is dripping with mockery, and her eyes narrow slightly, but these blue eyes have nothing on the dark blue eyes I was peering into earlier.

The thought of Genevieve is like a bucket of cold water, and I force myself to be in the present, to do what it is I have to do, to wipe her face out of my mind. I flip Carrie around, pressing her down onto the pool table, and creating the perfect arch of her ass in the air. Then, with an exaggerated wink to the brother who had just finished fucking her, I undo my belt. He laughs and shakes his head as he rolls his used condom off his limp dick, chucking it to the floor at his feet. Carrie's body stiffens, knowing what's about to happen. She doesn't complain, if anything, she widens her stance a little, curving her back just a little more, and those blood red fingertips sink into the felt of the pool table.

I'll fuck her, but first, this ass needs to be reddened.

With one firm yank, the belt comes free of the loops in my pants, and I fold it in half, letting the two sides snap together. The sound causes Carrie to startle and the rest of the guys to laugh. Goose bumps break out along the skin on her back, a sight I have come to learn is anticipation. This isn't the first time the leather of my belt has bitten into the skin of her ass.

With one swift, fluid motion, I snap the belt against her sun-kissed ass and groan as the welt immediately swells. "Your cheeks look so good blushing for me, baby," I tell her as my hand glides over the redness.

The next one crashes in, creating the perfect *x* when paired with the first. A scream erupts from her throat, but it quickly ends in a moan when my finger slips between her ass cheeks. I'm following her crack to her sopping pussy. Carrie always gets off on a bit of violence.

The belt hits the floor with a loud crash as I pop the button and release the zipper of my pants, motioning to the same brother who fucked her minutes ago to hand me a condom. He stands, reaching into his back pocket and pulling out the silver foil packet. He tosses it over onto the table, his face filled with a mischievous look. Every one of us has fucked someone in this very room with an audience. It's nothing new, but tonight, there's something a little extra added to the reasons why I'm doing this. Every time I blink, *her* eyes pop up behind my lids, every time I inhale, the scent of strawberries clouds my mind, and when my fingertips glide along the surface of Carrie's skin, I imagine it's a few shades darker and so irresistibly smooth.

I can reverse the damage, at least that's what I tell myself as I drop my pants and boxers. I swallow down the ball of emotion that's gathering in my throat as *her* bath soap scent is still lingering on my skin, and as it wafts up under my nose. I roll the condom down my semi-hard dick because I can't stop now. Everyone's watching, and with Laith already suspicious, I can't afford for my recent tryst to come to light. So for a few seconds, I let Genni crowd my senses. Her scent, her touch, and the way her lips tasted. I let it all consume me, and when my dick is throbbing hard, I ram it inside Carrie, reveling in the way she screams my name.

And as my brothers watch on, I quickly fuck Genni's image out of my mind, praying I don't find myself back in her orbit.

THIS BODY IS
TEMPORARY
BUT THIS SOUL IS
ETERNAL
永遠
JAEGER

JAEGER

Two hours outside of Phoenix, there's a warehouse the Steel Dragons own. Kind of like a drop-off depot for the things we move, for the people we're hiding, and right now, it's being used as some sort of father/son excursion. When Vic asked me to take this ride with him to check on the warehouse, I knew what it was instantly. He's sensing my withdrawal, and even though I tried my best to hide it, I'm not a fucking stone man. It's hard to mask the pain of family betrayal.

Apparently, we're here to take inventory on a recent drop-off, but I swear Laith had mentioned doing this last week with a few of the other brothers. Despite that, I gave in and followed him here. I'm doing this with him because he's my dad. He will always be my dad.

"When my father made me Vice," he says, as he steps up to the table beside me. "He told me not to piggyback on the respect the brothers give him, but to earn my own."

"This is a new story," I say to him, my eyes flicking to the side, watching as he strokes his fingers through his beard.

"I only ever have stories to tell if it pertains to a lesson that needs to be learned. I don't burden you with things that won't help you on this journey." I want to scream and rage, to tell him I know what he's done. I want to release this pent-up fury that's been festering inside of me for the past few weeks, because the longer I keep it trapped, the more it's changing me. When I look into a mirror, I don't know who the fuck is looking back at me anymore.

"Loyalty to the club has always been the most sought-after attribute when we are picking our prospects. Then the skill comes with training, and ultimately, the sacrifice of laying your life down for a band of brothers who would all do the same for you." He turns around and leans his back against the table, crossing his arms over the cut on his chest. My eyes flick to that worn President's badge, the same one that's been handed down. My fingers itch to touch it because I don't think it'll ever truly be mine. "When my father told me to earn my own respect, I didn't know what that meant. I thought I had their respect already. I was Sergeant at Arms, a position that holds as much importance as Vice in my opinion, but it wasn't until I took a bullet in the name of the Steel Dragons that I'd realized what he meant."

"So you're telling me I have to shoot myself?" I look him in the eye and work my brow as his head tips back on a laugh.

"No, it wasn't about taking the bullet. It was about proving the oath I had taken. It was about protecting my brothers as if they were my blood. Do you know who shot me that first time?"

"No." I shake my head as my brows furrow with confusion.

"Now, this is a story I told you before." He smirks, his beard moving with the sentiment. "It was Chino's uncle. He was also a Steel Dragon for most of his life, and he thought he was a shoo-in for Sergeant at Arms, but when I gave it to his younger brother, he was real angry."

The story is one I know well, and probably one that haunts Quinton to this day.

"Because I took the bullet, my father made me make the choice of what would be Chino's fate. As much as I want to take my gun and shoot him between the eyes for trying to kill his own brother, I decided exile would be something much worse to endure. He was stripped of his cut, flayed of his branding, and driven out of Arizona."

"You've never heard from him since?" I ask.

"I have heard things, but I have not laid eyes on him since that day. The respect came after that. My brothers saw me as someone who made tough decisions, but I made them based on what the club needed, and not what my best friend needed. Being the President of a motorcycle club is difficult. You hold the life of its members in your hand. If you grasp it too hard, you'll crush it." He holds up his hand to show me a fist, and then slowly his fingers uncurl. "If you hold it too loose, it'll all fall away." It's almost like he's teaching me how to be the best President for the Steel Dragons, but I know what his actual plans are, and the only thing this little lesson is doing is firing me up hotter. I drop the clipboard on the table and turn on him, my arms over my chest. I let him see it, the raw anger radiating from every single pore of my body, then I watch as he stands up straighter, facing me. "What is it?" he asks.

"Shouldn't I be asking you that?" I tip my head to the side. "Shouldn't I be questioning you about what you're hiding from me?"

His face instantly falls, and that's when I see how weary he looks. Every wrinkle is pronounced, the bags under his eyes are dark and puffy, and even the whites of his eyes are looking a bit yellow.

"There are some things I'm not telling you." He nods. "But it's not because I don't trust you, or that I feel like you couldn't handle it. It's because I have to clear up a few things first." His hand comes out to land on my shoulder. Those eyes of his, so much like Genni's, begin to fill up with tears. "You're my son, Jaeger." He squeezes my shoulder. "My only son, and Genevieve's only brother. Do you know what that means?"

At the mention of her name, my anger flares again, and my hand itches to slap his off my shoulder. Instead, I hold it together, staring at those eyes, willing him to give me some sort of explanation.

"I'm going to need you to protect her when I can't. I'm getting old, and I know you guys have this connection. I can see that lately it's been strained. I'm hoping you guys will find it again, because there's no one else I trust with my daughter. Jaeger, promise me you'll always take care of Genni."

Guilt swirls at the bottom of my stomach as the thoughts of what I've been doing to her recently flip through my mind, but it only lasts a few seconds before the same insecurities I've been living with for the past few weeks reappear. How can I be the one he trusts the most with his daughter when he can't even give me his motorcycle club to run? If he needs me to protect Genni, then I should be President of the club, not her.

"There are some things happening, and I want to be able to tell you, but I haven't even spoken to your mother yet."

He wants to involve my mother in club business by telling her he plans to make his only daughter the first female club President. I can understand his apprehension about it. He doesn't seem like he's in his right mind, yet, my mouth is still firmly shut, and I'm not voicing a single grievance. I want to, but every time I look into his eyes, something tells me this is a lot bigger than what I originally thought.

"Dad." I finally find my voice, only for it to crack on the word. "I don't understand what's happening. Did we come here to count inventory? Or did you bring me here because you have something to tell me?"

"Do you remember the first time you told me you wanted to be an astronaut?" His mouth tips upward in a tired smile. "Do you remember why you wanted to be an astronaut?"

He's saying all the things a father would to his son, but none of the words are making sense with his recent betrayal.

"Not really." I shake my head.

"You wanted to be on a spaceship because it blew up before it got to outer space. You were always fascinated by explosions and fire, and I think those are the things your soul is made of. You burn so fucking hot, it's an inferno, and you incinerate anything in your path. You are the one true dragon in this club." My eyes begin to burn as my throat swells with emotion. We all like to joke and say I have daddy issues, but the fact of the matter is, I fucking do. Vic has been a great father to me, but I guess I've always been waiting for the other shoe to drop since I was a kid. Nothing could be this good, and recently, he's proven me right. I know why my anger has festered and burned so fucking hot with this certain betrayal. It's because Vic has somehow made me feel small again. Just how my biological father did when I was a kid. "Now you're angry with me, I can feel it," he says as tears collect along his bottom lid. "But I need to hear you promise, Jaeger. Promise me you'll take care of my little girl, if and when I'm unable to."

"So you brought me out here to twist my arm to look after your full-grown daughter?" I don't want to make any promises I know I'm incapable of keeping, because even though it would be an easy revenge to do the opposite of what he wishes, I still need all the facts laid out in front of me.

"I needed you away from the club." He shrugs the leather cut off his shoulders and throws it onto the table. My eyes widen at his actions, nearly popping out of my head. "I'm here, standing in front of you as your father, not some fucking President of a club."

"Dad—"

"Yes, your dad," he cuts me off. "I'm here as your dad. I'm asking you, Jaeger, please look after my little girl."

And that's when I picture the two pigtails on her head, her dark hair curling into ringlets at the ends with the biggest grin on her face that's smudged with dirt, and those blue eyes twinkling with mischief. I see the little girl I first met, and I remember the immediate bond I had with her.

Before I can stop myself, the words fly out of my mouth, "I promise."

"Take off that cut, Son. You and I need to have a heart-to-heart. This is a conversation between father and son, not a President and his Vice."

Dad told me to go home without him. He has an appointment in the morning, and that was what the ride was really for, only he wanted me there to unload the burden he has been carrying.

Now I'm enduring a two-hour bike ride while my focus is shot to shit. My mind is like a never-ending reel, replaying the last few hours on a continuous loop.

A constant, torturous loop.

I don't know if I'm angrier than I was before, or if I'm angry at myself for understanding exactly what it is he's doing. We didn't speak about Genevieve becoming President because there's no need. I didn't want to stress him out further, and when the time comes, I already know how to fight for my rightful place.

When you're fighting with fire, the odds are never fair, and I'm a fucking inferno.

I finally pull up to the clubhouse and signal for a prospect to open the gates. My ears are assaulted by the sounds of heavy rock music as I pull into my spot and haul off my helmet. I tip my head back to look up at the sky, letting the rush of the music roll over me, and shutting down my mind. There are some things that can't be fixed, and in this life, we're meant to live each day as it's given to us. So that's what I'm going to do.

I hang my helmet up on the bar and reach into my pocket for my smokes, then I head inside as I bring the zippo to the tip of my cigarette. As soon as the doors open, I'm blasted with an angry tempo, a thick cloud of smoke, and the heady scent of pussy. I'm home.

"Jaeger!" Quinton calls out, somehow managing to slur my name. "I thought you were going to be gone for the night."

"Nah, Victor didn't need me that long."

Carrie is sitting snugly in his lap without a stitch of clothing on, with what looks to be red fingerprints on her neck and waist. She's been thoroughly fucked already tonight, and it looks like maybe multiple times. A few of my brothers are at the pool table, and Laith is there too, his eye lining up a shot precisely as he motions to the pocket he's about to decimate the boys with. No one can touch Laith on a pool table.

"Y'all having a rager without me?"

A few of the guys laugh, but my eyes are on Quinton. He and I haven't been on the same page lately, and I'm hoping we can bury whatever's growing between us and threatening our family dynamic.

"We were planning to keep going until you got back." Quinton's mouth tips up into a smirk, and I feel myself doing the same.

"Oh, yeah?"

"Yeah. Tell me you brought some of that inventory from the warehouse," he calls out, as a few brothers snicker.

"Oh, you want me to dip into our stash?" The music dies as my hand slips into the pocket of my cut. "You're asking me to steal from our livelihood?"

"Yeah!" a couple of the brothers exclaim. They're fist-pumping the air as I haul out the large baggy from my pocket, waving the white powder back and forth.

"Is this what you guys want?"

I toss the bag toward the guys, letting it hit the center of the table, and a few of them lean forward, readying to cut it up into nice thick lines. I'll partake tonight because I need something that's going to take the edge off of everything I've learned today. I want to spend one night completely obliterated just so I can forget, and when tomorrow comes, I'll face it all again.

Chip brings me a beer as if reading my very thoughts, and when I chug it back in one draw, he has another ready to go. The music is turned back up, and I saunter back to the table just as Angel comes walking out of the back. Her lipstick is smudged, her hair tousled, and just like Carrie, not a stitch of clothing on her body. By the way she's walking, she's already been thoroughly fucked as well.

"Hi, baby," she says just as I'm sitting on the couch beside Quinton and Carrie. "Where have you been?"

I pat my leg, and she sits down, her seeping pussy wetting my pant leg.

I can smell the cum leaking out from between her legs, and I take this moment to remember why I wrap my dick up so tight when I'm fucking her. Angel will take any dick, any pussy, with little thought. That's why I like her so much.

I ignore her question and pinch a bit of the white powder between my thumb and forefinger, sprinkling it along her full tits. She juts her chest out, ensuring it stays there in a nice thick line, and as I run my nose along the surface, sucking up each bit, my tongue dips out to lick her nipple.

My night to forget is just starting, and when Chino reaches across to grip my hair in his fist, giving my head a shake, it's the freest I've felt in weeks. I won't let anything fuck with that tonight. My problems will still be there tomorrow. I'll deal with them then.

"Baby, are you gonna fuck me soon?" Angel whispers in

my ear, her tongue dipping inside.

I give her ass cheek a sharp slap and motion for her to get up off my lap. "Doll," I drawl. "Why don't you get up off my lap? Your cum dumpster pussy is leaking through my pants."

She rolls her eyes and stands, leaving behind a large, wet patch on my leg. Chino's boisterous laugh hits the ceiling.

"You let me know when you're ready to fuck this dumpster." She winks as she saunters over to the bar, the insides of her thighs glistening under the fluorescents.

Carrie stands and gives me a wink as well. "Let us both know. It's always so much fun when the four of us get together." Then I watch as she walks away, her red ass swaying with the music.

I point to the globes and look at Chino. "Did you punish her tonight?" I grin.

"You know it," he says as he leans forward, sniffing a line of the coke. "Oh, this is good shit."

My eyes zoom in on those thick white lines and they do nothing to elevate my mood. They only serve to remind me of exactly what happened in the warehouse I scooped the baggy from.

I'm going to need an entire bottle of whiskey.

GENEVIEVE
BMW Motorrad Milano

EIGHT

I fell into a deep sleep after Quinton left, but I awoke a few hours later from a nightmare. Though the details were based on real life. In my dream, Jaeger had his hands wrapped around my throat as his cock thrusted in and out of me, and the pain that radiated from my core was also a reality, but it wasn't Chino who caused it, it was my brother. His skin glistened with sweat and his jaw tensed with each thrust.

I sat in bed for an hour, my mind reeling over the images of my dream. I don't know what it meant, but I'm left sick to my stomach because I didn't necessarily hate it.

When it became apparent that I wasn't going to be able to fall back asleep, I decided I needed to leave the house and its quiet oblivion. I needed a distraction and something that would help this dream fade from my mind.

I throw on my leather jacket and put on my bike boots, deciding a late night, or early morning rather, drive around town will do the trick. Only when I step out onto the driveway, I find a patch of oil staining the asphalt underneath my bike. A groan spills from my mouth, echoing around the quiet street as my eyes meet the dark sky. My father is not here to check the bike, and I know he's not home until late this evening. So that only really leaves one person.

Well, maybe two.

I could hit up Chino. He just had his dick inside me. I can't imagine he wouldn't want to help fix my bike. With that plan in mind, I hop on my bike and head to the clubhouse. I would bet anything they're still awake, those guys rarely sleep. The only reason I've worked up the nerve to head that way is because I know Jaeger and Dad are out of town. I won't have to see my stepbrother or deal with his hatred.

I love riding through the streets during this time, just before the sun crests over the horizon. It's still pitch-black, but the birds are waking up, their cacophony of sounds adding to the ambiance of my relaxing ride. My stomach flips with excitement as I think about seeing Quinton again. At the same moment he admitted to catching feelings, I realized the same thing within myself. I've always had a thing for my brother's best friend, but I never ever thought it would get this far.

My brother will fight us being together tooth and nail. He wouldn't want me to have anything to do with the club, and again, it sends a wave of despair over me, knowing what my father has in store for my future. I'm about to rip the rug out from under Jaeger and take away his pride when it's announced I'm going to be President. If I think he hates me now, I can't imagine what his reaction will be when that happens.

I ease the throttle of the bike when I see a couple of Harleys parked up ahead at the local bar. The guys don't tend to drink at the bar. They have their own bar at the club where they're safe and have each other for protection. This is either a meeting, or it's not the Steel Dragons at all. So since I'm about to become President, I take it upon myself to investigate. I'm going to have to deal with this shit anyway. Might as well start now.

There's an alley that leads to the backside of a nail salon a few buildings down from the bar, one I know very well. I park my bike there and walk up toward the bar, keeping my helmet firmly in my hand. If I need to protect myself, this can pack a hard hit.

I can hear the muffled music grow louder as I approach the building, and when I'm about ten feet away, the door swings open, revealing a staggering Laith being held up by Kennedy and the Steel Dragons medic, Cash. Laith is a big guy, and with how old Cash is and how lanky Kennedy is, I can see why both of them are needed. I slip into the shadows between the two buildings and watch as they hail a cab, the three of them piling into the back seat and leaving their bikes parked on the road in front of the bar. I've never known any of the Steel Dragons to leave their bikes unattended like that, and something's telling me this whole situation is off. I'm sure of who they were and of what I saw because all three of them were wearing their cuts.

Instead of going back to my bike like I probably should, I end up swinging open the door to the bar and stepping inside. Thick smoke hits me in the face, and taking a deep breath is like swallowing acid. I hold my hand over my mouth to stop myself from sputtering as I slip inside and head toward the bar. It's not busy tonight, but there are a few people that are still lingering, even though it's well past last call.

"Hey, miss. Are you here to pick up someone?" the bartender calls out. I give him a small nod and point to the back of the bar, to where the booths are. He replies with a thumbs up in the air.

The back seating area is shrouded in darkness and heavily condensed with cigarette smoke, but I hear a few voices over the sounds of the music, which is a little more reserved back here. I head toward the bathroom sign, bypassing a few of the tables, and notice some black bandanas and leather cuts. These are club members, but they're not Steel Dragons, which is odd because no other club dares to set foot in our town. They may pass through, but no stops. I reach the bathroom door and push it open, giving them one last look over my shoulder, and that's when I see the cut that says Hell's March.

The prospect who opens the gate steps forward, blocking my way into the club. I heave out a breath inside my helmet and flip up the visor, giving him a narrowed look. When he sees it's me, his eyes flash with fear as he quickly scrambles backward, ushering me inside. Perk of being the President's daughter, I guess. I park my bike on the far side of the clubhouse, away from where the guys park their motorcycles, not wanting anyone to know I'm here. As soon as I pulled up, I heard the music blaring, and I can only imagine the debauchery that's going on inside. With my brother and my father gone, it's probably a shit show.

I was sixteen the first time I walked in on a club party, and it was the first and only time I saw my brother naked, his ass flexing as he fucked a Club Bunny on top of the pool table. Needless to say, I was traumatized and ran out of there screaming, begging for someone to bleach out my eyes. The memory has me stilling as I drop my helmet onto my handlebar. Chino is in there. I know we didn't establish anything; I didn't tell him we were exclusive now or anything like that, but the thought of him touching another female after he just left my bed a bloody fucking mess sends jealousy scorching through me. I get off my bike, ready to storm the fucking place.

I stop about two feet from the door and drop my chin to my chest to breathe through whatever emotions are ripping through me at the moment. I just lost my virginity to my brother's best friend without him knowing I was a virgin to begin with, and I gave it to him willingly. The Steel Dragon men don't like to be held down until they're ready, so technically, it's none of my business what he's doing. We didn't set ground rules, and he is a biker, after all.

So with that thought in my mind, I haul open the door, and much like at the bar, I'm assaulted with secondhand smoke from both weed and tobacco. The music is blaring, but the first thing I hear above the noise is the sound of females giggling. There it is again, the jealousy that's threatening to rear its head and bowl me over. I scan the room quickly, looking for his long, dark braid, and when I don't find him, I slip along the wall, keeping to the outer perimeter of the room. The guys are all too busy getting fucked up or fucked in general to notice the President's daughter. As I make my way to the bedrooms, my feet are sure because I know which one is his, and even though there's something in the back of my mind that's telling me to turn around, to get my ass back home, I continue forward.

His door is looming in front of me, and the noise of the main room is fading behind me. My hand lands on the door handle just as it's opened, and there, standing in front of me, is that Carrie bitch.

"Are you lost?" Surprise highlights her features, but she

quickly recovers as her hands land on her hips and she juts one out in all her naked glory. My eyes take in their fill, because why not? I appreciate the female form, and Carrie has an amazing body. Unfortunately, it's her mouth that pisses me off, and my fist cracks into it, making her fall back into the room on her ass. I shake out the slight sting in my knuckles, knowing all the pain is worth punching her.

"Whoa!" I hear Chino exclaim. "What the fuck?"

Carrie groans while her hand grips her cheek, her tears of pain slipping over her fingers. I can already see the skin turning a dark red, the sight of it sending pride rushing through me.

Quinton runs forward with just a towel wrapped around his waist, his hair wet and hanging down his back. The sight of him naked and her naked sets me off, and I stride into his room with a growl. Carrie has enough sense left in her knocked brain to scramble out of the room and run down the corridor, her bare feet hitting the floor with dull *thuds*.

"Wait, Genni." Quinton's hands are raised in the air, but it does nothing to squelch my anger, and my fist once again flies out, cracking him on the nose. The burn is immediate and then shots of pain skate up my hand and along my wrist. The pain intensifies when I try to shake it out, but it's worth it when I see the blood squirting from between his fingers. "Are you insane?" he screams as he rips the towel off his waist and holds it to his nose.

"That little dick,"—I point at his soft cock to drive my point home— "was just inside me a few hours ago. Then you get back here, and you stick it in that whore?" My words are spoken with a shrilled edge as my anger pours out.

His eyes become hooded as they narrow in on me, slowly traveling from my face down to my feet and back up in a seductive once-over, but not once does he apologize or deny any of the accusations. His soft cock hardens, rising to point straight out toward me.

I can't ignore how my still sore pussy clenches at the sight, and it only enrages me further. Since I've already given in to every impulse when it comes to my emotions tonight, I let it go one more time, and I'm once again coming at him. This time, with both fists swinging. He's quick as he grabs my wrist and flips me around, throwing my back against the wall. My head hits the plaster, jarring my vision, and I let out a whimper as soon as he's on top of me, his chest pressing into me and his legs kicking mine apart.

"Did you think because I fucked you and made you bleed, that somehow you have some sort of ownership over me?" he sneers, his top lip curling up toward his nose. "Tell me, Genni. Did you think I fell in love with you?"

The phrase that he said into my ear as he was fucking my tight, virginal pussy clicks in my mind in that moment. So I let my lips curl up into a slow smirk, and I look him in the eye. "You were the one that said you were catching feelings, not me."

His confused face has the crown of my skull connecting with the wall behind me with the force of my laugh. He can try to deny it, but my night comes spinning back in perfect clarity. When Quinton decided to come into my home, I was fearful it was Jaeger. I was petrified that my stepbrother was back to physically assault me like he did the first time, so I set up my phone as proof, and even though it's probably dead now, I'm more than certain it holds a lengthy video chockful of proof.

His thick, tattooed fingers skim up over my jeans, gripping my thigh, and hauling it up and over his waist. Then his nose skims along mine, his breath dusting over my mouth as he crowds in closer.

"I know what I said," he whispers, "but, you and I? It can't happen."

"I know." I shrug my shoulders with indifference.

I do know. I came to that conclusion the moment his cock slid inside me. Even so, as I look into his hazel eyes, sadness pouring out and flipping all over me, I still feel like Quinton Chino is mine. I slip my hand up over his shoulder, skimming along his neck as my fingers sink into his thick, black hair, and then I curl it into a fist and pull him forward, making our lips press together. He tastes so fucking good, like the sweetest ambrosia, like my own brand of drug. Something I'll be addicted to for the rest of my life.

But it doesn't fucking erase the fact that he had a naked stripper in here hours after he fucked me. With that thought in mind, my teeth sink into his plush bottom lip, drawing blood. He yanks back with a hiss, his tattooed fingers rubbing into the crimson fluid and dragging it down over his chin.

"Is that what you want, baby? You wanna see me bleed? Does it turn you on? Or is it something now that's between us, the sight of blood during sex?" he taunts me, his words used as a deterrent for his actions.

"I am not having sex with you," I snap back.

Even as I'm saying the words, he's undoing my pants and pulling them down over my hips. I pull off my boots and kick the restraining material to the side. He curses when his fingers dip into my panties, finding me soaked and ready for him, and two of those thick fingers push inside of me. My head once again hits the wall as a moan slips up from my throat, escaping my mouth. It hurts because it's still sore, but there's no denying how much I want him, not when the evidence of that is coated all over his hand.

Quinton drags his hand out, making sure to skim my clit along the way, chuckling when my hips jerk forward, chasing those calloused tips. He holds his hand between us, my juices glistening in the dim light. It's still tinged with red from the brutal fucking I endured earlier. Those two fingers land on my bottom lip as he drags my essence down over my chin, matching the markings he gave himself.

"I want to fuck you so bad, Genni," he mutters, his nose dabbing at mine. "I want to fuck your mouth, then fuck these tits." His hands gather my breasts as he pushes them together with a groan, and then they slip down over my waist, and around to the small of my back, inching their way into the crack of my ass. "Then I want to fuck this tight asshole." My hands hang at my sides as I watch him with disinterest, making sure he can't see the effect he has on me.

I know the sweet man who fucked me earlier is no longer here, and this man who's standing in front of me, whispering filthy things, is the real Quinton Chino. This is the man who fucks with a lust-filled fury and then can easily turn his back to walk away. It scares me because the feelings that are gathering inside of me are not the type that can be shut off easily. Despite all of that, when he slips those fingers into my mouth, running the musky taste of me along my taste buds, I open up for him. When his cock jerks against my lower stomach, I shimmy my pants further down my legs. It doesn't matter how much I'm hurting, because the desire to have him between my legs once again and his hard cock inside of me is overriding everything else.

He drops to his knees and drapes one of my legs over his shoulder, leaning forward to press a chaste kiss on my pelvis. His eyes flick up to look at me as my fingers wind into the thick strands of his hair, and then his tongue flicks out, slipping between my pussy lips and brushing along my clit.

"Please, Quinton," I'm begging him to give me something I've only just experienced, knowing his expert tongue can take me there and make me forget his indiscretion.

His hands bite into the thick meat of my thighs, forcing me open, and then he answers all my prayers as he sucks me into his mouth. His tongue pays close attention to my clit, but his sneaky fingers slip inside my wet cunt, thrusting in and out in time with the circular motion of his tongue, only to slip up toward my rear hole and tease it with slow, methodical circles.

I clench my ass cheeks as he chuckles against my heated flesh. "Don't worry, Genni. Not tonight."

Then he drags his fingers back down to slip them inside me. I feel myself tightening, readying for an explosion and a whole new euphoria that I crave from him.

Just as I'm about to come, just as my pussy tightens, his mouth pulls away from me, and his fingers slip down the inside of my thigh. "Quinton," I warn.

His mouth drags up over my belly button and then on top of my shirt. It's only then that I realize I'm still wearing my leather jacket. It makes no difference because he quickly spins me around, forcing me to face the wall, and the only thing stopping my nose from smashing into the plaster are my hands as they slap against it.

He opens his bedside table drawer and the distinct crinkle of a condom wrapper sounds throughout the room before he's propping my ass into the perfect position to line himself up with my pussy.

"Twice in one night, baby," he moans as the head of his cock teases my opening. He pushes into me, the burn immediate. It's his turn to slip his fingers into my hair, yanking my head back and extending my neck to the point of pain. His lips land on my cheek, his teeth nipping the skin as he forces me to take every single inch of him. "I came home intending to forget you, Genni," he admits just as his hips connect with the thick globes of my ass. "And do you know what I did?" he asks, his voice lined with a smug arrogance. I whimper through the stinging hold he has in my hair. "I fucked Carrie."

It takes me about two seconds to fully absorb the words he whispered into my ear, because surely, I couldn't have heard that right, but then I realize she was in his room naked, and he has all but made me forget about it with his devilish tongue and skilled fingers. All of that fades as I push away the lust cloud and process the situation.

I try to pull back, to move myself away from him. The hold he has on my head and the grip on my waist keeps me in place though, and with each forceful thrust of his cock, he's driving me to the brink. I wish I hated every single second of it, but that would be a lie. As painful as it is, it also feels amazing. The evidence of that is saturated all over my thighs and the sounds my pussy is making around his cock is bouncing off the surrounding walls. There's no way I could deny the effect he has on me. So I let myself enjoy it. I'll take pleasure from his cock, but when I'm done, this will never happen again.

So as he's pounding into me, my pleasure climbs, and when my pussy begins to pulse, I can feel my orgasm right there, dancing in front of me. He slams in and stops, his mouth landing on my shoulder and his lips pressing a sweet kiss to my skin.

"Don't let this be it, Genni," he pleads. "I already know I'll never feel this with anyone else."

Before I can reply, he thrusts into me with force, knocking me off that ledge. My extended throat screams through my release, and then he's right there with me, his cock jerking inside me as my pussy milks him.

But now it's over, and with the cloud of lust dissipating, the quick rush of anger takes over. As soon as his hand loosens on my hair, I spin around fast and connect my palm with his nose and my knee to his groin, just like he taught me.

He drops to the ground like a sack of potatoes, and as he's moaning and sobbing, his hands gripping his balls, I quickly pull on my pants and shove my feet back into my boots.

"Fuck you, Quinton," I tell him, my voice shaking with emotion. "I never want to see you again." Then I yank open his bedroom door, step out into the corridor, and let it slam shut behind me.

The music hits me, and I remember there's a whole-ass party happening out there. That's where I go. Fuck Quinton, fuck Jaeger, and fuck this club. I don't even want it.

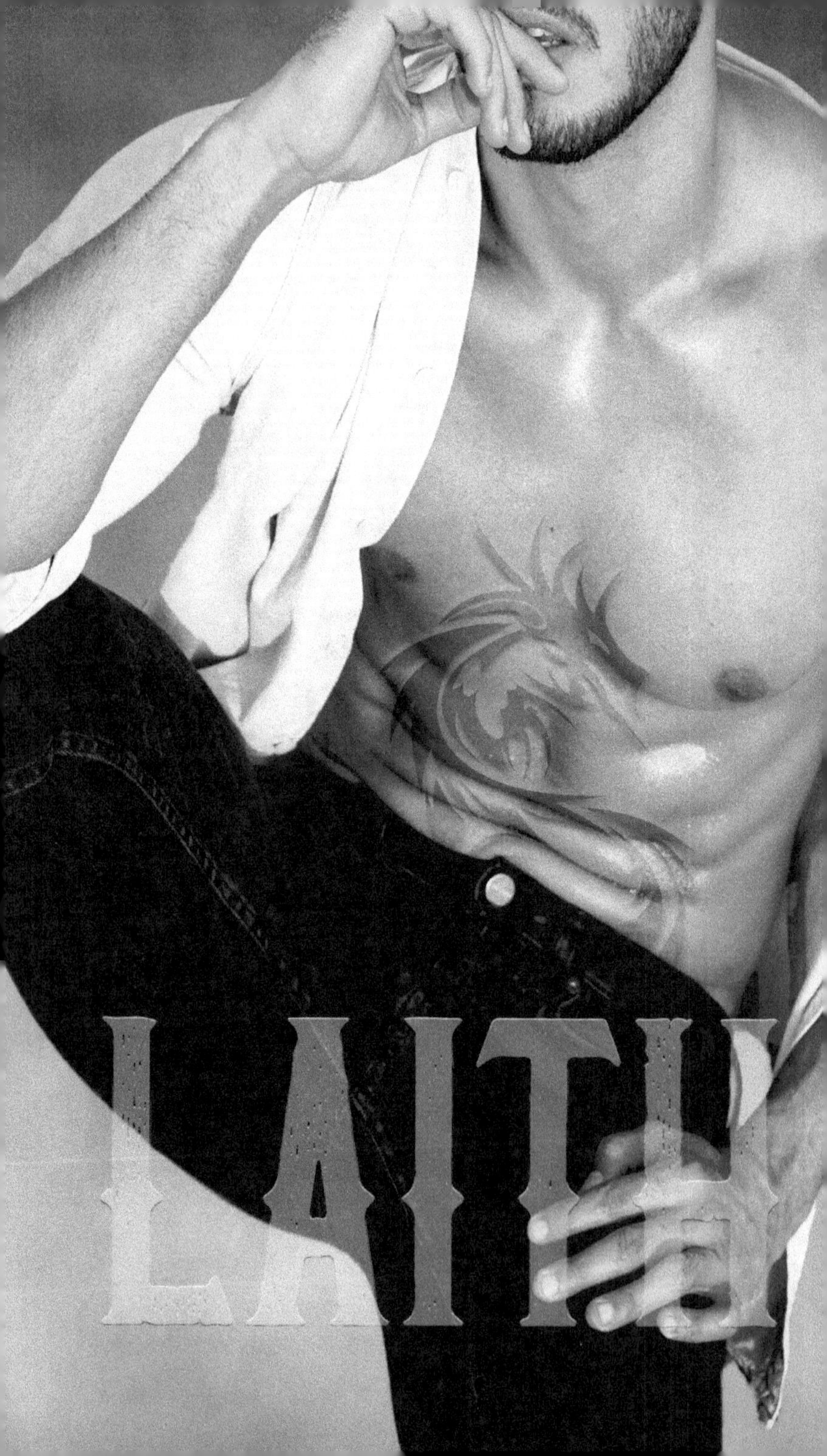

LAITH

LAITH

She comes stomping out of the corridor, her hair a tangled mess around her shoulders, her cheeks flushed with anger, and that jaw of hers clenching, making those plush lips pout. Genevieve Varga is a vision. She has her father's tall stature and their eyes are the same shade, but everything else is Wendy.

I've only ever been in Vic's office twice, but he has a picture of Wendy on his desk. The woman was breathtaking. She had radiant skin, much like Genevieve's same dark olive tone which turns into a beautiful brown beneath the sun's rays. The lips, the nose, and the shape of her face all belong to the woman who lost her fight with cancer. Wendy left a piece of herself behind in the pissed off woman who's heading toward me right now.

Genevieve slips onto a stool at the bar. I don't miss the wince as her ass meets the wooden top. I'm openly staring at her, but she hasn't noticed because her anger is overriding everything else. Her hand hits the bar top with a loud, resounding smack, which soon gets eaten up by the music in the room, but Chip is perceptive, and he hurries down the bar when he sees his President's daughter waiting impatiently.

"Hey, Genni." He looks around, and when his eyes land on me, his brow quirks up.

Genni doesn't come here often, and when she does, it's usually with Claire or her father, never during a club party. The things that go on here during a party, no President's daughter should ever witness.

"I need a whiskey, Chip," she says, her pink nails tapping quickly along the bar top.

Chip nods and grabs the whiskey off the shelf, pouring it into a clean glass, then sliding it across the bar. I turn on my stool and take a quick look around the room. If Jaeger saw his sister here, I don't think it would end well.

Thankfully, it looks like he left with the stripper named Angel, and if that's the case, he'll be gone for a while. That doesn't mean Genni should continue to stay.

My eyebrows skate upward when she downs her glass of whiskey in one gulp, running the back of her hand over her swollen lips, and that's when I really take in her appearance. She's disheveled, a red rash lining her cheeks where stubble may have caused friction. Her red lips are swollen, like maybe someone was brutally kissing them, and her hair tangled from fingers gripping the thick tresses.

Her leather jacket sits precariously on her shoulders, one side nearly falling down her arm, and her boots have been put on haphazardly, the zippers undone.

"Genevieve." Her name flies out of my mouth before I have a chance for second thoughts.

She hits the bar again, motioning for Chip to refill her glass as I stare at her profile. When her head turns, and those dark blue eyes are spearing into my own with a despair-tinged anger, I can't help but find her irresistible.

"Hey, Laith." She gives me a nod as her eyes narrow on me suspiciously.

"What are you doing here?" I find myself leaning forward. I want to hear everything she has to say, but not just the words. I want to hear the tone, needing to absorb everything about her.

"I came to speak to Chino about fixing my bike." She bites into her lip as if she's just revealed a large secret. "But he's busy." Her cheeks darken with a red hue, and I lean farther, finding myself utterly entranced by this young lady.

"What's wrong with your bike?"

"It's leaking a lot of oil," she says as Chip places a second glass in front of her. Before her fingers can wrap around it, my hand cuts it off, then pushes it back.

"You shouldn't be drinking if you're riding your bike, and we both know it's not safe for you to stay here."

She finally gathers her bearings and looks around the room. Some brothers are already partaking in Club Bunnies, some even doubling up, and even though it's a common sight for us, this is not what she should be seeing. The bag of coke Jaeger brought still sits in the center of the table in the corner of the room. Now and then, a brother will set up a line, snorting it into his nose as he watches a woman get fucked in whichever hole is available. This is no place for the President's daughter.

"You're awfully sober." Her brows come together in confusion. "How did you sober up so fast?"

"I don't drink often." I shake my head, which only has hers tipping with more confusion. "What am I missing?"

"I saw you earlier," she tells me. "At the bar in town, with Kennedy and Cash."

Kennedy and Cash have been away on a mission to find out more about the Junior situation. So I'm not sure why Genevieve saw them here in town at a bar, and supposedly with me. Then it all hits me. There is one other person who looks exactly like me. I keep the shock from spreading to my face, but I know I need to get her out of here. Shit's about to go down.

"Is Claire at home?"

"I shouldn't have come here." Tears gather along her eyes, lightening the blue just a little. "I don't know what I was thinking."

"How about this," I tell her as I get up off my stool, clasping her hand in mine. "I'll come by your house tomorrow and check out the bike."

"Oh, I couldn't ask you to do that." She shakes her head, her dark hair curtaining around her shoulders. "I'll just wait for my dad to get home."

The thought of Vic having to work on his daughter's bike in the driveway, when I know how tired he is, doesn't sit right with me.

"Go home and get some sleep," I tell her. "I'll be by around ten o'clock." Her eyes scan over my face. My first thought is she's going to be able to see my scars and be disgusted by them, but to my shock, she reaches up and runs her finger along my right cheek, feeling the disfigured skin. My hand comes up to wrap around hers, gently removing it, and then I turn her around, giving her shoulders a little shove. "Go on home, little lady," I tell her as she spares me a glance over her shoulder. "I'll be by later."

"I'll make you breakfast." She gives me a small smile, and it's like a bolt of electricity hitting my heart. She doesn't know just how deadly she is.

I smile and nod at her, and when she finally starts heading for the door, I release a sigh of relief, but not before my eyes fall to her ass, perfectly rounded in her skinny jeans, and legs that seem to go on forever.

Once she disappears out the door, my eyes skip toward the corridor she came storming out of. I didn't miss the scent of sex on her, and it was fresh. I smell it every day here, and she did reveal a few secrets.

She's been fucking Chino, and my brother is in town speaking to Steel Dragons.

THIS BODY IS
TEMPORARY
BUT THIS SOUL IS
ETERNAL
JAEGER

JAEGER

Angel's here, still sprawled out across the picnic table, her ass stretched open, and her tears pooling along the wood's surface. I was a little rough with her tonight, but it's nothing she can't handle. She's endured it many times before, and she still keeps coming back for more.

Nothing is working though. No matter how much I drink, how much blow I snort, or how many assholes I rip apart, I can still hear the words Dad said to me earlier at the warehouse.

I haul the condom off my dick and throw it across the yard, knowing either a prospect or a Bunny will find it in the morning. I didn't even come that time. I really don't give a shit right now though. I stand, pulling up my pants, then I grab the near-empty whiskey bottle, leaving my belt buckle undone to jingle in the silent night.

Angel's soft cries continue as I slap her ass. "Go inside."

She pushes herself up off the table and gives me a quick glance, her eyes red and swollen, saturated with fear. My still hard dick jerks against the confines of my pants, and the look she receives back has her scrambling into the clubhouse.

I grab my smokes from my cut pocket, pulling one out and lighting it before dropping the pack and the Zippo to the table. My vision swims in front of me, distorting further every time I blink. Even so, my hand wraps around the neck of the whiskey bottle, and I bring it to my mouth. Just then, the clubhouse door opens, and I nearly choke on the liquid when I see my fucking sister slink outside, heading around the side of the building.

"What the fuck?" I breathe out.

What the fuck is Genevieve doing here at the clubhouse this time of night? Is this where she comes, thinking she's the President and she can be here whenever the fuck she wants? Anger slips over me like an old friend, a relationship so toxic that I know I should end it, but never really succeed. Now I embrace it, giving myself over and filling my soul with murderous intent.

I stumble after her, the whiskey bottle in my hand, and it's like everything was meant to be as she slips into the shadows of the night, providing the best cover for when I confront her. As I round the corner, I spot her yellow fucking bike, and the scene in front of me coats with red shadows. I begin to shake, and when I stumble, kicking up a bit of the gravel, she turns with a gasp.

The whiskey bottle in my hand flies across the space between us, smashing into the brick wall beside her head, and she screams. The sound only makes me laugh with glee because no one will hear her out here.

"Jaeger." Her voice is pitched too high with fear, but it does nothing to quench the anger, just adds a little something to it. My cock springs back up as I storm toward her, and that's when I really take in her appearance. Her hair is a mess, her cheeks are flushed, and when I stand about a foot in front of her, I can smell it.

My hand wraps around the thin column of her throat, and I shove her back against the wall. Her breath pours out of her as her back connects roughly with the brick, and then I'm on top of her, my mouth just over hers. Her surprise renders her useless as her hands press against the brick at her sides.

"What the fuck are you doing here?"

Her hands come up to wrap around my wrist, but she's no match for me tonight. "Where's Dad?"

"Why do you smell like a cum dumpster?" I snarl in her face. "Who are you fucking here?"

Her eyes widen and her body trembles just as my fingers tighten around her pretty throat. "I'm not."

"Don't lie to me, you filthy slut." My lips brush against hers with every foul word I spit out. "I can smell it on you."

My cock is painfully pulsing against my open jeans, my boxers effectively creating a barrier between us. I don't know if it's because I can smell how much of a whore she is, or because I'm so drunk I don't give a shit, but I would like nothing more than to sink my dick into my sister and fuck her against the brick wall. Even as the disgusting urges flow through me, I step into her and the hand not gripped around her throat runs down the side of her body, gripping her waist.

"Jaeger," she whispers, but I don't want to hear her. She can't speak, it'll only make this worse. So I tighten my hand once more, ensuring another word doesn't slip from her mouth.

I pull her hip in close to me, arching her back and settling my cock to the apex of her thighs, and just because I can, my hand slips around and grabs onto her ass. I grind into her harder. I'm so fucking hard it fucking hurts, and I could come right here in my fucking underwear as I watch lust and fear war in my sister's eyes.

"You're a filthy little slut," I tell her, and her mouth opens as she tries to drag in air. I pull her leg up over my waist, opening her pussy up and settling my cock into the warmth against her pants. So fucking warm.

Her face is a nice, bright red when I loosen my hold on her throat, and when she sucks in a breath, my mouth is on hers, inhaling all the air and depriving her lungs further.

She doesn't reciprocate as I force her lips open and slip my tongue into her velvet-soft mouth, running it along the surface of hers sensually. She tastes as good as I imagined, and when her tongue moves against mine, her head tilting to the side, I know she's just as depraved as I am.

I swallow her moans as I drive my cock between her legs, rotating in time with each thrust of her hips, and I've just about lost myself… Just about, but then her moan grips me through the haze and yanks me back into reality.

I'm kissing and dry humping my fucking sister.

With one last spear of my tongue into her mouth, I yank my lips from hers, and stumble back, righting myself to glare into her shocked-looking face.

"Jaeger, what—"

The impact of my palm against her cheek cuts off any of her words as her head whips to the side with the force of my slap.

"You disgusting little bitch," I spit at her feet. "You filthy fucking slut. You would have let your own brother fuck you. Here, outside in the open, wouldn't you? Anything to have a cock inside that loose pussy of yours."

Her shaking hand covers her cheek, her kiss-swollen lips hanging open in shock as tears skate down from her eyes. Genevieve Varga can never become President of the Steel Dragons because the only thing she'll be good for at leading is how to open her legs to fuck every man here.

"Get the fuck home," I snarl out and turn as I do up my jeans and belt buckle. I hear her quiet sobs behind me, and when I round the corner, her bike revs to life. That's when it hits me. I would have fucked her against that wall.

I open the clubhouse door as her bike flies by and turn my head to see the prospect scrambling to open the gates. Good, I never want her to come back here. Every time she thinks she may become the President of this fucking club, I want her to remember how easily I could have defiled her outside its walls.

The inside of the clubhouse looks just the same as when I left it. Brothers fucking women, smoke clouding my vision, and music blaring to cover the lewd noises. The room spins in front of me once again as I head for the corridor toward my room, knowing I need to sleep this shit off, but a large hand lands on my shoulder, spinning me around.

I come face-to-face with Laith, and the look in his eyes has me stalling as my mind scrambles to figure out what's going on.

"We need to talk, brother," he says, giving the room a quick look. "I have information I think you're going to want to hear."

GENEVIEVE
BMW Motorrad Milano

NINE

The sun slips through the blinds on my window, attacking me with its late morning rays. I turn over, trying to ignore it when everything from the night before comes spiraling back like a horror film. Losing my virginity, catching the man I thought I was falling in love with naked in his room with another woman, and then being attacked by my brother, again. Only it wasn't so much an attack as it was the moment my ungodly soul left my body. Even now, as I think over our exchange, I don't know who that girl was, the one who arched her back to press her core into his hard cock, the one who slid her tongue along his with a breathy moan, or the one who wished it went further than what it did.

I'm thankful for the slap he gave me to the face because I deserved it.

With sleep fully abandoned, I throw off my covers and get out of bed. The space between my legs is still pulsing with soreness, and I'm once again reminded of the moment Chino stole my innocence forever, becoming the man I gave my everything to.

I stand in front of the mirror, and glare at my throat dotted with fresh bruises, settling beside the ones that are yellowing with age. Instead of shrinking away from it, I stand there and force myself to see what it is I deserve. I'm telling myself it should have been worse. Jaeger was drunk, clearly not in his right frame of mind, but me? I have no excuse. He'll probably wake up in the morning having forgotten it all, but I don't have such a luxury.

I take another bath, trying to soothe my sore muscles and sensitive flesh, and then I throw on a tracksuit to head downstairs. Ma's still not home, Dad won't be home until later tonight, and Jaeger, I would assume, is back at the clubhouse sleeping off the booze that was potent on his breath. I stand at the kitchen counter, trying to decide if my stomach could hold down toast when I look out through the window and find Laith under my bike with no shirt on and his dragon branding shining bright against the tanned skin of his stomach.

I remember him saying he would come by to fix my bike, but I didn't think he'd actually go through with it, and now that I see him out there, the last thing I want to do is talk to him. So I admire his flexed muscles as he cranks the wrench for a moment and then I pull myself away.

The gun my father left me in the house is kept in his safe in the office, and I retrieve it to head out to the backyard, planning to do the same thing I've been doing every morning since he told me his plans. I refuse to be a weak leader, and if I ever have to shoot anything, I want to be sure I don't miss.

I line up the rusted cans on the fallen log in my backyard, and then I retreat back to the line I've dug into the earth, slipping the silencer on the gun. The neighbors around here know my father is a dragon, and they've accepted that. Something tells me they wouldn't like to hear gunshots every morning though.

My eye travels down the barrel of the gun, settling on the first can as I widen my stance and loosen my arms, and then I fire. The cans topple over in quick succession, and when the final one hits the ground, I drop my arms and take a deep breath. I imagine my brother's or Chino's face on the reflective tin, and my aim is spot-on.

I put the safety on the gun and lay it down on the table, then head back to the line of cans to set them up again. For what feels like the hundredth time, I wonder if Laith has finished with my bike and left. The thought of seeing a Steel Dragon after last night makes my stomach flip with anxiety. Everything is ruined, so many lines are blurred, and I don't know how I'll ever fulfill my father's wish. How can I lead as a strong, independent woman if these men know my most vulnerable parts?

When I turn back around, a scream bubbles up my throat before I swallow it back down. My body tightens with adrenaline as it prepares for an attack. Laith is standing at the table, leaning on it with his arms crossed over his chest. He's put his shirt back on, but those biceps are still on display, he's a big man. I'm still trying to figure out how he sobered up so fast last night, it was like seeing two different men from the bar to the club.

"Hey." I raise my hand in a wave, and he gives me a slow nod. "Thanks for helping with the bike."

He nods once more as I begin to walk toward him. I guess he's not much of a talker. When I get about two feet in front of him, he picks up the gun and points it toward my head, his eyes darkening as he looks at my throat.

"What are you doing?" I ask him as fear settles over me, freezing me in my steps.

"Shooting those cans is easy enough," he says, his voice deep and raspy. "But what do you do when someone has a gun pointed at your head?"

LAITH

LAITH

With anger coursing through me, I'm having a hard time holding the gun steady, but my eyes do not leave the marks that are lining her throat. I can't remember if they were there last night. The room was too dark, but there's enough on display that I can see some are older than others.

The President's daughter is being abused by somebody, and I have a feeling that's why she's out here shooting tin cans in her backyard.

"Tell me,"—I pull the safety off the gun, and grin when her eyes nearly pop out of her skull—"does Vic know about those marks around your neck?"

Her hand creeps up to touch the long, straight column of her throat, her fingers gliding over the sensitive skin with a wince. "No." She shakes her head. "And I don't want him to know. He has enough on his plate."

"I agree with some of that, but that's why he has the rest of us to pull up the slack when his shoulders begin to slump under the pressure. So you're going to tell me, princess, who the fuck is leaving bruises on you?"

Her throat works on a swallow, the bruised flesh moving with the motion. "I can't tell you that, Laith."

"I didn't think so." I shake my head. "So this is what we're going to do. It's easy enough to shoot a couple of tin cans, but what you really need to learn is how to fend off someone who wants to lay their hands on you, and how to disarm them."

"You don't have to—"

"Yeah, princess, I do."

"Okay, I have one condition," she says as she lays her hand on my forearm. "Please, stop calling me princess."

"All right, Little Varga." I give her a small smile, her tenacity reminding me a lot of Vic, but her vulnerability shines through everything she does. I like that. "I can see your aim is good, and you've been working hard on that," I compliment her. "But a huge part of defending yourself is using the weapons your attacker owns against them."

"What do you mean?" Her brows come together in confusion as her hand drops from my arm. The sudden loss of her warmth sends shards of ice along the surface of my skin.

I put the barrel of the gun against her forehead, reminding her I am armed and pointing a gun at her head. She takes a step back, her brows crinkling and raises her arms. "How would I stop someone from shooting me if they're already prepared to do so?"

"That's a good question. The best thing you can do in this situation is to be quick and to know certain pressure points. See this?" I lower the gun as I point to the soft area of my wrist. "This is sensitive. Not much muscle here to protect the flesh encased between two bones. If you poke it, my hands will automatically curl."

"Here?" she asks as her long, pointed nail scrapes my inner wrist, and goose bumps dot my skin at the contact.

"Exactly." I give her an encouraging smile. "Now use two fingers and jab it."

"Wouldn't that make them want to pull the trigger?" Her eyes bore into mine, the intensity of the blue making my throat tighten.

"Not if you do it fast enough, and you make it a surprise." I take a small step closer to her, letting the citrus musk of her perfume wash over me.

She does as I instruct, and my hand curls inward, pulling a huge smile to her lips. "I did it." I find myself smiling at her enthusiasm.

"That's only the first part. Now, while my hand is curled, you're going to punch the top of my hand right here." I point just under my knuckles "There are a lot of small bones, and again, not a lot of muscle here. It's sensitive, and if those bones are bruised, cracked, or broken, it's extremely painful."

"Okay." She bites into her lip, and then her little fist hits my hand, sending shards of pain up my arm.

"Very good," I say with a cringe. "Usually at this point, the fingers will relax, and you can either grab the gun, or they'll drop it. The trick is you have to be quick. So let's do it a few times."

She masters it within fifteen minutes, and I'm pleasantly surprised at her dedication. She's a quick learner, and once she commits herself, she doesn't quit until she has it perfected.

"Next," I tell her. "You need to know the places someone could have a weapon that's easily accessible for you." I flick back my shirt to show her my belt and the holster attached to it. "See here?" I point to the flap that's holding the gun into place with a simple clasp. "Any type of holster is going to have this clasping that you can easily open with a single flick, but again, you have to be quick."

She nods, her eyes eating up everything I'm showing her. "Quickly," I remind her and show her how to quickly flick it open and pull out the gun. "Honestly, you just have to get past opening the clasp and sealing your hand around the handle. Sometimes a person's own weapon is the best to use against them."

After a couple of attempts, she gets that down pat, and I find myself looking down the barrel of my gun as she points it between my eyes. The triumphant look on her face has me laughing, and then she's throwing herself in my arms, the scent of strawberries washing over me as her head lands on my chest. My nose slips down to burrow into the soft strands of her hair. The second my arms come around her waist, a sob erupts from her chest. She tries to hide it by pressing her mouth against my shirt, but it does nothing. Her anguish is now mine.

"Little Varga," I whisper, my hands running down the back of her head, and my fingers tangling into her thick strands. "Tell me what I can do." My mouth presses to the crown of her head as her body shakes with the force of her cries.

I continue to hold her through the agony seeping out of her every pore, then when I don't see an end in sight, I bend down and pick her up in my arms. Her face lands in the crook of my neck, as her tears run down under my shirt and her fingers curl into the fabric against my stomach. When I get back to the clubhouse, I'm going to kill Chino. I've seen how rough he can be. I've seen

Carrie leave with similar bruises, and even though I know she asks for it and enjoys it, Genni clearly does not.

Once I bring her inside, I set her on the kitchen counter and open the fridge door to grab her a bottle of water. Her arms don't loosen from around my neck, and the surrounding air is tinged with her sorrow. It only makes me angrier.

"Little Varga." I put the bottle of water between us. "Here, drink."

"I'm so sorry, Laith." She shakes her head and finally releases me to wipe the tears off her cheeks. "It's been a really rough month or two."

"I'm here to help you, if you would let me."

"I know," she says as she opens the bottle, a hiccup breaking up her words. "I know I just… I have to learn to take care of myself. I need to be tougher."

I can't argue with her there.

I grab my cut from the back of the chair, where I left it when I ventured into the backyard, and I shrug it on over my shoulders, watching as her bruised throat moves when she gulps down the water.

"Do me a favor," I demand. When she looks up at me, those dark blue eyes of hers shining with unshed tears, I continue, "The next time anyone tries to put their hands on you, you do what I've taught you."

Her shoulders straighten as her chin lifts, pride shining in her eyes. "I will."

Her hand reaches out and fists the material at my chest, dragging me back in between her spread legs. It's my turn to swallow down the moan that wants to break free, and I pray my body realizes this is not the time nor the place to get excited.

"Thank you, Laith," she whispers, her arms wrapping back around my neck. "Thank you so much." Her soft lips press into my cheek just as my hands settle on her waist. She lingers there for a few seconds too long, but I don't dare move either. Everything about Genevieve Varga is intoxicating, and if I don't watch myself, I'm going to find myself falling for the President's daughter.

It's me that finally breaks the moment as I step back, instant regret burning through me with the embarrassed coating of red that dots her cheeks. I pretend I don't see it as I give her a smile. As much as something inside of me finds itself explicitly tied to this girl, there's no way in hell I would survive the fallout of our entanglement.

QUINTON

I'm hauled up off the stool I'm sitting on in front of the bar and come face-to-face with a furious-looking Laith. His teeth are bared, and his cheeks are stained a dark red with pure fury.

"What the fuck?"

Before I can ask him what the hell is the matter, his fist plows into my mouth, knocking me back against the bar. My spine ricochets off the wood, and the air in my lungs rushes out, leaving me gasping for breath, but that doesn't stop him. He grabs the front of my cut, wrenching it in his hand, and the complete lack of respect leaves me speechless. Blood coats my tongue as my split lip bleeds into my mouth and over my chin, and he drags me close so that our noses bump together.

"You put your fucking hands on her?"

"On whom?" I rear back, my own hands fisting at my sides. "What the fuck is this about?"

"Wait until I tell Vic, his Sergeant at Arms is bruising his daughter."

"Genni?" Again, shock tears through me as my body goes lax. "Are you talking about Genni?"

"How many women are you fucking beating?" He throws me once again against the bar, the impact finally jarring some sense into me. He thinks I'm hurting Genni.

The room has fallen eerily quiet, not even the sound of a lighter flicking permeates the silence. As soon as my brothers heard Genni and Vic's names, it became everyone's business. Only I can't let anyone know about Genni.

"Can we go talk somewhere?" I pray with everything inside me that he sees the earnest look in my eyes. I'm not above begging at this point, because I'm about to be devoured by wolves if this carries on. Thankfully, Jaeger left early this morning, and he's not here to witness this exchange, because where Laith is brutal, Jaeger is cunning. I wouldn't doubt for a second that his knife would have been through my neck already.

By the grace of the Creator, Laith steps back and looks around the room, realizing just how quiet it's become and knowing we are now the center of attention. No matter what is said, it'll be spun into a million different stories by evening. So he juts his chin toward the corridor and strides that way, heading toward his room. I push off the bar and follow behind him. As soon as we're out of sight, the conversation kicks up behind us again, and I can bet the brothers are trying to figure out what exactly is going on.

So the fuck am I.

Laith steps into his room, holding the door open as apprehension stalls my steps. I meet his gaze as he rolls his eyes. "I'm not going to kill you, Chino."

"Promise?" I hold up my finger and point at him, but my humor flies over his head as his stare becomes more menacing.

"Not if you don't get your ass in here." So I step over the threshold, throwing caution to the wind, and hoping that our vows sealing our brotherhood is something he's remembering at this moment. "Why is her throat riddled with bruises?" Each word is spit through his teeth, his lips pulled back taut, and his eyes narrowed with accusation.

"I know what you're talking about." I hold my hands up. "I was just as angry when I saw them, but they're not from me."

"I know you're fucking her. I know you fucked her last night." He jabs his forefinger at the air between us, punctuating every word.

"Yes," I admit, and then to rub salt in the wound, I continue, "I did fuck Genni. It was a one-time—okay, fine—two-time thing. We both know it can never work out, but I swear, I was not the one to put those bruises on her throat."

"I see the way you are with Carrie."

"Carrie's different, man. She likes that stuff, but Genni was a virgin—"

He cuts me off with a scream. "You took the President's daughter's virginity?!"

"I didn't know it at the time." My hands slowly raise

up, worried he's about to attack me again. "She hid it from me. I swear, if I knew…" My thoughts trail off because I don't know if they're accurate. Even if I knew Genni was a virgin, I don't know that I could have stopped what happened once it had started.

"Do you love her?" he asks. His eyes focus in on me, paying close attention to what I'm about to say, but his stiffened shoulders tell me he's worried about his answer.

"I care about her." I give him a nod before continuing, "I'm not sure about love, but there's something between us."

His ass hits the mattress of his bed as his hands grip his hair, his elbows resting on his knees. "I'm feeling something too," he confesses.

"Have you guys been hanging out?" Jealousy, raw and potent, hits me in the gut. My stomach burns with it, and now it's my turn to want to punch him in the mouth.

"No," he replies, shaking his head. "I went over there to fix her bike, because it's leaking oil, and I found her shooting tin cans in the backyard. Then I saw those bruises, and I was sure you were abusing her. So I taught her a few things as well."

Tension bleeds from my muscles, but the jealousy remains. I love Laith like a brother, but I don't know how I would feel if he began hooking up with Genni. I know I have no rights. I'm not her boyfriend. I made it very clear last night that we were not exclusive. Despite that, it doesn't change how I'm feeling, as irrational as it is.

"You have feelings for her." My hands curl into fists as I watch the way his face falls.

"She's gorgeous, vulnerable. She wears her heart on her sleeve." He looks up at me, confusion filling his eyes. "It's been a while since I've had any interest in a woman. Life has always been too complicated." He drops his head back down again with a chuckle. "Leave it up to me to want the one female who would cause the most complications."

Out of everyone in the club, I think Vic would be the most accepting of Laith for Genni. He's mature, he doesn't drink, doesn't party, and he's not sticking his dick in every woman around. He'd actually be perfect for her, and that only makes the jealousy boil hotter.

"Jaeger and Vic are pretty protective over her," I warn him. "So if you're planning anything—"

"Nah." He stands from the bed, cutting me off once more. "I just needed to make sure you weren't hurting her, man, and I guess everything else just flew out of my mouth."

"I want to know who's hurting her too. Vic had asked me to give her shooting lessons, and that's who I was complaining to you about having to babysit a few days back," I reveal to him, and his eyes widen in shock.

"Do you think Vic knows someone is hurting her?"

"Maybe." I shrug my shoulders. Although it doesn't make sense because Vic would kill anyone that would hurt her, but maybe he feels there's a threat, and since he's not around all the time, he wanted her to be able to protect herself.

"Well, you taught her well." He stands from the bed and makes his way over to me, his hand landing on my shoulder. It takes everything in me not to shove it off. "Her aim is pretty fucking good."

"She practiced hard." I nod, and then another bout of sadness pours over me because I don't think there'll be another session between me and Genni. No matter what I'm feeling, I know whatever it was between us is over. It doesn't mean I'd be okay with Laith having her though.

"I feel like we should speak to Jaeger about the bruises, because I don't know if he's been home lately to even see his sister to know what's going on."

"I've been wanting to tell him," I divulge as I fall against the wall at my back, crossing my arms over my chest. "She begged me not to, and I didn't want to break her trust, so I made sure to train her as well as I could in the time I was given."

"Well, maybe we just wash our hands of it," he responds with a shrug. "Vic will be back soon. I'm sure he'll see her neck, and then all shit will hit the fan. We may be sent out on a mission to bring back heads." His vicious grin has my mouth reciprocating with one of my own.

"Maybe."

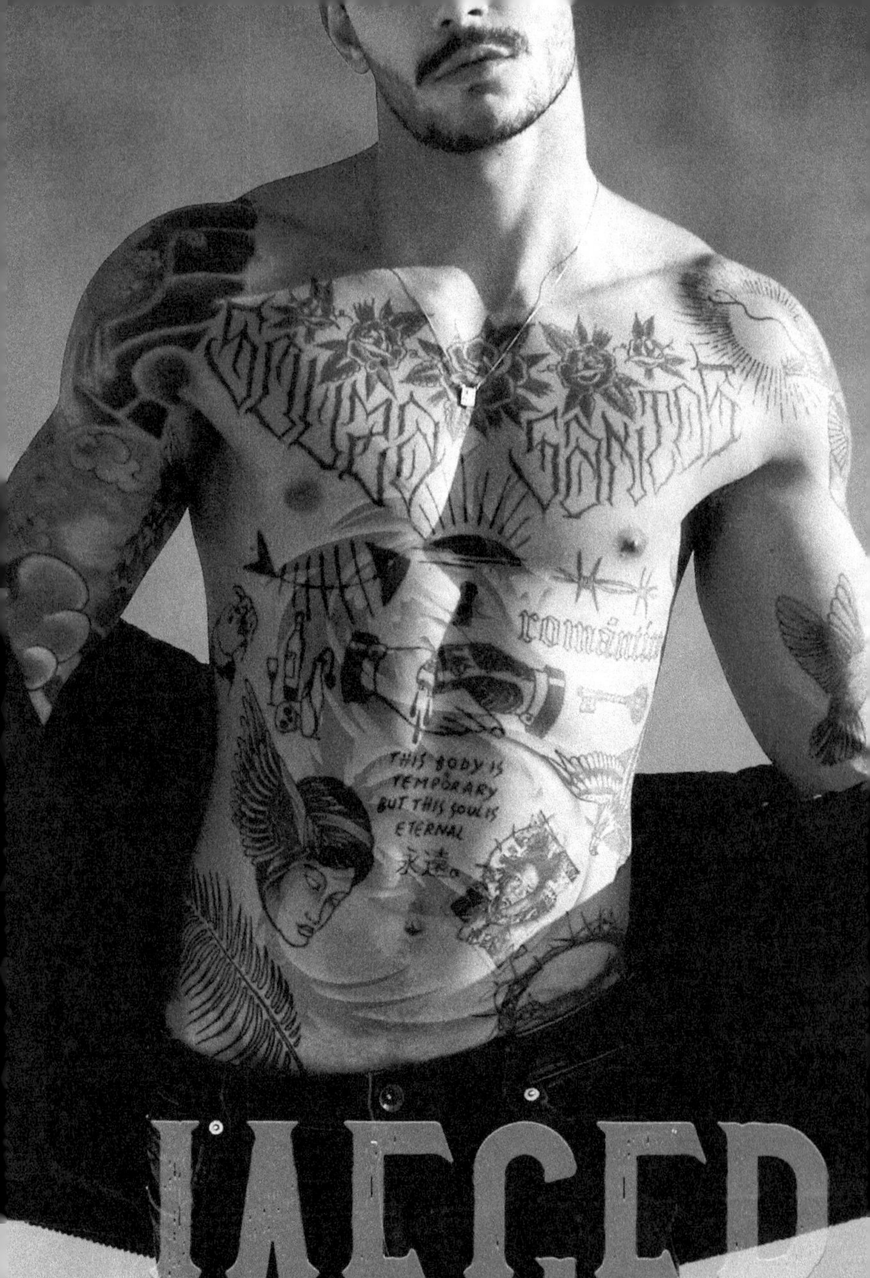
THIS BODY IS
TEMPORARY
BUT THIS SOUL IS
ETERNAL
JAEGER

JAEGER

After Laith filled me in on knowing his brother was in town and chilling with a few of our brothers, something didn't feel right, and after multiple unanswered calls to Bear and Malik, I knew I was being ignored. I could always chase down Kennedy or Cash and force them to tell me what it is they were doing, but then I'd be blowing the entire operation wide open without getting all the answers.

So now I have to play detective.

All of this, first thing in the morning, that coupled with a killer hangover, has me wishing I died of alcohol poisoning last night. I can remember bits and pieces of the night, but there's one detail that stands out in stunning clarity.

I kissed my fucking sister.

Everything after my lips on hers is a blur, but today, I'm a little more confused than I was this time yesterday, because even though I still hate her, my cock doesn't get the message. Every time her face pops up in my mind, I'm throbbing in pain in my fucking pants.

As much as I'd love to sit here and jack off to the thought of my naked sister, yeah, I know that sounds fucking filthy, I need to make sure Hell's March isn't about to renege on our deal. I'm handing them over something very important to this club in exchange for their security. They're meant to have my back for when this mutiny begins.

My boot digs at the gravel, and I curse under my breath. Why would they keep up their end of the bargain with me, the son of the Steel Dragon's President? Everything that seemed so perfectly clear a few weeks ago is completely muddled and distorted now. I'm ashamed because this is the very thing my father warned me about, that my explosive anger does the thinking for me, and more times than not, errors are made.

I want to be able to go to him and ask him for help, but I know the problems he's suffering from, and I can't bring myself to do it. I made this mess. I'm going to have to clean it up.

That's when the familiar rumble of his Harley sounds from up the road, and I turn in my seat on the bike and watch the gates. I've been sitting here for over an hour, unable to bring myself to go inside and face my brothers who think I'm going to be the one to lead them, and until this morning, I thought I had that secured and in the bag.

I fucked up.

It doesn't mean I'm giving up though, because I will not let this ship sink without trying my best to keep it afloat. If Genevieve mans the helm, we're crashing into rocks before she even hits the sea.

The gates open and Vic's bike comes into view. He slowly rides up toward me and parks in the empty space, cutting the engine. His movements are slow as he works to take the helmet off his head.

"Maybe you should consider taking one of the vans when you go on a long ride from now on," I suggest as he hangs his helmet on the bar.

"I'll die first," he mumbles as he reaches into his pocket to pull out his smokes.

I chuckle at the irony and light my own with him.

"Did everything go okay after I left?"

"Same old, Son." He reaches over and clasps my shoulder, giving me a solid shake. "Don't worry your pretty little head over it."

"You think I'm pretty, Daddy?" I preen, and the sound of his laugh has both pride and despair running through me.

"I need to call Church." He nods his head toward the clubhouse. "Is everyone here?"

"Not sure, to be honest. I just got back myself."

"What were you doing?"

"Laith told me some Hell's March were spotted in town last night at one of our local bars." I omit the fact that Kennedy and Cash were there as well. "I thought I'd go see what I could find out."

"Hell's March were here last night?" His brows come together as he takes a drag on his smoke.

"Yeah, but don't worry about it. I'll take care of it." The last thing I want is him digging into Hell's March, because if he finds out my association with them, I'll be praying for death.

"I was thinking of swearing in a few of the prospects today," he tells me. "We should bring the brander in from the shed."

Just the thought of getting the brander out brings me back to the day I was sworn in, and my hand instinctively rests against the skin of my stomach. Under my shirt, the smooth scars meet my fingertips, the rough edges creating the outline of a tribal dragon, the same one that's stamped on the back of our cuts.

"I have a few ideas for a couple of new prospects," I tell him as I inhale the smoke. "I had to kill Junior though, so we need a new drug runner."

"That fucking sucks," he says as he gets off his bike. "But I know you can take care of it. I'll meet you inside."

I want to tell him he has no other choice, because his daughter, who he wants to be President, couldn't fathom how to take care of it. I kick up the gravel once more before standing and watch as his back disappears inside the club. My club. This is my club, and nothing is going to change that.

"I called Church here today, because we have a few things to go over, and I plan on taking this weekend off to spend time with my family."

That's news to me.

Maybe he's talking about his only family, which is his daughter. In that case, it makes sense.

"When I get back, we need to discuss a few things. If any of you know of any potential prospects, let's get them in here. It's time we started building this club back up to the glory it once was. We need some young recruits." A few brothers' hands hit the table, smacking out a clapping rhythm. Vic's mouth widens into an excited grin, one that doesn't quite meet his eyes. "Today, we're going to swear in our prospects."

Excited hoots and hollers are chorused around the room, but my eyes don't stray from the tired man sitting to my left at the head of the table. He watches everyone with the type of happiness that can only be described as fleeting. My stomach churns with anxiety.

"Who's ready for a barbecue?" Vic chuckles as a few of the prospects swallow uneasily. It's not like they haven't been warned about our type of swearing in. Other clubs do tattoos, but we brand you. That scar is for life. There's no laser that can remove it, and the pain is something you never forget. It's the only thing that's kept me going these last few months, remembering the pain I endured to enter this club, and I did it willingly, with pride. That's why I won't let it go so easily.

Vic carries on about the warehouse we visited, about the inventory we currently have, and the profits we should see in a few months down the road. We talk about club expenses, and then we settle on Hell's March.

"As you know, we rode up to the cartel's warehouse a few weeks back," Vic says as his fingers brush through his long beard. "The cartel isn't loyal to Hell's March. They'll accept anyone to run their product from point A to point B. We just happen to be dead center. So after a lengthy conversation, the cartel informed me they're not completely opposed to working with us, but we'll need to do a couple trial runs. With that being said, our income would literally triple."

My brothers' palms hit the table once more in an excited rhythm, all of them loving the promise of more money. Who wouldn't?

"Jaeger and I will go over the details of it, and the potential fallout it will cause with Hell's March. As you know, we have a tentative cease-fire with them as long as they stay out of our town's borders, but they haven't been abiding by our rules." Vic pointedly looks at Laith. "Be prepared, Son. We may just be killing that brother of yours."

"If it comes down to that, I will gladly put a bullet in his head," Laith says calmly, not a ripple of emotion in his tone.

Vic nods his approval and continues on. "It would mean more rides, and I need members who can endure these lengthy, out-of-town trips. This is why you, prospects, are getting sworn in today, and one of your first missions will be doing a run for the cartel."

More excited cheers erupt around the room, and I wish I could go back to the time I was ignorant to my father's plans and be excited with my brothers. I should be excited. This is a new chapter for us, growth and opportunities we've all been wanting are now sitting there in front of us, but instead, I'm sitting here trying my best not to crumble beneath it all.

When the gavel snaps against the wooden base, I'm jarred from my thoughts as chairs scrape across the floor, and my brothers begin to fold out, talking animatedly about the branding. Laith rises with Chino, and when I rise, Vic's hand lands on my arm.

"Stick around a minute?" he asks. I settle back in my chair as Chino and Laith close the door behind them.

"What's up?"

"I plan on taking Genni up to the cabin tonight. I'd like you to come too."

It's been a long time since I felt the burning tingle in my eyes and the swelling of my throat that comes with melancholy, but there it is as I stare at my father. I swallow down past the lump and lower my eyes to the tabletop for fear of what he'll see with the moisture gathering in them.

"I don't think that's a good idea." I'm proud of how even my tone sounds, despite the turmoil that's raging through me. "Someone should be here with the brothers."

"There were some things I wanted to discuss with you and your sister. As you can imagine, it's time sensitive."

"You go ahead with Ma and Genni to the cabin," I tell him, my eyes still cast down firmly on my hands as I pick at my nails. "Then you and I will talk when you get back."

"Your sister too, Jaeger."

"Sure."

I nod, already knowing what it is he's going to talk about. It's a little too late. I should have been spoken to as soon as he made the decision to override me as President, giving it to my baby sister, who knows nothing about this club instead.

"Everything I do is for you and your sister. All I want is for the both of you to look after each other and to always be together. I don't want her to be alone, Jaeger, and I fear that's going to happen if I don't take certain steps."

"I get it." I hold up my hand. "But let's get this branding done. You go on your little trip with Genni, and when you get back, we'll have a family discussion."

To my shock, his hand wraps around mine in a grip so tight, and then he's tugging me over the table to wrap his arms around me. My face sinks into my father's hair as I hug him back, and I commit his scent to memory.

"I love you, Son," he says as he claps my back.

"I love you too, Dad." I push up to stand and hold my hand out to help him out of his seat when he lets out a booming laugh.

"Get the fuck out of here with that." He chuckles as he slaps my hand away. "I'm no geriatric."

"Whatever," I scoff. "Do you remember that goat we had a few years ago?"

He pushes up out of his seat and gives me a narrow look, his face a mask of amusement. "Don't you fucking even say it."

"That old billy goat had more spring in his step than you do."

He suddenly grabs me in a headlock, his strength shocking and startling a laugh out of me.

When I step out of the room, I find Chino leaning against the wall waiting for me, and his eyes give me a slow once-over.

"Is everything okay?"

"Yeah." I shrug, falling against the wall beside him. "Feels like I haven't spoken to you in a while."

"Because we haven't," he admits. "Vic had me on some secret missions, and I was told to keep it to myself, but I don't want it to drive a wedge between us."

"What secret missions?"

"Laith was talking about seeing Genni today." He ignores my question. "Said something about her having bruises around her neck. I saw them too, last week, and I wanted to tell you, but she begged me not to." There is no reason to lie to my best friend, it will only widen the space growing between us.

"She begged you not to because I'm the one who put them there."

He straightens and pushes off the wall, his face growing hot with fury. "What? Jaeger, are you fucking kidding me?"

"No, I tried to kill her twice now," I admit as I lean against the wall, my arms crossed over my chest.

His eyes dance with rage as his jaw ticks like a time bomb. "Make it make sense."

"Dad plans to make her President soon. He'll probably make the announcement in a few days. He hasn't told me yet. I overheard it. Both of them have just been keeping secrets from me, biding their time until they pull the rug out and leave me on my ass."

His hands drop from his chest and his mouth opens in shock. "I couldn't have heard you right."

"Genevieve plans to become President, she plans to take my spot," I say a little slower, keeping my voice low. "I've never been so angry in my life. I've never felt so used."

Recognition dawns on his face, and then his features drop, and anger slips over like a welcoming friend. His eyes move around the room at the same moment I look over my shoulder.

"Vic had me training her to shoot. She knew this whole time." His fist slams into the wall as his face distorts with rage. "She used me."

"Not for much longer, brother."

After the branding, Dad and I ride home, still feeling high off the morale in the club. It's always like this when we swear in new members, and we see our brotherhood growing. So when I pull into the driveway, the sight of Genevieve's bike doesn't send me into a pit of rage. It helps that I know she'll be going away with Dad for the night. It'll give me a chance to snoop through her room.

We head inside to find Ma in the kitchen, stirring a pot of spaghetti and meatballs. I take a deep breath, inhaling the savory scent.

"That smells good, baby," Vic says as he slides up behind my mother, wrapping his arms around her waist.

She giggles as his beard tickles her face, and while she's distracted, I sneak a meatball out of the pot and pop it in my mouth, cursing when it burns my tongue.

"How about you, me, and Genevieve go up to the cabin tonight?" Vic asks her as she slaps my hand away from the pot.

"Oh, baby, I can't tonight." She turns in his arms, holding his face between her hands. "I have that charity ball I'm helping coordinate down at the town hall. The meeting is real early in the morning. I can't get out of it."

"Fine." He kisses her cheek soundly. "I can't compete with charity."

"No, sir, you cannot. Someone in this household needs to be on good terms with God if we're all going to Heaven."

I hear Genni's footsteps coming down the stairs, and again, my mind travels to her being locked between my body and the brick wall of the clubhouse, the scent of strawberries making my cock thicken. Then my anger swoops in with it, my reaction so visceral for the girl who is supposed to be my fucking sister.

"Genni!" Dad exclaims as he holds out his arms. Genni folds into them, her eyes meeting mine over his shoulder. I barely contain my laugh when I see she's wearing a turtleneck. "How about you and I head on up to the cabin tonight?"

"Really?" She perks up as she averts her eyes from mine. "Just me and you?"

"I wanted it to be a family thing, but your mother and brother are too busy for me."

"Someone's got to run the club." I give Genni a pointed look, letting her know that's what I'm good at, running a motorcycle club.

"Okay, Daddy." A stunning smile lights up her face, completely ignoring me now. "I'm going to go pack."

Mom puts the cover on the spaghetti and dries her hands off on a towel. "I'm going to go help her," she says, then she leans in to kiss my cheek. "Don't you dare take any more meatballs out of that pot."

As soon as she's out of sight, Vic lifts the cover, sticking his hand in for a meatball and giving me a wink.

"YOLO," he says with a laugh.

"Oh, hell no." I shake my head with embarrassment.

GENEVIEVE
BMW Motorrad Milano

TEN

Our cabin is the same one my father bought my mother during their first year of marriage. They came here during the summers for a weekend at a time, and then when my mother became sick, this is where she wanted to be.

I don't know if Claire really had a charity event early the next morning, but I know she probably feels like this place isn't hers.

I step up onto the front porch and a calming energy flows over me. My eyes shut as I soak it all in. The sound of insects, birds, and rushing water, coupled with the soft breeze, puts my soul at ease. I truly believe my mother's spirit surrounds this place, and every time I come here, she makes everything better. The stresses of life melt away as if she's showing me there's more to live for.

"Did you want to go out on the boat today?" Dad asks as he slips the key into the door.

My eyes eat up every wrinkle on his face, the puffy bags under his eyes, sunken cheeks, and my stomach twists with a fear I'm not ready to face.

"No, Daddy. Maybe we could just build a fire out back. I'll make s'mores like we used to." The way my chest becomes heavy and the tips of my fingers tingle with numbness are ways my body is warning me about what's to come. Not having the strength to face something else, I bury it all down.

"Okay, princess."

I want to tell him not to call me princess, that the name invokes an angry stepbrother with murderous intent, but I swallow that down too, because to Victor Varga, I have always been his princess.

"It was a long ride," I say as I follow him inside the cabin. His walk is slow and imbalanced, and his shoulders are hunched. "Do you want to lie down while I start the fire?"

"We're only here for one night, Genni." The sound of his voice is so saturated with exhaustion. I honestly don't know when it changed, and it instills fear inside of me. "Let's make the best of it. I don't wanna sleep it all away."

I don't argue with him. Instead, I grab his favorite lawn chair and set it up by the fire pit, then I get to work starting the fire. It takes me a little longer, but I get there, and when the flames are rushing upward, attempting to kiss the sky, Dad claps with an excited chuckle.

"Look at that fire," he says. "Is there anything my princess can't do?"

My first instinct is to beg him to take back everything he's asked me to do, because I don't think his *princess* can run a motorcycle club full of men. Men who are only ever used to a woman being bent over and naked. But then I take in his appearance. How small he looks in the lawn chair he once filled beyond capacity, the bones in his elbows jutting outward, his cheekbones sharper than they've ever been, and those blue eyes of his look extremely tired and defeated.

My silence forces his attention from the fire onto me, and when he leans forward in the chair to rest those protruding elbows on the very baggy pants engulfing his knees, he gives me a pointed look.

"Genevieve Varga, you come from a long line of men who are inherently stubborn, whose fists do most of the talking because their mouths are pursed with frustration. A line of men who are so quick to fury, but slow to love. You also come from a line of women whose first instinct is to nurture, to love, to provide. They trusted their men to protect them. I can see both sides in you, and my advice would be to continue walking on that thin line. The one that travels straight down the center of both personalities. Be strong, be fiery, love with your whole heart, and protect everything that's yours."

"Daddy, what's happening?" My voice is so small, the sound quickly being eaten up by the cracking of the burning wood.

"I know it seems like a daunting mission," he reassures me, "to become the first female President of a motorcycle club. It's not going to be easy, but if I thought you couldn't handle it, I would have never asked this of you. I will tell the men, and I will tell them my reasoning."

"What is your reasoning?"

"To give you a family. One that will swear an oath to protect you with their own lives, to place your brother on your right-hand side, where he can never doubt the value of family. It's been a long time since Jaeger came into our home, but he still carries the demons of his past. In his blood, there isn't an ounce of Varga, but his soul is made up of all those things I told you that come from the Vargas line."

"He's so mad at me." I shake my head and run my fingers along my chin. "He hates me right now."

"I think that's because he knows what's happening. He overheard us, or maybe Chino let it slip, and for that, I can't be angry. I want those men, our club, to be loyal to both of you. So I won't fault Chino if he let the cat out of the bag."

"Chino doesn't know I'm going to be President, Dad."

"No, but the training you're receiving is exactly what Jaeger received when he joined the club, knowing he would one day run it."

"Why not marry me off to one of them? Make me an Old Lady? They'll still take care of me, and you'll never have to worry. You can retire and stay home. You could feel completely at ease."

He falls back into the chair with a boisterous laugh, the

sound echoing around the forest. "Genevieve, we both know you are made for something greater, and if I marry you off to a man to take care of you, the day I meet your mother in Heaven, she'll dropkick my fucking ass."

The image of my mother doing just that pulls a laugh from my chest, and I join him, my high-pitched cackle to his low chuckle.

"After me, you're all that's left of the Vargas, of the pure-blooded Vargas, and there has never been a leader of the Steel Dragons that didn't have the Varga blood. It's an honor to lead those men, one I feel blessed to have been able to do."

"Well, I'm definitely not ready yet," I mumble as my eyes skim over the raging fire.

"No one's ever ready, princess."

Dusk falls by the time we turn onto our street, our bike engines roaring in tandem, and both of us exhausted after a long ride. Just one night at the cabin has me feeling renewed. I have a new sense of pride in the family name I carry, and I truly believe I can stand at the head of the motorcycle club and lead them into something great.

And with all this newfound positivity, I also believe I can convince my brother to bury whatever hatchet he's carrying, and just somehow return to what we once were. The thought of going back to the way we were flips my stomach inside out, because how do you reverse making out with your stepbrother?

No one said it would be easy. Nothing about this situation is, but the way he kissed me that night and the way I gave in, I don't think we'll ever be siblings again after that.

"The lights are out at our house." I point straight ahead and yell over the engine. "Not even the porch light is on."

Dad slows down and holds up his fist, a signal for me to stop, and when both of my feet hit the asphalt, an ominous feeling comes over me, leaving a bitter coldness in its wake.

"Dad?"

He still doesn't give me an answer as I slowly look up and down the street. It's too early for Claire to be in bed. The sun has just set and sitting there in the driveway is Jaeger's bike. He definitely wouldn't be asleep yet, unless they threw a rager at the clubhouse last night and he's still sleeping it off.

"Genni," Dad finally speaks. "I need you to do everything I say. Am I making myself clear?" No longer is this my father speaking to me as his daughter. He's the President of an MC club, and I'm to follow his orders. He would only ever be like this if he, too, felt like something was wrong. We slowly approach the house and pull into the driveway, both of us cutting our engines and looking over our shoulders toward the street. There's no sound, and the eerie feeling has the hairs on my arms standing on end. This doesn't feel like the same house we left yesterday, nor does this feel like the same street. "Genni," Dad calls out to me, and I turn to find him holding a gun. "Stay behind me, no matter what happens, and get your phone ready in your hand. I don't know what we're going to stumble upon in there, but I need you to call the clubhouse."

With shaking hands, I pull my cell phone out of my pocket and dial Chino. He's the first one that pops into my mind.

The call goes to voicemail almost instantly, like he saw my name on the screen and canceled the call. If I wasn't so petrified of what's waiting inside our house, my heart would shatter into tiny shards.

"Chino, it's Genni. Something's wrong at my house. When you get this, can you come over right away? It's an order from my dad."

I end the call and look up to find my dad on the porch, looking through the window by the front door. I scramble off my bike and slide up between Jaeger's bike and Claire's car, taking a quick peek inside her windows. There, sitting in the passenger seat is her purse. It's a Louis Vuitton and expensive as fuck. I know she treats that thing like her own child and would never leave it out in the car in the driveway. As I round the hood of her car, my feet stop and the air surrounding me fills with static electricity. Goose bumps break out on my skin as I look around me. It feels like someone's watching us.

I force myself to move and scramble up the porch to find Dad staring at the front door. The red-painted, wooden exterior is cracked where the latch is, and the door is sitting slightly ajar.

"Dad—"

His hand snaps up, his finger hitting his mouth, warning me not to say another word, but I'm scared, and I'm afraid of what we're going to find when we open that door.

Dad motions for me to stand behind him as his hand grasps the doorknob, slowly pushing it open farther.

"Shit," he hisses.

I poke my head around his shoulder and look into the house, and at the end of the corridor, on his knees in front of the couch, is Jaeger. He's completely bound, twine wrapped around his legs and hands, and his own bandana stuffed into his mouth.

"Jaeger!" I scream as Dad rushes into the house, heading straight for his son.

I'm close behind, but as I pass the kitchen, something catches in my peripheral vision. I slide on my feet just as Dad reaches Jaeger and pulls the bandana from his mouth.

"Ma!" he screams out, his voice filled with anguish. "Where's Ma?"

All I see is red fluid rolling from a large puddle in the kitchen, the island effectively blocking what I know must be Ma. I run in, screaming her name, my boots slipping on the blood pooling along the tile. I fall to my knees, and my phone flies out of my hand, slipping along the floor and sliding under the fridge, but none of that matters, because the beautiful woman who's raised me as if I was her own, who's loved me despite the fact that I didn't come from her, is lying face down in blood. So much blood.

"Oh no, no, no. Ma, please." My hands slip on the tile floor as the blood oozes up between my fingers, and I sloppily crawl my way toward my mother. Just as I'm turning her around, I hear a shout from Jaeger down the hall.

"This is all your fault, you son of a bitch!" he screams at my father. "My mother was killed in the next room! I could hear her screaming!" he bellows, his words catching on his sobs.

"Don't be dead, don't be dead," I plead and beg, but as her stiff back hits the floor, I see the large slash across her throat, and her eyes staring unfocused at the ceiling.

"Claire!" I hear my dad yelling, his boots striking the hardwood floor in the hallway with each resounding step. "Claire?"

His frantic voice sends my heart ramming against my ribcage. Who could've done this? How will we ever go on?

Everything slows down, and suddenly, in the darkened kitchen, everything brightens with stunning clarity. The front door is kicked open, and men with leather cuts and bandanas wrapped around their faces stride into our home. Four of them, all around the same height and build. Their long hair is tied back in ponytails, and the image of a ram's skull shines brightly from the backs of their cuts.

Hell's March.

"No, you're early," my dad stutters as I push myself to standing. My hands are dripping with Ma's blood, my clothes completely saturated. Nevertheless, I walk toward the men standing in our front foyer.

"What did you do to my wife? What did you do to my son? This wasn't part of our deal." My father is a stoic man, not much fazes him, but when I hear his words being caught on choked sobs, my mind fights to see what's happening in front of me.

What deal?

The large beast of a man standing in front of the others laughs, the sound muffled by the bandana wrapped around his mouth. "You're not the only one we made a deal with."

I stop in the center of the kitchen, seeing my father to the left, his hands up in the air, and the four men to the right, their guns drawn and pointed at his chest.

"What are you talking about, Bear?" Dad asks, his tired face falling with confusion. "This makes no sense. You're early."

"You should ask your son."

Jaeger appears behind my father, my father's gun in his hand pointed to the floor, but it's the look of utter despair on his face that has my heart breaking. Our mother is laying in a pool of blood in the kitchen because of these fucking heathens, and he looks so lost.

"Listen,"—my father raises his hands higher, his eyes trained on the four men in front of him—"take me. Take me out of here, but don't hurt my children."

The one he called Bear laughs again. "I said…" He pauses as his eyes skip to the side, finding me standing and watching them while covered in blood before they flip back to my father. " I made a deal with Jaeger," he states.

My dad's brows crumble together as he stares down Bear. "What deal?"

"That Hell's March can continue to ride through this town as long as Jaeger keeps his position."

The only way Jaeger will keep his position is if I'm taken out of the equation, and it's then I realize these men are here to kill me on Jaeger's orders. Just as I take a step toward my father, Bear shoots his gun, the one pointed at my father's chest, and I watch as his body jars with the impact, flying back to hit the floor and landing at Jaeger's feet.

Jaeger looks down at him as Dad clutches his chest, and I'm frozen to the spot, because all I can see is each of us losing our lives here tonight. But when Jaeger lifts his hand, the one holding my father's gun, and aims it down at my father's head, a scream gets lodged in my throat. My mouth gapes open, and my bloodied hands form fists, but still, no sound escapes. The only sound is my beating heart pounding through my ears as a chill skates down my spine.

"It's okay, Son." My dad looks up at him, his eyes soft and his face serene. "Do it." What is he asking him to do? Why is he giving up so easily?

My dad's voice is barely a whisper, but I'm so hyper-focused on him that I can hear every syllable. He looks as if he's on the brink of death.

"Take her," Jaeger says, his eyes flicking to look at me. "Get her out of my face."

Two men rush forward to grab me, one of them tossing me over a shoulder, and I fight with my fists pounding into his back. I scream, making my throat hoarse with garbled words and sobs. They go through the front door as I look up, just in time to see Jaeger fire a bullet into my father's head, his eyes on me the whole time.

"No, Jaeger!" I finally scream, but it's no use. It's too late.

My body bounces off the shoulder of the biker carrying me, but the discomfort is nothing compared to the agony ripping through my chest. My father's lifeless body is laying at my brother's feet, and he's looking triumphant for being the one who's truly destroyed me.

"Chino," the man holding me rumbles out. "Put down that gun. Are we going to have a problem here?"

"Quinton!" I screech. "Jaeger killed Dad! Help me!"

A moment of silence stretches as the asshole holding me doesn't move, and Quinton remains quiet. I can't see him from how I'm being held, but the dread that begins to creep over me is threatening to crush me under its weight.

"That's what I thought."

We're moving once more, and I slump against my kidnapper's back. Chino will always be Jaeger's man, and I am completely alone. I can't bear to look at the man who's watching me being carted away. No one is here to help me. My family was gone in a matter of moments, and I'm being carted away by the enemy.

I'm shoved into a van as the Hell's March member chuckles. "I can't believe he went through with it. Killed his own father and watched his sister being taken away. He's fucking heartless."

One day, every Steel Dragon will beg me for mercy.

PART TWO

Present

GENEVIEVE
BMW Motorrad Milano

ELEVEN

I'm stirred from my fevered blackout by the sounds of boots coming down the creaky, wooden stairs. *Thud, thud, thud.* I can barely open my eyes, my mouth hangs open, the inside nearly completely dried out, and each breath I take rattles in my lungs. The feeling in my hands and feet has long disappeared, and the numbness is slowly working up my limbs.

I'm on the brink of death.

I've only had one visitor come down here periodically since I've been trapped in this dank basement. Just one. He wasn't one for speaking too much, although, when he would slam inside me, he did like to call out to God.

The mask he wears over his face has prevented me from seeing his features. His voice, however, is ingrained in my mind, and if I ever make it out of here alive, I'll kill him as soon as I hear him.

Not that I want to make it out of here. I no longer have a family, I no longer trust a single person, including every man who wears a dragon on his back. They will forever be my enemy.

"Are you sure he was coming down here?"

This is an unfamiliar voice. A new person coming to defile the Varga Princess, I'm sure. I should feel rage, fear, complete and utter despair, but I can't seem to bring myself to feel a fucking thing. It's as if my emotional well has been tapped dry.

"I swear. For two weeks, he's been coming down here every few days. I've been watching him."

Another voice. There are at least two of them. I can only hope they don't smell me festering over here in the corner, and maybe they'll go back upstairs so I can die in peace.

"Two weeks. That's around the same time the President of the Steel Dragons killed his wife and then shot himself."

My eyes snap open at the blatant lie. The crust lining my lids makes the movement painful as I grimace through it.

"They could never find his daughter," the first voice replies as his steps come closer.

"They say she ran away, Diego."

My leg muscle involuntarily twitches along the filthy concrete, causing a garbled noise to slip from my dry throat.

"Shit," the one named Diego calls out, his steps hurrying to my side. His form is distorted as I try to peer through the crust. "Who the fuck is this?"

A second pair of boots stands in front of me, and the air shifts as he squats down. I can't see his face because of the dark even though he's so close. In another life, I would have felt shame and discomfort by being gawked at while naked, but the only thing I'm feeling is the desire to leave this life and be reunited with the people who love me.

"This is Genevieve Varga, the daughter of Victor Varga, Steel Dragon's previous President."

"Shit," Diego curses again. "Her brother is the current President. This will cause an all-out war."

I wish I had the strength to tell him it wouldn't, that my brother doesn't give a shit about me. Even the thought of moving sends a wave of nausea through me.

"She's not looking so good, boss. She's real close to death."

"Let's get her upstairs where I can get a better look at her," Diego demands.

Rough hands scrape along my sensitive skin, the simple touch akin to coarse sandpaper, and when I'm lifted off the floor, I feel as though every bone in my body is broken. But the worst part of it is when he begins to ascend the stairs. The motion painfully jars my body, sending me right back into the blackened void.

DIEGO

DIEGO

It's been three days since I found the poor girl bound, naked, and filthy in our cellar. There are obvious signs of trauma with bruises decorating her very thin form, and also signs of her having endured repeated sexual trauma as well.

When I decided I wanted to be a doctor, a neurosurgeon to be exact, I had never thought this was where I would have ended up. I don't hate my brothers here at Hell's March, but I don't always see eye to eye with them, and in this young girl's case, I'm livid.

I've done everything I can for her. I've sewn her up, hooked her to an IV, and I've cleaned her body. The rest is now up to her. Her heartbeat is weak, but that's due to malnutrition. Her kidneys and liver are showing signs of failing along with respiratory distress… It's all concerning.

I was sure she was going to die the first night I found her. I stayed awake watching every slow, rattled breath she took. When the sun rose and she was still fighting to stay, I was surprised.

She's not out of the woods yet, but her skin tone is finally losing its yellow hue, and when I listen to the beat of her heart, it's a little stronger. The arrhythmia is not as pronounced and she still has a long road to recovery ahead of her.

I've also been taking blood samples, and checking for pregnancies and STIs, because again, I may love my brothers, but they're not the most careful.

So far, she's clear.

"Hey, boss." Ajani sticks his head into the room, his face filled with concern. "How's she doing?"

Ajani has been my assistant for the past two years, but he's been my best friend since we were in our early twenties and joined Hell's March. For the past two days, he's been walking on eggshells, too afraid to look in on our patient, but needing to know if she's making it. As much as Ajani is an asset as my assistant, he has a soft heart and death takes its toll on him.

"Still breathing." I give him a smirk over my shoulder, trying to calm his nerves.

"If any other doctor found her, she'd be dead."

He's always believed in me. We prospected together for Hell's March nearly eighteen years ago and we're pretty inseparable now.

"Thanks, Ajani."

He runs his hand over his close-cropped, coarse hair, his nearly black eyes filling with sorrow as they dart toward our patient, laying still on the bed.

"What's going to happen if she gets better? What will Barrett do when he returns?"

"When she gets better, we'll ask her what happened and find out what she would like to do. Barrett's due back tomorrow. I'll have a conversation with him then."

"He's been volatile lately," Ajani warns. "I'm worried about his reaction when you tell him we found that girl in the basement. He's going to want to know how we came to find her there, and then he's going to piece it together so that it would have to have come from me. My office is right next to the door for the cellar."

"Don't worry," I assure him. "Nothing will happen to you." I would easily die in his place.

"I'm also worried for you." He shakes his head and rubs his hand down his face. "Our President isn't the same anymore. He's not the same man I pledged my life to."

I know what he means. The last year has been difficult for us. Shipments have been derailed, our routes have been fucked with, thanks to the Steel Dragons, and now our cartel affiliations are precariously teetering on the edge. All of it has been forcing Barrett to face one glaring fact: Hell's March is losing their authority.

I press my fingers one more time to the inside of her small, delicate wrist, and then my eyes stay firmly trained on the watch on my wrist as I count her beats per minute. She's getting stronger every day. I'm starting to believe the hype that's been garnered around the Varga blood. There's a rumor that they're hard to kill.

I gently place her hand back on the bed. Her once pink painted nails are chipped and stained. I bet she was well taken care of before, protected, and now, just like those nails, she's broken and no longer pristine.

I step out of the room and close the door, walking to the next one. I step inside to find one of our brothers, who suffered from a gunshot, laying in the bed with his hand vigorously moving underneath the blanket.

"Jesus." I roll my eyes. "You claimed to have almost died, but still, you find the energy to jack your dick off."

"Sorry, Doc." The man opens his eyes and releases his cock, the sheets still tented, and brings his hand out from under the sheet, his voice not sounding apologetic at all. I step closer to check the bullet wound in his shoulder, and he holds out his hand for me to shake. "Thank you for saving my life. How much longer do you think I'll be in here?" I roll my eyes at the sound of dismay lining his words. It was nothing more than an in and out hit, not hitting anything major.

His chest is bare and a large patch is secured to the front of his shoulder and another on his back where the bullet went through.

"Chains, will you get that hand away from me?" I snap and step back, making him laugh.

Chains was one of our prospects who has recently been sworn in. On his first run to the cartel warehouse, he let his mouth run off and one guy shot him in the shoulder. He wouldn't have died from it, it was mostly a flesh wound, but he's been pretty dramatic about it. His fear of dying has been all I've heard.

"You could have been out of this room two days ago." I roll my eyes. "You're the one who insists on staying here."

"What if I, like, flatline or something?" Chains asks, his eyes filling with alarm and his hands gripping into the sheet pooled around his waist. "I've never been shot before."

"If you're flatlining, it's because I've held the pillow

over your face. Now get up and get dressed, then stick your dick in a Club Bunny. Give your hand a break," I tell him with all seriousness as I cross my arms over my chest.

"I can fuck?" He sits up quickly, groaning as his hand slips over his shoulder. "Are you sure?" His eyes narrow with suspicion.

"I'm signing your new bill of health." I give him a nod.

He's the only other patient I have on this side of the club besides the girl next door, and honestly, I just want him to leave. I don't want him to catch wind of who my other patient is, nor do I need him to become curious. I feel like I'm all she has, and I have to protect her.

Unfortunately, I can't erase what's happened to her while she's been under our roof, but I can make sure it'll never happen again.

GENEVIEVE
BMW Motorrad Milano

TWELVE

Her light brown hair flows in the breeze and the long, straight strands curl around her shoulders as the sun brightens the features of her face. Her dark brown eyes sort of remind me of Jaeger's, but when her mouth curls upward, I see myself in her. Standing there in front of me is my mother, my biological mother, and the way she's looking at me is as if she's been waiting for me forever.

"Mom?"

Her hand stretches out, her long, dainty fingers gracefully swiping through the air, beckoning me to come to her. I want to so badly. My life is not one I want to go back to. I don't belong there with the Steel Dragons. I'm where I'm meant to be now though.

"Is Daddy here?"

Her head turns slowly to look over her shoulder, and I watch as Claire steps forward. Her body is shrouded in white silk and her face is at ease. A drastic contrast to the way I saw her last, laying on our kitchen floor.

"Ma!" I scream, my hands steepling under my chin. "You're here too?"

Everything is falling into place. Everyone I love is gathering around me, welcoming me to a new life, one without pain and betrayal.

When I take a step forward, Ma's hand comes up, her palm facing me, the outline shimmering like iridescent diamonds. Suddenly, her face doesn't look as serene, her eyes clouding over with worry, as if she's trying to tell me something. Why isn't she speaking?

"Ma? Mom? What's happening?"

Then his body begins to appear, no longer gaunt and skinny. His pants are filled out, and his hair hangs past his shoulders in thick, dark waves. He's wearing a suit and looks so different from the Dad I know. His cut is missing, the tattoos that adorned his fingers are gone, and his neck is completely clean. No sign of ink anywhere. When I look at his face, I know with all my heart he's my dad.

"Daddy." My heart soars with hope as I step forward again, and now it's his turn to hold up his hand.

He gives a firm shake of his head as his mouth curls upward into a soft smile. All three of them are standing in a line in front of me, and I just want to rush forward and take them all in my arms, to tell them how much I love them, but I'm no longer feeling welcomed.

"Princess," Dad calls out, his voice echoing around our heads as if we're standing inside a cavernous room. "Remember what I told you?"

"No, Daddy." I shake my head. "I don't want to do the things you told me. I want to stay here."

"You have Varga blood." His voice begins to fade, but I can still hear him like a whisper in the wind. "Make me proud. Remember where your blood came from."

Slowly, their outlines fade, and a frantic feeling comes over me, like I'm losing them all over again. I sprint forward, only I could run forever because no matter how fast my feet hit the cold floor, they're not bringing me any closer to them.

I fall to my knees as sobs choke their way up my throat. I don't want to be left behind, and as their forms slowly dissipate, I hear my father's voice like a distant echo.

"Show them what you've got, Princess Varga."

My sense of hearing comes to me first. The room I'm in is eerily quiet. I can hear the air conditioning system pushing the wind out of the vent that's over my head, gentle swooshing paired with a steady beep of a machine to my left.

Next, I spread out my fingers, keeping my palms down, and let myself feel the sheets I'm laying on. They're soft and supple, and after the rough treatment I've endured, this feels decadent. I straighten my toes and let the sharp ache of my muscles travel up my body. Feeling the pain only confirms that I am indeed alive and does nothing to reassure me.

I take a deep breath, and for once, the air is clean and sterilized. I'm no longer in the basement with the smell of damp concrete and musty air. It's long gone, but the memory of it will stay with me forever.

I want to open my eyes, but I know the pain of not seeing my room or my family standing around me will be too much. I want nothing more than for this to be a terrible nightmare. So instead, I leave my eyes shut and decide to do it all again another day.

While I let whatever medication they've given me seep through my senses and numb them all again, I dread having to repeat this when I wake up. The thought of my heart breaking every time I'm forced to face reality only makes me want to stay asleep forever.

You have Varga blood.

I repeat the phrase over and over in my head, creating a mantra. There will be a day I'll have to open my eyes and face whatever it is I've been thrusted into, and at that time, I can decide whether to fight or let it all go. If I choose to fight, then I'll be sure to remind myself of everything my father said.

But that day is not today.

DIEGO

DIEGO

Her vitals are now stable, and she's regained consciousness, I can tell by her accelerated heartbeat, but whenever I come into the room to check on her, she's either actually sleeping or she's faking it. I don't call her out on it though. I don't blame her for not trusting anyone here, and if the only way she can protect herself is to keep herself guarded, I'll respect that.

With that being said, she needs to start eating soon. An IV drip only does so much. Soon, she will wither away without proper nutrition.

"I know you're probably sleeping," I say out loud, watching as her heart rate spikes just a little. "But you do need to eat. I will make sure a tray of all sealed products comes to you today. If I was in your position, I wouldn't want to eat anything from here either. I hope you realize I'm trying to help you, and that if I wanted you dead, I would have left you in the basement."

Again, at the mention of the basement, her heart rate spikes. My insides pool with guilt, but it needed to be said, and she's going to have to face what happened to her in that basement.

"My good friend, Ajani, will bring you a tray, and he'll be watching you today as I have an important meeting to attend to."

I step back out of the room and motion for Ajani to come over from his place just outside the doorway.

"What's up, boss?"

"Her catheter comes out today," I begin to list off while holding up my fingers. "Bring her a tray of Jell-O, keep it in the package, sealed, apple juice, and don't stay in there with her for too long. I'm hoping she eats without too much prompting."

"Will do." Ajani nods. "Do you think she's awake?"

"I know she is. Her heart rate reacted to me talking to her."

I pull off my medical jacket and hang it up on the wall next to my stethoscope, then I pull down my leather cut, slipping the supple leather material over my arms and letting it rest on my shoulders. When I first joined Hell's March, I was bitter, but now I'm proud to be a part of this organization, except for a few bugs needing extermination.

"I heard their bikes pull up a few hours ago," Ajani informs me. "But he hasn't gone to the basement. Do you think someone told him we brought the girl up?"

"It's a possibility." I shrug, watching as his eyes roll.

"I should be in that meeting with you." Ajani begins to pace. He hates being left out but he has to stay here whenever we have patients. "What if his crazy-ass draws his gun?" It's not a crazy notion when our leader is hanging onto his sanity by a thread.

"Then that's what happens." I give him a stern look. "Even if you were there, and he drew his gun, there's nothing you would do because it would jeopardize your place here in the club. They wouldn't just kill you, Ajani, they would need a reason to."

"Is this girl worth it, Diego?" Ajani asks as he finally stops pacing to look me in the eye. "She's nothing to us."

"She's someone's daughter. She's someone's sister. How would you feel if it was Delia?"

At the mention of my sister's name, the tension in his shoulders bleeds out and he exhales a long breath. "I'm sorry," he replies, shaking his head. "It just feels like we're all on edge lately."

"I know Barrett and Bear have been acting strange lately—"

"Malik too," Ajani cuts me off. "I mean, he's always been a psycho bastard, but lately he's looking secretive. A psychopath with secrets is fucking dangerous."

"I agree. Everything you're saying is correct, but regardless, I can't go in there guns blazing. I have to give our brothers the benefit of the doubt," I placate him, holding my hands out in front of me as he drops his chin to his chest.

"I know we're a rough bunch." Ajani tips his head back

and closes his eyes. "We've always been a rough bunch, but we've never been rapists. What they did to that girl…" He opens his eyes as his arm stretches out and his finger points to our patient's room. I don't miss the slight tremble along his limb. "What she's been through is catastrophic. They left her there to die, Diego."

"I know," I say on an exhale before repeating myself. "I know that."

"And when you go in there today, when you tell them you found a girl in the basement and you saved her, what do you think will happen then?"

"I will tell them I'm just doing my job." I put up my hands.

"Your job is also to be a sniper. What if he decides to fire you as Medic and sends you on the road again?" His hands drop to his waist as mine drop to my sides.

"He wouldn't—"

"Or better yet, what if you've just helped this girl recover so that the cycle can start all over again?" he cuts me off, his voice growing in tenor as he stiffens.

"At this point, everything you're saying is speculation. I won't know any of those answers until I speak to our President. In the meantime, I'll need you to take care of our patient. Do not let anyone in that room, but most of all, do not let her out." I soften my tone and step forward.

"You got it." He nods and walks toward our patient's room, his body still stiff with tension.

Ajani is the only one I truly trust, and he's right, everyone's been acting a little strange lately. Our President is aging well beyond his years. His mind is murky lately and it's making him feel inadequate, making his outbursts more frequent.

Even though Malik is Vice President, a role given to him because of his ability to switch off his humanity, Bear is sure he will become President. To be honest, he probably will. Malik doesn't seem to ever want to be the President, nor does he have the capacity to do so. He shows no interest in running this club. If we were left in his hands, we'd be nothing more than a bunch of uncivilized barbarians.

Not that we're too far from that now with our current President.

Barrett and my father were very close, and they created Hell's March together. We're a fairly new club, but if my father were alive to see what Barrett's become, he would be deeply ashamed.

I head toward the back of the club, going through the main room and finding it empty but seeing evidence of a party from the night before. The cleaning crew has yet to start the cleanup. Usually, when Barrett is out, the guys feel a little more relaxed, and they use that time to have parties and let loose.

My boots hit the tiled floor of the wide corridor with endless doors on either side. All of them are small rooms with adjoining bathrooms for the brothers who live here at the clubhouse.

There are a lot more recently since we've had a large influx of prospects, but for us older members, most of us have our own homes outside of the club.

It was necessary for me to separate myself and treat the clubhouse like a job. I know it sounds apathetic or detached, but it's the truth. I've made it no secret that this isn't where I wanted to end up in life. Being a biker, killing people, and then saving others wasn't how I wanted to rip my soul in two. For the days that I'm not here in the medical ward, I'm setting up my sniper on top of a building, in the woods, or anywhere that will get me the shot. I need to kill whoever it is that I'm ordered to.

Thankfully, there haven't been many recently.

We've been at a cease-fire, a volatile truce at best, with the Steel Dragons. So my life as the club's assassin has been quiet enough. I have a feeling though that all of that's about to change because if we're right and the girl laying in that bed is Genevieve Varga, then her brother will probably be the first to blow this place up.

I've been on the receiving end of some of Jaeger's bombs. We've lost a few good brothers because of the intricate designs he's put together. I've dealt with the carnage of every blast here in the medical ward, and none of them were pretty. He has a gift with shrapnel. I'll give him that much.

The large, double, oak doors appear at the end of the hall with a big, golden plate sealed to the surface. It has the etching of the ram's skull, and beneath it, it says *Welcome to Hell.*

Most motorcycle clubs have Church when they attend their meetings. Hell's March goes to Hell.

I open the door to find the most prominent brothers sitting around the table. Some of them are drumming their fingers along the wooden surface, sneering at me as I come in. "Sorry, I'm late. Chains has been whining in my medical wing for two days now about a flesh wound to his shoulder. I had to discharge him before I came."

Malik laughs as he brushes back his curly, brown hair. "Man, who picks these pussies? We're not Hell's March anymore, we're Hell's Kittens. *Meow.*"

"Watch it, Charles," Barrett warns, his voice taking on a dangerous edge. "I'm not in the mood today." The table dies down and silence descends on the room as I take my seat. Malik likes to skate along the single nerve Barrett has left, flirting with death constantly. I feel everyone's eyes on me as I take my seat across from Bear and Malik, and I know exactly what's coming. "Do you have something to tell us, Montez?" Barrett fingers the ram's skull etched into the table, his eyes never wavering from mine.

"I do, actually." I place my hands on top of the table, linking them together before taking a deep breath. "While you, Bear, and Malik were out on your run, I found a body in the cellar. She was on the brink of death, and I did what any other doctor would do. I got her medical attention." Apprehension skates along the nape of my neck as I wait for his reaction.

"There was a girl in the cellar?" Malik's eyebrow raises and then the corner of his mouth tips up in a devious smirk. "You kept her here?" he asks Barrett.

"She was mine," Barrett grits out between his teeth.

"Did you forget her or something?" Malik asks, always willing to dance with death. Sometimes I think he wishes to die.

"I wanted her to die down there," Barrett snarls. "And then, I wanted to send her body back in pieces to the Steel Dragons."

"Her dad's dead." Malik shrugs. "He would have been the only one to care. Her brother, Jaeger, runs it now. He's the one who asked us to take her, to kidnap her. He wouldn't give two shits if you sent her back in pieces."

See what I mean? The motherfucker is begging to be shot in the head.

"Malik, if you weren't my Vice, you would be taking her place in the cellar and the place she had on my dick."

"Kinky," Malik mutters.

"And how is my prisoner doing?" Barrett asks me, his eyes flaming with rage.

I refuse to back down and keep my body relaxed. I won't show him fear. "She seems to be recovering."

He leans back in his chair as his hand scrubs down his long, gray beard. It's the most hair he has on his head as his scalp gleams under the lights overhead.

"Wouldn't it be funny if we trained her to become a Hell's March member?" Bear laughs. "And then send her to war with her brother? That would be a spit on the Steel Dragons Club." His palm slaps the table as his booming laugh echoes around our heads.

"It's not the worst idea," Malik replies with a smirk. "Jaeger hates his sister, and I bet after he had let us take her out of that house, she hates him too."

I can feel Barrett's glare hitting the side of my face, the heat of his rage slowly making the temperature in the room rise as the tension crackles around us like static electricity.

"Since you decided to save her, are you willing to train her, Montez?" Barrett sneers. "You gonna teach the pretty girl how to shoot a big ole gun?"

"If that's what you want." I shrug my shoulders, finally meeting his eyes with my own. I would never take the chance of refusing him anything, not yet anyway. "But I would assume she was quite pampered."

"Nah." Bear shakes his head with a chuckle. "Her daddy

was going to make her President."

The room falls quiet with disbelief as I shake my head, my shoulders shaking with subdued laughter.

"No way," I say on a laugh. "That's the most absurd thing I've ever heard. There's never been a woman MC President before."

"It's true. That's why her big brother begged us to come and take her away."

I lean on the table and look Bear in the eyes, incredulity coursing through me. "You're telling me Victor Varga wanted to make his daughter the President over Jaeger Varga? He was already his Vice, that doesn't make any sense." My brows come together as I purse my lips.

"Victor Varga asked us to put a bullet in his head because his body was riddled with stage four cancer, but not before we were made to promise him we would end our war once and for all, so that his little girl could play house at the MC club."

"Who gives a fuck about all that?" Barrett says, his voice sharp as I fall back in my seat. "I was never going to keep any promises to that piece of shit. So that's why I kind of like this idea. Montez, you and Ajani will be in charge of the Varga Princess. She'll live with you, and you will train her to shoot."

GENEVIEVE
BMW Motorrad Milano

THIRTEEN

I'm just finishing off my Jell-O when Diego comes into the room. This time, I don't bother to pretend to be asleep. It's obvious he knows the difference. He stands at the foot of my bed as a smile creeps over his tired face. He has dark brown hair that hits just under his ears. It's thick and wavy, the ends slightly lighter than the rest. I think the chaotic, messy look is natural. His skin is dark and golden, making his crystal blue eyes pop out of his face. He's clean-shaven, leaving those plush, cupid-bow lips free of any distraction. He's tall, around 6'1 or 6'2, and lean under his hospital jacket, but I would bet he's toned and muscular, just like every other motherfucking biker I know.

"I'm glad to see you awake." He continues to smile as I drop the spoon and Jell-O back onto the tray. There's no mistaking the kindness in his eyes, the way the blue radiates with compassion. I bet he really stands out here in the sea of rapists and kidnappers. Saving lives seems like such a blatant contrast to Hell's March's behavior. My jaw tightens and I blink, making the movement overly exaggerated. "I'm sorry about what happened to you," he says. "Do you know for sure who held you in the basement? Are you able to describe him?"

I continue to stare at him, refusing to open my mouth and utter a single word to these people. First, they had the audacity to kill my family, and then they dragged me away from my home, only to leave me to die. When I had accepted my fate, this one came along and decided to ensure I survived, forcing me to live with every terrible thing that's ever happened to me.

"Are you a mute?" he asks, his brow lifting. When I don't answer, he gives a slight nod. "Fine. I won't force you to speak, but are you willing to nod or shake your head? I'm trying to help you here." Against my better judgment, I give him one brisk nod. "Okay, good," he says with relief as his hands land on his waist and his head tips forward, his messy waves flipping over his forehead. "Do you know who brought you here?" The four men who stormed into my home wearing Hell's March cuts and waving guns pop into my mind, but I don't remember names or faces, so I shake my head slowly. "Okay." He paces at the end of my bed, his fingers sinking into his hair, a habit I bet he does whenever he's frustrated. "What about the basement? Do you know who put you there?" He releases his hair and watches me as he paces.

Again, I shake my head because I don't know who put me there, but I committed his voice to memory, not that I tell Diego that.

He stops pacing and stares at me, his straight teeth biting into his bottom lip as he tries to think of questions that would only require me to nod or shake my head.

"Are you Genevieve Varga?" I nod once. "Would you like me to contact your brother?"

He didn't even say his name. Despite that, I can feel the blood rushing to my head, the sound like waves crashing on the shore. My ears are buzzing and pounding with my heart rate at the same time. Nausea swirls through my stomach, churning the Jell-O I just ate. I snap a hand over my mouth while I viciously shake my head.

Diego begins to blur in front of me as tears gather in my eyes, but I blink them back, forcing myself to swallow down every emotion. I will never be the soft girl I once was. Never again will I fall victim to any man, and that includes my brother. No matter if he's standing in front of me or if someone is speaking about him.

With that resolve, I drop my hand and stop shaking my head as he stares at me wide-eyed, surprised by my visceral reaction. I take a deep breath, willing myself to calm down, then I slowly shake my head.

"So the rumors are right. Your brother made a deal to have you kidnapped so he could have the presidency?" I nod and watch as his face falls. "Was your father planning to make you President? Or was that a rumor too?" I nod again, the movement making me feel like a bobblehead. "Shit," he curses as he begins to pace again. "That's fucking strange, you know? Why would your father do that to you? Putting a woman in a place of power where no one would respect her. No offense," he tosses over his shoulder, and I give him a simple shrug. Really, there's none taken. I've already thought of all this. "Do you know why he wanted to do that? To give you the Presidency?" I slowly shake my head, staring at him as he walks back and forth in front of me. "I'm sorry this has happened to you. I'm sorry your family turned on you, and I'm sorry one of my brothers hurt you. You have to make the choice to either break or take it,"—he stops pacing to slam his fist against his chest—"and use it to make yourself stronger." He's staring at me, waiting for a sign of my wanting to fight for my life.

I think about seeing Ma, my mother, and Dad, and everything in me begs to break, to give it all up, but then I hear my father's words. *You have Varga blood.* I remind myself with his words that I'm the last living Varga descendant, not even Jaeger deserves the Varga name. I look Diego in the eye and place every bit of determination into it, giving him a nod as my fingers twist into the bed sheets.

"Alright then." His lips curl up into a slow smile as he watches me. I really must be broken because even though I can see he's physically attractive, nothing inside of me responds to him. "I'm going to train you. Tell me, Genevieve, do you know how to shoot a gun?"

Chino's face appears in my mind, and I congratulate myself on the fact that I feel nothing but cold rage. The man who took my innocence, the one I trusted with my heart, let them take me without putting up a single fight. So I do as Diego says, and instead of letting it break me, I take everything I'm feeling and let it burn hot inside of me as I give him a single nod.

"That's good." He nods back, his hands landing on his waist. "Self-defense? Can you fight? Do you know how to throw a punch?" I shrug my shoulders. I know a little, but nothing worth admitting to. "That's all right." He gives me a smile, the dimple in his chin deepening. "I have a baby sister who's been fighting her whole damn life." A chuckle escapes him as he speaks about his sister, but I can't seem to find the humor in what he's saying. "She'll teach you."

As my lids begin to grow heavy, I give him another nod, the single cup of Jell-O I ate making me feel like I've gorged at a buffet. He notices my fatigue and his hands drop from his waist.

"You'll be in here a few more weeks," he tells me. "You need to get your strength back, and we need to bring up your weight. Once you're ready to leave, you can come live with me and my roommate, if you choose. If by then you change your mind and you would like to go home, I won't fight you."

I'm already passing out before he finishes his sentence, but I shake my head lightly as I sink into the pillows under my head.

The only time I'm going home is when I'm ready to exact my revenge.

DIEGO

DIEGO

By the sixth day, Genevieve started getting out of her bed and pacing the length of her room, determination shining in her eyes. Ajani has been keeping a close eye on her, and he says each day she gets a little less winded and can walk a little longer. I like that she's smart and knows she has to bring up her endurance. She has to slowly get her body used to the exertion.

Now it's the tenth day, and I walk into her room to find her sitting on the bed. Her hair is washed and brushed, the color of wet mahogany shining under the lights. Now that the bags have receded from under her eyes and her skin is back to its natural, olive tone, I can see she has beautiful, dark blue irises framed by thick, black lashes. Genevieve Varga is breathtaking.

She's dressed in the clothes my sister donated, and I'm surprised to see them hanging off her frame, but the pants are extremely short, looking like a pair of capris on her long legs.

"Let me guess," I say to her. "You want to leave?"

I've gotten used to this no words communication. I do all the talking, making sure to ask very specific questions which only require a yes or no, and if it's a maybe, she gives me a shrug.

Her facial expression doesn't change, but the quick nod and earnest look in her eyes tells me this girl wants to get out of here, whether she's completely healed or not. It must be difficult staying in the same place you were violated, and she's been working hard toward getting better.

"I live about fifteen minutes from here, and about twenty minutes from the Steel Dragons' clubhouse. You are welcome to stay with me and my roommate, Ajani, or if you've reconsidered and want to speak to your brother, I can drop you there."

If she chooses the latter option right now, Barrett will absolutely put a bullet in my head, but I can't hold an innocent person hostage. It's not who I am.

Her arm lifts, the bones prominent in her wrist and elbow, then points directly at my chest. "You'd rather come stay with me?"

Another quick nod.

"All right." I look over my shoulder and figure out a plan of how I'll get her out of here without her having to lay eyes on any of the brothers. I can only imagine she would be triggered if she saw her attacker again. I'm almost certain it was just Barrett, but I wouldn't put it past Bear or Malik either. "Stay there," I instruct. "I'll be back in a few minutes." I find Ajani speaking to Malik at the double doors of the medical ward, his hand resting against the door jamb, effectively blocking off the entrance. Malik never comes to Medical, so I can only assume he's only here for one reason. "Malik Charles," I call out. "Are you finally here to clear up that chlamydia?"

His head tips to the side so he can look at me in the space between Ajani's shoulder and the door jamb, letting loose a manic-sounding laugh. "It itches something fierce, doc." I can't help the chuckle that wells up inside me and slips past my lips. Nothing ever fazes Malik. "Actually, I'll be honest with you," he says, his face falling serious as he leans on the door jamb, right next to Ajani's arm. "I came to see the girl."

"What do you want with her?" I ask him, crossing my arms over my chest as a protectiveness courses through me. "You're the brother who took her. What makes you think she's going to want to see you?"

"I may have taken her, but none of that was my idea. My options were few." He shakes his head. His voice is even and his body is relaxed. I believe him instantly because Malik is never one to lie. "I didn't know we were going there to kill her father, but I also knew Bear had his own plans with Jaeger. They'd been talking back and forth for a while."

"All right." I shrug my shoulders. "I don't know if she'd believe you, and I don't think it's a good idea for you to see her."

"I wanted to tell her I have some information about her family's little club." He smirks as if he has a secret. "I know who their mole is. I've been visiting them to get information."

"What information?"

"That's none of your business." His brows come together as he straightens. "Just something I was ordered to do, to collect information on the Steel Dragons."

"Is this in relation to you robbing their little drug runner? What was his name?"

"Junior." Malik nods. "Yeah, something like that, but there's a lot more going on that's leaking from that club. More than just some low-level drug runner."

"She doesn't give a fuck about that club anymore," I tell him as disgust coats my words. "It would be a waste of your breath." My brow lifts, letting him know this conversation is useless, and Ajani hums his agreement.

Malik steps back from the door, his hands raising up in the air and that ominous smirk still plastered on his face. "If you say so." He turns on his heel and strides back down the corridor, his boots hitting the tiled floor with echoing thuds.

"Do you think he's being honest?" Ajani asks me as we watch Malik walk away.

"When have you ever heard Malik lie?"

"Plenty of times," Ajani admits. "But only when it serves himself."

His words leave a disgusting taste in my mouth. Malik is no doubt a monster, and it's true, maybe he wouldn't be above lying if it was for his own personal gain.

GENEVIEVE
BMW Motorrad Milano

FOURTEEN

He lives in a small bungalow on the outskirts of Phoenix. I'm just about to compare his house to the one I was raised in when I immediately shut down my mind. That life is dead to me now, and no comparisons will make it any less tarnished.

The hardest part about leaving the Hell's March compound and coming here to Diego and Ajani's house was the actual ride. Sitting on the back of a motorcycle again resurfaced my longing for my own. I'll probably never see it again though.

"Home sweet home," Diego says as I swing my leg off his bike and pull the helmet from my head. The desire to die isn't as strong now as it was a few days ago, but the prospect of living this new life still hasn't completely diminished the fantasy of being with my family. "You'll have your own room," Diego continues to talk as he leads me up the driveway. My eyes skip over the trimmed bushes and small flower bed just to the right of the front door. "It's usually the bedroom my sister stays in when she comes home, but I figure she's rarely here now and when she does stay, I have a pull-out couch."

If I were speaking, this would be the moment I'd say, 'Oh no, I couldn't take your sister's room, give me the pull-out couch instead.' But the thought of sleeping in a space without a door I could lock isn't very appealing. So thankfully, I just keep my mouth shut.

"My sister is going to come by tomorrow. Are you okay with that?" He turns to look at me over his shoulder as he slips his key into the door.

I chew on my bottom lip and shrug my shoulders as I wring my hands together. I'm not really up for visitors, but I can't tell this man, whose house I'm staying in for free, who's going to be protecting me, that he can't have his own family over.

"I can tell her to come by another day." He nods to me before turning around and opening the door.

I step inside and look around, pleasantly surprised with how clean the place is given two men live here. It's an open-concept floor plan where the kitchen kind of bleeds into the living room, and the living room bleeds into a small hallway. Four doors line the wall, and I would assume those are the bedrooms. For a small house, it looks really spacious on the inside.

"There's only one full bathroom." He gives me an apologetic look. "But Ajani and I clean it, and if we ever leave the seat up, I give you permission to punch us." He winks and leads me over to the four doors and opens the first one. "This is Ajani's room."

The room is organized and clean, his bed is made, and he has a large screen TV mounted to the wall. His king-sized bed is adjacent to the TV with many pillows on its surface. I like Ajani's room for its simplistic comfort.

"This would be your bedroom," Diego says as we go to open the next door.

Inside is a simple, double bed, a small dresser, neutral painted walls, dark hardwood flooring, and a mid-size TV mounted on the wall. The bedspread is dark blue, matching the sheer curtains which hang over the blinds, and a fluffy, white mat sits on the floor beside the bed, something to protect my feet from hitting the cold wood first thing in the morning. It makes me miss my room back home, and as soon as the thought slips out, I grind my jaw to force myself to forget. That's not my home anymore.

"Do you like it?" he asks. I turn to give him a nod and his face lights up with a smile. "Good. Now, right here is the bathroom." He opens the door to the right of my room, revealing a large, fully marble-tiled bathroom. He was right, they do clean it. Every surface is pristine and gleaming. I nearly moan when I see the deep-set tub with jets.

"My room is at the end," he says sheepishly. "It's a mess right now. I'd rather not show it."

I shrug and head back toward the room he said was mine.

"I think my sister has some clothes and pajamas in the closet, but whenever you're ready, I can take you shopping for more."

I look down at the clothes I'm currently wearing and cringe. His sister is wider than me but much shorter. I do need clothing, but the thought of taking any more from this man makes my stomach swirl with nausea. I don't know how I'll ever repay him.

He must recognize the look of guilt on my face because his softens with sympathy. If it was anyone else besides Diego, I would accuse them of pitying me, but because it's him, I know it's sympathy.

"Would you feel better if I told you it would come from club funds? The very same club who ripped you from your life and violated you?"

Well, when he puts it that way, it does make me feel better. So I let my lips tip up into a wide smile and his does the same at the sight.

"That sure is a pretty smile you got there, Miss Varga."

I pick out a set of pajamas; the shorts are like satin, boxer shorts, and I find a long-sleeve shirt in one of the drawers. Then I fill up that deep bathtub with near scalding hot water and turn on the jets. When my body is finally and completely submerged, I let those jets pummel my tender muscles and my broken soul until I'm pruned and waterlogged. There was a time when I was privileged enough to have a bath every night before bed, to ease my pampered body into salt-scented waters as essential oils dotted the surface. Though it wasn't due to my muscles being sore, or because I was so filthy and weak that I could barely stand in a shower. No, it was all because I could.

I now have a new appreciation for warm water and soap.

Diego stays with me for the evening while Ajani is at the club, preparing me a simple, chicken caesar salad, and as soon as the sun sets, I drag my feet to my new bedroom. When I pull back the blanket, I'm assaulted by the scent of freshly laundered sheets, and I smile, knowing Diego was ready for me. He wanted me to feel welcomed and completely comfortable.

I ease between the blankets, letting my body soak up the cool sheets as my head sinks into the soft pillows, and let myself feel peace; I force myself to accept peace, and it's all at the hands of Diego, whose heart is ten times bigger than anyone else's I've ever known.

I let myself feel it and then I shut it down. The images of the last three weeks of my life flip through my mind. I see Jaeger standing over my father. I hear the gunshot. I feel the biker's shoulder digging into my stomach. I remember Quinton not bothering to help, and then I let myself sink into the torture I endured day after day inside Hell's March compound.

"I have Varga blood," I whisper, the words sounding rough and strained due to the lack of using my voice, but I repeat that phrase over and over until my eyelids slowly seal.

"I have Varga blood."

The water flows down over my hair, washing the shampoo out and making it slip down over my body to gather around my feet. The shower has five different heads, and I can turn each of them on simultaneously, or I can pick which part of my body I want to hit with the pressure of the water. It's opulent.

When my fingers are pruned and the water feels like it's running cold, I finally step out of the shower and wrap myself in the thickest, softest towels. I hug the velvet material to my chest as I sink my nose into the fabric, inhaling warmth and fabric softener, the scent of comfort. I don't know how long this bubble of safety will last, so I'll soak it in for as long as I can.

I open the bathroom door and look out, making sure Diego and Ajani aren't up. The house is still quiet as everyone sleeps. I was up really early this morning to ensure no one would see me and rushed into the bathroom before I lost my chance to be the first one in there.

My feet squeak along the wood floor as I run back to my room, the stress of being seen in a towel all-consuming. I slip into my bedroom, nearly tripping over my own feet and slamming the door shut. I rest my forehead on the painted white surface and let out a long exhale. I don't know if this fear inside of me will ever subside.

"You must be Princess Varga."

I turn and my body startles as a scream wrenches from my throat to find a girl lying across my bed with her hands behind her head. "What the fuck?"

"Hey, did you speak?" She straightens, shock lining her features. "I thought you were like mute or something? That's what my brother said." Her head tips to the side and her tight, brown curls spring with the motion.

This must be Diego's sister.

I don't answer her as I focus my eyes to the floor, and instead, place my hand over my heart, feeling the rapid beat pounding against my palm. I try to swallow down the fear that's worked its way up my throat as my body begins to vibrate with the adrenaline coursing through me. I don't think I'll ever get over the fact that I was so easily taken from my home. A sudden realization comes over me, I screamed loud enough to wake the guys.

"It's okay, I'm here because they left for the clubhouse early today," she states reassuringly as she sits up. Her skin is a couple shades darker than her brother's, but they have the same, crystal blue eyes framed by the same, thick, black lashes. She's short. I can tell by the way her feet swing just above the hardwood floor when she's sitting on the edge of the bed, confirming why her pants are so short. She's also muscular, her body looking like it's toned to perfection with very little body fat. She's a beautiful girl. I envy her, and yet, I don't know anything about her. "You don't have to speak," she declares. "It was stupid of me to startle you like this. I wasn't thinking." Kindness radiates from her eyes, much like her brother's, and I fall back against the door, willing my heart to slow down as I try to breathe evenly. My hand finally falls from my chest as I begin to relax.

Maybe it's that kindness encased inside a woman's body that puts me at ease, but I shock us both by opening my mouth and saying, "You think?"

A cute, tinkling laugh escapes her mouth as she shrugs her shoulders. "I've never been one to respect boundaries, but I can see something bad happened to you." She stands up and the top of her curly head just about hits my shoulders. "If you need someone to talk to, I'm here." She smiles sweetly.

"I appreciate that," I whisper, my throat already feeling tight from weeks of not being used. I clear it and say, "Thank you."

"I've been told I need to toughen you up." She claps her hands, her mouth slipping into a slow smile. "Fighting is my favorite thing to do. I'm a boxer." She's about two feet in front of me as she begins to punch the air, her biceps bunching with the motion.

"I have to admit,"—I clear my throat again, trying to chase away the cracking dryness—"I don't have much experience with fighting."

"We'll change that. I'm Delia, by the way." She nods and then grabs her purse off the bed. "I got my brother's credit card, and he told me to take you shopping. You need clothes." Her eyes skim over my body. "You're way taller than me. There's no way you can wear my clothes without looking like a fool."

I laugh and then slap a hand over my mouth to stop the sound immediately. I never want to feel at ease enough to laugh. At least, not until I've taken care of the people who broke me.

"It's okay, it's our secret. I won't tell anyone that you're speaking or laughing, but with me, you can be yourself."

"Thank you," I whisper.

"Now get dressed and let's go shopping. After that, we'll start on some basic self-defense. My brother has a wicked gym in the basement."

MALIK
DIESEL

MALIK

"What the fuck is she wearing?" I mutter to myself as I watch Princess Varga get into a compact car with Montez's younger sister. "There are no floods in Arizona right now."

I bet she's missing her pretty, little, yellow bike.

They back out of the driveway as I watch from the spot I've picked up the street. I'm not really hidden. I mean, if they looked in the fucking rearview mirror, they would see me here in my leather cut and jeans, leaning over my handlebars and playing with the chunky rings on my fingers. They'd also hear my bike as I start it up, and notice the rumble of my engine as I follow them to wherever they're going.

Look, I'll admit it, I might be slightly obsessed. What did Vic Varga see in this fragile woman to want to make her President? I need to find out. She's also put her own brother in such a tailspin that he had to get rid of her. Despite being raised as true siblings, that's just heartless.

I know what it means to be heartless. It's an affliction manifested through parental trauma. When you're raised in a household with other siblings and your parents favor one over the other, it plants a seed in the child's mind who's looked at as a problem.

And do you know what happens to seeds when they're watered and nurtured? Those motherfuckers grow into trees.

I have a fucking giant Sequoia inside of me.

So I wonder what made Jaeger hate his sister so much. Could it have just been because Vic decided to make his little girl President? Or was it something that was planted years before Jaeger showed up, and Vic nurtured that seed into a fucking tree?

I'll never know, but my mind won't leave it alone. I need to know what it is about this girl that has everyone so fucking obsessed with her.

When they turn into the shopping mall parking lot, I chuckle over the noise of my engine.

"She better be buying some fucking pants that fit," I mumble as I park a few spaces down from Diego's sister.

Princess Varga unfolds herself out of the small car, those long fucking legs stretching out, and for two seconds, I imagine myself between them. She looks around the parking lot, her dark eyes flicking quickly, looking for any signs of danger. The look makes me want to raise my hand to show her the most dangerous thing around here right now, but I don't. I'm not ready to expose myself. I haven't found out enough yet.

Delia grabs her hand and drags her into the mall. I get off my bike, place my helmet on the seat, and follow the girls inside, keeping back about ten feet. I fucking hate malls. People talk too much and stand too close, but when they touch me, it makes my fingers itch to grab my gun and put a bullet in their head. That's why I avoid high-traffic areas with many people, because my tree inside of me does most of the thinking.

They head into a department store that has women's clothing on mannequins in the window, so I park my ass on the bench across from it and pull out my phone. I don't know how long women usually take to shop, but I'm already bored as fuck. I take a picture of the storefront and of Princess Varga entering with Delia, then I send that bitch to Jaeger.

Me: The life of the rich and famous.

I haven't heard from Jaeger since we watched him kill his daddy and then took his baby sister out of the house on his orders. He's been staying pretty quiet, but I like to stir the pot. Life is boring otherwise. I slip my phone back into my pocket and look around the mall. I've always been fascinated by the interaction between people. I enjoy watching facial expressions and body language, then deciphering what it is each person is feeling as long as I'm on the sidelines and not in the middle of a crowd. I'm hyper-focused on that mostly because I have yet to feel much beyond indifference myself.

My father was much the same way when we were growing up. I know a lot of me comes from him, and even though my twin brother, Laith, and I look identical, we're two very different people. He is more like my mother. She was calm, sweet-mannered, respectful, and she loved Laith. She planted the seed.

They finally come out of the fucking store right before my mind slips too deep into the past, and I shake it off, my hair tumbling around my shoulders. There's no way it would be safe enough for me to reminisce about my childhood in such a public place.

Their next stop is a lingerie store, and this time, I follow them inside. I want to know what type of panties Miss Varga wears, and if she sleeps in the nude or not. Maybe she'll buy those cute, little, lace nighties. Unfortunately, I won't be able to look in her window at night because she's been keeping the blind shut. It's annoying really.

Are those all cotton? I wonder as she begins to throw random underwear and bras into a basket. Not one thing has lace or color. Just whites and creams. This bitch is boring. She grabs a couple sets of cotton pajama shorts and T-shirts, and I throw up my arms in disgust. I stride back out of the store, declaring to teach her how to be sexy. That's the mother's job, isn't it? Not that I would really understand what roles a mother truly encompasses, but I mean, I'd like to think that's common sense.

Unless you want your daughter to be handed over to the church. Maybe that's it. Maybe she was going to be a nun. Mother Varga, President of the MC Club, Steel Dragons.

And I'm hard.

Not necessarily about her running an MC club, which, to be honest, is pretty hot. It's more about the fact that she'll wear one of those hoods on her head like a nun. I don't know what they're called. Now that's some sexy shit.

They finally leave the mall, much to my relief, and I continue thinking about nuns and convents. Maybe I need Jesus. Maybe the fact that I'm getting a hard-on about nuns means I should go to church. I'm thinking that as I watch them pull out of their parking spot, and I swear for the briefest moment, Princess Varga and I lock eyes, but Delia speeds out before I can know for sure.

I sit on my bike and strap my helmet to my head, stopping to think about church, Jesus, and the cross. I mean, I know a way to use the cross, but I don't think that's how the Catholic Church intended it. I'm thinking it might be a little different, but I'm intrigued nonetheless. Maybe I should go to church.

I didn't grow up in a religious household. We were atheists, not believing in any higher power or lower power, but given how we all turned out, maybe we should have.

Mindlessly, I'm back on Diego's street just as the girls get out of their car. I cut the engine, leaning back over the handlebars to watch them from the same spot up the street. Thank God Princess Varga got some new clothes. Those flood pants are atrocious. Is she wearing men's shoes? Weird. I could always go by her house and get her clothes for her. Maybe some shoes. I can do that.

So while the girls head in and do whatever it is girls do, pillow fights and painting toenails and maybe some pussy eating… Okay, I'm hard again. What was I saying?

Oh right, maybe I'll go by her house and get some of her shit. That would be nice. See? I can be nice.

DIEGO

DIEGO

"Montez!" Bear yells out as he comes in through the double doors. "We got one here who's dying! We need you to bring him back."

I fly out of my chair and rush toward the man being held up by Bear and another one of my brothers. I grab a handful of his sweat-saturated hair and lift his face. "Who is he?" I ask.

"Someone we need answers from," Bear growls as he drags the kid forward. "Take him and fix him so we can do this all over again."

I point to a room that has been disinfected and roll my eyes as I throw on my jacket and slip on a pair of latex gloves. Bear has always been really creative with his torture, so I can't even imagine what I might find under the kid's clothes.

What I end up finding is a badly beaten and tortured Steel Dragon. As soon as I cut the T-shirt away from his body, I see the fresh-looking branding on his stomach, the edges still red from healing.

He's the same as when they dropped him off, stable, but still unconscious, and he's young. This isn't something I ever wanted to be a part of. No good ever came from harming another human being, but sometimes we do what we have to do to survive. The people I had to kill boiled down to it being their lives or mine. I've never been that selfless to give up my life for someone I didn't know.

"When will he be up, doc?" Bear asks as I exit the room. He's leaning against the wall on the other side of the corridor because he knows my rules about not being in the room with a patient.

"I don't know if he'll ever wake up," I admit to him as I pull off my bloodied gloves and toss them in the trash. "What were you trying to get out of him anyway?"

"The cartel warehouse was raided by the cops."

"So we pay them off." I round the desk and sit in the chair, avoiding Bear's eye as he stands on the other side.

"They're not our cops," he snaps, then falls into the chair on the other side of my desk. "And now it looks like the FBI might be involved. This little bitch was found scoping out the place."

"I see. How much did we lose?" I run my hand along my chin, watching as he squirms.

"Not much," he huffs. "We had just cleaned it out, but that place is compromised now, and the cartel aren't too happy with us. From what I gather, they're looking to work with the Steel Dragons now."

"Well, I'll let you know if he wakes up," I tell him.

He rises from the chair with a nod, his hands still coated with dried blood, splatters of it lining his shirt and face. "Make sure that you do," he says as he walks out.

Ajani is home with Genevieve today and my mind keeps traveling back to her, wondering if she's okay. Has she spoken to him yet? I can't explain the jealousy that bubbles inside me when I think that maybe she'll choose Ajani to talk to first. It's silly, but I want it to be me. There's no denying I've grown protective of the girl, and every day, I worry Barrett will ask for her back. Then I'll have to make a choice.

A groan sounds from inside the room with the Steel Dragon, and I grab another set of gloves as I rush over to him. His head is moving back and forth, his hands are clenched into fists, and his moans are filling the room. The pained sounds send shards of ice through my veins. I hate to see anyone in pain.

I grab a syringe of morphine and apply it to his drip, hoping it keeps him comfortable.

"Please," he pleads, his eyes hooded and filled with pain. "I just need to find her."

His words have me stilling, the syringe still stuck in the IV, and my heart starting to pound. He hasn't said a name, but he doesn't have to. I know he's speaking of Genevieve.

"You need to find who?" I ask him as I lean over his face.

"The boss' sister," he mutters.

"Fuck," I hiss out as I put the syringe on the bedside table. This isn't good. "Why are you looking for her?"

"They… Want…" He chokes on the blood that's pooling in his mouth and I tip his head upward. "Kill her," he finishes and my heart plummets into my stomach.

I can't let that happen and I can't let Barrett or Bear find out that the Steel Dragons are sending their men to sniff around our compounds looking for Genevieve. It's a surefire way for her to end up with a bullet in her head while pieces of her are shipped back to her brother in warning.

The kid is just gripping onto the last vestiges of life. It looks like his spine is broken, he'll never walk, he has severe internal trauma, and the blood that's pouring from his mouth is coming from a punctured lung. He will not live long anyway, so I do the most humane thing anyone could do in this situation. I plug his nose and watch as he chokes on his own blood, his eyes widening as he struggles.

Bear will have to accept that this time, he took the torture a little too far. The Steel Dragons can't find out Genevieve is staying at my house. She's not strong enough yet, and I can't be with her all the time.

Maybe there's a way I can trick Jaeger into believing we killed his sister already. It was always a possibility. If I hadn't found her in that basement, she would be dead.

So why not just let him believe that?

I step out of the room and pull my cell phone out of my pocket, sending a text to Bear, letting him know he's on body cleanup, then I shut the place down.

I need to get home and stage Genevieve's death. Then I'm going to resurrect her like a phoenix and teach her to burn everything down to the ground.

Ajani is in the kitchen making dinner when I storm in through the front door. His immediate reaction is to haul the gun out of the top drawer and turn it on me, the safety undone and his finger pressing precariously on the trigger.

"It's just me. We need to come up with a plan." I wave off his gun.

He pops the safety back on the gun and drops it in the drawer. "You almost gave me a heart attack," he mumbles as he shakes out his hands. "What plan? Didn't we already have a plan?"

"Her brother sent a man to look for his sister. Bear got ahold of him and tortured the kid to within an inch of his life."

"That is a problem." Ajani nods as he leans on our kitchen island, his face looking pensive. "Why would her brother be looking for her if he's the one who let her go?"

"Maybe he wants to make sure she's actually dead," I supply as I begin to pace in front of the island, running my fingers through my hair.

"We need to make sure he stops sending men to look for her. Okay, we can do that. Do we scout him so you can put a bullet in his head?" Ajani would follow me to the pits of Hell if that's what I asked of him, and he knows I would do the same for him.

"We can't kill him," I say, even though it's against my better judgment. "I would like nothing more than to shoot him in the head as well, but it won't solve our problems. In fact, it'll increase them, and we'll have another war on our hands. Maybe we can make him believe she died already."

"Oh," he replies, straightening to his full height. "Yeah, I mean, she would have died in that basement had we not found her."

"Exactly. So what do I send back to him that will convince him she's dead?" I run a finger along my chin in thought.

"Her pinky finger." Ajani nods, his face completely serious.

"We can't take her fucking finger." I stare at him, aghast.

"Does that go for toes too?" He's fucking stony-faced like

he's not suggesting we disfigure her.

"No appendages."

"Teeth?"

"We're sick fucks," I growl out.

"Her hair!" He snaps his fingers as he straightens with excitement. "We'll send him her hair."

"Will it be enough?"

"We'll cover it in blood." He nods.

"Where is she, anyway?" I ask as I look around the room.

"Looks like your sister's got a jump-start on teaching her self-defense. Most likely that little hellion is teaching Genevieve how to collect testicles with her bare hands." Ajani's mouth spreads with a warm smile.

GENEVIEVE
BMW Motorrad Milano

FIFTEEN

My back hits the mat for what feels like the hundredth time this evening. My body is sore, and my muscles are trembling, but I get back to my feet and back into the stance Delia has taught me.

"I want you to think of every weakness on your body. Where would it hurt to be hit, or maybe you already know," she instructs, shrugging her shoulders. "And then I want you to attack me, trying to hit each of those spots."

My chest is heaving with each labored breath, but I won't give up. The new Genevieve Varga would never give up.

My bare feet grip the foam mats as I take off, each footfall pounding into the cushion and springing me onward. This time when I attack Delia, I don't go for her face or her chest like she expects. I bend down and kick out her feet, watching as her back hits the mat, then I get on top of her and grab her lightly by the throat, surprise washing over her face.

She taps my wrist with a laugh, the sound full of pride and giddiness. It feels good to have someone be proud of me again. "I think we can break for today." I push up off of her and grab her outstretched hand, yanking her up as well. The smile she has across her face is contagious. "You're a fast learner. I can't believe you knocked me on my ass, and it was unpredictable as fuck." What Delia doesn't understand is, this isn't an eagerness to learn something new, and yeah, I may be a fast learner, but that has nothing to do with this. It's about survival, and most of all, it's revenge. I'm eagerly awaiting the day that I stand in front of Jaeger and burn his fucking world to the ground. "I feel like I need to come up with a nickname for you." Delia snaps her fingers as my breathing calms, her mouth tipping upward mischievously. "Genevieve is a mouthful."

"Just don't call me Genni." I shake my head, my voice still a rough whisper.

"V," she says. "Yeah, I think that's what I'll call you."

I shrug my shoulders but give her a smile. The name doesn't bring any images of people I hate or miss with my whole heart, so it works. Besides, it feels almost like I'm a whole new person, with a new family.

Footsteps sound upstairs as someone walks back and forth, and I grin, knowing it's Diego. Delia catches the grin on my face as my eyes look up at the ceiling.

"He always does that when he's thinking," she remarks with a smile as she watches me closely. "He will pace a hole through the floor until he figures out whatever it is he's thinking of. You know, you're safe with him, right? He's not like the other bikers, neither is Ajani. They're different, but our families have been a part of this stupid club from the beginning, and my brother can't just leave. I'm thankful I'm a girl and wasn't forced into it." I look at her with a grin.

"Sometimes that doesn't stop it either," I mumble as the basement door opens.

Delia gives me a look but thankfully keeps her mouth shut as Diego comes down the stairs. I turn to look at him with his simple, black T-shirt and his dusty, black jeans. He walks with confidence, but it's lacking the arrogance that's usually attached to a leather cut. Diego is like no one I've ever known.

"We need to talk." His eyes flick from me to his sister, his face looking grim. "Thank you, Del, for doing this today."

"That's my cue to leave," Delia singsongs as she picks up

her hoodie from the nearby bench. "Did you want a few days to rest?" she asks me. When I vehemently shake my head, she lets loose a chuckle. "This one's dedicated," she tells Diego before looking at me once more. "I'll be back tomorrow. Same time, okay?"

I nod as she walks by, her hand laying on my forearm and giving me a gentle squeeze. Diego and I wait as her footsteps disappear up the stairs, and the door shuts behind her.

"Something happened today," Diego says, and my head snaps to look at him. "I don't want you to worry, but at the same time, I think you deserve to know everything."

The way my heart beats and my ears get that familiar buzz has me even more fearful of what he's about to say. Despite all I'm feeling, it doesn't penetrate the outside. My face remains even, and my body relaxed.

"We had a guest at our clubhouse today," he begins as he motions for me to sit on the bench. I shake my head, preferring to remain standing as he shrugs and sits himself. His elbows hit his knees as he leans forward, keeping his eyes on me. "He was from the Steel Dragons." My heart beats a little faster and my throat swells, but I refuse to give in. I won't swallow past that feeling. I'll let it stay there so I can grow accustomed to how it feels. Fear and I will have to learn to get along. "He had been tortured, of course." Diego's fingers brush along his five o'clock shadow, the scraping sound nearly as loud as the buzzing in my ears. "I spoke to him while I was trying to treat him, and he said something about being sent to our warehouse to look for you."

He was sent by someone from Steel Dragons to look for me? Maybe Jaeger was sending him to finish the job. Or maybe the guilt of not helping me has been eating Quinton alive and he sent him? Then there's Laith. Maybe he found out what happened to me and he's trying to find out where I could be.

Or all three of them decided, along with the rest of the club, that I would be better off dead than alive with the enemy. That seems like the most probable option.

"I have an idea," Diego continues when I haven't given him a reaction. "Ajani and I think if we cut off your hair and send it to them with some sort of ominous message, they may back off.

Seeing your hair may not be enough, so we're also hoping for some of your blood." He pulls out a syringe from his pocket.

That could work. I shrug my shoulders and give him a nod. Luckily, needles don't freak me out.

"Are you okay?" he asks.

Another quick nod and then I point up the stairs while motioning to the clothes I'm wearing. I'm sweaty, and internally, I'm on the verge of a breakdown.

I need to get out of this basement when I'm not working out. It's drastically different from the first I was held in, but being in a windowless space still sends my senses in a spiral. The scent of mold or a draft has the power to revert me back to that broken girl if I have too much time to think about it.

"Yeah, of course, shower." He waves for me to go upstairs as he continues to sit on the bench.

I don't rush. I take slow, measured steps while my heart is flailing inside my chest. I keep my breathing even, despite my lungs barely filling to capacity, and I will my eyes to stay dry. I'm no longer Genevieve Varga.

I step out of the basement to find Ajani in the kitchen, his eyes flicking over me and giving me a small smile. He and I haven't really interacted much, but I think it's more because he's uncomfortable and I don't blame him. I'm the daughter of a rival motorcycle club's President, and even after everything I've been through at the hands of his club members, I guess in a way I'm still the enemy.

"Delia says you're going to be kicking our asses soon." Ajani chuckles.

I take a deep breath and blow out the fear still lingering throughout my body and release the tension in my shoulders as I give him a returning smile. I lift my right shoulder up toward my ear, then turn toward the bathroom.

I just need to be alone so I can once again convince myself to forget everything, to bury it down deep. I've gotten pretty good at compartmentalizing.

After my shower, I dress in my new track pants and hoodie, then meet the guys in the kitchen. I slide onto my stool at the island and smile softly when Diego hands me a plate. My stomach is still knotted with stress, but I try to ignore it as I force myself to eat.

"Are you okay with what we talked about in the basement?" Diego asks as Ajani's head pops up from his plate to catch my answer.

I nod and force another forkful into my mouth, keeping my eyes on my food.

"Good, we'll do that before you go to bed tonight."

My head hits the pillow later that night as my finger wraps around the shortened patch of hair behind my ear. The thought of why it's there has my stomach still twisted, and my chest feels heavy, preventing me from being able to take calming breaths. On top of that, all of my muscles are burning, and my mind won't shut down. I don't know that the hair and blood will be enough to convince Jaeger of my demise. The thought of having to look over my shoulder for the rest of my life is terrifying.

Just when I think I've grown stronger, I find myself once again wishing I fucking died in that basement.

DIEGO

DIEGO

My eyes snap open as the loud shrill penetrates through the wall. I leap out of my bed, still half asleep, and run toward Delia's room. Why is she screaming? Who's hurting my sister?

I rush in through the door and stumble when I find Genevieve thrashing on the bed instead of Delia. Slowly, I come to my senses as Ajani comes running in next, his gun cocked and pointed at the window. He stops too as Genevieve sits up, her eyes blinking open to gaze at me.

She's drenched in sweat, her white tank top clinging to her full breasts. Her tears have soaked the skin on her cheeks and her mouth hangs open as she sucks in heaving breaths.

Ajani lowers the gun, giving me a look as he backs out of the room. He's not wanting to encroach on her personal space any more than he already has. To him and me, she's still delicate. Despite that, I can see how much tougher she's become since she's been living here and training with Delia.

"It was just a bad dream," I tell her as she continues to gasp for breath. "It's normal after everything you've been through. You're safe." I stand at the end of her bed, longing to hold her.

I turn around and head for her door because the overwhelming need to comfort her, to gather her in my arms, is becoming harder to deny.

"Diego." Her voice is like smooth honey, the rough tenor adding a husky note. My hand lands on the door jamb as my chin hits my chest. I need to hear her speak again just to convince myself I didn't imagine it. "Please, Diego."

I turn to look at her over my shoulder as my cock betrays me and hardens in my boxers. I should've at least put on a fucking shirt. The way she says my name, how the syllables glide off her tongue even as she's struggling to breathe, I've never heard anything so perfect in my life.

"Say it again," I demand as my hand drops from the wall. "Say my name."

"Please don't leave me here by myself." She shakes her head. "Please, Diego."

How can I deny her when her eyes are filled with anguish and her body trembles with fear? Her voice is begging me with words I've been longing to hear from her. Walking back, I pull up her blankets on her bed and slip between the sheets behind her, wrapping my arms around her too-thin waist and pulling her back against my chest. Her scent is uniquely hers. It's my shampoo she's using and my bodywash, but mixed with her essence, it changes into something more tantalizing.

I know I shouldn't want her like I do, but I can't help it. I think Genevieve Varga was always meant to land in my medical unit.

"Tell me," I whisper in her ear. "Tell me your dream. Don't let it break you." My arms tighten around her waist as her body finally eases its trembling. "Let it strengthen you."

"It's my dad," she sniffs, her voice like a symphony of agony. "My mind replays him being shot in the head repeatedly, but sometimes, instead of it being Jaeger standing over him… it's me." Her words end on a sob, the sound catching in her chest.

"You have some guilt to work through," I inform her. "But you're strong, and I'm here to help you every step of the way."

"Why?" she asks, keeping her back to me. The sound of her voice runs over me like warm sunshine on an early spring day and warming my chest.

"Because I've seen the absolute worst thing that can happen to someone when they decide to let themselves break." I slam my eyes shut, refusing to let *her* enter my mind right now. I need to be strong for Genevieve. "All I want is to see you flourish, and to be strong."

"Do you think it'll work?" she questions. "Do you think Jaeger will believe I'm dead?"

"Deep down inside? No," I admit as my arms tighten around her. "I don't think he'll be convinced that you're dead, but he'll want so badly to believe it that maybe he'll let himself carry on as if it were true."

"When are we going to practice shooting?"

"We'll start tomorrow," I tell her. "Now get some sleep."

"Do you promise to stay with me?"

"Only if you promise to keep speaking to me."

Silence engulfs us as my heart sinks into my stomach. I don't want her to revert to silence.

"Okay," she whispers.

"We need to make a run out to that warehouse." Barrett's voice sounds exhausted as he runs his finger over the etching on the table. "Diego, I need you to go this time, along with Ajani. Bear will lead you guys. I have a feeling more of those Steel motherfuckers are over there, and I may need you to set up a point to pop them off as they come out like little cockroaches."

I look at Ajani and our eyes clash with the same knowing look. Could Barrett have set this up so that Genevieve would be left home alone?

It's not as if we could refuse him, he's our fucking President.

"Am I going on this run?" Malik asks, his bored tone obvious as he slouches in his seat.

"No," Barrett says, leaning on the table to face Malik. "I got something else I need you to do."

Again, another shot of apprehension hits me. Malik would have no problem breaking into our home and re-kidnapping Genevieve if that's what Barrett asks.

"Are we good with that, Montez?" Barrett breaks me from my thoughts, his eyes drilling into mine.

"Whatever you want, boss."

"And how's our newest recruit doing?" A few snickers

sound around the table at his question.

"Still recovering," I lie. "I haven't even put a gun in her hand yet."

"She's a soft, little thing, isn't she?" His knowing smile sends hot fury through my blood, but I remain stoic as I give him a small smile and a nod.

"Real soft."

The guys all laugh again, but Barrett's eyes are narrowing on me, probably wondering why I haven't jumped to his bait. He can't know how my feelings for Genevieve have gone well and above being her caretaker or trainer.

It doesn't matter how I feel, or how Barrett feels, or what they think they're going to gain once that girl is trained, because I'm beginning to realize I will break all the rules, at any cost, to make sure she gets out. I never want her to be a slave to an MC again.

"You let me know if you need some help to toughen her up." Bear leans forward with a wink.

"Will do." I curl my hands into fists under the table.

I still haven't figured out who it was that violated her, or even if it was just one, but right now, my money is on Barrett or Bear. Both of whom seem to be slipping further into a dark place. Barrett's age is showing, but it's the frequency of his forgetful moments that's making me wonder just how far the decline has gone.

I don't disclose the fact that I sent Genevieve's hair and blood to her brother, nor do I let them know that for the last week, she's been hitting every target with stunning accuracy. Also, my sister says she fights like a feral animal. She doesn't let up until her mouth is around the jugular and her teeth sinking precariously into the skin.

I don't know if Victor Varga saw these things in his daughter, or if he just hoped they were there, but I bet he's shining proudly from wherever he is.

"All right, that's it." Barrett waves this hand, dismissing

us. We all stand to the clashing sounds of scraping chairs, and I sigh with relief. No one was shot in the head today. That's always a good sign.

"Malik." Barrett's voice cuts us all off as we stand still. "Stay behind for a minute, will you?" Malik is still in his chair, not having risen when the rest of us did. Almost like he knew he'd be asked to stay.

Nothing about this feels right, and now I'm more worried than ever about leaving Genevieve tonight. Ajani comes up beside me as we walk out of the room, our shoulders brushing, but we keep looking straight ahead and don't utter a single word until we get behind the large double doors of the medical wing.

"They're planning to grab her," he says as soon as the doors close behind us.

"We don't know that." I pace as I flick my cut out behind me, preventing the leather from rubbing along my arms.

"I know you heard the same words Barrett said." Ajani stands there, his eyes narrowed on me as they flit back and forth, following my pacing. "But did you hear the suggestion that laid just beneath? The fucking threat in his tone?"

I groan as I run my fingers through my hair. I did hear those things, but admitting them out loud would only serve to ramp up this uneasy feeling inside me. "I need to keep my head on straight, and we need to figure this out," I tell him.

I've noticed over the last few days that Ajani and Genevieve are starting to warm up to each other, and even though she's speaking to me, she has yet to say a single word to him. I know her voice is directly correlated to her trust, and once you've earned it, she graces you with that honeyed tenor.

Jealousy is an emotion I'm not familiar with, but when I think about Ajani hearing Genevieve speak, I can admit it's there. Its sticky tendrils are threatening to slip through me, making me want to push her to be mine. I don't have a claim on her, nor can I imagine trying to claim her, but I don't know how I would handle it if my best friend fell in love with her.

"Please tell me you're thinking up a foolproof plan,

brother," Ajani murmurs. "Because the hole you're wearing into the tile tells me it's going to be a good one."

"Okay." I stop with my hands on my waist as I face him. "We have an amazing security system, top of the line." He nods for me to continue. "And we have Delia. We could ask her to stay for the night."

"That's the best you got? An alarm system that takes over twenty minutes for someone to respond. And your sister? Who has to sleep with headphones on?" He falls back to the counter with a huff. "I guess we don't have any other choice."

"It's just one night."

GENEVIEVE
BMW Motorrad Milano

SIXTEEN

"How would I kill someone?"

"I've heard poison is good," Delia says as her hands land on her knees, her words sounding breathy as she drags in air.

"No, I mean, if I'm fighting someone. How would I kill someone if I didn't have a gun or a knife?"

"I'm not a killer, V," Delia tells me as she straightens, her eyebrows coming together in confusion. "I've never been put in a position where I've had to kill someone with my bare hands. I've never killed anyone. Don't get me wrong, I'm not judging you for how you're feeling because I know you've been through some real awful shit, but I think that question is best suited for my brother."

"Yeah. I'm sorry." I exhale audibly before I shake my head, then shake out my hands. "It was silly of me to ask you that."

"You're already an amazing fighter," Delia praises. "I've never witnessed someone learn so fast. Can you be better? Absolutely, and I think you will be, but I've taught you everything I know at this point."

Disappointment slips over me, and then immediately after, I feel ashamed. If it weren't for Delia, I wouldn't know what

I do right now, and I'm happy to at least be able to protect myself if I should need to.

"I appreciate everything you've done for me. I hope you know that. I don't want to learn how to kill someone so I can go on a killing spree," I tell her. "I've been having these flashbacks at night, and each time I'm back there in that basement, bent over a filthy table with intense pain..." My words sound disconnected with no feeling, nothing but apathy, but deep inside, I feel like I'm dying. "I just thought if I knew or had the skill to kill someone with my bare hands, then maybe I could sleep easier at night."

"I'm so sorry, V." Delia deflates as tears cloud over her eyes. "I don't know that having the capability to kill someone with your bare hands would take away the trauma you're experiencing. You've already taken an enormous step by talking to me and telling me what little you can, but maybe if you could speak to my brother, he could help you more."

"He ends up in bed with me a couple nights a week," I admit to her as her mouth drops open. "Oh, God!" I hold up my hands, a laugh escaping me. "Not like that! I guess I wake him up with my screaming, and he's been making sure I feel safe enough to get some sleep."

"You're totally going to marry my brother." She grins.

"I'm not marrying anyone." I let loose a sarcastic chuckle, maintaining eye contact. "Ever."

Marriage is not everything it's cracked up to be, and I'd have to be willing to divide my attention. I don't have such luxury.

"But you are speaking to him?" Her voice flares with hope.

"Yes, only in the bedroom after my nightmares, nothing else."

"That's so good." She smiles. "It's progress."

"I just need the nightmares to stop and then I can just forget everything."

"They may never stop." She gives me the cold, hard truth. Her eyes widen to emphasize what she's saying as her hand stretches out between us. "Or they won't stop until you've faced everything you've been through, from beginning to end. The mind is an intricate thing and learning how to master it is something very few discover, but first I think you need to take the time to find yourself again. You've already come so far."

"Genevieve! Delia!" we hear Diego yell out as he comes into the house, his voice sounding a bit panicked. "I need to talk to you guys!"

We rush upstairs to find him once again pacing his usual line in front of the island.

"Brother," Delia says on a chuckle. "Now I know why you never gain weight, no matter how many tacos we scarf down on Tuesdays."

"Something has come up." He stops pacing to look at us. My heart dives as the words slip from his lips, and then I curse myself. No matter how tough I try to be, my insides still quicken with fear. "Ajani and I have to go on a run to the warehouse tonight, and we have to camp out to keep a lookout. I won't be back until tomorrow morning."

Oh no. I can feel sweat forming along my spine, the droplets slowly running down toward the base of my back, but I continue to look at him with a blank expression.

"Delia, you will stay here tonight, and if you guys lock up and use the security system properly, everything should be okay."

"We'll be fine." Delia gives me a wide smile. "This girl can seriously kick some ass."

"I'll be leaving you my gun," Diego tells me. "Keep it beside you while you're sleeping, and if you hear anything, don't hesitate to shoot." I give him a nod. "Delia, give her your cell phone tonight so I'm able to text her, or she can call me if something happens." Delia nods as he gives me a pointed look. He's talking about my nightmares, so I give him another nod. "I promise it'll be okay, and Delia won't let anything happen to either of you."

"She can take care of herself." Pride shines in Delia's eyes when I look at her. "You should find out for yourself," Delia says. "She could probably take you down."

"I might just take her up on that when I get back." From the moonlight pouring in from the window I see he gives me a sweet smile, but his eyes burn with the same desire I saw the first time I said his name.

Feelings are brewing between us, and I know if I gave myself just a bit of leeway to feel them, Diego would own me heart and soul, but I'm not ready yet. I haven't avenged my father or Ma, and until then, I can't give myself over to someone just in case I don't succeed.

"Ajani is waiting for me back at the clubhouse. I came to throw a bag together for us." His eyes are still boring into mine, begging me to tell him I'll be okay. I soften my eyes and briefly nod, hoping it relays the confidence I'm not feeling.

"Seriously, Diego," Delia huffs out. "V is hella strong. She's got this."

"V, huh?" He grins at me. "I like it."

I nod to him, letting him know I like it too, and he chuckles. "All right, V. Make sure you call me if you need anything."

Delia and I watch her brother leave, and he warns us for what feels like the hundredth time to make sure we set the alarm for the house.

"Let's go finish out our lesson for the day," Delia says as she heads back down toward the basement. I give one last look at the front door, my heart pounding up somewhere near my throat. "I'll sleep in Ajani's bed tonight," Delia calls as she goes down the stairs.

A few hours later, we drag ourselves up the stairs, both of us utterly exhausted. I pushed myself a little harder this time so I would be that much more exhausted tonight. I'm hoping not to be awoken by another night terror.

Delia claims the shower first as she complains about the sweat clinging to her body.

"Fine." I roll my eyes and head to my room. I open the door and stop short when I see familiar-looking luggage on the floor at the end of my bed. "What the fuck?" I hiss as I step closer.

The pink-lacquered exterior is reminiscent of a girl who no longer exists, the bright hue making nausea swirl in my stomach. Did Diego bring this here?

Maybe my brother received my hair and threw away my things?

It really doesn't make sense.

I swallow down my fear because I'm so tired of feeling it, and grab the suitcase by the handle, throwing it up on my bed. I quickly open it up and gasp when I see the contents. It's filled with my clothes. My old clothes, but not what I wore daily. It has lingerie and stilettos, pantyhose, and thigh-highs ribbed with black lace.

Did Diego break into my old house just to steal my lingerie?

My heart picks up again at the thought of wearing any of this for him. Is that what he wants? Does he feel like that's what he deserves for all he's done for me? Angrily, I begin to throw the contents onto my bed, whipping the fragile material piece by piece until I see one of my old, leather miniskirts and a white, lace crop top.

"What the fuck?"

On the other side of my luggage are my hibiscus shampoo and conditioner, my coconut bodywash, and a razor that was probably sitting in my bathtub.

Now this part I can appreciate.

DIESEL

MALIK

I bet she smells of flowers right now, I think to myself as I lean against a tree across the street from Diego's house. I was told to monitor the Steel Dragon's compound, but fuck that, this is where I need to be. As much as he is my President, I don't answer to him. I didn't feel so good after that meeting with Barrett. Something tells me he may be here tonight. As much as he denies it, he seems a little obsessed over Princess Varga.

It probably has something to do with how many times he dipped his dick into her.

Surprisingly, I'm jealous of that dick. I want to dip my dick in her too, but I want her to want it. I'm not big on rape. I like a warm, wet pussy. I want it to milk my fat cock dry. What's the point otherwise?

The sun went down about an hour ago, and my phone has been pinging with messages. No doubt Barrett wants an update, but fuck him because I don't got one. He knew what he was getting into when he made me Vice, but it wasn't like he had a choice.

I keep my eye on her bedroom window and watch as the drapes blow gently in the breeze. She has her window open. It's just a crack, inconspicuous to any passerby, but I'm not any passerby, and neither are any of my brothers.

That's another reason I can't leave. For the life of me, I can't figure out if she was just very pampered or dumb as nails. I don't need a girl to be intelligent. I've never cared beyond what's between their legs, but it's a pleasant surprise when they speak and use words over three syllables long.

She still has her light on in there, so maybe when she gets into bed, she'll close the fucking window. Then I can head over to the Steel Dragon's compound to see what I can find out there. Otherwise, I'm stuck babysitting and Barrett can suck my dick.

I know Diego's little sister is in there with her. That one I could never figure out if she was a lesbian or not. She's been out to a few compound parties, but she was never interested in any of the guys, and I swear her biceps are bigger than Diego's.

Although the thought of having her slap me around in bed is making me grow hard. I blame it on mommy issues. The house to the right of Diego's has a car suddenly pulling into the driveway, and then idling. It's not one I recognize, but I don't like that no one is getting out and that driveway provides a perfect view into Princess Varga's bedroom. I'm just about to get to my feet when the car pulls back out and speeds down the road.

"Motherfucker," I mutter, because that had Barrett written all over it. Whoever it was probably caught sight of me over here, forcing them to tuck their tails between their legs and head back to their old geezer of a leader. I'm sure I'll have to face him tomorrow.

But that's a new day. I still haven't accomplished what I wanted to tonight.

My eyes land back on her window, and I curse when I notice her light is out and those lacey fucking curtains are still blowing in the breeze. I get it. These Arizona nights can run a little hot, but that's what the fucking AC is for.

I guess this means I need to make sure everything is okay. Just one little peek won't hurt anybody. Once I'm on my feet, I saunter across the street. The breeze kicks up my hair, brushing the strands across my face. Now I understand why she leaves the window open. I can admit the breeze is refreshing. The days are hot and dry, but when those breezes come through at night, it's nice. I get it. Nevertheless, she's a stupid bitch.

This is what happens when you grow up with privilege. You forget that you have a certain bubble that protects you from the dangers of the world, and even though Princess Varga had her bubble popped in a sick way, she hasn't really learned her lesson.

Right under her window is an annoying bush. I don't know why Diego doesn't just cut the fucking shit up because it's dying, brittle, and also has fucking thorns. I don't even know what this bush is supposed to be. It has no flowers, and it's fucking ugly, not to mention dangerous. It's a good thing I'm wearing my boots.

Standing in front of her window, the sill hits the top of my shoulders, and when I look inside the room, I see her face illuminated by a cell phone as she smiles at the screen.

Again, that weird feeling of jealousy bubbles inside of me, creating a feeling similar to gas. Only it's more annoying because I can't release it unless I slap my fist into Diego's face. I could do that.

She releases a long sigh and turns off the phone, dousing her pretty face in shadows as she places it on the table next to her bed. That's when I notice she has her bras and panties thrown about the room. It's pretty careless. I went through a lot of trouble breaking into her fucking house to get that shit. She's not very appreciative.

She turns over in bed, her back facing me and her leg swinging over her pillow as she hauls it in to cuddle. The blanket slips off of her and I see her ass is looking a little too skinny in her boy-cut shorts. There's not enough meat on there, which is a shame. Princess Varga would look stunning with more than a handful on each ass cheek. Does Diego not feed her? Can she not cook? That's a problem because I can't either. We'll starve to death if it's just the two of us.

Her shoulders rise and fall as she succumbs to sleep, and then I watch a little longer for no real reason but to stare at her ass again. It's still a hot ass, even if it is a bit on the small side. *Yeah, now it's getting a little weird.*

I'm not a stalker or anything. I just want to make sure she's okay and everything is looking good so I can pat myself on the back. Job well done.

I kick aside the stupid bush and sit on the wooden frame encasing it. I don't really feel comfortable leaving here after seeing the car earlier, but now I'm going to get bored because what more can I do when everyone is sleeping? Nothing interesting is happening, and I don't really feel like going over to the Steel Dragon's anymore. I let out a loud sigh just as a whimper filters out through the window.

Is the Princess crying?

After everything she's been through, she's going to cry because Montez isn't home? It's strange. Jealousy rears its ugly head again, and I begin to feel similar to how I felt as a child. Princess Varga likes Diego more than me, not that she's had a chance to get to know me. I should rectify that.

This time, the whimper ends on a loud moan, the sound anguished and frightened. Once again, I'm on my feet, kicking aside the mangey bush and looking inside the room. I find her on her back with the blanket wrapped around her legs as her body contorts with fear. Immediately, I recognize the symptoms of having a nightmare. I've had so many of my own. I'm unprepared for how affected I am when her head tips back and a scream rips from her throat. My reaction is immediate as my blade slips through the screen of her window. I rip it apart and push her window up farther.

I haul myself over the ledge just as her legs thrash against the mattress and the blanket billows down toward the floor. Her head swings back and forth and the cries that erupt from her chest sound like a siren's cry, the pitch squeezing my heart as I run toward the bed.

"Hey, Princess Varga," I say as I stand beside her. She continues to thrash as tears begin to slip down her cheeks. "Genevieve." My hand lands on her shoulder as I gently shake her.

Her eyes pop open on a loud wail. When her pretty, blue eyes meet mine, she sucks in a breath and her fist flies out, connecting perfectly with my dick.

My vision explodes in brilliant hues of red as pain spreads up and through my stomach. It takes everything in me not to throw up on her fucking face, but while I'm concentrating on my gag reflex, I can't control my physical reaction. I wrap my hand around her throat, pressing a knee into her solar plexus as I bring my face down to hers. Our noses brush as she struggles to breathe and her little fingers grip onto my wrists as she tries to free her throat.

"Why the fuck did you do that?" I grit out between my teeth, my spit flying all over her face.

GENEVIEVE
BMW Motorrad Milano

SEVENTEEN

Laith Charles is in my bedroom with his hand wrapped around my throat, squeezing the very life out of me. His nose brushes along mine as he growls something into my face, but the buzzing in my ears is so loud that I can't decipher a single word he's saying. Not that I care, because he's literally killing me. So once again, I ball up my fist, and in my last act of desperation to save my fucking life, I slam it into his temple.

That does the trick, forcing him to stumble back and his hand finally releasing my throat. I suck in a breath, my choking gasps filling the air around us as his dark chuckle intertwines with the sound.

"That was a good hit." He pushes himself off the wall and rubs his temple. "That was actually a great hit." He winces a few times and I can only imagine the pain he's feeling in his head and balls.

His voice doesn't sound right and there's something about his face that's off. I scrutinize him in the moon's illumination, my eyes quickly roving over his torso and up toward his face. Something's not right.

"Oh." He nods as he points his finger in my face. "You're trying to figure out who I am." His voice is wrong. Too deep and almost whimsical. The way his mouth tips up into a mocking grin isn't what I remember of Laith, and those eyes, their dark depths brimming with mischief, are nothing compared to Laith's gentle browns. He steps forward as I push myself up to sitting in the bed, scrambling backward until my back meets the headboard. "Like what you see?" he asks, his eyes looking manic.

I shake my head, words escaping me, rendering me speechless. I couldn't speak, even if I wanted to. He looks around my room, at the mass of my bras and panties, and then flicks his eyebrow up. When he does look at me again, his face breaks out into a wide smile, and that's when it hits me. I don't see any scars on his cheeks. "Do you know how hard it was to get into your house when your brother wasn't home? Then to find which room was yours and take all this for you?"

My jaw drops in shock as I stare at Laith's twin brother and absorb the information he's telling me.

"You broke into my house?" I ask incredulously.

"Hey, did Diego's younger sister teach you how to fight like that?" He rubs at his temple again, changing the direction of the conversation. "It's not bad. I bet if you put a little more meat on your bones, the hits would be a lot harder. What else are they teaching you?"

"You're Laith's brother." I tip my head to the side, feeling more shocked than scared.

"Right, we haven't formally been introduced, but you do know my brother, Laith."

"He's a good man." Even though I hate them all, I won't lie about Laith's character.

"He's pathetic and weak. Something I thought you were," he says matter of factly and snaps his fingers. "But just like that, you've changed into a tough girl now, huh?"

"I've had no other choice."

"We all have choices. So did you, but you picked the right one." He shrugs and then bends down, picking up my leather miniskirt. "Speaking of choices, do you want to go have some fun?" I shake my head as he finds the crop top, holding both items up, pinched between his thumbs and forefingers. "Tell me I didn't pick out a hot outfit." He gives me a wink.

"How do I know you're not here to kill me?" The way this man flips back and forth from interrogating to conversating is hard to keep up with.

"Because,"—he shakes his head as his thick hair tumbles around his shoulders—"you'd already be dead."

"What are you doing here? Why did you bring my stuff? And why did you cut through my screen to get in my room?" I rapidly fire questions at him, hoping he'll answer at least two.

"Because the man who was raping you repeatedly was waiting for the perfect moment to slip inside. He knew Diego and Ajani weren't home, so I was here protecting you." He sounds so nonchalant about it, his body relaxed as he stares at me.

"I don't understand—"

"Come on, Princess Varga, let's go have some fun," he cuts me off.

"Don't call me that." I feel my cheeks heat with anger.

"I'll call you whatever the fuck I want." His eyes flash again with a manic energy. "And if you don't like it, you'll have to rip my tongue out of my mouth. Go on," he taunts me. "Rip my fucking tongue out." I vibrate with anger, my fingers curling into a fist. "That's what I thought."

That's what I thought.

He's the one who threw me over his shoulder when we left my house that night. He's the one who taunted Chino.

"It was you." My heart begins to pound with the recognition as I bring my knees up to my chest.

"Is this a guessing game? I hate games. I must warn you, I don't like to lose—"

"You're the one who grabbed me that night," I reiterate, cutting off his attempt to redirect me.

He throws the skirt and top onto my bed as his head tips to the side. "We all have choices," he repeats. "Mine were to obey or die, and no one is killing me but myself. So I made a choice. Now, will you get the fuck up out of that bed? I have an idea."

"You're crazy." I shake my head.

"Maybe." He nods before speaking once more. "I mean… probably. But if we stay here all night debating that, I promise you, that's a terrible choice."

My mouth tips up involuntarily as I slowly look around the room. "I can't leave the house, Delia's here."

"Delia's dick is probably bigger than mine. She can take care of herself."

A snort flies from my nose as I slap a hand over my mouth. It feels good to be carefree again, but the weight of my guilt quickly tampers it back down. This man had a hand in what happened to Ma and Dad.

"Did you kill my father's wife and tie up Jaeger?"

He pauses as his brows come together and his mouth turns downward. "I had no part in that." His features are clouded over with anger. "I don't kill people who don't deserve it."

"Did you see her get killed?"

"No." He rubs a finger along his lips. "We showed up to do what we did and that was to take you. That was the deal. What happened before then? I know nothing about it."

I don't know why, but I believe him. I feel like he would have no problem admitting to things he *chose* to do.

"She didn't deserve to die."

"Baby girl, she is dead, whether she deserved it or not. That's out of our hands, but do you know what's in our hands?" I raise my brow at his question. "Deciding on if we should have some fun. I know this place. It's a strip joint run by a bunch of pussies called Glitz. Have you heard of it?"

He knows I've heard of it. My eyes narrow as I retort, "That's the Steel Dragon's strip club."

His finger wags toward me as he chuckles. "Yeah, you know it."

"They think I'm dead. Diego and Ajani sent them my

hair and blood. I don't think I should suddenly show up alive. Wouldn't that defeat the entire purpose?"

"Jesus rose from the dead on the third day. I did my research."

"What?" Confusion hits me at his words. Is he religious?

"You'll be revered as the girl who can't die. Maybe they'll write you a third testament." A snort flies from my mouth as I shake my head. "So answer me, Princess." He falls forward on the bed, his hands sinking into the plush comforter, and bringing his face mere inches from mine. "Are we going to have some fun?" The way his mouth curls upward and his eyes sparkle is beginning to sway me.

I take a deep breath, inhaling sandalwood from his cologne as my teeth sink into my bottom lip. The thought of seeing any Steel Dragon sets my anxiety off, but at the same time, I have nothing to be afraid of. Malik is right, we all have choices, and Jaeger and Quinton both made theirs. I would love nothing more than to see the fear in their eyes at seeing me alive and well.

"That's what I'm talking about." Malik claps and throws my skirt and top in my face. "Wear that. Oh, and,"—he bends down, picking up the smallest g-string off my floor, and tosses it at me—"with that."

Then he walks out of my bedroom and into the kitchen. I hear the fridge door open, then the hiss of a beer can.

"Hurry up, Princess, we don't got all night."

The neon sign blinks a bright pink, the word *Glitz* illuminating the top of the entrance. I step out of the cab behind Malik, mindful of my skirt riding up as the heels I bought earlier today click against the pavement. Trepidation and anticipation swirl together in my gut as Malik reaches behind him and clasps his big hand around mine. I'm actually doing this.

"Come on, Princess. You see that bouncer up there?" His

chin juts toward the large, bald, white man standing in front of the door, his bulging biceps crossed over his chest. "He always mistakes me for my brother."

"Well, you guys are identical."

"No, we're not." He gives me a grin over his shoulder. "I put holes in his face so people could tell the difference."

"That's sick," I snarl at him as his shoulders shake with laughter.

"It was a choice," he tells me, "and he knows why I did it. That's all that matters." Malik leads us straight up to the bouncer, bypassing the large line and says, "Let us in."

My heart is in my throat as this guy looks over the both of us. Malik doesn't have a cut, and thankfully, this guy doesn't know I'm Vic's daughter. So after five of the longest seconds of my life, he nods and moves aside, motioning for both of us to go inside.

Malik's stride doesn't break as he eats up the floor, walking through Glitz like he owns the place. He's not worried about being recognized, he literally doesn't care, and I feel myself relaxing. For the first time, I forget everything that's happened to me, and right here, tonight, I'm somebody else.

Malik heads directly for a private booth in the back corner, his shoulders swaying with the exaggerated swagger of his walk. I'd be lying if I said I wasn't feeling every step in my lower belly. He has the sort of confidence that only comes with being dangerous, knowing you are the single, most apex predator in the room only equates to possessing a God-like complex. It seeps from Malik's very pores.

He slides into a booth, and when I move to slide in across from him, he yanks on my arm, dragging me back to sit beside him.

"If we both sit here," he whispers in my ear, the sound muffled by the music around us. "Then we both get the perfect view of the stage."

The way his lips brush along the shell of my ear sends goose bumps along my skin. It's the warmth of his breath combined with the velvet feel of his lips that's creating an inferno inside of me. It's not a sensation I'm accustomed to, given what happened with Quinton and then in Hell's March basement, but tonight I'm soaking it all up.

"What can I get you, Laith?"

I look up to find the girl Jaeger likes to toy with. Angel is her name. She's not paying me any mind as her eyes eat up every inch of Malik. She's so fucking dumb for not seeing the differences between the twin brothers.

"A bottle of champagne," he demands and then waves her away. "Be quick about it." That's not even how Laith speaks. He would never be so disrespectful. He must see the questions in my eyes because he says, "Yes, she's got shit for brains, but she thinks I'm Laith because my brother would never come here. To her, I am him because she knows no better."

"She sees him frequently at the clubhouse," I counter as I pull back to look at him.

"That's a different atmosphere."

"Then there are the two holes you put in his face."

"Lighting, Princess." He throws his arm over my shoulders as smoke rises around the stage.

Sensual music begins, the drumbeat low and steady, amplifying the lust that's laying thick around us. My core is heated and pulsing to the beat as Malik's fingertips glide along my shoulder.

"Did you want to kill him?" I ask, the words sounding husky with desire.

"Are you my psychiatrist?" He sounds slightly amused.

"No, but you certainly need one," I retort.

The bucket of ice holding a champagne bottle is placed in the center of the table at the same time Malik's arm slips around my waist and hauls me into his lap, my back meeting his chest. My heart picks up with the heat of him surrounding me. Angel's eyes finally settle on my face, widening with what I can only assume is recognition.

"Let me tell you what I *need*, Princess," he croons in my ear, his hardening cock resting against my ass. "I need to make some sort of scene, because when that bitch goes running to the back to call your brother, this will be the last time I can step foot in here."

"You want to make a scene?" I ask over my shoulder. The way my body ignites with his touch is hard to ignore, and my hips move of their own accord, grinding down onto his cock.

Angel begins to back away just as the curtain on stage opens, and out walks Carrie. The last time I saw her, she was running out of Chino's room after I popped her in the mouth. Looks like she recovered fine, no bruising or evidence of lifelong trauma. Then again, Quinton didn't watch her being kidnapped and did nothing about it.

"Know her?" Malik's breath hits my ear, making me moan.

"Yes," I answer him as I squirm on his lap. Angel's presence slowly disappears as Malik takes over.

"Do you want my cock inside of you, Princess? Here in a crowded strip joint owned by your brother? Do you want that stripper on stage to watch?"

Once again, my hips jerk, moving over his steel length, and this time, I'm hauling a groan out of him. His calloused fingers grip the short hem of my leather mini as he drags it upward, exposing me inch by slow inch.

Do I want Malik to fuck me? I don't fear it as much as I thought I would, but I don't have feelings for him beyond lust. Which is clouding all my thoughts at the moment, effectively making me crave this man's touch.

The man who took me from my home, dumped me in the back of a filthy van, and shut the doors on my face with a grin. But that girl was a different me, not the one gyrating her hips on top of the man who helped break her.

They broke me, but I'm building myself back up, stronger than I've ever been.

My skirt is bunched up around my waist as Malik lifts me

slightly, just enough to run his fingers over my panty-clad pussy.

"You're so wet, Princess," he rasps. "Are you going to let me taste this?"

Am I?

Using my palms as leverage on the table, I hoist myself up to sit in front of him, facing him and opening my legs wide. His reaction is priceless as his mouth falls open, giving me a peek at a pierced tongue.

I no longer feel like myself, but if I'm being completely honest, I like who I am now more than I ever liked the girl who always wanted to please her daddy and big brother. I just wish it didn't take being kidnapped and brutally raped to find her.

My elbows hit the table as I lean back and grab the champagne bottle, the top already popped for us. As the mouth of the bottle hits my lips, I finally sever the last remaining ties to the girl I once was.

No more fear, no more hesitation.

The bubbles hit my tongue as they skate down my throat, warming my insides, and Malik watches me with rapt attention.

His brown eyes flare with an intensity so penetrating as the heat from consuming the alcohol washes over me. Never has anyone looked at me like this, and it's powerful, making me feel salacious. Something I've never felt before.

Malik has an energy that screams danger and after everything I've been through, I should heed the warning, but I can't seem to help myself when I spread my legs farther and tip the champagne bottle, letting the bubbling liquid course down over my mound and hit the table with loud splashes.

I can feel the attention from a table beside us filled with men. Their stares hit the side of my face, but I don't care right now. Everything is tunneled on Malik with that bar through his tongue. He has my sole attention.

Malik's finger runs over the soaked material of my g-string as his tongue flicks out to run along his plump lower lip. "You're gonna let me feast right here at the table, Princess?" His smirk literally sets me on fire.

His hands grip around my waist as he drags me to the edge of the table, and then he's pulling my underwear off in one motion, ripping the delicate lace in the process.

The heavy beat of Escort by Chase Atlantic flows over me as Malik slips a thick finger inside my pussy. My head tips back, providing an upside-down view of the stage and Carrie's naked body moving with the beat.

Just as the smoke billows up around the stage, Malik removes his finger and his mouth seals around my clit with a suction so strong, my ass leaves the table and a scream erupts from my throat.

A vision of long, luxurious hair appears in my mind, his head between my legs, and the sensations threaten to pull me back in time. I don't want to think of him though. I try my hardest to suppress it, but Chino is here with me because his is the only other experience I can compare this to. Where he devoured me, opened me up, and craved me, Malik is worshiping me. I'm starting to understand how this man operates, and I've barely spent any time in his presence. I don't need to though. He doesn't hide behind a facade. What you see is what you get.

I don't think this man does anything with half effort. If I were to judge him based solely on this one instance, based completely on the way he's using his tongue, fingers, and teeth, I would say Malik Charles gives a hundred-and-fifty-percent to any task laid in front of him. And I am currently that task.

His wet lips run along the inside of my thigh as his devilish eyes meet mine. The spark ignited in their dark depths brings heat to my cheeks.

"Your stripper friend is watching you," he murmurs against my skin. "She's watching you as I eat your pussy. Do you think she's jealous?"

His words only serve to make me widen my legs farther, and as he brings his mouth back to my aching core, I pour more champagne down over my mound, letting it slip between my lips and his. If Carrie is watching like Malik says she is, then I want this scene she's witnessing to be retold to Chino in stunning clarity.

Malik laps up every bit of champagne from between my legs as I bring the rim of the bottle back to my mouth and chug as much as I can before my throat burns from the carbonation. I've never been much of a drinker, but I've never been this version of myself either.

My lower stomach coils, my body gearing up for a combustion at the hands and mouth of a sinfully delicious man. A man whom I can only imagine relishes in all things evil. He latches on to my hardened nub and sucks as he slips two thick fingers deep inside me. When our eyes meet, I let go of all my restraint, exploding around him.

My legs shake with the force, my mouth hangs open in complete euphoria, but my eyes never waver from his. That mischievous twinkle is still there, but beyond that, I see something pure and beautiful. I decide right here and now that Malik Charles is mine. He must see the sentiment reflected in my irises because his eyes widen a fraction with surprise before he pulls himself from between my legs and stands up to hover over me, our mouths barely a breadth's width apart.

My release lines his lips and chin, the moisture glistening from the low, ambient lights. I can smell myself on him as it intertwines with champagne and something uniquely Malik. The mix is enticing. I close the distance between us, just so I can covet the taste. Malik Charles kisses with the same intensity I see in his eyes. His lips burn hot, his tongue scorches, and his hands trail flames over my body.

He was always meant to come and bury the last vestiges of Genevieve Varga, and like the Phoenix, I'm now rising from the ashes a new person. A woman free of the confines of grief, empowered by the atrocities I've endured, and never to be the victim ever again.

Thanks to Delia, I think V Varga will stick.

The kiss turns brutal as he grabs my hips, pulling my core against his rough jeans and grinding his cock between my legs while our teeth clash in a war of fueled lust.

He pulls away, his mouth curving upward, and his teeth nipping at his bottom lip, but his eyes still radiate with a vulnerability buried deep under his trained, hardened stare. I'm going to make it my mission to find out every little thing about Malik, because I can feel the very core of his soul mirroring my own.

"We have company, Princess." He leans forward to nip at my lip before continuing. "We need to get going before we're both bleeding out on the strip joint's floor."

"What?" Confusion makes me sit up straight.

"Let's go, baby. Our Uber is waiting outside."

"Uber? When…" I stare at him, trying to decipher what he's saying.

He hoists me up over his shoulder, the very same one I hung off of once before, but this time, my hands run down over his muscular back then follows the curve of his ass. I grab it in handfuls, making him laugh as he hurries through the club. I hear the sharp sound of metal clanging and then the fresh night air on the back of my legs as my name is screamed out from behind us.

"Genni!"

Malik steps outside, his boots hitting the cement sidewalk as the hinges of the metal door squeak. I look up just before it closes to find Chino standing about twenty feet away, his hair a tangled mess around his shoulders and his face pale and haggard.

My heart soars at the look of utter desolation on his face, and I lift my hand, wiggling my fingers in a gleeful goodbye as the door finally shuts.

I'm tossed into the back of a car, my ass hitting the seat just before Malik is on top of me. He shuts the door as his hand travels from my thigh up to my stomach, and I realize my skirt is still up around my waist. He gives the driver a nasty look, and the car begins to move.

"Stay with me tonight?" I ask as my fingers slip up and into his hair.

"Diego will kill me."

Diego.

My heart beats a little faster at the thought of the man who risked everything to save a girl he knew nothing about. Just as it beats faster for the man who's pressing his lips to my neck.

I want them both.

DIEGO

DIEGO

Ajani opens the door just as the sun is cresting over the horizon. We're both dead tired and all for a deadbeat errand. Nothing happened, and Ajani and I truly believe we were sent out there on a fool's mission just to be separated from Genevieve. The only reason I hadn't rushed home was because she was texting me for most of the night, and her last message I received from two hours ago still warms my heart with the thought.

Come to my bed when you get back.

My cock has been hard the whole time, and even though there's still a part of me that remembers the broken girl I found in the basement, I can't help but feel this way toward her. I can't help but want her, and if she is feeling the same, I won't hesitate.

My leather cut hangs heavy on my shoulders as I kick off my boots and unstrap the holster from around my waist. Usually I take it to my room and put it away in my drawer, but exhaustion has my eyes nearly sealing shut as I make my way to her bedroom door.

I quietly open it, not wanting to wake her since she fell asleep quite late. A yawn steals my breath as I step into the room, my mouth wide open and my eyes closed, but when I open them, the sight before me has me wide awake. Panties and bras are littered all over the generally pristine floor, and two forms lie still in her bed. I grab my gun, letting the holster hit the floor with a loud clang. Still, neither of them moves. I round the bed to press the barrel of my gun to his forehead as my eyes skim over the ripped screen in her window.

"Man, I've been laying here and waiting since I heard that front door open. You're getting slower, Montez," Malik rumbles as he stretches his arms over his head, not bothered in the slightest having a gun pressed to his forehead.

I don't miss the content way Genevieve has her head on his bare chest, or how her hand is gripping his waist. I'm thankful he has his pants on and she is wearing what looks like his T-shirt because even though this is suggestive enough, I don't know that I would be staring down into Malik's still-formed skull if she were naked.

"You broke into my house," I whisper harshly as Genni stirs.

"Came in through the window. I didn't break anything." His eyes finally crack open to look at me. "Fine, I ripped the screen. *Whoopty doo.*"

"Diego?" Genevieve moans, stretching as she turns onto her back, those dark blue eyes slowly opening to focus on me. "Come to bed." She pats the very narrow space on her other side.

"Yeah, Diego,"—Malik grins, shoving the gun from his forehead—"come to bed."

I continue to stare into Genevieve's eyes. I can instantly tell there's something different about her. She's not the same woman I left here yesterday. I have recognized the strength in her and how much it grows each day, but I won't deny the heartbreak I'm feeling at seeing her cozied up with one of my brothers, and the most dangerous one at that.

My stomach sours when I think of her letting him into her bed, and then the acid threatens to shoot upward at the thought of him between her legs.

Maybe Ajani was right, maybe I am falling in love with Genevieve.

"Diego," she repeats, her voice raspy with sleep as she pushes herself up to her elbows. "I missed you." My eyes flick to Malik and the small smile he has playing around his mouth. Genevieve turns her head to look at Malik, and then she's looking back at me, her eyes begging for understanding. "He was looking out for me while you were gone," she begins her explanation, but it's hard to hear her words over the pounding of my heart in my ears. "Someone pulled up, but they saw him and left." I nod, unable to deny how grateful I am to him for being here, but the feeling doesn't stay. I'm once again drowning in misery. "Will you say something?"

Hearing her say that and the hypocrisy of the situation pulls a startled laugh from my chest. At the sound of my laugh, her giggle chimes in, and Malik looks back and forth between us with a confused look on his face.

He gets up out of bed, his toned chest flexing with his movements and the ram skull tattoo moving with the motion. "She wants you to lie down with her," he says. "Get on in there."

I'm not a stranger to threesomes. I've shared women, but the thought of climbing into bed with her after Malik has had her doesn't appeal to me.

"Malik and I…" Genevieve shakes her head. "We didn't… you know…" Does her admission make me feel better? Maybe, but it also makes me feel irrational. She's not mine and I have no ownership over what she wants to do, even if I would like nothing more than to make Genevieve Varga my Old Lady. "The way I feel about you, Diego," she says as she pushes up to her knees, Malik's T-shirt pooling around her body. "I'm so grateful for everything you've done, for giving me back my life. If this was the old me, I would be head over heels in love with you, but this new version of me has other priorities to take care of first. That doesn't mean I don't want you."

"Forgive me for being confused," I finally say as I scrape my gun's barrel against my temple. "You were just in bed with one of my brothers."

"I want him too." She shrugs her shoulders. "I know it's not normal, and maybe I'm nothing more than a used-up Club Bunny, but I don't want to have to choose."

She doesn't want to choose between Malik and me. I look over my shoulder to find the psychotic man leaning against the dresser, his thick arms crossed over his chest.

"I'm fine with it." He waves his hand between us. "I'm man enough to share her with you, and trust me, once you have a taste of her, you'll want to share too."

"You've tasted her?" I ask just as Genevieve's hands land on my stomach, her fingers digging into the T-shirt's material.

"He did," she admits as she begins to tug my shirt up over my head, revealing my own ram skull tattoo across my chest. "He had me spread on a table."

"Like a proper meal," Malik chimes in.

Her fingers skim over the piercings in my nipples, her black-painted nails scraping through the hair on my chest, matching Malik's. Did they paint their nails together?

"Don't you want to taste me too?" she whispers.

My hands wrap around her wrists as I pull her away from my body, her eyes widening with shock, and then quickly coating with dismay. I shove her back onto the bed, her body bouncing on the plush mattress as I unclasp my belt buckle.

"Spread out on a table, huh?" I undo my pants, letting the zipper slowly come unfastened on its own as my hard cock pushes against the metal. "My table? Did Malik Charles eat *my* woman on top of *my* table?"

"*Your* woman?" Genevieve asks, her eyes widening and her mouth inching upward as her hair fans out around her head and that T-shirt rides up high on her thighs. "Did you call me *your* woman?"

"You've been mine since the day I pulled you up out of that basement. I've just been waiting patiently for you to see the truth."

"This is sweet and all, but my hard-on has deflated, and I'm bored," Malik drawls, his voice filled with humor.

"You really want this one?" I thumb over my shoulder. "After he breaks into your window, and you spend a few hours with him?"

"The old me would want love, a foundation of loyalty and honesty. The old me would want one man to profess their life to me, to love me forever, but all of that is bullshit," she spits out as she drags up the hem of the T-shirt, revealing a lacey pair of panties. "I'm tired of living by the rules, of doing what everyone else wants me to do. I want both of you. Each of you brings something different to the table, and I would never force you to share me if you didn't want to." She had me at the lace panties. I yank my pants and boxers down, and she gasps as my cock springs free. "What is that?" She points.

I look down at the bar that's protruding through my skin, just above my cock, right where my pelvic bone protrudes. Malik leans forward, looking around to the front of me, knowing damn well what she's asking about. He was there when I got it done, and on the same day, he got the tip of his cock pierced.

"See these bumpy ridges?" he explains to Genevieve as he reaches around and runs his fingers over my piercing. A touch I'm not unaccustomed to. "When he's balls deep inside you, these two balls here will grind against your pretty little clit."

Her eyes widen as his fingers continue to glide over the bar through my skin. I'm not sure if it's because he's touching me or if it's because of what this piercing can do for her, but either way, I like how her legs spread open a little more, how color blooms on the peaks of her cheeks, and how that full, bottom lip gets sucked into her mouth, gripped between her teeth. If that's the reaction we're going to get, I can honestly say, I don't mind sharing her as long as I have her too.

Malik reaches into his cut that's folded on her dresser and throws a strip of condoms onto the bed and pats my shoulder. "I already got her off once," he says smugly. "It's your turn now."

"Just once?" I tsk and raise an eyebrow toward Malik before looking back at Genevieve and demand, "Take off those panties and spread your lips open. I wanna see how wet you are for us."

Her chest heaves underneath the T-shirt as my words have her both shocked and aroused. Few see this side of me, but I figure if we're in here being honest, I might as well tell her exactly how I like it in bed.

She drags those wet, lace panties down her legs, the material rolling as it descends, and with a quick flick of her foot, she sends them flying over my head.

"Get that shirt off too," Malik insists. "I want to see them titties." I smirk because she's picked two very dominant men, and even though my behavior is probably much of a surprise, Malik's shouldn't be. "Can you imagine those nice, dark pink nipples pierced?" he asks as he rubs his hands together. "I'd love to get her in the shop."

"You just like sticking a needle into anyone," I reply with a snicker.

She looks between us, her brows crumbling. "You're a piercer?"

"Who do you think did that?" He points to my piercing and then he's hauling down his own pants. "Look at this work of art." His thick cock is on display as he wraps his hand around the shaft, gripping it in his palm and pointing it at her face, giving her the perfect view of the three rings looped through his head.

"You did that to yourself?" she asks just as I fall on the bed, my face landing between her legs.

"Mm," I hum. "Look at this pretty clit." I spread her open with my fingers, my mouth watering at the sight. "How pretty would it look with a ring through it?"

"I could give her one to match the two hoops I'll put in those tits." With the first swipe of my tongue, her sweet essence floods my mouth, and her ass arches off the bed with a loud moan. "Isn't she so responsive?" Malik croons as he walks up to the side of the bed, pumping his cock in his palm, my eyes trailing his movements over her mound.

I dip my tongue deep into her core and scrape my teeth over her clit, forcing a strangled cry from her mouth. "Diego," she whimpers. "Please."

"She begs so pretty, brother," Malik tells me, and I look up to find him tweaking her nipples in his fingers.

I think I could share. My baser instincts were to claim her and own her completely, and that primal urge is still there deep inside, but as I watch Malik shove his fingers into her mouth, forcing a gag from her throat, I decide sharing will be a lot more fun. Her pussy clenches around my tongue as he continues to gag her, ripping a moan from my mouth.

I suck her clit into my mouth, furiously rubbing my tongue over the hardened nub, and slip two fingers deep inside her sopping wet core. The tips find the small, rough patch on the inside almost instantly. So, with the same rhythm as my tongue, I work hard to pull my very first orgasm from her.

She doesn't disappoint as her thighs lock up around my head, the muscles rippling and gripping me to her while her hips lift and her back bows in a perfect arch.

"Looks like Princess is going to come now," Malik teases just as she sucks in her breath to scream my name to the ceiling. Her core clenches around my fingers, steady pulsations making the grip tighten with every savage swipe of my tongue. I lean up and slowly pull my fingers out of her cunt, the juices dripping down my hand, and my chin is saturated with her release. I grab the strip of condoms just as Malik leans on the bed in front of my face, his eyes roaming all over my mouth.

"How good did she taste?" Malik's words are dripping with confidence. He already knows the answer.

I pull my bottom lip between my teeth, dragging it in a slow haul, gathering her essence from the surface of my skin as I stare at him. "So fucking sweet."

I can hear her whimpering on the bed, her legs shifting on either side of my thighs, but Malik shocks me when he leans in and swipes his tongue along my chin, collecting the drops of her release.

"Yeah, so sweet."

"Holy fuck," Genevieve whispers as I put a foil packet between my teeth and rip it open, my eyes never straying from Malik's.

"Next time you want to use that tongue on me, brother," I say as I roll the condom down my length. "Make sure it's around my fucking cock."

With my eyes still on his dark orbs dancing with humor, I yank Genevieve by her thighs until her pussy is pressing against my cock. She squirms, and in turn, receives a sharp slap to her clit, courtesy of Malik who's looking at her intently.

"Stay still," he grunts out as I grip my cock in my hand and slowly run it up and down her slit. His hand roughly runs back up over her stomach, and I sink into her just as he roughly grabs her tit.

"Oh, my god," she murmurs as I get halfway inside her and pump into her with shallow thrusts. "Yes, Diego."

"How many times did you make her come?" I ask Malik with a smirk.

"Look, we were short on time." He rolls his eyes, but his hand comes back down to furiously rub circles into her sensitive clit.

Her head thrashes back and forth and the noises coming from her throat are growing louder as her hands grip the bedsheets. Soon enough, Ajani and Delia are going to know exactly what's happening in here.

"Stuff her mouth and shut her up," I say to Malik.

He moves to stand above her head, one knee pressing into the mattress and his hands sinking into her thick hair. He yanks her head up to meet the tip of his cock, those three rings bouncing off her lips. "Open up, Princess, you're being too loud."

I slam the rest of the way into her as her mouth opens on a scream. Malik takes the opportunity to shove his cock right down her throat as I bend over and grind into her, my piercing hitting the right spot.

"She did say she wanted both of us," I say to Malik as he snickers.

"She did," he answers as he continues to thrust down her throat, her eyes watering and casting pretty tears over her cheeks. "Do you think she's going to regret it?"

Her pussy begins to tighten again, and her legs stiffen, forcing her ass to leave the bed. "I know her pussy won't."

I pull her pussy lips open, making sure that the pulsing little nub is pressed to the piercing as I grind into her, and just like that, her throat works around Malik's length as she tries to scream through her orgasm. Fluid runs down over my balls, hitting the bed in hot splashes, and I chuckle as her body vibrates with the force of her release.

"That was number two," I gloat when his eyes meet mine.

Malik's jaw tightens as his cock begins to jerk in her mouth, and I watch as her throat works to swallow every hot drop of his cum. He slips out of her mouth and gives me a dirty look. "I told you, my time was limited.”

Her pussy flexes with a few aftershocks as I dip my thumb into my mouth, swirling my tongue around the pad. I pull it out as a string of spit stretches between my thumb and my lip. “Let me see if I can’t get another one.”

“No, Diego,” she begs, her head flipping back and forth and her eyes landing on Malik standing at the side of the bed. “I can’t.”

I pull out of our wet, weeping pussy and flip her onto her stomach, chuckling again when Malik grabs her waist to prop her ass in the air. I get on my knees once more, lining my cock back up to her entrance as Malik slips a finger into her asshole, the tight hole saturated with her juices.

“One day, I’m forcing my cock in here,” he warns her.

“Yours wouldn’t be the first,” she snaps, and I see the flash of pain in her eyes when she looks over her shoulder.

His hand slaps down onto her ass cheek as I push into her once again. “But it’ll be the first one you enjoy.”

Malik has always been unbothered, but despite that, I can see her torment and I can feel the baggage she still carries from the time she spent in the basement, I think she needs him for things I can’t give her. I could never act so flippant about her being raped, but Malik can take it and show her she’s strong despite it.

So as Malik continues to fuck her asshole, now with two fingers, I pound into her and watch as she grips the bedsheets with her fingers and then stuffs her face into the pillow where she begins to moan and sob simultaneously. The sensations are becoming too much. She’s overstimulated, and even though I’ve only just begun, I decide to take pity on her this one time. I will have many other chances to work up her endurance.

“Why don’t you help me make her come this last time?” I ask Malik, and he obliges with a smile. His hand slips down under her pelvis, working that clit as I continue to plow into her. Just as I’m nearing my end, she once again tightens and sobs profusely as she crests one last time.

With one final thrust, I’m balls deep and coming inside

her. The tendons in my neck tighten and my teeth clench as the euphoric sensations wash over me.

She collapses to her stomach as I pull out and stand at the end of the bed, listening to her heavy pants. Malik comes to stand beside me, pulling up his pants and scratching the side of his amused face.

"Should have done this sooner," he says, holding out his fist. I rap my knuckles against his and laugh as we both look down at a spent Genni, her body spread out across the bed.

"Maybe we should have."

MALIK
DIESEL

MALIK

Her knuckles slam into the cartilage of my nose, the crack resounding around the room and the pain instantaneously scorching across my face.

"Oh, no! Malik!" she screams as her hands grip the sides of my face.

Blood pours out of my nose and flows down over my mouth to drip off my chin as I stand in front of her, but I can't help the huge smile that breaks out over my face. Even though I'm in pain, I'm so fucking happy she's finally mastered it.

"You did it." I begin to back her up into the wall. "You fucking did it."

It's been three weeks of teaching her Krav Maga, a type of martial art which uses aggression in its most primal form. To attack with no holds barred, and to cause the most damage in the shortest period of time. It's the epitome of self-defense, and my girl just mastered a move.

I could see when her eyes switched out, when her need for perfection switched off, and that animalistic instinct that lives in all of us reared its beautiful head. She looked at me as her enemy, and she did everything she could to incapacitate me.

"I did it." She giggles as her hands tighten around my face, making the pain in my nose amplify, and still, I just want to live in this moment for a little while longer, not caring of the agony that I'm in.

"Yeah, baby." I grip her chin in my hand. "You fucking did it." Then I slam my mouth into hers, smearing my blood on both of our faces. She laughs into my mouth, but kisses me back with passion.

My cock is hard and begging to be inside her, but like every other time, I pull back. I haven't been back in the bedroom with her and Diego in the last three weeks. I've only been stopping by to train her. We make out a little at the most, and then I leave again. I want to give them this time to bond, and to be honest, I want to make sure she really does want the both of us. Not just in the bedroom now and then either, because I'm ready to lay my life down for her.

Her dedication comes from her desire for revenge, but above all that, I can see she's enjoying the more violent aspects of our lives and maybe I'm seeing exactly what Vic Varga saw in her potential. Her muscles are leaner now, she's stronger too, and I'm realizing she'd be a leader worth following.

I promised her three weeks ago that I would help her exact her revenge, and I didn't just mean it through training. I would go to war with her, and I would lay my life down for her cause. The part I played in the destruction of her family will forever be a festering spot between us unless we face it, and the only way I can prove to her that I'm loyal is by seeing her dreams of revenge come to fruition.

Once we part, I grab a towel and press it to my nose as she grabs her hoodie and keys. "Let's get you to the hospital."

"Nah, Diego will set it, don't worry about it." I wave her off. "I have something for you."

"Then I'll text Diego now." She grabs my phone from the cut hanging on the chair, her thumbs flying over the screen as I imagine her frantically telling Diego to get his ass home. She finally sets it down and grabs my hand. "Let's go wash your face."

I yank my hand out of hers and wrap it around her throat, dragging her against my body. I love that she's so fucking tall, making it so easy to stand eye to eye with her. "Are you fucking ignoring me?" I growl out as I throw the towel to the floor, letting the blood run freely. "Did you not hear a fucking word I said?"

She could attack me right now. I've taught her how. She has mastered getting out of any hold, but she doesn't because my little princess trusts that I want her alive.

"What do you have for me?" she asks, her eyes twinkling with mischief and her voice cracking around my fingers.

I lean in and loosen my grip, giving her a quick kiss to her bloody lips. "I made something for you."

There's a foreign feeling fluttering around inside my

chest, something like fear. Maybe I'm kind of worried this girl won't like what I made for her. If she doesn't, I know there's going to be a problem and I might have to put a bullet in her head. I spent a lot of time making this thing, and I only ever wanted to give it to her when I knew for sure that she would be strong enough to wear it.

As I walk across the room, my footsteps falter as I imagine her face when I hand it to her. This isn't the life she wanted. It was forced upon her, but she's taking it in stride. Does that mean she's accepted it completely?

I sound like a fucking pussy. Great, I've become a fucking pussy.

I look over my shoulder at the girl who's made me into a pussy, and I haven't even stuck my dick in it yet. My hand scrapes down my face as a groan escapes my throat, both from the notion of being pussy whipped and the fact that my nose is broken.

"Malik." Her voice... Just the sound of her fucking voice has me melting. "What's going on?"

"I'm debating whether to give you this thing or to shoot myself in the head," I admit to her, my voice sounding whiny.

"Wow, that's pretty extreme," she says, snickering. "I think we've already made a mess of Diego's gym with your blood. I don't know how he'll feel about brain matter."

See what I mean? This girl was made for me, I have no doubt. We share the same humor, and sometimes, when I look into those dark blue eyes, I see a monster similar to my own.

"Fuck it," I mumble as I grab the bag and throw it over toward her feet. "If you don't like it, just fucking say so."

I hear the crinkling of plastic as she opens the bag, and then the sound of her pulling out the item as her breath catches in her throat.

"Is this a *property of*?"

"Fuck, no." I turn around with a growl. "Have you not read it? Have you not even looked at it?"

She holds the cut up in front of her, the back facing her

while the front flaps open. "It says Hell's March. I'm not a Hell's March member."

"The fuck you aren't," I snap. "Turn it around and look at your position."

It's as if time slows and she turns that fucking leather cut in slow motion, forcing my dead heart to pound with nerves. I'm never fucking nervous. Why do I fucking care so much? I barely know this girl, and even as I think about it, I know I'm wrong. Genevieve Varga holds the key to my soul.

"Oh my god," she whispers as she looks at me over the top of the leather cut, her eyes wide and glistening with unshed tears. "Malik, this is fucking perfect."

"Put it on, Princess."

She shrugs the leather over her sports bra, and I'm instantly hard. I know it's not a property of, and if I have my way, she'll never wear one of those. Genevieve Varga was never meant to be property to anyone.

Her fingers skim over the patch I sewed into the front, the touch almost reverent.

Dragon Slayer.

"You're ready, baby," I whisper as I swipe at the blood still running down over my lips. "You've risen from the ashes, and you're ready to raze them to the ground."

"Yeah." She nods as her pouty lips turn up into a sadistic smile. "I'm ready."

"When you wear this cut, I want you to become the leader your father saw you as." I can see her steeling her jaw, trying her damnedest to hold in the emotions that are threatening to pull her under. She has yet to deal with the grief of losing her family and the life she knew. I crowd against her, forcing her back to the wall as my fingers dip into the waistband of her leggings, seeking her hot cunt. "Spread your legs. I want to watch you come while you're wearing leather."

"Fuck, Malik. I want you to fuck me already."

It's become routine now. Every time I come over here to

train with the Princess, she ends up begging the peasant to fuck her.

"Not yet," I tease as I sink two fingers deep inside her, making her legs tremble as the back of her head hits the wall.

To be honest, I don't know why I haven't fucked her yet. Maybe it all boils down to the women I've had in my life, or the lack thereof. Mommy issues are a real thing. My mother wanted nothing to do with me from the moment I was born, and that feeling of abandonment has always stuck with me. It's the reason this tree grew so large inside of me, and now there's no room for trust or love.

I think if I were to give in and finally fuck my Princess, I'd end up hurting her. I jumped at the chance to share her with Diego because, like she said, both of us bring something different to the table. He's caring and protective, whereas I'm spontaneous and coldhearted, not really relationship material, but I don't need to be to make her come anytime she wants with my mouth and my fingers.

With my free hand, I pull her leg up around my waist, opening her pussy up and giving my fingers room to really fuck her with force. The scent of the leather and the way it complements her dark golden skin has my cock aching behind my zipper. I'd love nothing more than to pull it out and rip her pants off, just fuck her without abandonment.

I've never had such a visceral reaction to a material object before, but seeing my Princess in a leather cut nearly has me coming in my pants.

The sounds her greedy pussy is making echoes around the room, creating a melody of pleasure. Her pussy tightens around my fingers, her core trying to grip my hand in place. If this was my cock, I'd be pounding her cunt so hard, she'd be screaming through the most pleasurable pain she's ever felt. I don't have a slowdown tool in my repertoire.

Her screams hit the ceiling just as Diego's boots begin to descend the stairs, and just because I know exactly what he's been getting every night, I finger fuck her through her orgasm, stretching out her cries of pleasure.

"I was expecting a bloodbath," he says as he looks around the room. "But not expecting you both to be fucking in the middle of it."

I pull my fingers out of her wet pussy and step back to look at Diego as I slip them into my mouth, audibly sucking off her juices with a shrug. "Are you here to patch me up, doc?"

His eyes land on the cut hanging from her shoulders, his eyebrows hitting near his hairline. "Whose cut are you wearing?"

"Mine." She stands proudly, her chin lifting slightly. "This is mine."

Diego steps forward, gripping the leather in his hand and yanking her against his chest as he reads the patch roughly sewn into the front. "Dragon Slayer."

"That's me." She gives him a sadistic smile, making my chest brim with pride. With my blood still coated along her face, she looks beautifully feral.

His arms wrap around her back as he pulls her in for a hug, his eyes meeting mine over her head. His mouth curls up into a slow smile, his hand running circles on her upper back. "Yeah, baby," he coos. "You are a dragon slayer."

We share a secretive smile, both of us knowing we've created the perfect weapon to be used against the Steel Dragons. Now all we have to do is set the timer and watch her fucking detonate.

DIEGO

EIGHTEEN

When I rushed home today, I left Delia back at the warehouse because there's been something I've been working on for Genevieve, but Malik breaking his nose kind of put a wrench in the entire plan. That's why I'm so shocked right now, standing here and feeling the supple leather cut under my fingers. It's the perfect accent for the gift I have planned.

"I'm going to take care of Malik," I tell Genevieve as I give her a quick kiss on the head. "Why don't you go on up and shower? But I want to see you in that cut right after."

She giggles as she pulls it tight across her chest while an excited red blush coats her cheeks. "I love it so much."

"It's like you were always meant to be a part of Hell's March." I nod, then watch as she runs up the stairs. "Did you know?" I snap my hands to my waist as I stare at Malik, blood running freely from his nose.

"Know what?" His head tips to the side in question.

"The gift I had planned for her. My surprise."

"No." He shakes his head. "Should I have known? Did you have a cut made for her too, brother? Tell me it's not a property of because you may be fucking her every night, but she's not just yours."

I throw my hands up with an exasperated sigh. "No, never mind. Come here and let me look at that nose."

"I just need you to snap it into place. Breathing is a little hard right now. Let's get this shit done. We got things to do."

I stride forward, irritation still thrumming through me, and I grab his fucking nose, snapping it into place just like he asked. He gives a grunt of pain, but besides that, he's basically unaffected. Pain never bothered Malik. I've seen the way he fights. I've seen him pierce his own fucking dick. This motherfucker loves pain.

"The cut is nice." I give him a small smile as he wipes his nose on the towel he picked up off the ground. "But when were you going to tell me you took her to Glitz? Or better yet… that fucking Chino saw her?!" I bellow, my words echoing around us.

"Listen, she can't be cooped up here forever—"

"I needed them to believe she was dead! Now they'll keep sending people to kill her!"

"Stop fucking whining!" he screams. "We kill whoever comes for her! But she can't be dead if she's going to destroy them! They need to know she's their worst nightmare. How can she do that from the grave?"

My fist flies forward and smashes into his freshly set nose, breaking it once again. His holler of pain and vile curses fills the room, but I'm suddenly feeling a lot better about the situation.

"From now on, we will talk everything out. The three of us. No secret strip joint trysts in the middle of the night. We need to be a tight unit, now more than ever."

"Do you think she's ready?" His nasally words have my stomach turning.

"I don't know, man, but we don't have a lot of time. The hair and blood we sent to her brother was never retaliated. That piece of shit either doesn't care about what happened to his sister, or they're quietly planning something."

"Barrett said something to me today," Malik says as he swipes at the fresh blood on his face. "He told me he wants me to step down as Vice and hand my position over to Bear."

"You can't do that." I shake my head. "As crazy as you fucking are, we can't give the club over to them."

"I know." He nods before continuing. "Besides, if he forces me to step down, you know who will come back into the picture, and when that happens, our club as we know it will crumble."

"Would that be such a bad thing though?"

"I know what you're thinking," he says as he sits on the bench. "I've thought about it too, and yeah, I think it would be a bad thing. We think this war we have with the Steel Dragons right now is bad, but if *he* were to come back, this will be nothing but child's play."

"Barrett wants to break the treaty with the Steel Dragons." I scrub my fingers through the hair on my chin. "That's a war I'm not willing to fight, not for Barrett, anyway."

"But you'll fight it for our girl, won't you?"

"Without a doubt."

A week later, I pull up to the house with Delia finally coming up on my rear. We park in the driveway, and I give her a smile, the excitement inside me bubbling over on a steady boil.

"Do you think she'll like it?" I ask her for what must be the hundredth time.

"Big brother, you can't convince me you've not fallen in love with her." Delia smirks as she gets off the bike. "She's going to love it, but what I'm worried about is if she's going to love you."

I look my sister in the eye; her face so very similar to our mother's, and my heart cracks painfully down the center. Both of us were impacted the day our mother took her life. I've become overly worried about the people I let get close to me, scared of missing the signs that could save their lives, but Delia, she became angry, developing a chip on her shoulder that only fighting could combat. She felt abandoned and not worthy of our mother's love.

"I know why you're worried," I tell her as I gather her in my arms, my hand smoothing over the tight coils of her hair. "But you needn't be. I may feel strongly about Genevieve—"

"She likes to be called V, first of all," she cuts me off as she leans back to glare at me.

"Fine, I may feel strongly about V, but my heart is safe for now. I promise."

"Don't make me hate her." She gives me a small grin, her blue eyes twinkling.

"I have a feeling that could never happen," I say, leading her into the house. Delia and Genevieve have grown extremely close, and sometimes, I watch them and their silent conversations through looks and facial expressions. I'd be lying if I said I wasn't somewhat jealous. There's a barrier between Genevieve and me, one I fear I'll never be able to tear down because it was built with family betrayal and trauma, stronger than brick and mortar.

"Are you guys really going for a ride, and with Malik?" My sister's brow quirks as we step into the house.

"He's not so bad." I give her a wink.

"For a psychopath." She waggles her eyebrows.

I chuckle, but the sound is quickly stolen from me as the breath in my lungs escapes on a hard sigh. Genevieve comes out of her bedroom in a pair of black, skinny jeans, the tight material only accentuating her long, long legs. She has on combat boots, the chains wrapped around the ankle, jangling as she walks. She's wearing a tight, white, crop top, the material doing nothing to hide the two new piercings she has in her nipples, and then she's wearing her Hell's March cut. No one in the history of any motorcycle club has ever made a cut look so good.

She shakes back her wavy, brown hair, the mahogany highlights twinkling under the kitchen lights, and her face is free of makeup. Yet, she is still, so stunningly beautiful.

"What do you think?" she asks.

"I think I'm gay," Delia admits, breaking up the tension that's gathering in the room. The three of us laugh as I walk forward, gathering Genevieve in my arms.

"You look like a biker. Are you ready for our ride?"

Just then, a rumble pulls up outside the house, and she gives a little squeal. "I'm so excited to go on a ride with you guys. Who am I riding there with?"

I slip my hands into hers, interlacing our fingers and tugging on it, bringing her toward the door.

"Don't worry about me, I'll just hang out with Ajani tonight!" Delia calls.

"I'm not worried about you!" I call back.

"I love you, Delia!" Genevieve giggles, and once again, my thoughts roam to situations I may never have. I wonder if she will ever say those three words to me.

She opens the front door, her body springing with excitement, and rushes down the driveway to jump on Malik, who's still seated on his bike.

"Damn, our girl is fine." He grins as his hand grips a whole ass cheek.

"She looks like a proper biker."

"You're fucking right. She does, but she's missing something, right?" Genevieve pulls back and looks at me over her shoulder, then quickly skims over the driveway, seeing three bikes, an extra one parked beside mine.

"No fucking way!" she squeals as she runs to the small chopper. Everyone knew Vic Varga's daughter loved her yellow bike. The one she would speed around town on, but I knew if I were to get her something similar, it would only dredge up painful memories. So I'm hoping this bike gives her back something she loves without forcing her to remember what she lost. "Where are we going?" She grabs the bucket helmet off the handlebar, pushing it down on her head.

I quickly glance at Malik, his eyes already steady on mine. "Are you going to tell her or am I?" he asks.

"Guys,"—she looks back and forth between us—"I'm dying here."

"Are you feeling strong today?" My voice becomes solemn and my face serious as I look at her. "Are you feeling like maybe you could set the world on fire?"

We've talked about this, gone over the scenario, perfecting the details, and thinking out every probable outcome. Malik and I believe she's ready, but ultimately, it has to be her decision.

She doesn't say anything as her face loses any expression and her eyes stay downcast toward the driveway. I admire her most when she's like this. She carefully thinks out every decision, and once she makes a choice, she sticks to it. Malik and I give Genevieve her space, both of us knowing we'll follow her to the depths of hell if that's what she wants.

"Yeah," she finally says, lifting her head up to look at us with confidence. "I'm fucking ready."

My cock instantly thickens in my pants as sweat collects along the nape of my neck. She doesn't fucking understand just how fucking sexy she is.

"You heard our girl." Malik grins. "Let's get this shit started."

Malik and I are right behind her, each of us holding a canister of gasoline, the fumes clouding our senses on this dry, hot day. There's no breeze to dispel the scent, but it doesn't bother me because the sight of our girl riding ahead of us, her hair flowing out behind her in a beautiful fan, is the sole reason why I will tolerate anything.

The compound appears up ahead, and my heart spears up into my throat. No matter how hard she's trained or how far she's come, I'm so fucking scared of the outcome. Malik assures me nothing will happen to her, that they will be too shocked to react, but I know Jaeger, and I've seen the cold detachment in his black eyes. He's only ever cared about himself, and he's proven that once already by offering his sister in a trade.

"I can feel your worry over here, man," Malik calls out, snapping me out of my morbid thoughts. "It'll be fine."

Just like we've gone over, Genevieve stops about twenty feet from the gate, shutting her bike off and undoing the helmet on her head. There's no doubt they've heard bikes approaching, but we're hoping for the chance that they're expecting some of their own. I hate how our plan relies partly on luck, but I know our girl needs this to begin her healing. Her night terrors are only becoming worse, and each time I hear her shriek for her father, my heart breaks further.

We park our bikes, all of us getting up and removing our helmets, the sounds of our movements saturating the surrounding air. We don't speak. We're all in that zone of kill or be killed. The seriousness of the situation is haunting me, and possibly Genevieve, whose face is lined with apprehension and her body stiff with tension, but when I look at Malik, the motherfucker is giddy as fuck with a huge smile on his face.

Genevieve shakes out her hair, fluffing it up where the helmet has flattened it, and readjusts the cut on her shoulders. Then, without a backward glance, she purposely strides toward those large, ominous gates. If this wasn't so necessary, I would toss her over my shoulder and force her back to my house, never letting her leave again.

Malik and I stand to the side, waiting as she approaches that metal barrier just as a breeze picks up, blowing her hair to the side and making her look so fucking majestic.

"Open up!" she demands. "Do you know who the fuck I am?"

"I'm going to cum in my pants," Malik groans.

"Dear god…" I shake my head.

The sound of metal scraping alerts us to the gates opening, and we walk forward, the gas canisters heavy in our hands.

GENEVIEVE
BMW Motorrad Milano

GENEVIEVE

The two prospects standing at the gates are ones I've never seen before, but for some reason, they open the gates quickly, both of their faces flushed as they scramble.

I can hear Diego's and Malik's footsteps behind me, their heavy boots hitting the pavement in loud, resounding thuds.

I thought when this day would come, I would feel fear, apprehension, and a small part of me would grieve for my lost brother. I've never forgotten my time with Quinton or the feelings he thrusted upon me, but the one sore spot of this whole situation is Jaeger.

He haunts my nightmares, and he's a main character in every one of my daydreams. Sometimes I want to kill him, and others, I want to be right back there with my back scraping against the brick wall with his hungry mouth on mine.

It's sick and utterly disturbing, but just because I bury the forbidden thoughts, doesn't mean they go away.

I stride through the gates as the first prospect tries to intercept me, his large body crowding around mine.

"Are you here for the party?" he asks.

There's no point in using words because I've been training for this very moment. The tips of my fingers chop into his throat, forcing him to bend forward, his hands gripping at the tender skin. That only aids in me grabbing his head and bouncing his nose off my knee. Everything around me fades and my vision tunnels in, focusing solely on my opponent. He flies back onto the pavement just as the second prospect runs to my left, and once again, everything else around him fades. This one's more muscular and not as round as the first, but still, he has his weak points.

Like the soft tissue in his groin, the exact spot my foot hits, and his arms aren't fast enough to prevent it. When he falls forward to grip his precious balls, my hand slips into his hair, pulling his neck at an awkward angle so I can look him in the eye. There's surprise there lingering in the shit-brown hue of his irises, and it makes me want to giggle because I get it. I'm a fucking female.

My fist slams into his nose as my knuckles crush into the cartilage, the rough edges scraping against the smooth skin on my hand, and he drops like a sack of potatoes, heavy and fucking useless.

Diego and Malik come up behind me. One of them puts their hand on my shoulder while the other twists his fingers into my hair. Just by touch alone, I can tell them apart.

"You did good, baby," Malik says as he yanks my head back, his mouth meeting my ear. "So proud of you."

Diego's hand curls into the cut at my shoulder as he hauls me over, forcing our foreheads to touch. "You got this."

I grab the can of gas from Diego's hand and stride forward, my steps measured and my eyes on the line of bikes parked in front of the clubhouse. Music blasts out, some heavy metal beat, and all it does is ramp up the tension in the moment.

I start at the front of the line as I open the spout on the gas tank and begin to douse the bikes. One… Two… Three… Four are saturated in fuel, the rainbow colors shining prismatic in the setting sun. Then I grab the next canister from Malik and finish dousing each bike until I reach the last one. Emotion clogs up my throat as I stare at my father's Harley.

I don't know who has the audacity to think they can ride it nowadays, but I'm about to put it to rest along with the others, and maybe my father can ride into the sunset in Heaven. I pour the last of the gasoline on top of Vic Varga's bike and then I step back and wait.

Diego and Malik are well behind me, knowing this is my mission and mine alone, but ensuring I can feel their presence in case I need them.

The first one to slip out of the door with a cigarette in his mouth is Quinton Chino, and at the first sight of me standing behind the bikes, his mouth gapes open, dropping that cigarette to the ground. This is new, he doesn't smoke.

"Genni!"

"Hey, Chino." I give him a seductive smile. "Why don't you run back inside and get my brother? Go on."

I won't deny the pleasure that courses through me at the haggard sight of his face, the way his hair is messily braided, like he couldn't give a shit about his appearance. Maybe that's attributed to the party they're throwing, or the Club Bunny's pussy he was just fucking, but I'll let myself believe it's because of his grief at the thought of my death.

With shock emanating from the features on his face, he slowly walks back into the clubhouse, letting the heavy, industrial door slam shut behind him. I turn to look at the two men who have saved me, each in their own ways, but they've resurrected me when I was nothing more than a corpse praying for death.

I walk forward and snatch up the cigarette from the ground, the same one Chino dropped, and pop it in my mouth. I walk back toward Malik who already has the Zippo I was going to use in his outreached fist. He flicks the flame just as I hear the door opening behind me, and I lean forward to light the tip, the cherry burning a bright orange as the sky darkens.

I take a long drag on the cigarette as I turn around to face not only Jaeger and Quinton but also Laith, whose eyes are set angrily on his twin brother.

I grip the cigarette between my fore and middle fingers, slipping it from between my lips and letting the smoke billow up over my head with a long exhale, enjoying the burn that runs along my throat.

"Genni." Jaeger steps forward, his eyes wide, but it's not in surprise. The black pools of tar are shining with hatred. "What the fuck are you doing here?"

I bring the cigarette back to my mouth, taking a long drag, the corners of my lips tipping upward. "It's time for your reckoning, big brother," I call out as smoke puffs from between my lips with every syllable spoken.

That's when I see his nostrils flare as he takes a deep breath, the still air holding the heavy scent of gasoline.

"What the fuck?" he screeches as he steps forward, but

I've already extended my hand, the cigarette sitting precariously between my thumb and forefinger. As I hold out the cigarette, the burning cherry bright against the darkening backdrop, I flick the flap of my cut, ensuring he sees exactly what the patch says. "Dragon Slayer?" Jaeger questions, his brows coming together over the bridge of his nose.

It's in that exact moment Quinton holds out his hand, his tattooed fingers elongated and begging for me, that Jaeger understands exactly what I'm there to do.

With a flick, the cigarette butt soars through the air, rotating back to tip until it lands in the center of the line of bikes, suddenly combusting into a magnificent wall of flame.

I stagger backward from the heat that emanates off the bikes, and I feel both of my men grabbing my biceps to pull me back.

"Let's go," Malik urges as he hauls me away back toward the gate. We run past the fallen prospects, our boots hitting the asphalt in quick succession, and then the explosions sound behind us, one after another as each bike's gas tank ignites.

I mourn one last time for the family I once had before I seal it all up to transform into the new me.

I am the Dragon Slayer.

JAEGER

EPILOGUE

Genevieve Varga is a Hell's March member.

My fucking sister is in with my enemy.

When I was sent her blood and hair, a part of me wanted to be relieved, glad she was dead. But there, deep inside, my heart blackened further. I was so eager to believe her death, so glad she was finally out of my life that I let go of all the suspicions I had about the bloodied strands. Why not her hand? Her fucking heart even?

I know how ruthless Barrett can be, so seeing the hair and blood didn't confirm shit. Now I know for certain, the deal I made with Bear and Malik was never intended to end the way I wanted it to. She was supposed to be scared so badly that she would flee from Arizona.

Instead, Barrett and his men found out about the deal I made with Bear and amended it to his liking. They tied me up, then helped themselves to our fridge, waiting for Dad and Genni to get home.

But Ma was first.

The moment the door began to open, I knew it was her. The lack of bike engines on the street, and the obnoxious way her too-full key ring jingled all attributed to my mother being home early.

One look at Barrett and I could see the glee in his eyes. He had Vic Varga's wife here, unprotected, while his son, *his Vice*, was uselessly incapacitated. What's the one way to rip apart your enemy? By destroying their weakness. What makes a man weak?

Family.

Genni is the last of my family, and while I watched her flick her cigarette, the stick flipping through the air, my eyes couldn't move from her form. She looked stronger, more confident, and so fucking beautiful that it physically hurt to look at her.

All of it just made me hate her more.

Because of her, and the position she was so willing to steal from me, I lost my mother. There's no coming back from that. She can call herself a Dragon Slayer all she wants. It won't change a fucking thing.

Genevieve Varga has just started a war.

Carry on for the Prologue of Book 2! Dragon Strife

GENEVIEVE
BMW Motorrad Milano

PROLOGUE

I'm being held in the Slaughter Room, in the basement of the Steel Dragons MC. The cold, steel floor cuts through my clothing, eliciting goose bumps along my skin.

The room is bathed in pitch-black shadows, the temperature similar to a fucking fridge, and the soundproof interior is supposed to be fucking with my mentality.

They have no idea what I've endured this past year. Instead of going insane, this is as relaxing as a fucking spa day on vacation.

I rest my head back against the steel wall and begin to whistle, the tune jolly and fast paced, reminding me of the carnivals Dad used to take me and Jaeger to.

Jaeger.

He fell right into my trap, nabbing me when he thought I was alone and vulnerable, and now he says he has plans to break me.

I'm fucking excited because I have plans to be broken by him.

Jaeger Varga needs to believe he's ripped me apart, worse than killing my father, and I want him to plan my death, only to watch me rise like a phoenix.

Then I will make sure every Steel Dragon is gathered together before I raze the whole club to the ground, making sure Jaeger is watching.

When he thinks all is lost, I will just be getting started.

I will rush him to the brink of ultimate despair, only to drag him back by his stringy hair and start all over again.

A key slides into the lock on the door and I quiet my whistling, needing them to believe I'm truly fearing for my life.

The door opens, letting in the bright, fluorescent light from the corridor. I hiss at the sudden attack on my corneas when I hear his deep chuckle.

"That's just the beginning of your pain, sister."

"Goody."

ALSO BY C.A. RENE

The Whitsborough Chronicles
Through the Pain
Into Darkness
Finding the Light
To Redemption

The Whitsborough Progenies
Ivy's Venom
Carmelo's Malice
Saxon's Distortion
Gabriel's Deception

Desecrated Duet
Desecrated Flesh
Desecrated Essence

The Reaped Series
The Reaper Incarnate
Hunting the Reaper
Claiming the Reaper

Hail Mary Duet
Blue 42
Red Zone

Sacrificial Lambs
Sing Me a Song
Song of Tenebrae
A Verse for Caelum

Steel Dragons MC
Dragon Slayer
Dragon Strife

Mimic
Festum Mors

ABOUT THE AUTHOR

C.A. Rene lives in Toronto, Canada with her family, where most of the year varies from chilly to frigid. Most days you'll find her wrapped in her many blankets in bed while reading or writing her next dark, twisted story.

Her stories boast of inclusivity and refusal to be conformed in any small box. Writing across genres is a hobby and drinking wine is a must… Or coffee … with a splash of Baileys.

For all book updates and social platforms, check out my website

www.ingramcontent.com/pod-product-compliance
Lightning Source LLC
Chambersburg PA
CBHW060848210726
48293CB00006B/1717